CW01375720

THE LIONS OF
CATALUNYA

By
Jeremy D Rowe

Grosvenor House
Publishing Limited

The right of Jeremy D Rowe to be identified as the author of this
work has been asserted in accordance with Section 78
of the Copyright, Designs and Patents Act 1988

Cover photograph by Ian Jones of the church of Sant Miquel, in Barceloneta
and cover layout - Ben Rowe

This book is published by
Grosvenor House Publishing Ltd
28-30 High Street, Guildford, Surrey, GU1 3EL.
www.grosvenorhousepublishing.co.uk

A CIP record for this book
is available from the British Library

ISBN 978-1-78623-012-6

for Ian, Liz and Lynn

PREFACE

Through twelve generations of the Blanxart family, we follow the tumultuous story of Catalunya. From open warfare and terrorist atrocities to joyous celebration of a unique culture, the narrative of Catalunya as experienced by the Blanxarts, sheds light upon our experience of the modern world and its challenges.

This is not a history of Catalunya: readers who wish to know more about the fascinating and troubled history of the nation can find accurate sources, in English. What follows is fiction, and although many of the characters and situations in the story are taken from history, the Blanxart family and its exploits are entirely imaginative. Blanxart is a traditional Catalan family name, pronounced (approximately) "Blan-shart".

This story has been made possible by research at the Museum of the History of Catalunya, in the Palau del Mar, Barcelona; at the amazing Mediaeval building, Santa Maria del Mar, also known as the Cathedral of the Sea; and at the extraordinary church of Sant Miquel in Barceloneta. The sculpture of St Michael on the façade of the church was the catalyst for the story.

Jeremy D Rowe
January 2016

THE LIONS OF
CATALUNYA

CHAPTER ONE

The child's life was hardly different from that of a small foraging animal. Each night he would curl up to sleep in the filth and rubbish in some neglected corner beside the cathedral; by day he would beg and hunt for scraps of anything edible he could find. He stayed with a small pack of urchins, all equally stinking and unwashed, all hardly alive in the midst of the bustling affluence of the city.

His world was small, no more than a few lanes and alleyways around the walls of the cathedral. He would scuttle from place to place, never missing a chance to beg from the constant stream of pilgrims arriving to worship at the shrine of Santa Eulalia. He was tiny: perhaps no more than four years old. And his smallness was at times an advantage. Now and again, a grand lord or lady would arrive with a servant carrying alms for the poor, and he would be lucky, picked out for his smallness, and big brown pleading eyes. A coin would be dropped into his filthy fingers, a coin sufficient to buy a pie at Santa Caterina market. It happened occasionally that some pilgrim had decided his route to

1

heaven required him to bring a basket of bread to give to the urchins of the cathedral, and he would spend the day nibbling half a loaf.

He thought he had a name, since everyone called him Sucio. Little did he realise at the time, that it simply meant 'dirty-one', and it amused the clean and cultured visitors to the cathedral to see him answer eagerly to the insult. He understood speech, but never spoke, apparently quite dumb, and he knew little of the world beyond the cathedral alleyways.

Sucio knew his city was Barcelona. He knew he had a king called Philip, since he heard the nobles' calls of 'God save King Philip', and he often wondered which of the rich gentlemen entering the cathedral was indeed his king. He knew that God lived in the cathedral, and that along with the mysterious Santa Eulalia, God had many visitors. He'd often tried to creep into the cathedral to see this God, but he had never got past the fierce priests who were always guarding the doors. "Away with you," they would cry, kicking into the air as Sucio dodged back, "Filthy urchin, away from the door, this is God's house!" And Sucio would scamper away, turning only to pull a face at the pomposity of the priest, and then run on to find the next crust.

At night he would curl up with the other urchins he ran with. Like a pack of small animals, they huddled together for warmth in the winter, for companionship in the summer. And it was at night, lying in the darkness and filth, that he would see again the haunting last picture of his mother, after she was dragged from the tiny room they called a home.

They had come for her at night, crashing down the lane with shouts and curses. "Witch!" they had shouted, "Witch! You will not escape! Do not try to hide!" And at that she had bundled him into the corner and covered him with the rags they slept on. Peeping from the pile of torn blankets, he had watched the men, snarling like animals, burst into the hut; he had seen them grab his mother, and heard her cries.

"No, never, leave me alone. I've done no wrong, I've done no wrong!"

"You cannot escape, you whore. We've seen you in the market trying to sell your potions, claiming to have cures for sickness and stomach attacks. We know you make the stuff here, and we've been told of how you collect herbs and flowers. We know you steal from gardens, and grab plants from any corner. And insects. We have eyes everywhere and have been told of you crushing beetles into your evil concoctions. You cannot deny it."

"Surely I make remedies," replied his mother, "But it's with a good heart and good skill to give good medicine."

"Fie on your good medicine," interrupted the man leading the gang. "You are no expert in medicine, you are an expert in sorcery, and you bring black arts into our market place. And what is this?" he continued, bring the lantern up to his mother's face, "What painted harlot are you? What stuff is on your face, evil one?"

"I make cosmetics also," whimpered the woman.

"Cosmetics?" spat the man, slapping his hand brutally across her face. "What clever words are these from one so low? Words only a witch will know." And he slapped her repeatedly scraping the simple make-up from her face. As she screeched and whimpered, he continued to abuse her.

The boy cowered down in the rags, struck dumb by the brutality he was watching. The other men joined in baiting and attacking the woman, calling her whore and witch and filthy names. She would have fallen to the dirt floor if the leader had not been grasping her by the wrist. She twisted and pulled from him, but he was far too strong for her to resist.

"It's to Santa Caterina market you'll go, but not to sell your evil stuff. There you will hang by your scrawny neck. There are others too – and all will be put to death. You are working for the devil and now the time has come for you to meet him!"

With that, they dragged her from the hut. The tiny boy lay, quivering in the darkness, listening to her screams. Cautiously he crept out from the pile of rags and peeped around the ragged curtain at the door of the hut. Despite being in the grasp of four strong men, his mother was struggling enough to make progress down the lane very slow. Screaming like an animal caught in a trap, she did all she could to escape. It was useless. They continued on their brutal way.

From other hovels in the lane, nervous faces watched the progress of the brutes, but none came to the aid of their neighbour.

His silence in the hut had saved his life, and now the little boy continued dumbly to follow his mother. An instinct told him to remain inconspicuous. As he reached the open market place of Santa Caterina, he saw a sight of nightmarish horror. Other groups of men were dragging other women into the centre of the market place, which was lit by flaring torches. Set up, and well lit by the flames, was the gallows, with ropes hanging ready to hang several unfortunate women all at once.

Each chaotic group, three or four men dragging a screaming young woman, converged into the torchlight, until there were six women being held, struggling and cursing, with a gathering crowd of onlookers. The boy could see people he recognised joining the crowd and shouting for the deaths of the witches.

"Hang them all!" echoed around the market.

"I saw her conjuring a potion to ruin the vegetables in my garden," said one.

"And she bewitched my cow, and turned the milk sour," said another.

"That's the one who sent my boy mad, raving night after night, screaming that the devil was chasing him!"

"There's the one who looked into the face of my poor husband when he dropped dead before me. She killed him, I know, by her witchcraft. Death to the witches!"

"Hang them all." The cries grew, as more and more of the crowd joined the mass hysteria.

Suddenly a shout halted all the other cries and screams. "Stop this nonsense!" came the loud voice of one of the priests from the cathedral. "You do not do this in the name of God. These women have had no trial. You have no evidence against them. The church does not condemn them."

"Go back to your cell, cleric," came the voice of the man who had come to drag Sucio's mother away. "This is nothing to do with you. Your pope-ish ways could have rooted out the evil living in the midst of us, but you chose to ignore it. Your inquisition could have burned these witches, but you didn't. We can wait for you no longer. The time has come for these hags to die."

The priest stepped forward in front of the gallows, but one of the men stepped up to him. "Move aside my lord bishop," he said with a sarcastic sneer, "Move aside." The priest lifted up the wooden cross hung round his neck, but as he did so, the man struck him in the face, and he fell. "Get him out of the way."

A group of women darted forward and half carried and half dragged their priest away. The crowd, which had gone silent during this exchange, started their murmurings again. The sound grew and grew again, until all were baying for the lives of the women.

The little boy, bewildered by the noise, terrified by the flames from the torches and confused by the screams, stayed in a dark corner of the market. Something told him not to run to his mother; something told him to remain silent and hidden. And he watched the satanic ritual take place.

The women's arms were tied behind their backs. Their struggles brought forth much cursing and swearing by the men. Their shawls were pulled away from their faces, and each neck was placed in a noose.

"I have done no wrong!" came the loud clear voice of his mother.

"Nor I, nor I!" called the other women.

"Witches you are, and as witches you will die!" shouted the leader. And turning to the crowd, he said, "Let this be a warning to any others who practise the evil arts. Get out of Barcelona. Be on your way, for do not doubt, if you be caught, you also will die."

"I curse you," came from another of the women, "We curse you!"

"It is you who are cursed," shouted the leader. "And now you die."

Horses were brought into the market place, three of them, bucking and rearing in the torchlight. Their riders were having much trouble controlling them, but brought them eventually to the gallows. The ropes from the nooses about the women's necks were already hanging from the high gallows, and now the loose ends were knotted and brought to the horses. They were handed to the riders, who gripped them firmly, and tied them to their saddles. All went quiet, save for the snorting of the horses and the crying of the women.

"Now you die!" repeated the leader, bellowing so that all would hear.

Suddenly the horses were whipped hard, and bolted. This shot the women high into the air, hanged by the neck. A great cheer went up from the crowd. The women's bodies whipped and swung. For some the end was mercifully quick; for others, their death was lingering as they choked and retched. The women swung limply, like rag dolls.

The ropes were quickly grabbed from the horses, and several of the crowed darted forward to hold them and tie them to nearby posts, thereby keeping the women swinging high above their heads.

The little boy watched all. The sight was printed into his memory, and even if he didn't understand what had happened, he was numbed by what he had seen. The women were left hanging, and the crowd started to drift away. Unsure what to do, he went back towards the hut. As he shuffled slowly in the shadows, the smell of burning came to him; and as he turned into the lane, he saw the hut blazing. Hiding in a dark corner, he heard the shouts of the neighbours.

"Hang the witch and burn her hut! That's the end of all her evil ways. We'll have no more of her kind here."

He slipped down in the corner, and cried, a strange animal-like mewling cry. Numbly he curled into a tiny ball. In the darkness no-one noticed him, and the crackling and spitting of his burning home meant that the strange noises he was making were unnoticed and unheard.

Each night he had curled up in the same way: at first alone, and then with the small group of homeless orphans around the cathedral. He never spoke; remained quite dumb, the power of speech having left him when his mother was taken from him. He had little memory of her, nor understanding of having a mother, and it was only the horror of her death which remained with him. It was as if he had known her only at the moment she was taken from him. The only sound he ever made was the mewling cry which accompanied his midnight tears.

He had fallen in with the gang of urchins, and learned their ways: scrounging and stealing and begging through their days; waking with the sunrise; huddling together to sleep at sunset. Each child had his own nightmares, and each would cry out in his own way. They comforted one another roughly in the darkness of the night, but come morning, they never tried to tell one another what horrors haunted them.

Thus a year passed, and then another. Sucio shivered in the cold of winter, then broiled in the summer sun. His sun-tanned skin became dark with its constant patina of dirt. As the smallest urchin in the group, he stayed close to the older boys, and never ventured far from them. The oldest boy watched over him, ensured he got his share of the meagre pickings, and in a crude way cared for him.

It was a hot day in the height of the summer when a legless beggar arrived, dragging himself on his hands and settling himself at the cathedral door. The boys watched warily as the beggar stretched out his calloused hand for alms. They were surprised to see someone more filthy and more needy than themselves. The beggar was dressed in rags, and a shaggy beard added to his fierce visage. His crab-like movement on his hands gave an impression of someone not human, more some kind of creeping, dragging animal, low to the dirt of the road. The cathedral priests did not kick the beggar out of the way as they had kicked the urchins, nor prevent the cripple from calling for alms; the passing worshippers were clearly rewarding the beggar far more than they did for the urchins.

As evening came, the beggar moved towards the boys, and the oldest shouted to him.

"Hey, you! You've taken our place today. Give us some of what you got given!"

The beggar laughed. "Filthy kids. What do you take me for? Go try somewhere else."

But the boy persisted. "This is our patch. We live here. We can't try somewhere else. We don't know anywhere else. We've always been here."

"You can do better than here. You're wasting your time here. This is my patch now. All these rich lords and ladies like to give alms to a cripple like me. They just think you kids are a nuisance and in the way. It's giving alms to me that gets them into heaven isn't it?"

"We have nowhere else to go."

"Look kids, take some advice from someone who's been on the streets for ever. Go down La Ribera slums. You'll do better there. More chance to steal, more rubbish to pick through, more chances. I'd be there myself, but I can't run away like you can. Go on down La Ribera."

Sucio listened and watched with his usual wide-eyed attention. Was there really somewhere better than being at the cathedral?

"So where is this place?" retorted the boy.

"Not far," replied the beggar, "Go on down to Santa Caterina, go straight across the market and just keep going. Go past Santa Maria, and go on and on. You'll know the Ribera slum when you get there. It stinks. But then so do I! And so do you! Lots of narrow alleys, lots of shops and hovels all close together. Lots of chances."

The urchins withdrew from the beggar and talked together. "Is it true? Here in our city, a better place for us?"

The oldest boy decided: "I'll go and see. And if it's good, like he says, I'll come back for you."

The boys found it hard to trust anyone, even one another, and suspiciously a couple of them grasped his wrists. "You'd better come back. Don't just abandon us. If it's good, you come and get us – or else we'll come and find you, wherever you are."

He struggled out of their grasp. "I'm not going now, it's getting dark. I'll go in the morning. Now let's sleep."

Sucio crept up close to the bigger boy. He said nothing, but put his hand on the boy's shoulder. "It's OK little one, we won't leave you behind." said the boy, and Sucio slept close to him.

When he woke, the boy was gone. "We'll not see him again." muttered the other boys, and Sucio felt tears welling up inside. "Hey, we'll be alright little one," said the others, "Come on."

But Sucio stayed in the dark corner of the cathedral wall, rocking and mewling quietly. How could he run with the others, when yet again, he was so alone? Suddenly a fist knocked him gently on the shoulder. The oldest boy had come back.

"What're you crying for, little one? I said I'd come back. I've come to get you. It's true what the old bastard said. It would be better. And if it didn't work, we could come back here."

The gang crowded round. "This city is bigger than we know," said the boy, "but it's not too far. La Ribera is big, goes on and on, and it's what he said, full of chances. Look what I got." And from his dirty jerkin he pulled a grubby paper, full of squashed cake. The boys devoured it in just the way they gobbled all food. Sucio had never tasted anything so sweet, and he looked hopefully for some more. "Some more, little one?" laughed the boy. "There'll be more when we get there."

Despite their excitement, the urchins didn't run noisily through the market. They were used to moving silently, warily, keeping clear of trouble, watching always for opportunities to steal, or rubbish worth picking through. They moved from shadow to shadow, through Saint Caterina's. They skirted the open space where the tall gallows stood. Sucio grabbed hard at the hand of the biggest boy as they passed the site of his mother's execution.

"Get off me, little one," said the boy. "What's the matter?" But Sucio said nothing as usual.

They went down a long sloping lane that was little more than an open sewer, stinking in the dry heat of the summer, and skirted an enormous church.

"Is that another cathedral?" asked one of the boys.

"I think so," came the reply.

"I wonder if they've got a God living in there?"

A slight incline brought them out of the sewer, and into a wider lane. Here the buildings were grander, built on several floors, and the shops were bigger. An air of affluence reigned, and boys watched as merchants and their wives stepped from carriages to go to the shops.

"Is this La Ribera?"

"Not yet," said the oldest, "But we are getting near."

They continued to slip from shadow to shadow, crossing a wider road with horses and horse-drawn carts, and then plunged into a complex maze of tiny lanes and alleys.

"This is La Ribera, boys. Welcome to your new home."

They had never seen anything like it. Hovels and huts crowded close upon one another, like trees planted too close and gasping for sunlight; many of the huts had open fronts selling all kinds of things – piles of fruit, bright coloured cloth, strong-smelling spices, and shiney kettles, a living breathing bazaar. Tables piled with goods of all kinds spilled into the narrow streets. People lived and worked in desperately crowded conditions, but nevertheless an atmosphere of life and good humour seemed to pervade the choked streets. Terraces of shops, side by side and back to back, had mushroomed, creating a complex maze of narrow lanes. Here and there a small open space, sometimes with a water fountain, allowed sunlight and air to penetrate, but the lanes themselves remained in permanent shadow, and inside the shops and homes which crowded on either side, it was even darker.

The area around the cathedral had been busy, with nobles cheek by jowl with the beggars and urchins, but La Ribera was far busier. No grand nobles, but a complete cross-section of working people. Dusty stone masons and woodworkers hurried amongst the shopkeepers and housewives; errand boys ran with messages, unheeding of who they splashed or knocked into in the teeming street; occasionally a reluctant donkey was dragged down the road, piled high with faggots or logs; and everywhere there was noise – laughter, crying, shouts and arguments, jokes and gossip – and smells.

Such smells, the boys had not encountered before. Despite the open drains and rotten vegetation, another pungent smell filled the air, that of food being prepared. Bakers shops with pies and loaves, meat being roasted, and most of all the smell of frying fish. The boys stood open mouthed at a huge pan of fish cooking in front of a shack. The man cooking the fish saw them, and laughed.

"Want some, boys?" he joked. "Plenty for everyone. If you can pay for it!" And he laughed some more.

The boys turned away. It was unusual for them have let their guard down, and let themselves be so obvious. They retreated to the shadows.

"We must find somewhere to sleep," the oldest said. "Keep close."

They continued to wander deeper into the slum, turning corner after corner, through tiny alleys and lanes, penetrating the complex of homes, workplaces, and shops. Gradually they lost all sense of direction, all sense of where they were, or how they would ever get out. The heat of the day persisted into the evening, when oil lamps and tallow candles were lit, and the food stalls offered the last of the day's stock.

Turning a corner, Sucio saw a trestle outside a modest shop, with a small lamp lighting a few remaining cakes, just the kind his big boy had brought back for him earlier in the day. He stopped and looked at the cakes. He had eaten nothing all day since that morsel of cake, and the smell of the baking lingered in the air. The fat woman selling them turned away, and Sucio grabbed a cake. Holding it tightly to his chest, he slipped into a dark alley, found a corner, and ate it quickly. It was only as he finished it and looked up, that he realised the others had not seen him stop, not seen him steal the cake, not realised he was not with them. There was no sign of the gang.

Panicking, he ran to the next corner, and looked both ways. No sign of the boys. He ran back, past the cake stall to the previous corner. Still no sign. He turned back to the dark alley where he had consumed the cake. He felt sick. If only he had not been tempted. Now the cake felt heavy and leaden in a stomach unused to such richness. He retched. He knelt and banged his head repeatedly against the wall. He was in an unknown part of the city, in this vast maze they called La Ribera, and he was entirely lost. Lamps were being put out around

16

the slum, as the people settled for the night. It was getting darker and darker. He slumped into the corner, and cried his pathetic mewling cry until he fell asleep.

He tossed and turned, fighting the usual nightmare demons, which now included the other boys running away from him, and he woke at dawn. He was hungry and very frightened. Crawling out from his corner, he looked around. The cake stall with the fat woman was still closed up, but from it he could smell the delicious aroma of baking. He ventured a little along the alley, hoping he might see the other boys, but of them there was no sign. Creeping a little further, he heard the splash of water, and came out into a small open space with a fountain. Early risers were filling various containers from the several brass spouts of the fountain, and he advanced with great caution and managed to get a drink of water. He wandered back, determined to remember at least this small part of the slum, and once more stood in a quiet spot, watching for the woman to open her cake stall.

Gradually he took in his surroundings. Many small dwellings were squashed together on either side of the alley, and from many of them came the sounds and smells of the new day starting. The alley was becoming busy with early morning errands, boys running, women chattering and men hurrying by. No-one seemed to notice the little urchin with the big brown eyes. He peered cautiously between the shacks, and saw the heaps of rubbish and refuse thrown out by the various small businesses. This, at last, was something he knew about, and soon he was sorting out various bits of crust and vegetables – the kind of food he was used to scrounging.

He went back to drink some more from the fountain which was becoming increasingly busy, and when he returned the second time, the woman had opened the front of her shack, and pushed the small trestle table halfway into the lane. He watched as she brought the day's baking from the oven; he watched her eat one of her own cakes which had broken as she took it from the oven; and he continued to watch silently from the shadows as the day unfolded.

Once or twice he felt the woman's eyes on him, and he turned away. He'd stolen a cake the day before, and he didn't want her to notice him and remember she had been one cake short at the end of the day.

Thus he passed his first day in the Ribera slum. The legless beggar had been right – there was more chance to eat from the rubbish dumps of La Ribera, and it was easy to drink water from the ever-flowing fountain. As evening drew on, and lamps were lit, he sat in the alley, and when the lamps were extinguished, he crept back into the same corner to sleep again. This night there were not so many demons, and although he cried and mewled a little, it was not for long, and he slept.

The next day was the same. He found good pickings from the food waste behind the shops, drank unmolested from the fountain, and steadfastly watched the fat woman at the cake stall. He felt unable to drag himself away. Without him understanding it, she had become a fixed point in his chaotic universe, and watching her made him feel safe. The routine of the day passed just as the previous had passed, and once more lamps were being lit in the darkening alley.

"OK, you scrappy little thing, what have you been looking at?" Suddenly the woman's voice made him jump. He must have dozed and hadn't seen her coming. She had come out from behind the trestle of cakes, and was bending over him. "What are you looking at? I said," she repeated. He froze, horrified that she was addressing him directly, and stared back at her, speechless.

"You are a skinny little thing, aren't you? Come on." And with that she held out a hand to Sucio. Very slowly, he raised his hand, and let her take it. He let himself be led round the trestle, where she indicated for him to sit on the floor in the shop.

"Hungry, aren't you? I suppose you're always hungry. I've watched you for two days now, and I saw you sleeping round the back. There's not much I miss in this street young man. Now, are you hungry?"

He nodded his head. She reached behind her and brought out another broken cake. "I can't sell this one, and I don't need it, fat as I am," she laughed, "so you can have it."

He hesitated for a long time, looking from the woman to the cake and back. "Go on, it won't bite you."

Suddenly he grabbed the cake and stuffed it into his mouth.

"That was quick!" she laughed again. "Did it taste as good as the one you stole?"

His big eyes opened even wider. She knew! She had known all along. Now he knew he was done for.

"Don't look like that, I'll not send you to the constable. My little boy was just like you...." and she paused. "Was just like you," she repeated.

"Now then, when did you last have a wash?" He continued to stare at her in silence. A wash? He didn't wash. "OK, let's start again. What's your name?" Another silence. "Are you deaf and dumb? Can you hear me?"

He nodded slowly. "That's good then. Now can you speak?"

He nodded slowly again, then whispered, "Yes."

"That's good. And where d'you live?"

He stared vacantly around. He didn't live anywhere – he just lived where he was. He stared again at this extraordinary big woman. And the tears started to flow. He didn't know why, but they just started to come and trickle down his grubby face. He collapsed in a heap on the floor.

The woman found a small stool from the room, and lowered her great bulk onto it. She leaned forward.

"Do you have a name?

Again he nodded, his eyes big and round and full of tears. "Sucio" he whispered. This appeared to send the woman into fits of laughter, which frightened him more; but when she stopped and mopped the tears which flowed down her cheeks, she said, "We can't call you that. Sucio indeed! It might be true, you are indeed a very dirty little one, but that's no name for a boy. We'll have to think of something else."

There was a pause as she looked at the tiny boy crumpled on the floor at her feet, and the little boy looked up at the big woman towering over him. Suddenly jumping up, she called out, "Father, come and see what we have here!"

To Sucio's surprise an elderly man shuffled from the shadows at the back of the shop. "Look," she said. "This is the little street urchin I told you about."

"He looks just like....." started the old man.

"That's what I thought," she replied. "Come on, stand up. Let's have a proper look at you."

She stood him up, and looked him over. The old man looked from Sucio to the woman and back again. "OK," she said, "now talk to me."

She lowered herself back onto the stool so that her face was almost on a level with Sucio's. He found himself staring into two blue eyes, round rosy cheeks, and a smiling mouth. Her dark hair was piled on top of her head in a kind of big bun, from which wisps and strands of hair escaped, to be pushed back constantly with one of her chubby hands. In a city where women dressed always in black, it was a rarity to see a woman in calico white. The rounded shape of the woman, swathed in the cotton cloth, resembled an enormous cottage loaf, and her round face with its rounded mass of black hair was like a gigantic currant on top of the loaf. In every direction, she was round, and Sucio's instinct was to bury himself within her.

She held out a hand to Sucio, and picking up the corner of her apron, wiped his tears. "Now, little man, tell me the truth. Do you have anywhere to live?" He looked puzzled. "Do you have anywhere to sleep?" She tried again. He shook his head. "Does anyone look after you?" Again he stared vacantly at her. She tried again, this time more firmly. "Where is your mother?"

The tears started again, with alarming sobs. He started to shake, and she pulled him against her. "OK little one, you can tell me another time."

He stared around the shop. The room was small, and dominated by a large brick oven, which gave tremendous heat. There were plastered walls, painted ochre, and a wood-beamed ceiling. The whole room, including the baked earth floor, was warm from the oven. There was a table and a shelf with large containers, and the simple items of the baking trade arranged tidily. In a back corner of the room, an archway led to a very dark inner room.

"Sleep here tonight, by the oven. Perhaps tomorrow you can tell me the story. Father, keep an eye on him while I shut up the shop."

She brought the few unsold cakes in and put them on the table; she lifted the trestle top off, brought the trestles in, and used the top to make a kind of makeshift door. Turning to Sucio, she smiled. "Now some supper."

Leaning over the little boy, she took a cloth and reached into the oven. She pulled out an iron pot containing a steaming stew of oysters and beans. The little room was filled with an aroma Sucio remembered. This was something his mother had made. He knew that smell, and he knew that what was coming would be good. His mouth watered.

"Father, bring your stool here, we'll eat in the shop tonight. We'll not risk his fleas and nits indoors."

For the first time since the death of his mother, Sucio was under a roof, in a clean dry room, sitting on the floor, with a bowl of hot food, with someone who seemed to be ready to look after him. The old man seemed to be equally kind. Yes, the beggar was more right than he knew. Perhaps La Ribera would be a good home for a street urchin! He took some mouthfuls of the hot soup. It was delicious, but he could not keep his eyes open, and he rolled gently into a ball on the floor and fell asleep.

He awoke to find a forest of feet and legs surrounding him. It was still dark, still night, but there was much movement in the tiny bakehouse. He lay still, unsure what to do.

The old man was loading logs into the oven, and others, unknown, seemed to be in the room bringing bread or pies to be baked. Abruptly the shuffling was interrupted by a shout. "Hey, you've got one of those street urchins sleeping in here. Who knows what vermin he's brought in?"

"Leave him be," came the voice of the fat woman. "I know he's there. I'll get to him in a minute."

"If there's fleas and nits in my pies, you'll know it," came the first voice.

"There's fleas and nits in you, you old fool," replied the woman. "Now get your pies in here and get out of my way."

Once the strangers had gone, the fat woman bent down to Sucio. "Are you awake, little one?" she asked. "It would be hard to sleep with them all trampling about. Now let's get you up and sorted out. Fleas and nits indeed! Of course you have, but not for long."

With dawn breaking over La Ribera, Sucio found himself standing to attention in the centre of the little room, with the fat woman and her father inspecting him.

"Right father, my mind is resolved. We'll take him in and hope he's good. With you getting older and slower, I need to train up a good boy to help me, and I think he'll do."

The old man grunted his approval.

"We'll get him out of these rags and burn them." She felt his matted hair. "And I think we'll have to cut most of this off." And with no hesitation, she started to undress the little boy. Despite his street life he was only filthy, not diseased, and as she pulled him out of the rags, she revealed a wiry little body. As she undressed him she continued to talk to him.

"Now, we'll get you cleaned up. And find something decent for you to wear. I'm going to have to cut your hair, and once that's done we'll get you washed. It's still early, there won't be too many at the fountain! Hold him father, while get my scissors." Wide-eyed, the boy stared at the scissors – something he'd never seen before – and soon his matted hair was joining the pile of rags on the floor. "You are a skinny little thing, aren't you? Cat still got your tongue?"

Sucio nodded, his mind a whirl of fear and apprehension. Things were happening too fast for him to have any reaction other than to stand mutely.

"I think under all this dirt, you've got good blond hair, you lucky boy. We'll soon see!"

Sucio continued to stand, dumb and confused.

"Come on then!" announced the woman, and grabbing the naked and shorn child by the arm, she propelled him out of the bakehouse and into the street. Looking back at her father, she called, "And burn the rags and hair – but not in the oven, they'll stink when they burn and spoil the baking. Take them round the back!"

The sunrise was promising another glorious Mediterranean day, and to his surprise, the boy liked the feeling of nakedness as he ran beside the woman towards the fountain. He did not like the cold water, however, and squealed when she thrust him under the gushing pipe. From her pocket she produced a lump of soap, and a familiar smell came to the boy. His mother had made just such soap when she was alive. That had been one of the skills which had led to her downfall.

The jolly woman rubbed him all over with the coarse soap, removing the dirt and grime of two years on the streets, together with anything living on his skin or in his hair. Rinsing the spluttering boy under the fountain, she rubbed his shorn head affectionately. "OK," she said, "no more nits!"

There was laughter from the small group which had gathered. Coming to fill morning vessels with water, they had not expected to see the spectacle of the big woman washing the tiny boy, and it had provided an amusing diversion to start the day.

Wrapping him in a rough cloth, she tucked him under her arm and carried him back to the shop. Her father had cleared the rags and hair, and swept the floor, and she stood him in the middle. "Now we can see what we've got," she pronounced. "And I think he's delicious!"

Sucio began to smile. His serious little face rarely smiled, and laughing was even rarer – but now the smile broadened into a grin, which became a giggle, and soon he was dancing naked in the bakehouse and laughing. The fat woman gathered him up to her ample bosom, and laughed with him.

Abruptly she stopped. "Now let's get sorted out. Come with me." And taking his hand she led him into the back room of the shop. There was only one room, where she lived with the old man, and it wasn't very big. Sucio looked around. It was dark, and quite like the small room he lived in with his mother, but this was tidier, and contained all manner of things he'd never seen before. Rugs were neatly piled on a bed, shelves with cooking pots and jars lined one wall, and most surprising for such a humble dwelling, a modest clothes press stood to one side.

She knelt down and put her hands on his shoulders. "Now listen. They call me Viuda Marta, but you can call me Auntie. This is my father, and you can call him Abuelo, grandfather. He will like that."

The boy looked solemnly into Marta's face. "Auntie" he said. Turning to the old man, he stated seriously, "Abuelo."

"Yes, I think he'll do, father. I really think he'll do."

Shuffling on her knees, Marta went to the clothes press and opened the lid.

"Are you sure you want to do this?" asked her father.

"Quite sure," she replied. "God sent this little one to us, I am sure, and tomorrow at Santa Maria, we will thank God for him. But he can't go naked as a heathen."

Turning to Sucio, she explained. "I had a little boy, and a husband. My husband was a good man, and built this baker's shop. Everyone knew him, Blanxart the Baker! Oh, we were always fat! I was fat and I married a fat man! We would laugh together as we cooked. From nothing, we made a good living together, and we had a little boy. This was a happy bakehouse and we were always busy. My little Jordi played here with Abuelo, and we worked all day, making cakes, and baking for others as well.

"And then one day my husband got sick and took to his bed here in this room. Little Jordi stayed with him, and watched as he got thinner and thinner. And then Jordi got ill with him, and grandfather and I watched them both fade away and die. I made soup and got all kinds of cures, but none worked. They both just died. I laid Blanxart the Baker and his son Jordi to rest.

"Grandfather and I waited to see if we would get sick, but we didn't. And all through the sickness, I kept the oven going. Grandfather had to help with the logs and carrying the flour, and I kept it all going. God knows how I did it, nursing my man and my boy, but I did. God stayed by me, even if he wanted to take my husband and my son. He spared me, and he spared Grandfather. Perhaps this is why – he spared us for you. Yes, we must go to Santa Maria in the morning and thank Him for our blessings."

Sucio stood trying to understand all that Marta was saying, and shivers started to run through his naked body.

"The boy is cold, Marta," said her father. "Don't kneel there all day; save the kneeling for the Virgin tomorrow. If you're giving him the clothes, get him dressed."

"You're right father," she replied, and leaned into the clothes press. Bringing out Jordi's clothes, carefully preserved since his death, she presented them to Sucio. "It's not much, but it's good stuff and will fit you well."

With Sucio dressed in Jordi's clothes, scrubbed clean, shorn of hair, and even Jordi's clogs on his feet, he was unrecognisable from the scruffy urchin of the day before.

A smell of burning started to waft into the little room.

"Oh God, father! We've forgotten Senor Valdes' pies! Quick, before they burn to glory! He'll never forgive us!" and rushing from the room, she opened the oven and started to pull out the scorching pies. Left alone,

Sucio felt his head, with the strange feeling of the short stubble of hair left from his shearing. He looked down to his clothes, and smoothed them carefully. And he looked at his feet in the clogs, hardly daring to move. Years of going barefoot, even when he was with his mother, had left him unable to imagine walking in clogs, and he was unsure if he could move at all.

The crisis in the bakehouse averted, Marta and her father came back into the room. "Our routine is all messed today," she said. "Father find us some breakfast; I must get the shop open; and ...." she hesitated. "Sucio, take this jug to the fountain, and fill it with water for us."

"You may never see him or the jug again," warned father.

"The Virgin's brought him to us," said Marta. "We must have trust in Her as we have trust in the Lord."

She handed the jug to Sucio. He stepped out of the clogs, and went through the shop. The day before he had been desperate to find the other urchins from the cathedral, but now he hoped fervently they would not be around. How would he explain what had happened? Surely they would steal the jug, and probably his clothes as well.

They were nowhere to be seen, and he filled the jug, trying hard to avoid splashing his new clothes. He carried it proudly and quickly back to the shop, and as he walked in, Marta announced to her father, "Trust in

our Holy Mother, father, trust in our Holy Mother."
And she crossed herself. Turning to Sucio, she said,
"Good boy, and so quick. Go in now to Abuelo and
find some breakfast."

Sucio watch carefully as the schedule of the day
unfurled; he saw the batter to make the little cakes
going into the oven; he watched customers coming
to buy the cakes; he saw Senor Valdes and other local
shop keepers coming to collect the pies and loaves
Marta had baked; and he saw people who despite their
obvious poverty, were reasonably well fed, were clean
and respectable. It was different from the scruffy street
where he had lived with his mother; and it was certainly
a world away from life around the cathedral walls. Not
only was he given some breakfast, but another meal
later in the day.

At the end of the day, Marta told him to get some
rest, as in the morning, they would be up early to go to
church. He carefully undressed, folding Jordi's precious
clothes, and placed them, with the clogs, on the clothes
press. With a coarse blanket, he rolled up on the floor
in front of the oven. Tomorrow they were to go to
visit God, go into his house! What would he be like,
this man who everyone talked about? And would his
mysterious mother, the one called Virgin, would she be
there?

It was still dark when Marta woke him, but this time
there was no-one else in the room. "Dress quickly, little
one," she said, "We must be on our way."

Once ready he stood at the door, peering out into the dark. Sunrise seemed a long way off, and yet others were leaving their homes to hurry, he assumed, to the huge building they called a church. Marta took his hand, "Come on, she whispered, we mustn't be late."

Sucio shook his head, and looked down at his feet, immobilised in the clogs. Quickly he stepped out of the clogs, ran back indoors with them, then smartly returned to Marta, holding out his hand for her to take. She smiled, "OK for now: barefoot. But we can't let you do it for too long. What will people think if my little boy is running around barefoot?"

As they hurried through the slum, she continued to talk. "We have to get you a proper name. We can't call you Sucio – dirty one. It's not going to be good for the business to have a boy called that. And it's not true now. Oh I know you certainly were very dirty when I first saw you, but you're not now. I wondered if you would like to be called Jordi, like my own little boy, but grandfather says that would not be a good idea. After mass, we'll talk to the priest. He can give a name for you."

They hurried through the darkened maze of La Ribera until they reach the wide street the urchins had crossed a few days before. Ahead of them, stood the vast bulk of Santa Maria del Mar.

For three hundred years, Santa Maria had been the working people's church. Towering over the surrounding streets and squares, the huge austere mass of

Montjuic limestone had been the spiritual home for hundreds and thousands of ordinary folk who lived around it, artisans, shopkeepers and fishermen. True, they had lost Santa Eulalia when her bones had been taken to the Gothic Cathedral, but they still had the simple statute of the virgin, the focus of their devotions.

Sucio hesitated at the door. Previously, when he was a filthy urchin, the priests had kicked out at him when he tried to go into the cathedral. This time, however, the priest at the door smiled, recognising Marta, and nodded in his direction. Once inside, he was transfixed.

With its octagonal pillars stretching far overhead, its cavernous spaces of darkness, and the hundreds of flickering candles, Santa Maria del Mar was unlike anything in Sucio's experience. As he got used to the darkness, Sucio become aware that the vast stone floor of the church was full of kneeling people. Some were coming, some were going, and all were whispering. Who were all these kneeling people? The smell and smoke of incense, mingling with the aroma and faint smoke from candle wax created an extraordinary and dramatic atmosphere, and Sucio clung tightly to Marta's hand.

"Auntie, Auntie" he whispered urgently, "Where is God? It's so busy in here, I can't see him."

Marta, leant down to him. "He's all around you, and he's watching you now. Just be good and he'll be pleased." Sucio looked over his shoulder, and pressed himself closer to Marta.

Marta led him to one of the numerous side chapels. A small group was already gathered there, on their knees, and Marta knelt, indicating to the boy to do the same. He knelt and watched the others nearby. They didn't seem to be doing much except hold their hands in front of their faces, so he copied, leaving cracks between his fingers to watch what else would happen. After a while, a priest came to the group and went from one to another, blessing them. Sucio cringed, remembering the kickings he had got from other priests, but none came. Instead he felt a slight touch on his forehead and then the priest had gone by.

At last the worshippers got up and dispersed, leaving Marta and the boy kneeling alone. He went to stand, but Marta pulled him back down. "Wait, little one."

He looked from Marta to the priest who was now standing by one of the giant pillars of the church. Marta nodded in the direction of the priest, who came to her and put out his hand. Kissing it, she looked up.

"Do you need confession, Viuda Marta?" asked the priest, in an unexpectedly warm voice.

"No," replied Marta, "but I need some help. Can we go outside and talk?"

The priest helped her to her feet, and walked ahead of her to the door. Other worshippers were still arriving, and looked strangely at the unusual group: priest, baker, and barefoot boy.

"Viuda Marta," said the priest, "Ever since the Lord took your husband and your boy, you have been a good Catholic woman, and I have noticed your piety. I find it odd for you to need help, you who are so calm and well organised." Smiling the pirest looked down at Sucio. "And who is this little chap?"

"It's for him I need help," began Marta hesitantly, and she told the priest of how she had found Sucio hanging around the bakehouse. She thought it best not to tell the priest that Sucio had stolen a cake, but instead explained how she had decided to take him in as an orphan, and raise him as her own.

"You are a good woman, Vuida Marta," said the priest. "But I'm sure you don't need my help. What can I do?"

"That's just it," said Marta, "He says his name is Sucio." The priest smiled. "But I can't call him that. How can I find him a good Christian name?"

"We must name him for his saint's day." replied the priest.

He doesn't know how old he is, nor if he has a birthday," replied Marta with a sigh. "If he did, that would have been easy."

"Then we'll name him for today," announced the priest. "Today is the twelfth of June, of our Lord's mercy, in the year 1606. Today shall be his birthday, and I say he shall be five years old this very day. Thus will he have been born on the twelfth of June, 1601, the very day our Lord Pope Clement, recognised the blessed Saint Joan Gonzalez de Castrillo. This boy shall be Joan. And knowing what we do about the Blessed Saint Joan Gonzalez, it is an apt name for a boy saved from the streets in the way you have saved this boy."

"I confess I do not know the story of Saint Joan Gonzalez," said Marta. "Please tell me, and I will explain later to the boy if he does not understand."

"Blessed Joan was born in Burgos," began the priest, "And lived a life of poverty and chastity. He saw Our Lord Jesus in many visions, and Our Lord exhorted him to dedicate his life to the poor."

Marta nodded and smiled.

"One day, the Blessed Joan came upon a crowd of people surrounding a well. 'My child has fallen down the well,' cried a woman, 'and we fear him lost.' The Blessed Joan knelt in prayer for a miracle to save the boy, and as the villagers watched, a miracle happened. The well filled with water, rising up and rising up, and carrying the boy up with it. At last the water reached the top of the well, and the boy floated unharmed into his mother's arms. Thus does Our Lord move in mysterious ways. Thanks be to the blessed Virgin."

"Thank you my Lord, oh thank you," cried Marta, bending and kissing the hem of the priest's surplice. "Joan Blanxart. A good name."

The priest smiled. "Come back into the church, and let us give thanks for Blessed Saint Joan Gonzalez."

Crossing herself, and holding the little boy firmly by his hand, Marta followed the priest into the church, where he led her to the chapel of Saint Joan the Baptist. "Saint Joan the Baptist was a gift of God to Our Virgin, and Saint Joan Gonzalez, similarly was a Gift of God. That's the meaning of the name Joan. And this little boy has been sent by God to bring light into your life Vuida Marta, he is your Gift from God. Kneel and give thanks, and ask the Virgin to grant you mercy to look after this precious soul."

Marta remained on her knees for a very long time, and Joan, who once was Sucio, knelt beside her. He was not sure quite what had occurred with the priest, but he knew Marta, his own special Auntie, was happy, and so he was happy too.

As Marta prayed, Joan looked around at all the extraordinary sights in the enormous church. Suddenly he gasped, as the statute of Saint Joan the Baptist turned into a vibrant glowing red. He could not remain quiet. "Auntie, Auntie! Look, look!" he whispered urgently. Marta raised her head.

"Praise the Blessed Virgin," she said, "The sun is rising, and shining on us all." And she rose to her feet, and little Joan stood with her, and they looked around, and the sun was shining through all the vast spaces of Santa Maria del Mar, beams of coloured light cascading though the stained glass, filling the lofty building. The red light falling on the statue of Saint Joan the Baptist, was one of many beams of coloured light.

"Come quickly," Marta said to Joan, "I will show you a miracle."

She took his hand and walked rapidly around the apse to the altar steps. The shafts of coloured light filled the buildings in a dramatic and spectacular way. There in front of them was the focus of the whole church, the statue of the Virgin, glowing brilliantly in a golden light from one of the highest windows. "This is the miracle of Our Lady of the Sea," she whispered to Joan. "See how Our Lady glows. I have seen it many times. She is telling us how much she loves us. Our Lady is giving us her blessing. Now let us hurry home and tell Abuelo the news."

Joan Blanxart learned the baker's trade quickly, and soon was working hard in the bakehouse. Slowly the nightmares of his early years faded. He never saw the other urchins again, and grew to love the kindly woman who had taken such a risk adopting him, and her gentle father. Gradually he took over the chores of the business, and the old man could potter around in the shop, no longer struggling with armfuls of logs, or staggering back from the fountain with water jugs.

With good regular food, the little urchin boy grew taller and stronger, and soon was carrying the main work of the business on his shoulders. Even Marta could start to slow down, letting Joan's developing muscles take much of the strain. She delighted in the way the boy became a young man, and one day realised that he had become as tall as she.

He grew into a handsome youth, strong and tall. With no knowledge of his mother or father, Marta could only speculate where his strength and good looks came from. Most Catalan young men of his age had dark, often black hair, but Joan's hair was unusual and distinctive: he had a full head of luxuriant blond curls, marking him out as different and unusual in La Ribera.

As he had grown up, he had learned all the alleyways and lanes of La Ribera. He would duck and dive from alley to alley, delivering a cake here, collecting a bag of sugar from there, drawing water from the fountain, carrying a bag of logs on his back as if they weighed nothing, never stopping, rushing through the lanes, always on the move. And at night he continued to sleep on the floor beside the oven, with auntie and grandfather beyond him in the little room they called 'indoors'.

One thing, however, remained beyond Marta's control. As he grew, she had adapted her husband's clothes for Joan, with much joking about how much fatter the old baker had been; and she would pull out the baker's clogs, and Joan would smile, and put them on. But as soon as he went out on an errand, the clogs would remain behind. Despite all her best efforts, he continued to go everywhere barefoot. Marta would look at the strong young man, and remember the tiny boy she had adopted. Sleeping on the floor, and running barefoot, these were the legacy of his early years, and they would remain with him.

CHAPTER TWO

The sixteen-year-old Joan Blanxart was the mainstay of the baker's business, not only running all the errands for Viuda Marta, but increasingly taking responsibility for the whole operation. Life in the baker's with Marta taught him all there was know about the trade; and life in La Ribera taught him a great deal more about the world, and the realities of Barcelona.

Most of all, he learned from the old man, Abuelo. As a tiny child he had sat at the old man's feet listening to tales of Catalunya, tales of the Catalan heritage. Abuelo was passionate in his story telling, and little Joan absorbed all the stories with relish and excitement. Hanging in front of the little baker's shop was a small Catalan flag, yellow with its four red stripes. Many of the little shops in La Ribera had similar flags. The story of the flag was one of Joan's favourites, and often he would ask Abuelo to repeat it.

"Tell me again about the golden shield!" he would clamour, and Abuelo would reply:

"Many years ago, when Catalunya was a new country, we had a great hero, Guifre el Pelos. He was not our king. Ramon Berenguer, Count of Barcelona was our king. Guife el Pelos was one of his knights, and a fierce warrior with a golden shield."

"Golden like my curls!" Joan would interrupt.

"Yes, golden like your curls! Well, Guife el Pelos was a brave bold knight. First he defeated the armies of Castile, and then he defeated the armies of France. Catalunya was at last a free country, free of the yoke of the Castilians, free of the tyranny of France. But in the last great battle, Guife el Pelos was mortally wounded. He had given his life for Catalunya."

"Tell me about the shield, and the fingers of blood," demanded the excited boy.

"I was coming to that," continued Abuelo, "As he lay dying, the King of France, Louis le Pieux, dipped his hand into the wound in the side of Guife el Pelos, and taking the Count's golden shield, dragged his four bloodied fingers down it, giving us the four red stripes on our yellow flag. We call it our senyera."

"Our senyera: and to this day, we have the four red stripes for Cataluyna," exclaimed Joan, "And Castile only has two stripes!"

"The four blood red stripes from our first great hero!" rejoined the old man.

"Do you think he really was hairy?" asked the boy, knowing that the question would send the old man into fits of laughter.

As he grew older, Joan's patriotism grew stronger and stronger, and with it, a growing awareness of the divisions and inequalities in the city. Unlike many other such feudal societies, Barcelonans, and indeed most Catalunyans, were acutely aware of the iniquities in their lives. They did not accept their station in life as God-given and there was a constant ferment of unrest in La Ribera, which sat unhappily alongside the general good nature of daily life. Marta had little or no interest in politics when younger, but was gradually brought into the discussions as Joan got older and grandfather continued to tell the stories of the history of Catalunya.

"Always remember, my boy," said the old man, "When I am gone, and you younger people take up the fight, we have enemies on all sides. Castile would like to grab us back and France still has designs upon us. Barcelona is a wealthy port, and a great city, and would be a great prize for either of our neighbours. We must never let our guard down."

"And who would fight for us, Abuelo?"

"We fight for ourselves! When the call goes out we must all be prepared!"

Joan found the politics of his city and state hard to understand, especially within the context of all the problems he saw daily. As he ran around La Ribera on one errand or another, he saw all the cruelty and casual violence of his feudal inheritance. Sometimes he wondered if he was the only one horrified by the vicious punishments meted out by greater and lesser nobles upon their hapless servants.

He was even more horrified and angered that witch hunts continued in the city. Now and again, the cry "Witch!" would be heard, and the people of the slums would rush to see who the wretched woman was, and if she would be hanged. Marta would watch the anger in Joan's face, as he would turn away, clench his fists, and grind his teeth. "No more," he would mutter. "When can this madness stop?"

As he got older and stronger, Marta was fearful that he would take matters into his own hands, and intervene in one of these witch hunts. If ever he was foolish enough to do so, he would himself surely perish at the hands of the hysterical crowd.

When in one of these private rages, Marta would pull him towards her, hold him against her warm bosom, and rock him gently, calling him again, "Little One" even though now he was as tall as she. He never told her the story of the death of his mother, indeed he did not remember it clearly himself, but Marta guessed the cause of his anger and fear, and held him tight during such times.

Thankfully the witch hunts were infrequent, and despite the many political pressures upon Catalunya, life in the Ribera slum was mostly peaceful. The winters were mild, and the summers hot, and rain or shine there was always demand for the oven and the baker's skills.

No-one seeing Joan striding through the lanes would dream how skinny and emaciated he had been when Marta rescued him all those years ago. The light dusting of flour which constantly followed him, gave an added glow to his rich tan complexion. His unruly blond hair grew into a lion's mane. His strong arms became accustomed to the massive weights of bags of flour, and his muscled legs developed with the constant rushing back and forth in the neighbourhood. Famous for being barefoot all the time, he became a well-known character of La Ribera, popular and admired. His big baker's hands often had a morsel for a beggar or street urchin, and as he went about the business of the shop, he would often be followed by one or two hopeful waifs and strays.

Aduelo grew older and more frail. He had, after all, expected to do little in the shop once his daughter had married her strong baker husband, and it had been a stressful and exhausting time supporting Marta though the deaths of her husband and child. Once Joan was big enough and strong enough to carry all the heavy work of the baker's, Aduelo was pleased to take a back seat once again. Gradually he had spent more and more time in bed in the darkness of 'indoors', with Marta and Joan checking him regularly, bringing him food, and listening to his stories.

Joan loved the old man, and forgot that he wasn't his grandfather, and when he quietly slipped away from them, was as distraught as Marta. Marta sewed her father into a cloth, and Joan carried him in his arms to the burial ground at Monjuic where he was laid to rest alongside Blanxart the baker, and little Jordi.

With the old man gone, the little room indoors, seemed empty to Marta, and she asked Joan to sleep there, but he couldn't. After so many years of sleeping on the floor, he couldn't sleep in grandfather's bed. Indeed, when he was at last persuaded to try, he didn't last half an hour, and crept back to his usual hard floor beside the oven.

At first he did not notice the admiring glances from many of the young women in the barrio, and when Marta told him of his admirers, he was bashful, and in denial. He tried to tell auntie that she'd be the only one for him, but she would laugh, and push him away, and tell him that one day soon he will be caught.

His routine took him twice a week to the flour merchant, where Violeta would pout and prance before him; regularly to the fishermen on the beach near Santa Maria del Mar, where a certain Anna would be waiting for him; and once a week to the wine merchant, Senor Dominguez, where Emilia would peep from behind a curtain whilst her father let him taste the recent Rioja. Senor Dominguez was a fellow businessman in La Ribera, and was much respected for his successful wine shop deep in the centre of the slum, not far from the Blanxart bakehouse.

Violeta repulsed him; he hated all that make-up and perfume, so incongruous in the miller's dusty warehouse.

Anna had no attractions for him either, and when she got close, she smelled of fish. For Emilia, however, he showed some interest. From the little he saw of her, he could tell she was demure and pretty, and she didn't thrust herself at him like so many other girls. One day, the wine merchant took the initiative. After the usual small talk and wine tasting, he suddenly said, "Have you met my daughter Emilia?"

The girl immediately vanished behind the curtain from whence she had been peeping, but the merchant turned, and pulled the curtain to one side, revealing the girl. Joan was shocked by the merchant's unexpected behaviour, didn't know what to say, and as in any such crisis, remained dumb. Emilia curtseyed and Joan made a funny little bow, desperately trying to think of something to say, but managing only to stutter.

The merchant smiled to himself, and pulled the curtain back as if finishing a performance of some kind. "Well, young man," he said, "What do you think?"

"I know not what I think," muttered Joan, "But she is indeed pretty." And with that, he lifted up the flagon of Rioja and fled into the street.

Hurrying back to the bakehouse, his mind was in a whirl. Why had the wine merchant behaved like that? Why had Emilia looked at him that way? And why had he been so completely speechless? At the shop, he dumped the flagon, and turned abruptly on his heel, and ran to Santa Maria del Mar. Marta watched him go, smiled, and said to herself the single word, "Smitten."

Once in the church, he trod quickly over the flagstones to a side chapel, and knelt; but no words of prayer would come into his head. Instead it was full of Emilia. Emilia's smile, Emilia's eyes, Emilia's hair, all he could see was Emilia. A priest started to approach him, and he quickly crossed himself and stood and left the church. Instead of going home, he turned the other way towards the sea, and walked briskly along the shore, carefully avoiding Anna the fisherman's daughter.

Eventually he found himself at Monjuic, not far from the resting place of Abuelo. "Oh Grandfather, whatever's the matter with me? I'm never like this. I get on with the job, I'm a good baker now, and I'm making a good life for Auntie." He stopped and sat on a large rock and stared out to sea. "I could run away to sea," he thought, and then shook his head and laughed out loud at his own stupidity. "What will be, will be," he told the circling gulls, "What will be," he shouted, "Will be." And standing and stretching, he let himself whisper the name, "Emilia. Emilia Blanxart. Yes, I like that."

That evening he was humming and singing as he went about the chores of the bakehouse, and even continued to hum loudly during their late meal. "Are you OK?" enquired a much-amused Marta.

"Yes indeed," replied Joan, "It's just this stew is so good, it makes me feel good."

"It's the same stew we always have. Beans and oysters. We've been eating the same stew for years."

"But tonight it's especially good!" he assured her, and she laughed with him.

The time came for his weekly visit to the wine merchant's, returning the empty flagon to be refilled with Rioja. He found himself anticipating the visit with a mixture of excitement and apprehension. Would the same little ritual take place again, with the merchant showing his daughter with a flourish of the curtain? And would he be capable of speech this time?

To his surprise, the merchant was not there, nor was there any sign of Emilia. The merchant's wife served him at the shop, with a great deal of smiling and even winking at him. He smiled back, but thought it inappropriate to wink.

As he turned into his own lane with the full flagon on his shoulder, he thought he saw Senor Dominguez, the wine merchant, leaving the baker's shop. And surely that could not have been Emilia with him? He started to run, but the heavy flagon made it hard for him to hurry without spilling the precious Rioja, and the merchant and his daughter were gone before he could catch them.

Entering the shop, he found Marta in a state of excitement.

"Put down the wine before you drop it." she said.

"Was that...."

"Yes indeed, it was. I have had the most extraordinary conversation with Senor Dominguez. How shall I tell you? Where shall I start? Oh dear, such a conversation."

Joan picked up the flagon and poured a cup of wine for her. "Drink this, and then start from the beginning," he said.

"Senor Dominguez has only one daughter, Emilia, and no sons. It seems many children died in childbirth or as babies. You know Senor Dominguez is a successful wine merchant, and he has no-one to leave it to. Oh my goodness! Give me some more of the good man's wine!"

With increasing anxiety, Joan refilled the cup. His heart was beating hard.

"Senor Dominguez has been looking for a son to marry his daughter Emilia, and inherit the wine business. He has been here to talk to me about it. Me, a widow who knows little of these things. I had no idea. He has been watching you, watching us, and he likes what he has seen. He is offering his daughter to you, with his business as a dowry!"

Joan reacted as he always did at times of great emotional stress; he was struck dumb, and simply stared at Auntie. Silently, he reached for the cup from her hand and drained it himself. He continue to stare.

"Well, say something," said Marta.

"I know not what to say."

"That my little boy the baker, should become a wine merchant as well. You will be the greatest business man in La Ribera. The grape and the grain. What a marriage. But you will always be my little one. Come here."

And she pulled him into her bosom as she had done some many times before, and the tears and laughter flowed, and they danced a little jig right there in the shop, and were interrupted only when a customer called out, "Are you selling these cakes, or shall we just help ourselves?"

As soon as the customer had been served, Marta turned to Joan with a more serious look on her face. "He had just one question I did not expect," she said. "He asked if you are a good loyal Catalan. Of course, I said to him, of course he is. He has his grandfather to thank him for that."

Joan spoke at last. "And is Emilia a good Catalan?"

"She will do as her father says. And he has the flag with four blood red stripes outside his shop, does he not?"

"Then, with your blessing Auntie, I shall marry her!" and he hugged her again.

Thus it was that in a few short days, their lives were turned upside down. Auntie and Senora Dominguez met, and had a great deal to speak about, and supervised a number of meetings between Joan and Emilia; and Joan in turn had several meetings with the wine merchant. It was easy to agree that they should be married by a priest at Santa Maria del Mar; and it was even easier to plan a wedding breakfast with the joint resources of a baker and a wine merchant. What was much harder, however, was the question of where they should live.

Joan should, of course, bring his bride back to his home; but his home was a small room where Marta slept. He could hardly expect his young bride to bed down with him on the bakehouse floor. Both Auntie and his future mother-in-law were adamant – the wedding could not take place until the problem of where they would live was resolved.

One morning, early, Marta was woken by noises overhead. Startled she jumped up and went to wake Joan, but he was not to be seen. Going out into the lane in the semi-darkness, she spotted him, standing on the roof.

"Whatever are you doing?" she called. "Watching for the sunrise?"

"This is where we'll live, Emilia and me, when we're married. Look around you Auntie, everyone's doing it, building up, and we can do it too. Why at Senor Dominguez's, Emilia is used to going upstairs to her bedroom. So shall she here!"

"And who will do all the building?"

"I will, of course, Auntie. I've seen it done, and I can do it myself. You'll see, we'll have a proper house, and the chimney from the oven will go right up through the room."

This gave the older women plenty more to gossip about, and Senor Dominguez gave the project his blessing: "As long as you do it well, and give my daughter a beautiful bedchamber, I can't see I can object. Get it right and you'll have the morning sunrise one side, and the evening sunset the other."

"It will be a love nest for us," whispered Joan to Emilia, "And I'll build it right across the bakehouse and Auntie's room. You'll see, it will be very fine."

After that, Joan worked harder than ever. Rising early for the regular chores of the bakery, he would get all the daily tasks finished by noon, and then he could start on building the house. Some days would be spent dragging timber from the timber merchant, other days would be hammering and sawing up on the roof. Progress was slow, and inevitably he fell clean through to the bakehouse floor several times. Auntie would screech that the dust and dirt was upsetting the baking, and he learnt to move slowly and carefully, and save any very disruptive work for when Marta had gone to church.

Poking around the back of the shop, to decide where to put the outside staircase, he disturbed a little dark corner, and a strange feeling came over him. What could be there to raise the hairs on his neck? Somehow a distant memory came to him – this was where he had slept those first nights in the Ribera slum. Looking up, he saw Marta nodding and smiling at him, sharing the memory, and it felt right to be building the next stage of his life on that special spot.

Emilia would come and visit some afternoons, and Auntie below would hear the work stop and a suspicious silence descend. She would bang on the ceiling with her broom, and hear the laughter of the couple, and work would resume.

Finally the job was done, with glass in the windows and a good rug on the floor; and first Auntie and then Senor and Senora Dominguez came to inspect the upper floor.

The wine merchant was impressed, telling them all that it was indeed, "a light and airy bedchamber that any noble would be pleased to grace." He then announced that he would like to give the young couple, "his second-best bed, and the hangings and bedclothes to go with it."

Joan Blanxart and Emilia Dominguez were married in the church of Santa Maria del Mar, on Emilia's saint's day, the eighth of May 1619. Joan was nearly eighteen years old, and his bride just seventeen. They prayed together at the shrine of his namesake, St Joan the Baptist, gave special prayers for St Joan Gonzales after whom he was named, and then enjoyed a remarkable feast of a wedding breakfast, held at the wine merchant's house. The couple went finally to their new bedchamber, just as the sun was setting, and as planned, they watched the sunset from the new room. Nervously they got into the 'second-best bed' and held one another tightly.

"This is magical, my love," whispered Emilia.

"And will always be so, I promise you," replied Joan.

With much kissing and fondling, they fell asleep. In the night Emilia awoke. Joan had vanished. "Where are you, my love?" she whispered anxiously.

"Down here, on the floor," came Joan's reply. "I've never slept in a bed before. Give me time. I'll get used to it – I hope."

"Come back, and embrace me some more. Goodness, it will soon be light, and you'll be going down to start your baker's day. Come kiss me."

Miquel Blanxart was born in February 1620. The extended family were delighted to see that he had inherited his father's blond curls, although as a baby he was often mistaken for a girl. Joan's mass of blond hair marked him out in La Ribera as different, and he was particularly pleased to see his baby son with similar blond hair.

There could not have been a greater contrast between Miquel's early years and his father's. The new baby was pampered not only by loving parents, but three doting grandparents. The sunny bedchamber built by Joan for his bride, became an airy nursery for his son. Emilia was able to focus all her attention on her growing infant, and whenever he could be spared from the bakery, Joan would run up the stairs to cuddle his precious boy.

As he grew, Miquel developed the same mane-like mass of golden curls, making obvious the likeness between himself and his father. His life was spent between the warmth of the bakehouse and the cool of his grandfather's wine shop, and soon he was running between the two with errands for the happy family. Joan similarly was spending his time between the two businesses, maintaining his flourishing bakery whilst learning the wine trade from his father-in-law.

Although the Ribera remained a slum, with most of the population crammed into shacks and hovels, the family lived between two of the grandest buildings in the barrio. The bedchamber Joan had created above the baker's shop was the envy of many, with glass in the windows, the ornate bed, and the winter warmth of the bakery chimney. Miquel's crib, which he quickly out-grew, was also in the chamber, and little did he realise how rare it was for a little boy to be growing up in such luxury.

More than this, he could explore the even grander premises of Grandfather Dominguez's wine shop. The huge barn-like doors of the shop front were unique in La Ribera: solidly closed at night, opening wide in the daytime to reveal the well-stocked shop. Miquel was always intrigued by the little door set into one of the big barn doors: it was as if it had been specially designed for a small boy, although all the family stooped through it when the shop was closed. In the shop itself, barrels and bottles stood neatly on shelves, and a rich warm smell filled the air. Behind the shop was the large living area for the family, with its ever-warm oven, the open fireplace, and the table around which the family would gather.

Down a steep ladder was the cellar, but the little boy was not allowed there on his own. More barrels were lying in the cool and dark cellar, wine which had been brought gently from the surrounding hillsides, mainly good Rioja but also a few small casks of precious brandy. Miquel was slightly afraid of the dark corners and cobwebs of the cellar, and preferred his grandfather's house when the trap door was firmly shut.

Upstairs, however, was another matter for him: a place of both safety and fun. The upper floor was reached, unusually, by an internal staircase: a small door in the panelling near the fire opened to reveal the spiral of stairs. Upstairs, the area was divided into smaller sleeping cubicles, giving the little boy many hiding places and unexpected alcoves to snuggle against his mother or grandmother.

Whenever he could, Joan would tell Miquel the stories of Catalunya he had learned from his beloved Abuelo. Miquel in his turn became as passionate about his inheritance as his father before him. The Catalan flag, the senyera, flew proudly over both businesses. Tales of fighting reached the family from many customers, but the war in the countryside seemed far away and did not affect daily life. Miquel, however, was excited by the prospect of the war, and often told his father that he wanted to be a soldier and go and fight for Catalunya. "Your time may come, my boy," replied Joan, "Indeed, one day we may all be called to defend our city and country. Bide your time – you are still young."

As Miquel grew older and stronger, Grandfather Dominguez grew older and frail, and increasingly unable to cope with the physical demands of the wine trade. The time came when Joan took over the wine merchant's work, and Miquel started to run the bakery. The two men were remarkably alike – sixteen-year-old Miquel had his father's mop of long blond curly hair, and his father, twice his age, was still a strong and handsome man. The gossips of La Ribera came to calling them the Old Lion and the Young Lion, and many a head turned when the two of them marched down the lanes together. Emilia had given Joan three other sons and a daughter, but it was her first-born who had all the charisma and good looks of his father.

Joan marvelled at being in the centre of such an idyllic life, and felt that nothing could go wrong. Unfortunately, nothing could be further from the truth.

There were early hints of trouble when deliveries of both wine and flour failed to arrived. Vague messages of difficulties in the countryside were hard to interpret. Farmers who were previously reliable grape growers would send less wine than expected, and in some cases failed to deliver at all. Millers would report similar failures in the crops from farms. It appeared marauding Castilian soldiers were making random attacks against Catalan farms. The farmer's lives were in danger and their farms falling into ruin. War was beginning to affect everyone in La Ribera.

At the same time, troubling demands for extra taxation arrived in La Ribera; it was rumoured that King Philip of Castile was trying the raise taxes for his Castilian troops, in order to mount an attack on France. Joan and other shopkeepers like him, got together and decided to ignore such demands, and sent a message to the Generalitat of Barcelona that they would not pay anything to the Castilian king. The Generalitat supported this refusal to pay extra taxes, and Canon Pau Claris himself, President of the Generalitat, visited La Ribera and met the leading businessmen of the area, including both the younger and older Blanxarts.

Matters came to a head in 1639. Miquel was now 19, and being chased by all the young women of the slum. Joan would joke with him, that by that age, he had been happily married for a year, and it was time to choose one of the enthusiastic maidens. Joan and Emilia were in the wine cellar when Miquel came bursting through the door.

"Come quickly, they're commandeering the bake-house. Grandmother is on her own, and she needs help!"

Telling Emilia to stay with her elderly parents in case the trouble spread to them, he and Miquel ran full tilt back to the bakery. As they turned into the lane, they could hear cries of many neighbours, and see much struggling going on in the street around the bakehouse. Pushing through the crowd, Joan found Viuda Marta blocking the staircase against a small group of well-armed Castilian soldiers. Behind Marta peered the frightened faces of Miquel's younger brothers and sister. The tall, strong baker commanded much respect and his neighbours stood back, knowing that Joan's authority would prevail.

"Stand back from my mother!" roared Joan, oblivious to the weapons of the soldiers. Surprised by his direct approach, the soldiers paused in their assault upon Marta, and turned to Joan. They were confronted by both the Old Lion and the Young Lion, and for a moment, even though they were soldiers, they hesitated, just long enough for Marta to pick herself up and resume some dignity, standing on the stairs.

The moment did not last long. Thrusting the sword, with which he had been threatening Marta, towards Joan, the leader of the soldiers replied with a similar roar.

"Castilian troops are now stationed in Barcelona. I am charged by his Majesty King Philip the Fourth of Castile, to requisition billets for my men here in this Ribera slum. My men will not hesitate to use whatever force is necessary to assert their authority. If this fat woman is your mother, tell her to move quickly, or we will slit all your throats!"

"Never!" growled Joan. "Catalunya does not recognise your king, and we refuse. We spit upon your king."

A great shout of support went up from the crowd as Joan lunged towards the soldier, but the unarmed baker stood no chance against the sword and the skill of his adversary. Before Marta or Miquel could move, Joan was stabbed through the stomach and fell to the floor. Miquel knelt at his father's side, desperate to do something to save him. Marta ran down the stairs to her son, whilst two of the soldiers laughed and jabbed at her with their swords.

Miquel and his grandmother desperately tried to staunch the wound, but Joan's blood was spilling freely, and a dark stain appeared on the ground beneath him. "I love you, my boy," groaned Joan, "and I love you Auntie. Tell Emilia I love her. Tell Emilia...." But he could not finish the sentence. His eyes closed, and Marta and Miquel stared horrified at one another.

"Father!" shouted Miquel, "Father!" And he shook Joan as if to wake him from a sleep.

"He's gone," said Marta. "Help me take him indoors."

News of Joan's murder spread like wildfire throughout La Ribera and beyond, and street fighting broke out in many places. Guerilla warfare developed in the city, and many groups of Castilian soldiers, despite being fully armed, were ambushed. Soldiers were killed and their weapons stolen. At the same time, many loyal Catalonians died themselves.

Nowhere was the street fighting fiercer than in La Ribera. Joan Blanxart had been one of the heroes of the barrio, popular and well-respected. His strong loyalty to the Catalan flag was well known, and his murder was seen as an insult to all that Catalunya stood for. Men who had never fought before, found reserves of anger and strength they didn't know they possessed, and formed vigilante groups, determined to kill every Castilian soldier they encountered. Even priests from Santa Maria del Mar, hearing of the rioting, rushed into La Ribera to assist, only to find themselves tending the injured and dying.

Whilst Marta and Miquel had been trying to save the life of Joan, one of the brothers had run to his mother at the wine merchant's. Great was the screaming and panicking with the realisation that Joan was dead.

Later in the day, Miquel's brothers, with one of the priests from Santa Maria, solemnly carried Joan's body to the wine merchant's house where Emilia was waiting. Senora Dominguez laid a white cloth on a table, and Marta and Emilia tearfully prepared him for burial. Miquel's brothers and sister and the wine merchant and his wife watched, tears flowing freely. When the body was ready, Emilia whispered, "Clogs?" and Marta replied, "No, he couldn't wear them in this life, he'll not thank us for making him wear them in heaven. He will want to meet his maker with bare feet!"

Everyone looked to Miquel, who nervously looked around the room. "Our father must not die in vain. We must all, everyone of us, swear to keep up the fight against Castile." Suddenly he stood up straight, and continued vehemently, " never will we live under the House of Austria. In the name of our father, Joan Blanxart, I swear to uphold the Catalan tradition, to speak the Catalan language, and to fly proudly, the Catalan flag."

"Well said, young man," replied Senor Dominguez. "Joan is now at peace, but here in La Ribera, the fight will go on."

Initially, the bakehouse was lost to the soldiers, who let the fire in the oven go out. Once they had eaten and drunk all they could find they settled in, and presumed to think they had secured the billet. One was posted at the stair whilst the others slept, desecrating Joan and Emilia's beautiful room. Silently from an adjacent rooftop, came the knife-men, slitting the throat of the guard, and waiting for the others to appear. One by one, they surely did, needing to piss in the alley, and one by one their throats were cut. The bakehouse resembled a butcher's more than anything else, and the neighbours sent word that the bodies could be retrieved by their fellow soldiers.

Shortly after, in the evening, a neighbour arrived at the wine shop with a strange bundle. Handing it to Miquel, there was a brief whispered conversation, Miquel took the bundle, and the neighbour vanished into the night. Without unwrapping the blood-soaked cloth, Miquel felt the hardness of the steel within. He nodded silently to himself, and climbed down into the wine cellar. By the light of one small candle, he unwrapped the bundle and revealed a large, sharp Castillian sword. He sat for a long time with the sword on his lap, his eyes closed, and his mind full. This was the sword which had killed his father, retrieved by one of the many loyal friends who had hunted and murdered the murderers. With a sigh, he re-wrapped the bundle and hid it behind the furthest barrel in the darkest corner. "Wait there," he muttered, "until our time comes."

The rioting continued for days, and weeks, and skirmishes continued to break out all over the city, and in the surrounding countryside. More farms were destroyed and rural livelihoods ruined. The Generalitat attempted to send messengers to Madrid, but they were murdered before they got there. Canon Pau Claris was at his wits' end, desperate to stop the killings, but unwilling to submit to the Castilian demands.

Miquel conferred with the family, and they agreed that the bakehouse was violated beyond repair. None of them ever wanted to live there again, and with the encouragement of the old wine merchant, they abandoned the bakery and all moved into the winery. The laughter and jollity of the family had vanished. It was as if with the death of Joan, a light had gone out.

The Dominguez's home, however, gave them a haven in which to regroup and recover. Although in the heart of La Ribera slum, it was larger than most of the surrounding buildings: the street frontage was, like all the neighbours, the open shop front, but behind it, the spacious living room gave the family a safe place to mourn the loss of Joan. The trap-door and ladder from the living room led down to the cellar, where Miquel had hidden the Castilian sword. Wine and casks of brandy were stored in the cellar, and Joan had used all his youthful strength to move the barrels of Rioja up and down the ladder, relieving his father-in-law of the tasks which were becoming too strenuous for him, in much the same way he had relieved Abuelo at the bakery. Rising from the living room the steep staircase lead to the bedchambers on the upper floor, which also provided private spaces where Emilia and her children could hide away when the grief became overwhelming. Senor Dominguez was much admired for achieving such a grand home, but he never expected his dwelling to become such a centre of such grief.

Time slowly started to heal the emotional wounds, although Joan and his memory was never far from the family's lips. Some semblance of normality returned to the merchant's house, which now contained all of Emilia's children. A further ladder led up to the roof – a space which was mainly used for drying the washing, but which became a favourite place for Miquel and his brothers to sleep on hot summer nights.

Usually, however, Miquel and his brothers slept in the large living room behind the shop, and the women and Senor Dominguez were able to sleep upstairs; Emilia returning to her old room from her younger years, and Marta enjoying the novelty of a small room of her own. The household also had the benefit of a servant, a bright young man who lived day and night in the shop.

One evening, a stranger arrived at the wine shop asking for Miquel. The two stepped outside for a while, and then Miquel returned, looking unusually grim faced.

"I have a chance to seek revenge for my father's death," he said. "There is a plot to kill King Phillip, and all of the House of Austria. Loyal Catalonians, those few of us with the courage and desire to avenge the murders, not only of our father, but the hundreds of fellow Catalans we have lost recently, have been asked to go to Madrid. This is the call. I am determined to go. You, my brothers, must help Grandfather Dominguez to run the wine shop, and my sister, I charge you with caring for our grandmothers and our mother. I alone will go, and avenge our father's death."

Grandfather Dominguez, with his characteristic and unswerving Catalan loyalty, spoke first. "This is a dangerous mission, and we are loath to lose you, my boy. But you will go with my blessing, and that of your grandmother."

"And mine," came the voice of Emilia. "There is no more noble endeavour than to seek revenge for the death of your father."

"And for the deaths of all loyal Catalans. We have lost so many," said grandmother Dominguez. "God speed you."

"God speed you," repeated the others.

Asking everyone to wait, Miquel climbed down to the cool dark cellar, and swiftly pulled the mysterious bundle from behind a barrel. Upstairs, and to everyone's horror, he appeared with the bloodied bundle. Looking around the room, he slowly unwrapped a sword. The family were silent, looking at him in confusion. With an ironic smile, he said, "You didn't know I had this. I have been waiting for this moment. This is the sword that killed our father, and this is the sword that will kill King Philip. Now it, and I, will do our duty."

June 7th, 1640 would go down in Catalan history as "Corpus de Sang" - the night a band of guerillas attacked the royal family in Madrid. Where they came from nobody knew, and they melted back into the night after the bloody business. King Philip survived the attack, protected by loyal soldiers, but several of his family, members of the House of Austria, died. Each time a prince or princess was slaughtered, the murderer would dip his hand in the blood and draw the four bloody stripes of Catalunya across the victim's face. The Castilian king could be in no doubt where the murderers came from.

At this time, impoverished peasants from the countryside, from farms devastated by the Castilian soldiers, joined with the workers and servants of the city in a general uprising against anyone showing sympathy for the Castilians. Many were the nobles and knights who met untimely deaths. Weapons were anything to hand, and the country folk showed many grotesque and deadly skills with such tools as sickles. History would remember this chaotic time as 'The Reaper's War' and it would take its place in the folklore of Catalunya, and in the history of the Blanxart family.

For many months, a guerrilla war raged in Barcelona and reprisals were severe in the city. Castilian agents, well disguised, hid themselves on roof tops and in dark alleyways ready to strike. Anyone showing the senyera, the Catalan flag, was vulnerable. No Catalan was safe as the random slaughter continued. Senor Dominguez knew he was a prime target, but refused to take down the senyera flying over the door of the shop.

The family were awakened one night by shouts in the street and a fearsome hammering on the door. Senor Dominguez had already gone to bed, and clambered down the stairs to see what the commotion was all about. Opening the small door, he peered out, and was grabbed by unknown assailants.

Before he could speak, he was dragged from the house, and his throat slit. Hearing the terrible noises, the family rushed down the stairs to see what had happened. As they climbed through the small door, they were horrified to be confronted by the sight of Senor Dominguez, half naked in his nightshirt, dying in the street, blood pouring from a hideous wound in his neck. With a terrible scream, Senora Dominguez's instinct was to rush out to her husband. Emilia tried to hold her back, but was not quick enough to prevent the older woman's headlong charge out into the street. In the melee that ensured, and despite neighbours attempting to intervene, the old lady received a blow to the head from one of the assassins, and Senora Dominguez crashed down and died shortly afterwards, falling beside her husband.

The sight of the two old people lying dead in the street, brought a silence to the crowd. The assassins disappeared into the night as Emilia knelt weakly by her parents. It had all happened so quickly. Neighbours helped her up, and the bodies of the old couple were carried into the shop. Numb with sorrow, Emilia watched as the bodies were laid on the long table, in just the way her husband had so recently been laid. Marta, who had stood paralysed by horror and fear, put her arm around Emilia, and held her tightly. There was a pause as if she was gathering strength for what was to come, and shakily at first, Emilia stood up.

Finding herself thrust shockingly and unexpectedly to guide the family, Emilia focussed on the enormity of the terrible task in hand, and gradually she found a calm inner strength. She invited everyone to a vigil for the grandparents overnight. She thanked the few neighbours who remained with the family, and they set candles around the bodies, finally settling down to a hushed calm.

As dawn broke, Emilia with Marta's help, watched by her youthful children, carried out the tearful and reverend task of cleaning and preparing the crushed bodies for burial at Montjuic. With a handcart borrowed from a neighbour, the young family took their grandparents to the graveyard. The old couple seemed strangely small and insignificant wrapped in sheets on the bare boards of the handcart, belying the importance and regard with which they had been held in life. Several neighbours joined behind them as Marta and Emilia led the sorry funeral procession across the beach towards the mountain. Emilia found the way to the Dominguez tombs. With help from the neighbours, the grandparents were pushed into the tomb, to lie side by side for eternity. After laying the old couple to rest, the family and their friends went to Joan's fresh tomb, to say further prayers.

"If it is the way of the world that Catalunya be defended with blood," said Emilia at Joan's graveside, "Then so be it. My father was proud to fly the Catalan flag, and his death must not be in vain. My mother also stood by him at all times, always proudly Catalan, and she died beside him in the fight for our country. All night I have been thinking. They died because of what they believed in. And we believe the same. In the name of my father, my mother, and Joan my husband, we must be strong and fight on. We pray for the safe return of Miquel. We pray that he has avenged his father's murder. We pray to the Blessed Virgin of the Dawn to give us the strength to carry on the fight."

Some weeks later the family were horrified by another sudden night-time hammering on the door. They went down into the shop, but did not dare to open the door. "Not again," whispered Emila to the children. "They cannot want the rest of us."

The hammering continued as the family cowered. Then came a shout, "Is anyone awake? Let me in! It's Miquel!"

Letting out a huge sigh of relief, Emilia pulled back the bolts, and peered round the door. It was with great relief that she saw her oldest son, grasping his sword. She opened the door just enough for him to slip inside. Miquel had returned unscathed but battle-weary, quietly pleased at the deaths he had achieved with the royal relatives, but frustrated by the survival of the king himself. The family could see immediately that he had changed: the violent experiences in Madrid had given him a maturity, although he still had a young body. He was horrified to discover that his grandparents had become victims of the bloodbath, and reacted with anger. "An old man." he growled, "And an old lady. What cowards are these Castilians to kill old people in this way?" Miquel's hand grasped the hilt of his sword tightly, his knuckles turning white. "If only I'd been here," he said. "They would have received a taste of their own medicine."

"You were doing greater work for our country, risking everything, Miquel. We won't forget that, and we don't regret that you weren't here when the assassins came. You will remember what your father told us," said Emilia. "Castile will stop at nothing to win Barcelona; and we must all be ready to defend our land. Your father was a proud Catalan, and showed the senyera defiantly at the door of the baker's shop. He always knew it was provocative, but he was determined to show his loyalty. He would not take it down – that would have been the action of a coward. In the same way, my father showed the flag at the door of the winery. I am proud of my father, just as you are proud of your's. The Virgin has returned you safely to us, and we thank her for that."

Canon Pau Claris, desperate to stop the killings in the city, sent to Louis, King of France for help. Louis XIII was delighted to offer French troops to protect the city from the Castilian soldiers, thereby gaining a foothold in the glittering prize that was Barcelona, and soon the city was teeming with the foreigners. The Castilian troops, with orders that they must not retreat, engaged the Frenchies in skirmishes throughout the region, and both sides were constantly attacked by the Catalans. Miquel, his hackles raised, wanted to join the guerrilla fighting, but this time was held back by Marta.

"You are the eldest, the first-born," she said. "Your duty now is to the family. With your father gone, and Emilia's parents also, we look to you for protection and support."

"But grandmother, I should go. I have tasted the blood of these Castilians, and have seen many bloody deeds. I must drive these foreigners from Catalan soil. Philip's troops must be driven back to Madrid; and the cost of having the French here is too high. We are forfeiting lands to France in the Pyrenees, and we will never get them back. I have no taste to live under the French flag any more than I wish to be Castilian"

"And who will carry on the fight here?" answered Marta. "Your duty is to marry, and have a son. Teach your son the stories of Catalunya that your father taught you, the stories that my father had taught him. It is up to you now to secure your family, this is your responsibility and duty."

"Tell the stories?" said Miquel.

"Yes indeed," said Marta. "They are not written down; they are stories that pass from generation to generation. Remember the senyera, the story of the golden shield. You would not know it, if my father had not told it to your father. That is why you need a son." she paused and smiled, "And we need you. You are the man of the house, and must settle to the job."

"Then who shall I marry, grandmother?"

"There are many eager young women in the barrio."

"Then find me one who has passion and fire and loyalty for Catalunya, and I'll wed her!"

Marta's optimism was a little misplaced, for Miquel rejected all of the young women she found. He had no patience for the small talk of the girls, and sent them, crying, on their way.

At last she found Elena, the daughter of a blacksmith. Elena was a big fierce woman, with a fiery temper, long black hair, and a suitable match for the battle hardened Miquel. She was a true daughter of La Ribera, and boasted to Miquel that she had played her part in the recent riots. She showed an understanding and knowledge of Catalunya that pleased Miquel, and vowed that when the time came she would fight alongside him.

"We shall raise our own army," she declared. "Many Catalonian babies, to grow up as soldiers for Catalunya!"

Miquel, as a young man, had learned the trade of baking, and run the Pujol bakery well. Now he found himself without a bakehouse, but with a wine merchant's. He was anxious to learn the vintner's trade. For some weeks, since the murder of Senor Dominguez, the business had been in the doldrums, with transactions happening more by chance than design. Emilia knew much from observing her father, but had always remained in the background and thus did not have the many personal contacts which were needed for the business to flourish. Miquel promised to marry Elena as soon as he had it back on its feet.

One evening, a knock at the door startled Miquel and the women. "Who calls at such an hour?" wondered Marta, and Emilia was worried, and frightened, remembering the terrible night of her parents' murder. "Don't fear, mother" said Miquel. "'Tis a friendly knock; I know the sign." Nevertheless, he picked up his sword before opening the door.

When it was opened, a handsome man of Miquel's age came into the shop. Dropping his sword, Miquel embraced him warmly. "My dear friend, I did not expect to see you here. I trust you do not bring bad news."

"On the contrary, brother Miquel, I come peacefully and cordially. Many of us have heard of the murders of Senor and Senora Dominguez; and we know that you are struggling to maintain your grandfather's business. It cannot be easy."

"I struggle here, I admit," replied Miquel, "but I believe I will revive this business. But first, come through to the parlour and be refreshed from your journey."

Calling to Marta and Emilia to meet his guest, Miquel explained in rather vague terms that the man was known to him as a loyal Catalan fighter, a 'man of the four stripes of blood', and a welcome guest. Marta produced pastries, and Emilia was sent to find a bottle of good Catalan Rioja.

"We don't have many of these left," she said as she returned from the cellar.

"But soon there will be plenty," replied the stranger, with a mysterious laugh. "Is it in order for me to talk in front of the women?" he asked.

"It certainly is," replied Miquel. "My mother and my grandmother are both loyal Catalonians. You can tell we speak no other language in this house, and we will all defend our Catalan heritage until death. I am sorry only that the girl I am to marry is not here also, for then you would meet three generations of good Catalan women."

"The word has been passed around," rejoined the stranger. "Of how your grandparents were murdered by Castilian thugs, murdered for showing the flag of Catalunya. The word has travelled over the countryside, and loyal Catalonian farmers send their greetings to you. It is hard to thrive in this strife-filled land of ours, and we are bringing messages of goodwill from many of your admirers."

Miquel looked startled, and Emilia clutched her son's shoulder.

"Do not be so alarmed," smiled the stranger. "The stories of your son's exploits in Madrid may have become part of Catalan folklore, but his identity remains a close-guarded secret."

"I am fearful you have come to take him away again," said Emilia.

"I trust not!" said Marta.

"Fear not ladies, your son, your grandson, is safe here in your care. I bring quite different news. Many farmers are rebuilding their vineyards, and need to renew the network of trade in wine. Despite all the best efforts of the Castilian fighters, and the supposedly friendly intervention of the Frenchies, some of the vineyards are already bearing fruit, and good Catalan wine will soon be flowing again. Now we need to find a way to sell the wine and bring some measure of prosperity back to our land regardless of the intentions of the Castilians or the Frenchies."

"I have come," he continued, " to challenge Miquel to be our channel through the port and to satisfy my brothers that he is ready and willing to deal with the growing trade in Catalan wine. There is much danger, as all his suppliers will be well-known to the Castilians as loyal Catalonians, and we do not wish to bring a spotlight to bear upon this house. There have been enough deaths for the cause already."

"Amen to that," whispered Emilia.

"And here is the crux of the matter," the stranger continued. "Senor Dominguez dealt in wine from the countryside, and supplied it to Barcelona. That was his trade, wine for the rich and the poor. We know that even Pau Claris himself and the rich of the city drank wine supplied from this house. We know also that the loyal people of this barrio, your own Ribera, looked to Senor Dominguez for the good Catalonian wine he sold them. But we are talking about a new and greater challenge. There will be far more wine than Barcelona can drink. If Miquel, our brother in arms here, is to support us and be the channel for rescuing the grape farmers of the region, he must prepare to ship the wine abroad; become a wine trader as well as merchant. What do you think?"

The family turned to Miquel, who did not hesitate.

"I cannot say anything but yes," he replied.

"It may not be as glamorous as wielding your sword in Madrid," grinned the stranger, "But it will be supporting the network of Catalunya, and by bringing wealth to the region, help to restore some dignity and strength to our people."

"A wonderful proposition," exclaimed Emilia.

"And a good basis for raising a family," laughed Marta.

"Let's drink to that, and to your forthcoming nuptials," announced the stranger, raising his cup of wine.

"Aye, good Catalan wine," said Miquel. "It's time the world found out about it."

The women went to bed, and Miquel and the stranger talked late into the night. Eventually the stranger disappeared into the darkness, but Miquel sat up thinking. He would need contacts at the port; he would need to understand how trade worked and he would need a network of foreign customers. England! The English had always been friendly towards the Catalans. They notoriously hated the Castilians, and were daggers drawn with the French. Yes, he would trade with London, and introduce good Rioja to the Englishmen. All would have to be done with a measure of secrecy. The daily local trade would act as a cover whilst he sorted out the international complexities. London! Could it be?

In the morning, Emilia found him slumped across the table, the candle out, and the wine finished. "Well," she said, " what shall we do first, marry or buy a boat?"

"Both, mother!" exclaimed Miquel, "Wait until I tell Elena; she will be mine, and we will sell our wine to England!"

The merchant's house was again the scene of some rejoicing for the marriage of Miquel and Elena. Although there was a deep underlying sadness, for the wedding would take place without Joan or the Dominguez grandparents, the family did their best to give Miquel and Elena a good start in life. Marta's old bakery skills, with Emilia's help, produced many tempting breads and pastries for the wedding breakfast. Miquel found a few more bottles of good wine, and he and Elena were married at Santa Maria del Mar just as his parents had been.

Meanwhile, Miquel had not been wasting time since the visit of the stranger, and at the wedding breakfast, he explained everything to the family.

"I have taken the lease on a warehouse in El Born, and we will start to fill it with good local wine, in barrels, which can age slowly in the dark and cool." Turning to one of his brothers, he said, "You, brother Javier, are to set sail for London as soon as you can, and will set up our trade in that city. There is an English boat leaving within the week, and you will sail on that." Javier was suitably astonished, and then excited. "Do not think the voyage will be a holiday, as you must learn the English tongue from the Englishmen on board. I will furnish you with a cask of good wine, and if I can find it, another of Catalan brandy, as gifts for the captain, to ensure your safe passage and co-operation from all on board, whilst you learn the lingo."

Turning to the next brother, he continued, "And you, brother Jose, are to go with him." Now it was Jose's turn to be surprised. "And as soon as you know we can sell the wine, you will find the first ship back to tell me. The sooner you return here, the sooner our trade will begin in earnest. Oh, and whilst you're on board, you will learn English too. In fact, not a word of Catalan from your lips, either of you. If we are to become traders, we will become great traders, and knowledge of the English tongue and habits will be crucial."

"Finally Jordi, my baby brother," he continued, "I will give you the names of many of our loyal Catalan farmers, and you can ride out and meet each and every one. Tell them of our scheme. Encourage them to help fill our warehouse ready for Jose's return."

The brothers shouted loud with their excitement, but Miquel quietened them quickly.

"Stay calm, my brothers, stay calm. Remember what we are doing is not without its dangers. The Castilians will be watching the seas, and sailing out into the Mediterranean is dangerous. And for you also Jordi, riding the countryside will arouse suspicions if you are not very careful. The Frenchies are watching you, just as much as the thugs from Madrid. There are spies everywhere. These are great adventures you are embarking upon, but maintain some secrecy, keep your own council, and trust no-one. And now, my bride, I had almost forgot this is our wedding breakfast. These brothers of mine are off to London and the countryside, but we are to bed!"

CHAPTER THREE

Miquel and Elena were good at producing babies. Miquel's bloodthirsty adventures in Madrid left him much in need of the comfort and rewards of a lusty wife; and Elena brought all the gusto and verve of being a blacksmith's daughter to their love making. Following their wedding, they moved into the room previously used by Senor and Senora Dominguez. At first, they were insecure about the ghosts of the grandparents lingering in the room, but soon their athletic love-making banished all such thoughts. The rest of the family were highly amused by the shrieks which echoed through the house, and indeed the vibrations which threatened to demolish the place, as Miquel and Elena matched one another in lust and stamina. Little Joan Blanxart was born in 1643, rapidly followed by little Miquel, little Jordi, little Jose, and little Javier.

"You produce babies just as you live life in every way, everything done at speed." joked Marta. The old lady was slowing down, and found all these great grandchildren rather challenging. The house was getting full, and the constant noise of children was hard for her to bear. She was, by now, well known throughout La Ribera; indeed she was probably its oldest inhabitant, and she would make an almost royal progress when she slowly made her way to a neighbour or friend.

She would sit in the sun, and tell stories to whoever would listen. "I remember Queen Anne visiting Barcelona," she would tell them. "I can't tell when it was, but fifteen-hundred and something. Before the new century. Before little Jordi died. Before he was born even. She was married to Philip, the king of Castile. Not this King Philip now, I spit on him, nor even his father, I spit on him. No, she was married to Philip the grandfather of the Castilian king. She came from somewhere else, a place called Austria, but I never knew where that was. That was a time. It was when they were hanging witches. Used to hang them at Santa Caterina, by the market. That was a time." And she would mutter on, mixing moments from her ancient history, and her listeners would humour her, not for a moment realising that all she said was true.

Emilia would worry that her mother-in-law's ramblings would betray Miquel's part in the Corpus de Sang, but Marta's memories were from her childhood and early years; she seemed to have forgotten the recent past.

Meanwhile the Blanxart family business was on the move. Jose returned from London full of extraordinary stories about the strange Englishmen and the enormous city. He told the family tales of King Charles, and how the English were fighting amongst themselves. He tried to explain how there were two different Christian churches in London, some Catholic and some Protestant, but he wasn't clear quite what the difference was. He told them how the Londoners hated Charles being married to a Catholic princess, and how the city seethed with plots and schemes. He amazed them that London was a greater city than Barcelona – "No, it can't be!" said Emilia – but most of all, he came back with stories of the riches of the great English capital. He'd wandered the streets with his brother, and seen the endless procession of rich and poor, prostitutes and businessmen, elegant ladies and tramps. The rich pattern of London life, the wide boulevards and elegant houses, had overwhelmed the brothers at first; and Jose told the family how they had found lodgings in Whitechapel – "very like our Ribera slum," said Jose – and met wine merchants, and been to the extraordinary London docks and watched the whole process. "We can do this," he told them, "London is a huge market for us. The local ales and wines in England are poor: rich Londoners are forced to drink cheap French claret, and even some rubbish Portugese wines, and I know they will welcome our Rioja."

"But here's the best news: the wines from Lisbon and Cadiz do not command good prices. I have made an arrangement with a vintner in London by the name of Mr John Paige. He specialises in wine imports, and has, as he says, far too much bad wine from Castile and Portugal in his cellar. He is very excited to get his hands on some of our good Rioja."

"Javier is investigating that we will rent or even buy a warehouse, so that we can unload and store our wine when we get it to London. We have great and ambitious plans. Let's hope it all works."

Jose had been surprised that even with political upheavals and parliamentary controversy, the commerce of London was thriving and growing. It was as if the two existed independently of one another. Whilst the king and the politicians and the church fought their battles, the traders continued to be very active and make many lucrative international deals. "Rather like us, here in Barcelona," commented young Jordi.

Jose delivered a long letter that Javier had written to Miquel, detailing the practical aspects of the wine trade in London, and introducing vintner John Paige, the merchant willing to buy the Catalan wine. A letter in English from John Paige himself confirmed his good intentions, but warned, "If you should send me bad wine, like the Jerez sent recently from Lisbon, do not expect me to pay more than twelve pounds per pipe." Jose explained the London traders' system of measuring wine, and that a Catalan barrel was equivalent to a dozen London pipes. As long as they could get the Rioja to London unharmed, they would command extraordinary prices. It seemed nothing could go wrong.

Jordi, meantime, had spent many days and weeks in the saddle, visiting farmers throughout the region. From Valencia in the south, up into the high mountains of the Pyrenees, he had worked his way through all the networks of loyal Catalonians, dodging Castilian thugs and French soldiers. He returned with many promises to supply the Blanxart warehouse with wines and some brandies, and was excited each time a cart arrived with a consignment for them. Miquel was impressed how his youngest brother remembered details about all his contacts, and was able to greet personally each cart as it arrived.

Mostly the consignments of wine arrived very early in the morning, or late into the evening, thus avoiding drawing too much attention to the large quantity which was accumulating in the warehouse. Farmers sent their carts lined carefully with straw to ensure that the wine arrived in excellent condition; and it was handled carefully as it was placed in storage. Jordi, who had seen the process in the fields, knew how important it was for the Rioja to be handled gently, and was worried how it would fare on board a ship. Would it arrive in good enough condition to sell for a good price?

Gradually the warehouse filled, and the time approached for the first shipment to London. This was a tense time for all the family. Their entire future lay in the warehouse. Miquel was in debt to his suppliers, who he would pay handsomely when the ship returned from London; and he was in debt to both the captain and owner of the vessel. Should the Castilians find the warehouse, or attack the ship; should a storm overtake the vessel in the notorious Bay of Biscay and the ship sink; or any other disaster strike, then all would be lost. Miquel would be the one locked in the bankrupt's prison, and the family would be reduced to begging on the streets. It was a huge gamble, and it was only once the scheme had started that they realised how much was at stake.

There was the further uncertainty of what Jose would find when he got back to London with the first shipment. Would Javier have maintained and developed their contact with John Paige? Could they trust a London merchant? Would a civil war have broken out? Would, indeed, Charles still be king, after all the whispering he had heard in the city about assassination?

At last, the vessel recommended by Mr John Paige arrived in the port of Barcelona. The Swan from Gravesend, owned by Mr John Shaw of that town, brought a small consignment of West Indian sugar. Miquel found himself trading in a commodity he knew nothing about, and consulted the elderly and ailing Marta. "White sugar," she told him, "is very special and rare. From Havana you say? That's the best. You must get a very good price for that. I remember baking good cakes for the nobles in their palaces on Carrer Montcada. So long ago now. And muscovados? Good brown sugar but not as valuable as the white. Well done young man, you have done well. I will bake many cakes with this sugar, so beautiful, so white....." and she drifted off again.

One night, a group of loyal neighbours from La Ribera, gathered to load the ship. Gently the precious casks of Rioja were passed from hand to hand down to the shore line, and then into small boats to be rowed out to the ship. Straw in each small boat not only kept the operation quiet, but also prevented the wine from rolling about too much. Nervously, the brothers watched the operation – Jordi at the warehouse, Miquel down on the beach, and Jose on the ship.

At one time, in the darkest part of the night, Miquel was startled to see someone approaching with a lantern. "Don't be alarmed," came the voice of his mother, "but I have brought a friend, someone to wish the wine Godspeed."

Miquel was astonished to find the lantern illuminating the face of none other than Canon Pau Claris himself, President of the Generalitat of Barcelona. "This is a great thing you are doing, Senor Blanxart. Catalunya is in safe hands with men like you. It is not prudent for either of us to meet publically, so I have come in the night. When your ship returns, there will be great rejoicing in Barcelona. Godspeed to the Rioja."

The ship was loaded by day break, and the warehouse empty. With a favourable wind, The Swan sailed as the sun arose, passing the little fishing boats returning with the night's catch.

Jose sailed with that first shipment. Miquel's local trade continued as it had done all through the first filling of the warehouse and the first shipping to London, and with Jose gone, Jordi went back out onto the lanes and tracks of Catalunya to tell his contacts that their good wine was on its way to England; and to encourage them to send further consignments to refill the warehouse ready for the vessel's return. Gifts of little paper packets of white sugar endeared him to all the farmer's wives in the region, and he secured even more contracts to sell Rioja and brandy in London.

Gradually, as Elena was lustily bringing new lives into the world, Marta's was ebbing away. She took to her bed, rather as her father had done many years before, and spent much of her time sleeping. When she died in 1649, she had five great grandchildren, supposedly a record for La Ribera, and the whole barrio mourned her passing. Her reputation for celebrating the culture of Catalunya made her a celebrity amongst the neighbours, and many came to her funeral mass in Santa Maria del Mar.

Elena was pregnant again when Marta died, and in 1650, Perot Blanxart was born. All of her other children had inherited Elena's black hair, but Perot was the exception, having his father's mass of blond curls.

"I am pleased, at last, to have a son with blond curls like mine," commented Miquel. "He continues a family tradition which started with my father. We used to be called the old lion and the young lion: the lions of La Ribera. Perhaps I'll become the old lion now, and Perot here will be the new young lion."

Elena looked at the tiny baby she was suckling and smiled. "I don't think he's a young lion yet; but his time will come."

Perot was born into a land of strife. Outside the carefree and loving home provided by Elena and his grandmother, nothing could be relied upon. It was difficult to know who were friends, who were enemies, and who was spying for whom. The network of treachery encouraged by both Castile and France created a web of deceit and nervous anticipation of what might happen.

Beyond the relative safety of La Ribera, dangers lurked at every turn. A minor scuffle could escalate into a riot; a riot could trigger involvement of the militia, and in the blink of an eye, French soldiers would come running down the lane, bayonets fixed, expecting to skewer Castilian thugs. Should an innocent Catalan get in the way, it was of little consequence.

Miquel and his family were, however, more concerned with immediate matters, and despite the sadness of losing Great-grandmother Marta, they talked constantly of when the ship would finally return. Each day one or more of them would go to Santa Maria del Mar and pray to the Virgin to bring their ship safely back to Barcelona.

In London, Javier was standing on the quayside, looking down to the muddy Thames. Below him, moving gently on the rising tide was The Swan. He smiled to himself, and turned to Jose.

"Father will be so pleased," he said. "Will he have imagined the success we have had? Will he even believe we have our own warehouse here in London?"

"I'd love him to see it," agreed Jose, looking up at the newly-painted sign, proclaiming for all to see, 'Blanxart and Sons, Importers of Fine Catalan Wines'.

"It's all happened so quickly," continued Javier, "Just one shipment of Rioja. Much of it sold before your return to Barcelona, and an amazing cargo to send back to Father."

"I hope he's ready and willing to deal with diverse goods," said Jose. "I'll work hard to reassure him that we'll make an excellent profit on everything. Besides, it makes sense to take the boat home with a good cargo: it would have been nonsense to go back to Barcelona empty."

The Swan sailed on the tide, moving quickly down the river, propelled more by the rush of water than her sails.

Meanwhile, the waiting in Barcelona continued. Despite the knowledge of the time such a voyage would take, and the unknown challenges faced by Javier in London, and Jose on the high seas, the family fretted day by day, waiting the boat to return.

At last their prayers were answered and The Swan was sighted in the Mediterranean. It anchored some way off the beach, and Miquel and Jordi were rowed out to the ship, where they found a jubilant Jose waiting on deck for them.

"At last we greet one another my brothers. Is my mother well? And all those boys of your's? And your wife Elena? And grandmother? What news? Is all peaceful in La Ribera?"

"Slow down my dear Jose," grinned Miquel, "There is much to tell you, and we will tell you all. But first,

I must know. Did you have success in London? Have we made our fortune, or am I destined for the bankrupt's jail?"

"I can report that our Rioja is a sensation in London. The trade was brisk and at auction, having tasted the wine, the merchants competed to buy it. We reached the top price for imported wine in the vintner's hall. We have beaten the Castilians and the Portugese at their own game. They do not pack their barrels in straw as we did, and their wine arrives in poor shape. It has to be racked before it can be bottled. Our wine arrived in good condition for drinking."

"You have been gone so long," said Miquel. "Will the voyage always be this slow?"

"We had easterly winds in the Atlantic, and crossing the Bay of Biscay was very slow. At least the winds were gentle; they told me terrible tales of gales and storms, and of ships vanishing beneath the waves. Once in the English Channel, we made good progress. We took some time in London, renting a warehouse to unload the wine, and then assembling the return cargo. It was very complicated, but we completed many deals very quickly. The English are good businessmen and move fast when they smell a good trade. Our return voyage has been fairly speedy, although it was a little rough in Biscay."

"We have another warehouse full of good wine for you to return to London with. Do you believe you will do as well next time?"

"As well?" laughed Jose, "No, we will do better, for next time our reputation will go before us. But first, dear brother, we have a cargo to unload."

"More sugar?" asked Jordi. "Last time we did well selling the sugar."

"Some sugar, most of it white this time," replied Jose, "but many other goods. Some bundles of a rare American wood called campeachy, and cochineal, and indigo, and ginger, and tobacco, rare hides and much more."

"So I am to be a general trader? A dealer in commodities I have never heard of!"

"The merchants of Barcelona will know what you've got. The weavers and the dyers will be astonished by the campeachy wood; it is the rarest and best of purple dyes, and can be used for ink as well as fabric. Cochineal and indigo will also command high prices; and the cooks of the city will clamour for the ginger."

"And talking of cooks," said Jose, "How is my grandmother?"

"A cloud lies over your return," said Miquel sadly. "Grandmother died whilst you were at sea. We have missed her very much. Your mother has taken it badly; but she waits for you on the shore. Come, let us row back and greet her. She will be so glad to have you in her arms."

As they neared the beach, Jose could see the two women waiting. "I see mother, and I see Elena. And is that another baby she carries? Miquel, tell me, are you a father again?"

Miquel grinned, "Of course, you know me. That's my little Perot. And wait 'til you see him; he has my blond curls!"

Although Marta's death cast a shadow over Jose's homecoming, the success of the first shipment of Catalonian wine to London was a cause of quietly intense celebration. Miquel had considerably under-estimated the value of the wine in London, and was astonished by the prices achieved by the cargo Jose had brought back on The Swan. He was able to pay all the producing farmers. And even after paying the captain and through him, the owner of the ship, he still had a remarkably handsome profit.

Jose noticed that the situation in Barcelona mirrored that in London – trade was flourishing despite the background strife between the politicians. Javier had sent letters from London: he found the English warring between the Royalists and the Cromwellians to be similar to that between the Castilians and the Catalonians, and he wondered if the socialist principles of the Roundheads matched the feelings within the Blanxart family, of the injustices in Barcelona. He did, however, admit that he didn't understand everything that was happening, but reassured Miquel that trade and commerce seemed remarkably immune to the English political shenanigans.

Miquel found the same in Barcelona. Despite being at war with Castile, and the very uncomfortable relationship with the French, the Blanxart businesses flourished. The warehouse was full, and so as soon as the mixed cargo was unloaded, another consignment of Rioja and brandy was gently placed on its straw bed in the hold of the ship, and Jose was once more on his way to London.

The wine merchant's shop began to resemble a rather exotic bazaar, and customers were delighted by the chance to buy the rare dyes, and enchanted by the little paper packets of white sugar. Speculating that he would make as much profit from the next shipment as the last, Miquel dared to think that the Blanxart family fortunes were secure. He and Elena felt optimistic; little Perot thrived, and Miquel smiled upon his peaceful family. At last they could live in peace. The Swan sailed continuously between London and Barcelona, taking the good Rioja and brandy, and returning with a variety of exotic goods from around the world.

But it was not to be. The family's fragile peace did not last long. Disaster came from a very unexpected direction.

Frightening news of the continued skirmishes between Castilians, Frenchies and Catalonians, meant that Jordi's regular trips to the vineyards were always dangerous. Emilia found herself more worried about him than she was about Jose on the high seas, or Javier in London, and was always mightily relieved when she heard Jordi's horse in the lane. She would rush out to greet him, and on this particular occasion, that's just what she did.

"Jordi, my son, welcome home, safe and well, welcome!"

"Safe," replied a grim faced Jordi, "but far from well." As he slipped down from the saddle, he was doubled up with an acute spasm of coughing. Emilia rushed to embrace him, but he pushed her away, spluttering between the coughs to warn her. "Mother, stay back, I think I am infected with the plague."

Emilia recoiled in horror for a moment, but then flung herself upon her son. "I am not afraid of my own son," she stated. "You may be a man in the countryside, but you're still my son at home. Come inside, tell me all."

Miquel and Elena rushed to greet Jordi. When the coughing had subsided, and he had managed a mouthful of brandy, he told his story.

"Last night I stayed in a farmhouse near Prat de Lobregat; simple good people, loyal to the Catalan flag. They have a smallholding and outbuildings where they produce some of our finest brandy. The quantity is not great, perhaps a dozen casks a year, but the quality is excellent and they earn, and deserve, a good price."

He stopped, racked by another coughing fit. Miquel and Elena stepped back, fearing the worst, but Emilia remained cradling her son. After a while, last he could continue.

"We talked late into the evening, and enjoyed some of the good brandy, and it was too late and just a bit too far to ride home last night. I lay in one of the stables, just as I often do on my country trips, and slept on the straw."

"I awoke at sunrise to see many rats running around; nothing unusual in that, but I awoke with a terrible itching all over, and realised I had been bitten by many fleas."

At that moment Perot ran into the room. "Uncle Jordi, Uncle Jordi!", but as he was about to fling himself into his uncle's arms, Miquel grabbed him and pulled him back. Elena took Perot firmly, and retreated to the far corner of the room. Jordi continued the tale.

"There's not much more to tell. Before I left, the farmer told me that there had been much talk of plague in the area; and that some distant farmers and their families were reported to have died; but he didn't think it had come to his farm yet. I fear, mother, he is wrong. As I have been riding this short distance from Lobregat, I have had this cough, and it's getting worse. Help me mother. I must undress and see for myself if I have been smitten."

As he went to stand, the coughing started again, and to the horror of the family, he spat a mouthful of blood onto the straw-covered floor. Emilia turned to the others. "Get out, and get right away. I will stay with Jordi, but you must keep well clear."

Miquel, Elena and Perot went out to the front shop, almost frozen with fear. "Plague?" asked Elena.

"It looks like it." said Miquel. "Oh God, not now, not with The Swan due any day."

They stood silently in the shop, listening intently, but hearing nothing but Jordi's coughing and groaning. Suddenly Emilia let out a scream. Indicating to Elena to stay where she was, Miquel rushed to the parlour. A half naked Jordi lay slumped across the table, with a splattering of blood on his torso and on the table. Emilia stood transfixed, and simply pointed to her son's arms. There Miquel could see clearly the buboes of the plague, fearful red swellings in Jordi's armpits.

Emilia, trembling, said, "It is, as he feared."

Miquel stuttered, all his bravado gone, and could only say feebly, "It takes hold so fast. He's a strong young man, but his body cannot resist the disease. Mother, stand back from him, or you will surely be infected."

Emilia smiled, "If that will happen, then it is already too late. I will nurse Jordi and comfort him, but you and your children must keep away."

Miquel shook his head. "Oh mother," he said, "I will go to Santa Maria; I will take all the children and my sister, and she and Elena and I will pray to the Virgin. Santa Maria brought Jose and the Swan safely back to us; let us pray she will give mercy to Jordi."

On the way to the church, they agreed to say nothing in order to avoid a panic, but they immediately encountered a neighbour with similar news. "There is plague in Sant Antoni. My daughter and son-in-law live there. I am going to pray for them."

Others were on the street, some hurrying to the church, others hurrying away, but the word from all was "plague". The dreaded disease was heading for La Ribera, and Jordi was only one of many.

They tried to sleep in the shop that night, but tossed and turned, unable to sleep, listening to the groans and cries of Jordi. The next morning, Miquel stood at the parlour door. His exhausted mother said nothing, but turned to Jordi. The red buboes had grown huge and turned black; he continued to cough blood and he was racked with pain. "I'm so sorry," he said repeatedly, "I'm so sorry."

"Hush, baby," whispered his mother. "Santa Maria is watching you and calling you. Soon you will be with grandmother Marta." And she tried to give him a sip of brandy. Abruptly there came a scream from the shop.

"My babies, my babies," screamed Elena. Miquel turned back to his wife. She was kneeling in front of the six children, undressing them one by one. Each revealed the horrifying red marks in their armpits of the beginnings of the disease. The five dark-haired boys were finally lined up, all crying, all clearly ill, all smitten. Finally she reached Perot. Miquel darted forward and pulled his jerkin over his head. No buboes. No plague. Perot, for the time being, had been spared.

"Take him," Elena said, "Take him to the church and stay there. Stay there with him. Stay there until you get a message. He is our only hope. Go quickly Miquel."

Stunned and numb, Miquel picked up the little curly haired boy, and went to the door. With tears in his eyes, he looked back at the rest of his beautiful boys, knowing he would never see them again.

Miquel ran full-tilt to the church. Neighbours stood back, seeing the tears streaming from the man, and the cries of the frightened little boy. Not pausing at the door, he ran into the church, skirting through the kneeling worshippers, until he was at the foot of the statue of the Virgin. "Santa Maria, take me, let me come to you, but spare my boys, spare my boys." Unaware that he was shouting, and disturbing the normal peace of the church, he continued in his panic and fervour, "I have sinned and deserve to die, but my boys are innocent; my brother is innocent, spare him, spare them."

He felt the hand of a priest on his shoulder. "Come with me, Senor Blanxart. I will help you to pray as you should. Let us go to the chapel of Sant Antoni. He understands disease, and will provide intercession for us." Picking up the little Perot, and guiding Miquel with the other arm, the priest took them to a small chapel to one side of the high altar.

Miquel and Perot remained in the tiny chapel of Sant Antoni for the rest of the day. The priest returned with bread and water, and Miquel fed the boy, but took nothing himself. They remained there all the following night. Whilst he tried to comfort the boy and coax him to sleep, Miquel kept up a vigil on his knees, praying to St Antoni. He did not let himself sleep, nor rise from his knees. In the morning, the priest returned with more bread and water, and Miquel tried to feed Perot again, but again took nothing himself.

A voice behind him startled him, and he turned to see an exhausted Elena. "My wife, my good precious wife, what news?"

Elena collapsed beside him, shaking her head. "All gone," she sobbed, "All gone. They were so young, the plague took them easily. Thank God their agony was short. Jordi lingers, but nothing will save him. His agony goes on and on. Your mother is strong, but I fear for her. I cannot believe she will escape. Your sister has gone to the nunnery at Santa Anna, where she will be safe."

Perot had wakened at the sound of his mother's voice, and climbed onto her lap. She held him tight. "Let us pray together that the Blessed Virgin will let us keep you, my pretty Perot. Let us pray together."

Miquel could only guess at the hell his wife had endured in the last two days. Sleepless, she had tended her five older boys, and watched as each one died in her arms. Gently she had laid each little body in the straw on the floor, found cloths to wind each in, and prepared for them to be taken. Day had turned to night and back to day again, but she had not noticed.

Jordi lingered for five days more; his strong young body fought hard against the disease, and his mother began to wonder if he would survive. The coughing, the shortness of breath and the agony of aching limbs never left him, and she watched the black buboes grow and burst. Jordi was decomposing before her eyes, and yet there was still life in him. At last the time had come. "Sleep, Jordi, sleep," whispered Emilia. "See the angels have come for you. Now is the time. Sleep my baby, sleep." and finally Jordi slipped away in her arms.

By a miracle, Emilia and Elena survived, and Perot remained immune. The three generations of the family clung together, marvelling at their survival, fearful that it was only a temporary respite.

Miquel was distraught that the bodies of his boys had been taken to the mass grave at Poblenou; and went there to search for them. The stench of the limepit and the scene from hell that he encountered, drove him back. Determined to avoid a similar fate for Jordi, he carried his brother's body to Monjuic where it was laid to rest close to his grandmother. Emilia, Elena and Perot walked with him on that sad journey, and the four of them sat quietly by the sea reflecting on the terrible disease and how it had devastated their family.

Suddenly little Perot leapt up. "Look, father, look! There's the Swan!"

Startled, they jumped up. Perot was right. The Swan was on the horizon, and with a fair wind would be with them within the day. "How can we tell Jose?"

wailed Emilia. "He will be full of excitement and news as he was before, and will have no idea of the misfortune that has befallen us."

"I will take a boat and go out to meet him. It is the least I can do after the sacrifices you two have made in the last few days. It is my duty. I will sit with him on the ship, and tell him everything, and prepare him for his sad homecoming. Then I will bring him to Santa Maria to pray for the souls of our lost boys, and of his brother. Wait for us at the church. We will pray at the chapel of Sant Antoni whose intercession saved the life of Perot."

"Father, take me to the Swan," pleaded Perot. "I'm big enough now to come with you." Smiling for the first time in many days, Miquel agreed to take the boy.

Waiting in the cool of the great church, the two women felt much calmer now that Jordi had been laid to rest; Miquel eventually arrived with a rather sleepy Perot in his arms; and the women were startled to see Jose carrying a small barrel, and looking very grim-faced. Silently he put down the barrel and embraced his mother and Elena. He then turned and indicated a pretty young woman standing a little behind him. Beckoning her forward, Emilia kissed the woman, who said not a word. Jose turned to the image of Sant Antoni, and knelt. The family knelt with him, and so did the mysterious young woman.

After a while Miquel and Jose stood and led the little procession out into the evening sun. The brothers walked silently down to the shoreline, and found a place to sit on logs between the rough working boats. Jose put down the barrel, and the young woman sat on it. The brothers stared out to sea for a long time, contemplating the Swan as it lay at anchor bathed in the glow of the setting sun. At last Jose turned to his mother, a trickle of tears running down his face.

"This was to have been such a glorious homecoming, mother," he said. "The Swan is laden with wondrous goods, the wine has sold well in London, better even than before, and best of all," and he paused, and put his hand upon the arm of the young woman, "I want you to meet my wife. Mother, this is Elizabeth."

The young woman smiled, and leaned forward to Emilia. "Please forgive her, mother, but Elizabeth is English and knows very little Catalan. She has been trying to learn from me on the voyage, but my English is now good, and we forget and speak English all the time."

"Welcome to our family," said Emilia. "I am only sorry you come at such a sad time. We will do our best to make you comfortable. Jose, please tell her what I am saying."

Jose translated, and the others were amazed to hear how fluent his English had become. "Me?" he joked, "You think my English is good? You should hear Javier! He sounds like a real Englishman! They call him Harry in London!"

"Let us go home," said Miquel. "Jordi and the boys are all now at peace with the Virgin. Let us go and make our home peaceful again."

As they walked, Jose described to Elizabeth, in English, all that they were seeing, and became quite animated when they reached the Ribera slum. Behind them, Elena asked Miquel why his brother was carrying a barrel. "It was hardly appropriate to bring it to the church, unless it was good wine for the priest. What ever is it?"

"Vinegar, wife, the finest!"

"Vinegar!" she exclaimed, "He's carrying a barrel of vinegar!"

"Yes," replied Miquel. "When I told him on the ship of the plague and all that had happened, he begged it from the captain. It is an old remedy for disease on ships. They wash the decks with vinegar to keep the pox away. We are to wash everything at home with it – everything. Jose tells me we will then be safe from the plague."

A strange mix of emotions swirled around the family for some time. The shock of losing all but one of her children was exceptionally hard for Elena to bear, and she prayed for them daily at the chapel of Sant Antoni. Miquel's way of coping with the devastation of his family was to throw all his energy into little Perot, constantly talking to him, amusing him, protecting him and most of all giving him the benefit of all his knowledge of Catalan culture, all he had learned from his father Joan. Soon Perot was a walking encyclopaedia of Catalan heroes, reciting their names and deeds to anyone who would listen. Little did he know, that the blood-thirsty story of Corpus de Sang included a central part played by his own father.

Emilia also found it hard to deal with the deaths; but she devoted herself to learning a little English, and teaching some basic Catalan to Elizabeth; thus she got to know her new daughter-in-law, and to hear something of life in London. She was particularly pleased to discover that the English dislike of the Castilians was as strong as her own.

For the first time, Miquel sent the fully-laden Swan back to London without Jose on board. Miquel had honoured all his debts to John Shaw of Gravesend, and trusted the boat's captain and owner to deliver the cargo to Javier. Jose worked alongside his brother developing the businesses in Barcelona.

Meanwhile, the war had rumbled on, and on. There were many who could not remember a time of peace in the land. At times the Frenchies seemed to be winning, and Barcelona was full of French soldiers, speaking their strange language which was not unlike Catalan, but wasn't Catalan; and at other times it seemed they had all vanished, and groups of well-armed Castilian soldiers would occupy the city, shouting orders in their hated Castilian language. The population of La Ribera hated both groups of soldiers with equal venom, and no opportunity was missed to quietly despatch one or two of them in a dark alley. Miquel displayed surprising agility at coming over a rooftop, and silently cutting the throat of an unsuspecting soldier. A small arsenal of weapons was accumulated in the wine merchant's cellars.

It was just before Christmas 1659, that Miquel, along with a number of other prominent businessmen of Barcelona, were summoned to the Generalitat. Perot was by now nine years old, and Miquel was involving him in all aspects of the business; he thus took both his son and his brother with him to the meeting. The newly-appointed president of the Generalitat, Canon Pau d'Ager from Lleida, looking distinctly uncomfortable and under some duress, welcomed them hesitantly, and they were outraged that his welcome was given in Castilian, not the usual Catalan. They had an ominous feeling that this was going to be a very uncomfortable meeting. The Canon had even provided placatory cups of wine – from Miquel's own cellar, of course – and invited them to sit. Beside him was an unknown nobleman, and a number of heavily armed Castilian soldiers.

Standing, and drawing himself to his full height, the strange nobleman announced, "I am the emissary and representative of the Count-Duke of Olivares, minister to his majesty King Philip." At this, the Castilian soldiers let rip with a loud shout of "God save King Philip".

"Gentlemen," said Canon d'Ager, "I have to tell you that the Castilians and the French have finally signed a peace treaty. It is to be known as the Treaty of the Pyrenees, and was finalised on 7th November, a month ago. This peace has not been won without a cost. A cost not only of lives," continued the Canon, with a nervous pause, " but of Catalan land."

Miquel and his fellow business men gasped, as the emissary interrupted the Catalan Canon.

"King Philip, through his representative the Count of Barcelona, and myself his emissary, has conceded much of Catalonian land to Castile."

There were increased murmurings amongst the businessmen.

"I would prefer to continue with you in silence," snarled the nobleman. The horrified men fell silent. "Thank you. Castile, in return, has given large tracts of Catalonian land in the Pyrenees to France. Catalunya has lost all of the county of Roussillon with its capital Perpignan, and we have given El Conflent, El Capicir," – the mutterings and murmurings were increasing – "El Vallespir and part of La Cerdanya, to France."

"These are all sources of our wine and brandy," whispered Jose to Miquel. "This is grim news indeed."

"In exchange, I am delighted to announce that Barcelona and the surrounding lands are now under the control and justiciary of Castile," continued the emissary, "and amongst my duties will be the raising of taxes for Madrid."

"This is not a peace for us," said Jose to Miquel, "It's as the English warned me. We cannot trust either the Castilians or the Frenchies.

Flinging their wine cups to the floor, and with a noisy scraping of stools, the group of businessmen started to stand indignantly, and prepare to leave the assembly.

"Stay just where you are!" ordered the emissary. The soldiers raised their weapons, and the atmosphere in the room became distinctly ugly.

"There will be a number of regulations relating to this delinquent region; the most significant is the abolition of the reprobate language of Catalan." There were further gasps of horror. "Castilian is the only permitted language for public use, and will be adhered to in all legal, political and commercial business. Further regulations will be posted, in Castilian of course, on the door of the Generalitat. Now gentlemen, go about your business. Canon Pau d'Ager, you will remain with me."

The brothers, young Perot and the rest of the businessmen shuffled out of the chamber. Once in the street, their anger exploded.

"Peace treaty! It's an abomination!"

"How dare they come into our parliament and behave this way?"

"To try to ban Catalan! I would they tore the tongue from my mouth first – I am a Catalan, and my language, my culture, my whole being is of Catalunya."

The men stood in an impotent group frustrated by the high-handed treatment they had received. Jose glanced around. "Gentlemen, I think we should move on. There are Castilian soldiers all around us, and who knows what spies amongst them. Hold your peace until we are somewhere a little safer."

Turning to one or two closer friends, Miquel said, "Come this evening to my shop. Let us reflect upon these happenings and consider what should be done."

Later that evening, over a considerably more friendly cup of wine, Miquel spoke to his friends. "I swore on the body of my murdered father, that I would never live under the yoke of the Castilians. I swore to uphold the Catalan language and traditions. Before you, my friends, I renew my vow. We are Catalans, and will always be so."

"And I swear also," came the youthful voice of nine-year-old Perot, "that I shall follow my father and grandfather. Grandfather was the first Lion of Catalunya, and my father here, is the second. I will grow up to be third, and Catalunya will never be destroyed whilst I am alive!"

"Well spoken, young man," replied one of those listening. "We all join you in dedicating ourselves to this most nobles of causes."

Miquel spoke thoughtfully. "Friends, I believe we must continue our guerrilla war against the Castilians. We are few in number compared to the hoards from

Madrid, and we cannot openly declare war. We can, however, continue to make life hard for Philip's men. We must undermine their resolve to dominate our land."

"We'll drink to that," came another voice. "It is us, not them, who will show resolve."

Jose interjected, "I don't think this supposed peace will last. Friendship and peace between France and Castile? They'll soon be at one another's throats. And Catalunya will again be their battlefield. I give it two or three years, and the Treaty of the Pyrenees will be ripped to shreds."

"You may be right, brother. We all pray that you are. Meanwhile, we fight on, and when the time comes we will be ready to rid our land of the Castilian curse. Just as we spilled the wine in front of that cursed emissary, so we shall spill Castilian blood."

Barcelona was a great prize for the Castilian king; and he wanted it as much for the riches of the international trade developed there, as much as the power and prestige. Perversely, therefore, he did not want action to be taken against the businessmen of the city, as without them the trade would collapse, and with it the possible advantages for Madrid. It was this policy, more than anything else, which saved the life of Canon Pau d'Ager, and prevented a manhunt in La Ribera for the Catalan guerillas. Miquel and his fellows were protected rather than threatened by the Madrid attitude, and much to their own surprise, were able to continue to trade, although with the threat of unknown taxes hanging over them.

Emilia, Elena and Elizabeth became good friends, and gave an impression that they would happily sit and sew together, gossip, and quietly laugh, enjoying the benefits of being the women in an affluent and successful family. Elizabeth, however, was becoming increasingly homesick for London, a feeling not helped by the dangers of living in Barcelona at that time. One day Elena took her husband to one side. "Miquel," she began, "you should know that Jose is talking of going back to London. Elizabeth misses her family, and misses life in London; she is becoming desperate to return. Jose thinks her anxiety is preventing her from bearing him a child. I think they will be going on the next voyage of the Swan."

"I had expected this, good wife, and we must wish them well. Life here in Barcelona is uncertain – heavens, the poor women has hardly known a time without wars of some sort surrounding her. Letters from Javier indicate that England is a great deal more peaceful than here, and it is not surprising that she wishes to return."

Jose confirmed his wife's desire to go back to London. He said that since the English had cut off the head of their king, the land was far more peaceful. "Old Ironsides, the Lord Protector in London, is a fierce man, but he brought peace with the execution of King Charles. Would that we had a Cromwell here, to lead us to a similar victory in Madrid. Would we not be glad to see Philip's head struck from his shoulders?"

"I would be that Cromwell," replied Miquel, "but I haven't the troops to command. Indeed we must wish Jose and Elizabeth well, and hope that their return to English soil will bring the issue of children from Elizabeth that Jose is hoping for."

"Perhaps," said Emilia, "I will have English grand-children. Better by far than have Castilians!"

The family group that gathered on the shore was in sombre mood. Emilia had not seen her son Javier for many years, and she feared she would never see Jose again either. She had grown to love Elizabeth, but understood her homesickness and gave her blessing to her. Instructing them to write long and detailed letters, to be sent back to Barcelona on the Swan, both Elena and Emilia embraced Elizabeth as she stepped into the boat. At the last moment, Jose turned not to Miquel or his mother, but to Perot. "Well young man, I leave the fate of Catalunya in your hands. My brother your father, is a strong and powerful man, but he will not always be so. The task will fall to you to take up arms when called; and to keep the traditions and language of our heritage alive. Farewell, little soldier, little lion!" And he ran his fingers through Perot's blond curls.

Turning to his brother, Jose continued, "And farewell Miquel; may God preserve you from the plague, the Frenchies and the Castilians."

"Farewell brother," rejoined Miquel, "and if you find out how Cromwell led his Roundheads to victory, come back and tell us!"

"If ever you cut off the head of Philip, I'll be back to help!" laughed Jose as he embarked.

They watched the couple being rowed out to The Swan, and then the slow and laborious setting of the sails, and the ship gathering speed as it headed for the horizon. At last they turned and walked back up the beach. "Well, little soldier-lion," said Miquel, ruffling Perot's hair as his brother had done, "We have a business to run, you and I, so you can put those thoughts of swords and fighting out of your head. With Jose gone, you are my right-hand man, and you are going to work at learning this trade until you know more about it than I!"

The trade in Rioja and local Catalan brandy remained the cornerstone of the Blanxart family business, and as Perot grew older, he became an expert. He expanded the trade of the business, and soon the Blanxart firm needed another ship. A letter was sent to Javier, who contacted the owner of the Swan, John Shaw of Gravesend, and The Woodbird was selected.

Although the company had an outstanding reputation as experts in the Rioja and brandy trade, and had almost a monopoly in providing high quality wines and spirits to London, Perot was concerned that they needed to diversify, and thus contacted other tradesmen in La Ribera, as well as making discrete enquiries in the countryside. He sent Javier and Jose samples of cloth from a number of cottage industries in small towns to the north, and discovered sources of high quality olive oil in a number of farms in the countryside west of the city. Perot maintained his father's passionate commitment for Catalonian commerce, and dealt exclusively with farmers and traders who had equal fervour for the cause.

Javier sent back very encouraging messages regarding the fabrics, but reported that the Londoners were rather confused about olive oil. He agreed to try to sell some for its 'medicinal' qualities, but advised Perot not to send too much.

The Blanxart warehouse on the shore near La Ribera was no longer the secretive place it had been when it was started, and whilst Miquel was almost always at the shop dealing with the wine trade customers, Perot was at the warehouse meeting and greeting traders and farmers as their goods were delivered. With the second ship, Perot was despatching large quantities of goods to London, and was pleased to learn from letters that his uncles Javier and Jose were kept fully employed selling the Catalonian products, and investing in a wide range of goods for sale in Barcelona.

The years passed. Emilia became a frail old lady, maintaining a dignity and earning respect throughout the Ribera. When she died in 1665, she had outlived her husband by twenty-six years. She died with Miquel, Elena and Perot beside her, and as she expected, she had never seen her sons Javier or Jose again.

"Perot," she whispered, "where are you?"

"Close beside you," replied her grandson, as he leaned towards her.

She run her fingers through his curls, and her last words were to Perot. "Always remember, my handsome grandson, the four blood stripes on the golden shield. Always remember."

At age fifteen, Perot was as tall as his father, and as strong, and asked to carry his grandmother's body to Monjuic, to lay it beside the grandfather he never knew. Walking behind him, Miquel and Elena studied the tall blond youth with the precious cargo in his arms.

"Our son is a man now," said Elena. "I feel very proud of him."

"Let us pray that we see him come of age in these troubled times," replied Miquel. "He inherits a flourishing business, and a fine tradition; he has been born into a rich culture, and showed strength in surviving the plague. He understands our love of our country, and we have passed to him all the stories and songs of our land. He is our only son and heir. He carries a large responsibility on those shoulders."

"He will do well," said Elena, "He is a true Catalonian."

CHAPTER FOUR

Jose's prediction that the Treaty of the Pyrenees would not last, was true. In 1663, renewed hostilities had broken out between Castile and France, and a sporadic war between them began that would last for over thirty years. The skirmishes were rarely near Madrid, nor in the South of France – they were invariably in Catalunya. Barcelona, the city, remained largely untouched, frustrating Miquel that he had only a few opportunities to continue his personal guerrilla warfare against both Castilians and French. The continuing war caused far more problems in the countryside, creating constant insecurities for all the farms, hamlets and small towns. Country folk thus formed small armed groups to defend themselves when necessary against the marauding soldiers. Such groups were generally thought of as bandits, and regarded as rather romantic, the stuff of legends and tales.

Just as his uncle had travelled the land seeking business contacts loyal to the Catalonian flag, so Perot started to ride from farm to farm, meeting grape growers, and learning about the origins of the family's flourishing Rioja trade. He travelled many miles and was greeted warmly. The farmers remembered the charismatic Jordi who had visited them previously, and Perot, so instantly recognisable with his blond curls, was a popular visitor throughout the land.

Perot was also the contact between the guerillas in La Ribera, and their bandit counterparts in the countryside. Many times he would arrive to find a farm occupied by a rough Catalan group, to whom he was always a hero.

One day, his curiosity got the better of him, and he asked one of the bandits why he was treated so royally. "After all," he said, "I'm just a businessman from La Ribera. You treat me so well, and I'm not sure why. I'm no more than my father's son."

The bandits laughed. "You are your father's son! That's enough, that's more than enough. Your father is our hero; and so his son must be treated well also."

Perot was still puzzled. "I don't understand. What do you mean? My father's just a wine merchant in Barcelona."

The bandits laughed even louder. "Listen to him! Just a wine merchant!"

Then one of them realised the mystery. "Wait," he said to Perot, "You don't know the significance of your father, do you?"

Perot shook his head.

"You know the story of Corps de Sang?"

This time Perot nodded. "My father told me the story. It was when bandits went all the way to Madrid, and murdered many members of the king's family. My father told the story very well."

"As indeed he should. He was one of those bandits. He wanted revenge for the death of your grandfather, and when the call came he was ready to go. The sword, you must know of his sword, the one used to kill your grandfather, was the sword he took to Madrid. It killed many of the accursed House of Austria. Your father dipped his hand in their blood and made the mark of four, just as Guifre el Pelos's blood was used on his golden shield to make our first senyera."

Perot shook his blond curls in astonishment. "My father the bandit. But that makes him a wanted man. This must remain a closely guarded secret. Wait 'til I get home; how could he not tell me? And wait, you said 'the sword'. What does this mean? It's all a mystery to me."

With a friendly punch on the shoulder, one of the bandits laughed again. "Just wait until you get home, then you ask him. But do it very privately: choose a very safe time and place."

Once back in La Ribera, Perot asked his father to join him in the cellar, where they could talk privately.

"You have a secret, father: a secret that I have found, quite by accident."

"I don't know what you mean, Perot," said his father.

"I think you do. All those times you told me the story of Corpus de Sang. You knew the story very well, and in much detail, didn't you?"

Miquel nodded, with a slow smile.

"Perhaps you knew it so well because you were there, father. You were one of those bandits, weren't you?"

Miquel nodded again. "My identity was always a secret, and we decided that we could not tell you when you were young, for fear you would boast to friends, and the story would get out. The Castilians would dearly love to know who killed so many of their royal family, but none of us have ever been found."

Perot jumped up and embraced his father. "Perhaps you were right not to tell me. I am so proud of you. I would have wanted to shout it from the rooftops if I'd known it when I was young. My father the bandit! And the sword! Where is the sword? Show it to me."

"I was the Young Lion of La Ribera once," said Miquel. "Your grandfather was the Old Lion. Now I suppose I'm the Old Lion and you are Young Lion." Turning to the darkest corner of the cellar and leaning behind a barrel, he pulled out a bundle, and unrolling it, produced the sword. "It's a Castilian sword, from a

Castilian soldier. It was the one used to murder your grandfather, and in turn it was used to murder many of the House of Austria. One day, this will be your sword, and you will keep it safe, and have it ready to defend Catalunya."

Perot took the sword from his father and held it reverentially. It was heavy and sharp, showing no sign of its age, or indeed the deeds it had been used for. There was a silence between them, and Perot passed it back to his father. Miquel wrapped it carefully, put it back into its secret corner.

Perot sought a wife the way he ran the Blanxart business, with enthusiasm and passion, but also with care. Miquel and Elena were perplexed at the way Perot was determined to continue to try to export olive oil despite Javier's problems selling it to the Londoners. Perot was particularly keen on one particular farmer near Sant Cugat del Valles, who, he claimed, had particularly good and productive olive trees growing on the hillside. One day Miquel took his son to one side.

"What's this passion you have for olive oil?" he asked. "And so much interest in that farm at Sant Cugat? You visit there more often than all the vineyards put together. Your judgement seems a little clouded on this issue!"

"Oh no, father," replied Perot. "I don't think my judgement is clouded at all. I have a passion all right, but it's not particularly for olive oil or the farmer. It's for the farmer's daughter. I think I am in love father."

"Perot Blanxart, you will inherit one of the most flourishing businesses of La Ribera. Despite your youth, you are already much respected in the barrio, and I suspect even in the city itself. I cannot have you falling for some country girl. I think you should forget all about this trade in olive oil."

"Anna's father is a gentleman farmer, father. He owns much of the Sant Cugat area, and lives in a splendid house, a great masia many times larger than our's. It is a former castle, standing proud on his own hill overlooking the lands of Sant Cugat. Who knows? Perhaps we may even need it one day to defend Catalunya. I would like for you and mother to visit Anna's family. May I have your permission to seek an invitation?"

"I do not know how your mother will feel about such a journey," smiled Miquel, "but you may ask your Anna to talk to her father. I will be interested to know if he is able to offer a suitable dowry for such an eligible young man!"

Anna's father was indeed a wealthy landowner with a surprisingly magnificent house. His fortified farmhouse dominated the Sant Cugat valley. Rising like a small castle on its own hill, it commanded excellent views over the surrounding countryside. Like a number of other landed gentry, for some generations his family had been gradually buying small plots of land from lesser peasant farmers, and accumulating a significant land holding. He also came from a tradition of very large Catholic families, and Anna had six brothers, all older than herself, and three sisters. Her father was thus anxious to get his daughters well married and away, and offered modest dowries for all four girls.

The Blanxart family were intrigued to receive a invitation to join Anna's family on their annual autumn mushroom forage. Miquel was unimpressed by the prospect, but Elena assured him that this was a country tradition, and it was an honour to be asked to participate in a party arranged by a member of the country gentry.

Thus it was that Miquel and Elena, accompanied by a very excited Perot, made the unfamiliar journey inland, Miquel and Perot on their horses, and Elena on a small pony. Their loyal servant was left behind to guard the shop which would be closed whilst they were gone. The road passed west out of Barcelona, and through the village of Gracia, before heading high up into the hills. For a family whose life was concerned with trade and the sea, it was unusual to be so far inland.

"Jordi must have travelled all these roads," reflected Elena. "This is strange and unfamiliar to us, but it was the background to his everyday life. He would have enjoyed this jaunt over the hills."

"A familiar road to you also," said Miquel to his son. "How strange that both my brother and my son know this countryside better than I; and it is all part of Catalunya."

"More than that," replied Perot, "This is where our wealth comes from. Look how you can see the terraces of vineyards on these higher slopes. See over there the hamlet of Horta. Those are the nearest vineyards to Barcelona; and they stretch for many miles north and west from here, around and beyond the mountains."

As they rose higher, Elena especially was amazed by the panorama. "Let us stop for refreshment," she suggested, "at a place where we can admire this splendid view. What a sight our city is!"

Perot showed where to tether the horses under some trees. He knew this route well, and had often stopped to enjoy the sight of the city below. He delighted in pointing out the landmarks to his parents. "There is Montjuic, and down below the beaches near our warehouse. There, standing tall in the smoky air, is the Cathedral of Santa Eulalia, and to the left of that, you see our own Santa Maria del Mar. Look further left again, and can you see the mass of houses and shops, all with their smoking chimneys? That's our own La Ribera."

"I had no idea Barcelona was so big!" exclaimed Elena. "And look how the sand of the beach stretches out into the sea. Those must be the sand dunes of Barceloneta, where I used to play as a child. I have often looked up to these mountains from the beach," she continued, "but have never looked down from the mountain to the sea. Do these mountains have a name, Perot?"

"Yes, mother, we are climbing the track over the Serra de Collersola. And see above there is a chapel at the top. That is the chapel of Tibi Dabo, the mountain top visited by Jesus, and given to us by Him."

"You are knowledgeable young man," said his smiling father, "Does this track take us right to the chapel?"

"No father, there is a goat path to the chapel, but we skirt round. See how there is a kind of saddle between the two high peaks? That's how we get through to the valleys beyond. Once over this saddle, we are very close. And we must ride on," said Perot. "We are expected before nightfall, and indeed this journey is hazardous in the dark."

As they drew close to the castle, Perot could tell that they were being watched from the castle, and that Anna's family had been alerted to the arrival of the Blanxarts.

Dusk was falling as the little party rode up the final hill into the farmyard at Sant Cugat. In the slight mist of early evening, the fortified building was impressive on top of its own hill rising above the valley. The main house, within the mediaeval tower of the castle, was surrounded by many outbuildings. Illuminated by flares held by the younger brothers, the family were ready in their best clothes to greet the Blanxarts. Miquel was particularly delighted to see the Catalan flag hanging from the top of the castle. The four blood stripes reassured him that this family would match his own in their loyalty to the Catalan state.

Having led the party into the farmyard, Perot hung back as his parents greeted Anna's parents; and Anna herself was nowhere to be seen. Once the formalities were completed, Anna's father sent one of his sons to fetch Anna, and she was presented to Miquel and Elena. Perot was brought forward, but of course he already knew Anna's family well from their business dealings, and he greeted both Anna, her parents and all her brothers and sisters warmly. Elena presented Anna's mother with a package of white sugar, which was in the form of a small solid cone. Anna's mother and her sisters were exceedingly delighted by this gift, and it was clear that the women were immediately warm with one another.

Anna's mother led the party into the hall of the farmhouse. The large room was lit by tallow candles, and roaring log fires, one at each side of the hall, filled the space with heat. A generous meal was set out on the long trestle table and several servants stood ready to serve the guests. Elena and Miquel tried to look as if they were used to dining in such splendour, but cast surreptitious glances at the wall hangings, and the furniture. Supper was a jolly affair, brought to a close only by tiredness from the journey from La Ribera. Elena was surprised by the size of the farmhouse and was shown to a guest bedchamber, the like of which she had never seen before. Perot was to sleep with the brothers in the main hall of the house, and the two fathers sat outside, a good bottle of wine between them, and under the stars, they discussed the future of their offspring.

Anna's father was aware that Miquel had lost many sons to the plague, and started the conversation in a very careful manner.

"Perot tells me he is your youngest and only surviving son." began the older man. "My heart goes out to you losing your sons in the way you did. May they be in heaven with Our Lady; and may the Virgin continue to comfort you in your loss."

Miquel thanked the old man, who continued, "I have six surviving sons, and I thank the Lord daily that they avoided the plague. In my case, it was my youngest son that was carried off, God rest his soul, and the others have all grown up strong and good. Alas with such a large family, I can offer only a modest dowry for Anna, but she has a goodly chest of linens and will bring further gifts to you."

Miquel smiled. "I am successful in my own way as a trader and businessman, and I do not look for a grand dowry. I believe my son is truly in love with your daughter, and I am sure they will make a good match. Although our wealth comes to us from very different means, we understand one another well, and the link between our families will be satisfactory. Your daughter will find life different in our small family after living with so many siblings, but I believe she will not find La Ribera dull. Life beside the sea, with all excitement of trade and commerce will be quite a contrast to this rural idyll. I trust your daughter will be as prolific as your wife and provide me with many heirs."

"I believe she will. And when we break our fast in the morning, we will announce the marriage."

The annual mushroom hunt turned into a kind of alfresco party, with all the young people running and jumping wildly through the undergrowth, watched by proud and delighted parents. For two days, the families were engaged in preparations for the wedding as well as much merry-making.

Perot and Anna were married in the church at Sant Cugat, and Anna returned riding her own pony, with her husband and his parents, the following day. They stopped at the same mirador in the mountains, and Perot excitedly showed his bride the city spread below them.

"I had no idea Barcelona was so huge," said the girl. "And the sea so blue."

"This is the dark blue of an autumn sea," said Perot, "You wait for the summer sun; then you will see the sea sparkle like sapphires; then you will know why we love it."

Perez Blanxart was born in 1680, followed rapidly by nine more children, most of whom survived childhood. Perez, the first born, however, was the one who inherited the Blanxart trademark: curly blond hair. Miquel had done a splendid job filling Perot with all the stories and songs of the Catalan tradition, and Perot in turn wasted no time in giving little Perez and his brothers and sisters an understanding and knowledge of their precious culture. Anna knew many of the stories told by her husband, and was able to add a few from her family that were new to Perot. At home, as always with the Blanxart family, the only language spoken was Catalan, and the children learned many of the old folk songs when they were still very young.

Anna may have thought the merchant's house quiet when she first arrived as a new bride, with only her husband and his parents, but the arrival of Perez and his siblings soon put an end to that. Passing the shop, neighbours would hear the singing as the children raised their voices in the songs their father and grandfather taught them. Anna, coming from another strong Catalan family, knew other songs to add to the repertoire.

Ringing out from the shop, passers-by would hear the great songs of the mountains, the songs praising the bandits, and of course, many sailors' songs. Miquel was in great demand as a story-teller for the children, and they had two favourites: the ancient story of the senyera, and the much more recent story of the Corpus de Sang. Miquel now an old man himself, would tell how he heard the senyera story from his father Joan, and how he used to tell it in the old baker's shop; and he would match it with a remarkably detailed account of the exciting time the bandits went to Madrid to assassinate the House of Austria. Just as he omitted his own role in that particular adventure when he told it to Perot, so he similarly omitted it when telling his grandchildren.

For a land pummelled and bruised by war, it was astonishing that trade flourished and grew. Perot had taken over the bulk of the work at the Barcelona end, and Javier and Jose were now in command of a major import and export business in London. Perot continued to diversify, but the export of fine Rioja and good local brandy remained the mainstay of the trade. The Barcelona warehouse was a hive of activity, with a growing workforce employed; the employees were very varied – some local men and some from the countryside, but they had one thing in common: Perot would only employ loyal Catalans, and he expected that all daily communication would be in Catalan, despite the official ban on the language. The lusty singing of his children added only to emphasise the political dimension of the business, and that it continued to do so well in the face of Castilian opposition, was little short of a miracle.

Letters were exchanged every time the Swan or the Woodbird docked and Miquel and the family followed with interest the fortunes of Javier, now a successful business man in London, with Jose managing the Blanxart warehouse. Both brothers had made successful marriages, and were clearly well established in England. The family were aware of countless cousins they had never met, and they were resigned to the fact that the "English" side of the family would grow away from them.

It was thus with some astonishment that Miquel received a message to hurry to the shore where he found a distinguished elderly man and his wife had disembarked from the Woodbird. It was one day in 1690. Miquel welcomed the strangers onto the beach. The two men looked at one another for a while and in slightly hesitant Catalan, the man said, "You must be Miquel. My, how your golden curls have gone grey!"

And Miquel, also hesitant, said, "Are you Javier, my brother?"

"Indeed I am," replied the stranger, "but I am having much trouble remembering my Catalan. I sailed away from Barcelona in 1642 as a young man; I return more than forty years later, with my wife, to make a pilgrimage to my birthplace before I am too old."

Miquel embraced Javier, and was introduced to his wife, who spoke only in English. At the shop, there were many introductions, and once the curiosity of the younger children was satisfied, they were sent to play. Perot, however, kept Perez, his first-born, who was now ten years old, to remain with the adults.

"So who is the Young Lion now?" asked Javier.

"I am," replied Perez boldly, running his hands through his golden curls. "Father is the Old Lion and grandfather is....." and he faltered, unable to finish the sentence.

"The ancient one," laughed Miquel. "It seems we Blanxarts live long if we are not murdered in our beds."

"I have been in awe of how long you have survived, Miquel. You have been a wanted man for over forty years. But Madrid has never identified you; the Virgin must be watching over you, of that I am certain."

Perez looked at his father with a puzzled frown, but Perot mimed for him not to speak. His Uncle Javier continued: "At home, we follow the fortunes of Catalunya. Your letters, and reports we read in the Times of London, give us much information. There is little love lost between the English crown and the kings of Castile or France. Should you need them, I believe the English would support Catalunya in a battle against either France or Castile, or even both."

"How ironic it is," said Miquel. "We live with our King Charles the Second in Madrid, and your English government has returned to the monarchy by putting your King Charles the Second on your English throne."

"A strange time to have lived through," said Javier. "Much of what Cromwell stood for was reflected in many of the ideals of Catalunya, but in the end he was a despot, and become much despised and disliked. There was great rejoicing when Charles came to the throne; of course many of those singing loudly, had been equally delighted when his father was executed."

"Philip died in his bed," replied Miquel. "I often wondered if he knew how near he came to his end on that night in 1640. He had twenty-five more years that he didn't deserve." Miquel paused and looked around the room, and put an arm around Perez's shoulders, smiling as he did so. "Perhaps your visit is a good time to enact a little ceremony here in the Blanxart family. I have been thinking about this for some time – and now seems the right moment. Let us go down into the cellar."

Puzzled by this instruction, they all clambered down the steep ladder into the cool of the cellar. Hastily lighting candles, Elena looked around her family in the flickering lights. She was the only one anticipating what was about to happen. Reaching behind the barrels,

Miquel pulled the dusty bundle into the candle light. Perot, at last realising what was to happen, put his arm around Anna, and Perez looked from one to another in bewilderment. Javier gasped, "Is that the sword?"

"Indeed it is." replied Miquel, "And now, in front of my brother, returned from London, the time has come to hand the sword to Perot. I am too old now; the responsibility lifts from my shoulders, and falls to you Perot. This is the sword that killed my father, your grandfather, and it was used on the night of Corpus de Sang to despatch many of the princes and princesses of Austria. It was I who carried it to Madrid, and I who joined with my loyal friends, the so-called bandits, in our attempt to rid Spain of the royal family." It was now the turn of young Perez to be astonished as Miquel continued, "It is to be used to defend Catalunya, and when the call comes, Perot, you will obey it." Turning to Perez, he went on, "So you see, Young Lion, one day your father will hand this sword to you. Meantime, learn all you can about our traditions, and the noble history of our land."

Perot took the sword solemnly and held it before him. "I swear to defend our land until the last breath in my body. And I swear that my first-born son Perez will inherit both the sword and the responsibility from me, just as I have inherited it from my father, and his father before him."

Turning to Perez, Perot told his son, in very serious tones, how important it was that he keep the secret of the sword, not even telling his brothers and sisters.

Javier patiently translated to his wife the significance of the little ceremony, whilst Anna and Elena emptied their larder to prepare a meal welcoming Javier and his wife to their home.

The sword was returned to its hiding place, and the family went upstairs to the parlour. Anna gathered the rest of her children, and they sang many of their much-loved Catalan folk songs to Javier and his wife. Javier whispered a commentary to his wife, "This song is telling us about the noble mountains of our country." And later, "Now they sing about the romance of the bandits who defend our land." Finally, chuckling, he said, "I think this is about us, my dear, as they are singing about sailors who return to defend our shores!"

Her eyes sparkling, Javier's wife asked him to tell the company how honoured she was to have been part of the day's events.

The priority for all of the family was a visit to Santa Maria del Mar. Javier's wife, brought up amidst the over-decorated gothic cathedrals of England, was at first surprised by the severity of the building, but as the family knelt in prayer, she was consumed by the peace and tranquillity of the vast space.

She particularly admired the tall octagonal columns rising far overhead, with the giant keystones holding the arches secure. Instead of kneeling, she sat back and gazed in awe at the lofty roof high above. She was amazed that such a simple but enormous building could contain such an atmosphere of peace, and she was sorry when the rest of the family rose to leave.

Standing and looking around, she whispered to her husband that she would like to visit each of the side chapels in turn, and slowly the family made a pilgrimage from saint to saint. They paused for a long time at Sant Antoni's statue, and once outside Javier translated to his wife the whole sad story of the deaths of his brother and the little boys. They walked back to the winery very slowly.

Several days of entertainment followed – a most unfamiliar experience for the family. Javier had become a wealthy man in England and was generous in providing for the daily feasting. He enjoyed hiring a cart, and going with his wife and Anna to La Boqueria Market, Barcelona's biggest and oldest food market, to buy expensive meats and other foods. Once, when Anna suggested going to the little shops in La Ribera which were their neighbours, he dismissed the idea. "Oh no," he said, "we can have far better than that!"

Even the markets of El Born and Santa Caterina were too humble for Javier; only the prestigious Boqueria was good enough for him. He presented Anna and her kitchen maid with huge cuts of pork, and sweetmeats, pig's hearts and sausages. He sought out unusual fruits and expensive pastries. Only the wine pleased him in La Ribera, and that was because it was from Miquel's own well-chosen cellar.

Miquel and Elena became quite exhausted by the constant holiday atmosphere, and Perot excused himself regularly to attend to the family business. At last it all became too much for Elena, who took to her bed, and she was relieved when Perot announced that the Woodbird was fully laden and the weather fair for the return trip to London. Javier's wife requested another visit to Santa Maria del Mar, and the whole family joined together in prayer for the safety of those about to embark on the journey to England.

The farewells on the beach were tender, a mixture of regret and relief. Miquel knew that he would never see his brother again, but longed to return to the daily routine of his life which had been so completely disrupted. He had also become increasingly uncomfortable with the ostentatious spending of his wealthy younger brother. It did not sit happily in his conscience to eat, drink and be quite so merry in the midst of the poverty of La Ribera slum.

On the day Javier was to sail, Perot took the sword from its hiding place, and carried it, keeping it hidden in its roll of cloth, for the first time, to the beach. Perez walked beside him, excited to touch the hardness of the steel under the cloth.

On the beach, Javier made a speech which he had clearly been preparing: "Miquel, my dear brother, and all of your family: my wife and I have had an extraordinary visit to Barcelona. We return to London to live out the rest of our days, peaceful now that we have been to visit you, my dear family, in our precious city of Barcelona. We have great memories and love for our Catalan heritage, and will tell the stories you have told us with pride and dignity. There will always be a small part of Catalunya in our house in London, and I proudly fly the senyera in Charing Cross. You will always be in our thoughts. Remember always in your struggles and strife, that the English will come to your aid when you need them. Long live Catalunya!"

Without unwrapping it, Perot held the sword aloft and repeated the words, "Long live Catalunya!", and Perez's shrill young voice echoed the sentiment again, "Long live Catalunya!" The words echoed around the bay. Anna's children, gathered closely on the beach, sang all of their repertoire of Catalan songs as Javier and his wife were rowed out to The Woodbird, their voices ringing across the water in the forbidden Catalan language. With the euphoria of the moment, none of the family noticed how much they had been observed.

Anna's family lived comfortably in their fortified farmhouse at Sant Cougat, and were generous to family and servants; but Javier had gained an Englishman's attitude to money, and clearly relished his expensive lifestyle. Miquel found it hard to know why he was uncomfortable with Javier, but not with Anna's parents. When he talked to Perot, he discovered that his son shared his disquiet.

"We strive to make a living," he began, "and we are successful. We are minor businessmen here in La Ribera, and we work hard to provide a good living for our wives and the grandchildren. So why does Javier's financial success upset us?"

"I'm not sure, father," replied Perot, "but I know we were embarrassed at the way he bought meat and sugary treats into the house. Somehow, I wanted to tell him to share it with the beggars and urchins in the street, not us."

"Yes, that's it," said Miquel. "I wanted to share, I didn't want it all just for us. Your grandfather Joan always had something to spare for the street poor."

"It seems unfair to me," continued Perot, "That some people in this world are so lucky, and have so much, whilst others are so poor and live such miserable lives."

"The priest would tell us to be content with our position in life," said Miquel. "We thank God and the Virgin for what we have, however little it may be."

"And the rich give alms to the poor, a tiny proportion of all their wealth," said Perot, "Is that enough? Should we not do more?"

"We must accept our lot," concluded Miquel, "but that does not mean I am without conscience. I remain uncomfortable. Somehow it seems to be part of our Catalan heritage that we feel concern and sympathy for the poor, and dislike the feudal system which gives so much to one and so little to another."

"Dislike is not the word in my mind, father," said Perot. "It makes me angry and I hate it, the poverty we see around us all the time, and wish with all my Catalan heart, I could do something about it."

Ironically, in the light of such sentiments, the Blanxart business continued to flourish with the two ships constantly sailing between London and Barcelona. The good Catalonian Rioja continued to provide the backbone for the trade. The weather favoured voyage after voyage, the skills they had developed to deliver the high quality wine to England ensured that the family remained ahead of other importers in their reputation and success in the London wine markets, and the Blanxarts continued to receive a healthy and regular income.

In 1697, the French reluctantly abandoned their attempts to control Barcelona, leaving the city to the Castilian army. The regulations outlawing use of Catalan became more draconian, and many families gave up their efforts to maintain the language, capitulating to the pressure to speak Castilian. The Blanxart family, however, remained a defiant stronghold for the Catalan language.

Miquel and Elena did indeed die in their bed, in 1697, of old age; Elena died within a month of her husband. For a man who had had a price on his head for over fifty years, living until the age of seventy-seven was a remarkable achievement; the Castilians had failed to identify the bandits of the Corps de Sang and had abandoned their efforts to do so. His wife, from solid blacksmith's stock, was a strong woman, and remained so into old age, surviving the horror and sadness of the plague, standing beside her husband in fierce defence of the Catalan language.

On his death bed, Miquel addressed Perot and Perez. "My son and my grandson. I passed the Blanxart sword to you Perot, some years ago, and at the time you committed to pass it to Perez when the time is right. The sword is a symbol of our Catalan heritage, and in this year of our Lord 1697, we are beset with efforts to stamp it out. Few are left in this great city to pass on the stories and songs of our past, and you, more than anyone else, are charged to do so. Perez, young man, to you falls the task of finding a loyal Catalan wife, and raising your children in the Catalan heritage. Even now, before you receive the sword, you must be thinking of the next generation to whom you will pass it. How old are you now, boy?"

"Seventeen, grandfather," replied Perez.

"Then you must be married within a year," smiled the old man.

"I promise, grandfather, that I will do my best."

"And now," continued Miquel, "bring in your brothers and sisters and sing once more the great Catalan songs. Sing to me of the mountains and the seas, the bandits and the sailors, and the land God gave to us."

The family crowded into the room, and started to sing. Quietly at first, in reverence to the dying old man, but gradually more and more lustily, the singing filled the room. Angels themselves could not have heralded a man more beautifully into heaven, and the young people finished with their favourite song, praising the resplendent mountains of Catalunya. At the end of the song, there was a silence. Perot pulled the sheet gently over his father's face, and Anna ushered her children quietly out of the room.

CHAPTER FIVE

Rafael Blanxart was Perez's first-born son, born in 1699. Perez had taken it as a duty to obey his grandfather's instructions, and had married Carla in less than a year. Carla was the daughter of Senor and Senora Macia, another Ribera family, with a small butcher's shop deep in the slum. Perez had seen the young Carla Macia occasionally at the pump, but had never spoken to her. He had even been sent once or twice to the Macia family shop to buy meat, and was rather repulsed by the smelly and fly-blown atmosphere of the butcher's. The Macia family were known, however, for having a small senyera hanging at the back of the shop amongst the offal, and Anna, who had visited the place more often, suggested the Macia girl as a likely match.

The courtship had been a strange one, with Perot and Anna quizzing Carla's parents about their understanding and knowledge of Catalan and the stories and songs of the land. The parents had passed this test with flying colours, and so Carla was deemed an appropriate wife for Perez.

When the question of a dowry had come up, Carla's parents were as surprised as they had been by the Catalan grilling they had been given.

"I am not a rich man," Carla's father had begun, "and with many other children, my daughter Carla cannot bring a rich dowry to your family."

"I do indeed seek a valuable and rich dowry for my son," stated Perot, "but not as you expect. I want him to inherit the richness of his Catalan ancestry, and I need your daughter to bring your family's songs and stories to the marriage. I must know that she will bring all the richness of our Catalan language, and ensure that my grandchildren are brought up in the tradition. That is all the dowry I seek."

Once more the vintners had echoed with a merry wedding feast: following their marriage at Santa Maria del Mar, the couple had returned to the wine shop to find a banquet. Perot had raided the best of the wine from his cellar, Senor Macia had sent a generous piece of pork and many varieties of sausage, and Anna's parents, in recognition of another excellent Catalonian liaison, had sent a whole basket of country treats from the farm at Sant Cougat.

The wedding feast was followed by the singing which had become a tradition in the Blanxart home, and Perez's brothers and sisters were joined by Carla's brothers and sisters who knew most of the same songs. There was further delight when they discovered that Carla herself could sing with a high clear voice, and there was a silence as she launched into a song which was new to the Blanxarts.

The singing vibrated through the shop and rooms above it, and out into the street. Many passers-by smiled to hear the twenty voices raised in joyous celebration of the marriage, but there were some who stopped, and listened and frowned. The family was unaware of spies in La Ribera, but reports of this unashamed celebration reached la Generalitat, adding to a growing file of notes and evidence that the Blanxart Wine Merchants were defying all the regulations banning the Catalan language.

The presence of the Castilians continued to cast a shadow, but failed to curtail the commerce and trade of the city and port. Carla and Perez continued to produce babies as rapidly as their forefathers, and soon Rafael had a dozen siblings. With his trade-mark blond curls, Rafael stood out from most of his friends, and even his brothers, and followed his father into the family trade. By the age of 13, he was fully engaged in the business and his hard work enabled his grandfather Perot to start to slow down and enjoy the fruits of his labour.

Perot cannot have known that his decision to enact the ceremony of handing the family sword to Perez came at a particularly significant time. It was the last day of 1712, and he was now sixty-two years old. He knew Rafael was old enough to witness the ceremony, and that Perez deserved his inheritance of ownership of the sword. He asked the family to gather in the cellar.

In the familiar candle-light of the old cellar, Perot reached behind the barrels, just as his father had done before him, and pulled out the bundle containing the sword. Anna put her arm around her husband, and Perez gasped, since they realised the significance of the moment. Carla stood with her husband and son, wondering what was to happen, and Rafael remained blankly uncomprehending. Unwrapping the sword, Perot announced, "This is the Blanxart family sword."

Perez grasped his wife's hand, smiling broadly. Perot continued.

"This sword is a Castilian weapon; it was used to assassinate my grandfather, Joan Blanxart. My father, Miquel, stole it from the murderers and swore upon it to revenge his father's death, and did so in Madrid. You all know the story of the famous Corpus de Sang. Miquel, my father, was one of those bandits who went to Madrid to kill the royal family, the members of the house of Austria. He did not kill the king, but found and murdered several members of his family, leaving the mark of the senyera on each of them. When he knew he was too old to wield the sword, my father gave it to me in a solemn ceremony here in this cellar. The time has now come for me to pass the sword to my son. Perez, I pass the sword, and the responsibilities it bears, to you. I do this in front of my grandson Rafael, so that he understands his inheritance. Rafael, this sword will one day be your's. Its existence and hiding place must remain a secret, and I have judged today that you are old enough to bear the responsibility of this secret."

There was a pause, and then Perez spoke first. "Father, it is with joy and pride I take the sword from you. I have waited many years for this day, since you were given the sword by grandfather Miquel, in the presence of your brother Javier. I have carried the secret honourably, and I know my son Rafael will do so also. I take the sword and swear to defend the precious state of Catalunya. When called, I will be ready."

"I too will be ready," said Rafael. "The knowledge I have gained today sustains me in my love and commitment to my homeland, and when the time comes to be given the sword from my father, I will be ready."

Unexpectedly, Carla spoke up, "I am the newest member of the Blanxart family, but I come from another staunch Catalan family. The Macias have always loved the songs and stories of Catalunya, but never did I expect to come so close to the great story of the Corpus de Sang. To be married to the grandson of one of the bandits of Madrid, I consider an honour, and with enthusiasm I swear to support my husband with his responsibilities of the sword, and to prepare my son Rafael to be an honourable successor in this astonishing family tradition."

"Well spoke, daughter," said Perot. "It is good to have you in our family. You have already proved your worth teaching my grandchildren the stories and songs of our land, and I know you will continue to do so with renewed vigour now you have witnessed our ceremony of the sword." Turning to Perez, he continued, "Now, son, it is time to return the sword to its hiding place;

and I think it appropriate to go upstairs and sample some of this new Cava you are so keen to export."

Perez wrapped the sword, and hid it again, and then turning to the family with a grin, said, "That's what it's for, this Cava. It's a celebration drink. And I think we may need more than one bottle!"

Upstairs, Perez poured the sparkling wine into glasses, the first the family had owned, and proposed a toast. "To our homeland. Long live Catalunya!"

"Long live Catalunya!" they echoed, and then, "Happy New Year!"

"I wonder what 1713 will bring?" mused Anna. "Let us hope for a peaceful year."

The family hurried through the streets to midnight mass at Santa Maria del Mar, with Rafael's younger brothers and sisters puzzled by the sudden air of excitement in the adults. Rafael held the wondrous new secret tight inside himself, and prayed for strength to keep his new knowledge safe and hidden.

The season was cold, and few ventured outside unnecessarily. During that winter, however, there were a number of visitors to the Blanxart shop, often in the dark of night. Mostly strangers, they spent much time talking in urgent whispers to Perot and Perez. As the spring arrived, they decided to bring Rafael into their confidence, and explained why the various strangers had been visiting.

"The news is not good, Rafael," began Perot, "We'll not worry the women and your young brothers and sisters, but we believe you should be aware of what's going on."

Handing his son a cup of wine, Perez continued, "There are many messages coming from the country-side that this new king, the fifth Philip of Spain, cursed Castilian king that he is, has made peace with the French court and Louis the Fourteenth. Louis's army is much depleted following many wars with the English, but with Philip's help, the two have set their eyes on a final defeat of Catalunya, and total control of the Mediterranean via our strategic port of Barcelona."

"I thought the Castilians already had a great deal of control of our land," observed Rafael.

"They control the Generalitat certainly," replied Perot, "but they don't have the absolute rule they crave. Many families such as ours defy the law, we are a thorn in their flesh, but we remain alive just as long as we are useful to the commercial life of the port. With greater control and influence, Catalan will finally be eliminated and Catalunya will be dead."

Perez sighed and spoke with resignation. "I have no heart for bloodshed, for I am a peace-loving business-man, but as long as I have the sword," said Perez. "I will fight to the end to defend our land."

"And I," said Rafael. "I hold your trust inside myself, and I have long known with certainty, that I will honour my inheritance. I will stand firm beside my father."

"I fear that time will be sooner than you expect," said Perot sadly. "Even now the French-Castilian army is massing in the countryside. I have word from the fortified house at Sant Cougat, that they are surrounded. I don't know how to tell your grandmother, but her family are in mortal danger, and their lands liable to be forfeit to the enemy."

As they spoke, there was a great hammering at the door, and they opened hesitantly. One of Anna's younger brothers tumbled breathlessly into the shop. "They're everywhere," he said, "I got through by luck. They're everywhere..." For a moment, struggling to hold back the tears, he gasped for breath: but then sitting, he collapsed with the horror of his news, and the tears started to flow.

Rafael had never seen a grown man cry, and was moved to comfort this unknown uncle who had suddenly appeared. With Rafael's hand on his shoulder, the older man looked up, "God and the Virgin preserve us," he said, "Young man, I am so sorry that you should witness such a moment as this."

"I'm so sorry," he muttered again as Anna brought her brother a cup of wine. Sitting with him, she tried to comfort him as he began to tell his story. Slowly the truth came out of how the farmhouse at Sant Cougat had been surrounded, and how the French-Castilian troops had battered down the door. Some of the family had fled, but he didn't know who had died and who had survived. Anna's father defiant to the last, had defended his flag with its four blood red stripes, and had been hacked down on the turret of the building, and thrown into the mud of the farmyard below. His senyera had been thrown down after him, and lay in the mud beside him. Anna's brother completed his story by telling how he had run to warn the Blanxart family, and had made the whole journey on foot, dodging into bushes and shadows whenever he had seen enemy soldiers. The family surrounded him in shocked silence, broken only by gentle sobbing from Anna.

"So," said Perez in slow measured tones, "They're at the gates."

The night was spent in anxious sleeplessness. An odd silence settled uneasily over La Ribera. The usual barking of dogs ceased, as if even the local hounds sensed the impending battle. As dawn broke, Perot went down into the cellar and organised bringing the weaponry he had amassed over the years up to the shop. Perez was surprised how many old swords and muskets his father had hidden, but was alarmed to find so many were too antiquated or damaged to be of much use. The old man was proud of his accumulated store, and Perez did not disillusion him; but he despaired of defending the city with such motley arms.

The Blanxart sword, however, was in excellent condition. Perez took it from its sheath of rags and the family were astonished to find it sharpened and polished ready for its bloody business. It gleamed as Perez held it before him.

Suddenly the uneasy silence was broken by thunderous canon fire.

"By all the saints, what's that?" muttered the old man.

"Castillian canons, I fear," replied Anna's brother wearily.

Across the city, dogs which had been strangely silent all night, started barking and howling, sending weird warning signals through the lanes and alleyways of the city; and almost at the same time, another hammering came at the door. Opening, they found two of Carla's brothers, armed and breathless.

"To the barricades," they shouted, "the city is besieged!"

The women and younger children crowded into the shop, and watched, horror-struck, as the men chose their weapons from Perot's collection. Perez thrust the Blanxart sword into his belt, and found a serviceable-looking pistol; Perot picked up a huge and fearsome looking musket, but realised he was not strong enough to use it, and changed it for a smaller weapon; and Rafael, uncertain how to load or fire any of the small arms, found a modest sword. Carla rushed forward to try to prevent her oldest son from going to battle, but Perot defended him.

"He is old enough to fight," he declared, "And he deserves the honour of playing his part. You others, barricade yourselves into the house." Handing the familiar senyera flag to Perez, he instructed his son to tie it to the sword and hold it aloft as they marched.

The three men, three generations of the family, opened the door cautiously, but were rewarded with a cheer from neighbours gathering outside. Breaking into a broad grin, Perez recognised many friends in the small crowd. Brandishing their weapons, they broke into song, one of their great Catalonian patriotic songs, the deep bass voices of the armed neighbours in the street and the treble voices inside the house joining in enthusiastic harmony. As Perot lead them down the street, with his son on one side and his grandson on the other, it was as if they were marching to a party or celebration, not to war. As they passed the humble houses and shops of La Ribera, others joined them.

Viewed from outside, the rag-tag army would have looked pathetic, with its mixture of assorted weapons, many too old to be useful, and lack of any armour: but within the group, the atmosphere was of optimism and enthusiasm. At last the moment they had been expecting had arrived. They would finally defeat the Castillians, and defend their beloved homeland.

The three Blanxarts at the head of the little army, complete with the blood stripes of the flag, were a particularly striking sight, with their manes of curly blond hair. "There go the Lions," mothers told their children, peeping from shuttered windows. There go the Lions of Catalunya!"

"We are marching for grandfather Joan; we are marching for my father Miquel; we are marching for Catalunya," stated Perot. Rafael, beside him, was too excited to reply, but simply grinned as he walked, overjoyed to be leaving his childhood behind, and relishing his new status as a fighting man.

Reaching Santa Maria del Mar, the three Blanxarts, called a halt to the marchers. Leaving guns outside in the care of a group of street urchins, but carrying their swords, they went into the church to seek a blessing from the priest. Back out into the sunshine, they found others waiting for them, anxious to join the band. Marching on past the sea gate, they headed towards Montjuic, splashing like excited children through the polluted stream that flowed to the sea. As they approached the city walls, they could see hundreds of other citizens, similarly armed, arriving with similar purpose and with much the same joyous determination.

The initial volley of cannon shot had died away, and again a silence held over the city. Clambering up to any vantage point they could find, the citizens' army could see guns massed upon Montjuic, the splashes of red uniform of the Castilian troops, and the blue of the French.

"By our Lady of the Sea," said Perez, "there's thousands of them."

Another roar of canon sent a mass of smoke into the air, and the destruction of several of the small outlying buildings in the rough land between the city wall and the mountain. The citizens watched impotently. Their ramshackle weaponry was useless against such canon-fire; not one of them had a gun which could fire as far as the army on the mountain. They could do nothing but stand and watch as the canons fired towards them. All along the wall fluttered the Catalonian flags, their defiant red and yellow stripes tantalising the distant enemy.

A disturbance in the street behind them distracted them from watching the enemy. Several men on horses had appeared, and one of them, recognising Perot, called to him to come down. Perot clambered down from the wall, and greeted the chief minister of Catalonia, Rafael Casanova.

"What news, Senor Casanova?" asked Perot.

"No good, my friend Blanxart," replied the chief minister, jumping down from his horse. "There's Frenchies up there as well as the troops from Madrid. We think there's forty thousand of them. They have overrun the countryside, and murdered many loyal Catalonians."

"So we have heard," replied Perot. "We got news only yesterday, of the deaths of my daughter-in-law's family up at Sant Cougat."

"A wretched business. God rest their souls," returned Casanova. "Is that your son I see on the wall above? Let us call him down. And is that young lion your grandson? I fear I have never met him. Call them both."

Perot was excited to greet the chief minister, and delightedly introduced his son. "Another Rafael, Senor Casanova!"

"A pleasure to meet you, young lion!" said Casanova, and Rafael, uncertain how to respond to the chief minister, simply responded, "Long live Catalunya!" The cheers from the group surrounding them were drowned in another volley of canon-fire.

Casanova moved close to Perez. "That's a fine sword, Senor Perez. It would not be a particularly famous one, would it?"

"I don't know if it's famous, senor," replied Perez, "but yes, it's very fine, and has been in my family for many years. It was my father's and one day will be my son's."

"I would love to know its history," stated Casanova.

Rafael looked towards his father, alarmed that he was about to betray the secret, but Perot simply laughed, "I expect you would, chief minister, but you will not hear it from me. The secret remains a secret."

Another massive volley of canon-fire roared over-head. "They're getting closer," shouted a voice from the wall. The chief minister remounted and his group rode on, as the Blanxarts resumed their positions on the wall.

In fact, it was clear that the enemy troops were not advancing, but simply using canon-fire to clear the ground between themselves and the city walls. With a wide strip of land laid barren, it would be impossible for anyone to leave the city without being seen, and thus killed, by the enemy. The word went along the walls. "We are besieged."

"Son," Perez addressed Rafael, "It looks as if nothing will happen for a while. The immediate crisis is over. Run home and tell your mother and grandmother what's happening, and bring back something to eat. God, we left home without breakfast. Tell them not to worry, and that we may even sleep in our own beds tonight."

As Rafael ran back towards the shop, Perot turned to his son, "Some of us may sleep in our beds, but others must keep watch. These bastards may attack at any time, and we must be vigilant."

"You're right. But by hesitating on the mountain, they are giving us time to get organised. There may be forty thousand of them, but we are strong, and our warehouses are full. We are in good shape to withstand a siege."

The day continued as it had started, with spasmodic firing of canons from the mountain, and the Barcelona citizens, lining the walls, watching the farms and small-holdings of the Raval reduced to rubble. Mid-afternoon a messenger came along the line inviting leaders of the little scratch armies to go to the Placa Sant Jaime to discuss strategy and make plans. Although Perot had led the Ribera group, he sent Perez, as the younger and fitter fighting man, to the strategy meeting. At Placa Sant Jaime, the fighters were addressed by chief minister Casanova, standing on a crate.

"Brothers in arms!" began the chief minister, addressing the crowd in Catalan, "When news of the advance of the Madrid army first broke, we made arrangements for those in power in our city, loyal to Madrid, to be put into a safe position in the cellars under the Generalitat. At this moment, that is where they remain." A cheer went up from the assembled crowd. "Our city is in the control once again of loyal Catalonians." A further cheer erupted. "Many of you already know General Moragues. He is to lead our strategy, and will lead us to victory."

The chief minister climbed down from the crate, and made way for General Moragues. As the most senior army officer loyal to Catalunya, the general was well respected in the citizens' army, and was greeted with more cheers, which were drowned out by more canon-fire.

"Citizens," began the general as the cheering and canon-fire died down, "many of us have known that the day would come when we fight for our land. That day has arrived, and the canons of the enemy are at our gates. I cannot offer you an easy fight, nor a quick solution. We face a siege, and we face a large and experienced army. We must fight them with cunning and guile. Our greatest strength lies in our passion for Catalunya. They fight for their king, but we fight for our women and children!"

The crowd, already excited by the atmosphere, cheered the general, but he waved them down.

"Do not shout so hard or long until the fight is won," he said. "We must bring discipline to our volunteer army, order to our defences, and a system of good communication. We must know always what our enemy is doing, we must anticipate his moves, and we must be ready to defend our city in the face of unknown firepower."

The men, recognising that the general did not want enthusiastic cheering, but rather a sober acknowledgement of the task ahead, simply murmured their assent, and leaned forward to hear everything he said.

"As volunteers, I know you do not have the discipline or experience of a regular army," continued the general, "but I believe your loyalty to your homeland is strong, and you will serve the cause of this war steadfastly and courageously."

"Our first task is to prepare to deal with a breach of the city walls. The French and Castillian fire power is such that they will, I am sure, aim to demolish the wall. This they will do with canon-fire without themselves coming within range of our small arms. If we allow them to breach the walls, they will then pour through and we will be defeated."

"At the same time, we must be watchful of snipers. They will undoubtedly bring marksmen within range of the city walls, and aim to demoralise us with random killings of our men. We will not see them, as they will hide in the rubble and ruins of La Raval. I need to know which of our men are good shots, and to post them on the walls as snipers of our own, ready to return fire if it appears, always, of course, keeping hidden as much as possible."

"Finally, we must be ready for a prolonged siege. Tell your wives to take care of their stores. Whilst we can maintain some communication by sea, there will be shortages and we must conserve all that is in the city. Those of you with storehouses will know we are well-placed at the moment, but this enemy is determined, and the siege could be long. Remain steadfast, and remain patient."

"My priority today is to set up communications and ensure we can get messages as quickly as possible from my headquarters here to all of you on the front line, and all along the line. Return now to your post and await further orders. May the Virgin and our own Blessed Saint Eulalia be with us all."

A loud "Amen" from the crowd signalled the end of the meeting, and the men hurried back to their positions.

Back at the walls, the general's speech was repeated from man to man. The realisation of a prolonged siege started to settle into their minds, and many messages were sent back to the men's families to start preparations.

By this time, Rafael had returned with provisions, and the three Blanxart lions conferred together. "We shall take it in turns to return home to sleep," said Perez. "We will ensure that there are always two of us on duty alongside our neighbours here on the wall. You go home now, father, and instruct the women to get ready for a long siege."

Suddenly their conversation was interrupted by another volley of canon-fire, but this time directed out to sea.

"What the devil?" said Perot.

"There's a ship in the bay," said Rafael.

"It's The Swan," gasped Perez. "She's very early. Must have made good time across Biscay I suppose, and sailed straight into the Castilian canons."

Abandoning their position on the city walls, the three men ran to the beach where they found Anna and Carla amongst the small knot of people gathering to watch the ship sail straight into the sights of the canons on Montjuic. Anna handed a telescope to Perot as canon shot peppered the water around the ship.

"Why are they firing, grandfather?" asked Rafael. "How do they know it's our ship?"

Screwing up his eyes, Perot peered through the glass. "They've a huge British flag flying," he announced. "Madrid cannot resist the chance to sink a British ship, especially such an easy target as The Swan."

Perez turned away from the sea, his head in his hands. "No," he moaned, "not this one. Not this time. Santa Maria save us."

Rafael grabbed his father. "They may escape, father," he said urgently. "The cargo may get to us yet."

"But a direct hit?" said Perez, "You alone know what's on that ship. It cannot survive a direct hit."

Trying to comfort his distraught father, Rafael repeated, "They may escape."

"Oh my God," spoke Anna, "There's no escape."

They watched, horrified, as the sailing ship, painfully slowly, attempted to turn and escape the range of the canon, but it was no use. Shot after shot rang out across the water, and the Blanxart family could imagine the gleeful laughter of the soldiers on Montjuic as they fired at their sitting-duck target.

The canon-fire started to shred the sails, and the main mast was demolished. Abruptly a huge explosion ripped across the water as The Swan exploded. A huge fire-ball rose into the air, with a roar beyond any they had ever heard. The noise echoed like thunder around the mountains, and a cloud of black smoke rose from the water. The group on the beach stood frozen by the shock. None had ever seen such an explosion before, and many crossed themselves, thinking that the world was ending, and they knelt horrified on the shore. A calm descended, and in the blink of an eye the Swan was no more.

"What the devil?" gasped Rafael, falling to his knees on the beach.

"What cargo did The Swan carry, son?" asked Perot suspiciously, kneeling beside his sobbing son.

His shoulders shaking, as he hugged the Blanxart sword, Perez choked and tried to answer. "Explosives," he answered. "I did a secret deal with our agents in London to smuggle gunpowder and arms to Barcelona. The British were always ready to help our struggle."

The noise of a horse clattering over the cobbles, and then onto the beach made them look up.

"What was that?" shouted chief minister Casanova, jumping down from the horse.

Rising to his feet, his clothes wet and muddy from the beach, tears still streaming down his face, Perez turned to the minister. "My ship exploded," he said simply. "It blew up."

"I don't understand." replied the minister.

"My father was smuggling arms and ammunition from London," explained Rafael. "The ship was loaded, like a giant bomb ready to explode. Only my father and I knew what the secret cargo was. A few bales of cheap cotton lay across many tons of explosives."

"There were even English canons on board, replacing the ballast at the bottom of the hold," said Perez. "What a difference they would have made to our fight."

"You risked everything to bring arms and ammunition from London?" asked Casanova. "The city is in your debt."

"But now all is lost. How did they know?" muttered Perez. "We have been betrayed."

"No: I think your secret was safe. The soldiers up on the vantage point of Montjuic could not believe their luck when a ship with a British flag sailed into their sights. They would have sunk everything coming into range." said the first minister. "I am sure they were as amazed as anyone when it exploded."

Looking out to sea, it was as if the boat had simply vanished. Where once there had been sails and cargo, and sailors, was nothing. The sea had an uncanny calm. Small fragments of the boat would be washed up on the shore for many weeks to come. It was clear there were no survivors.

The group turned away from the sea. "Go home," said Casanova. "You must recover, and our fight goes on."

Wiping his face, Perez spoke clearly, "We must go to our beloved Santa Maria del Mar, and pray for the souls of the sailors. Then we must to the barricades. This terrible victory for the Castilians will encourage them to further aggression, and we must be ready. God, if ever we needed something to strengthen our resolve, this was it."

Leading his horse, and walking with the family, the first minister spoke. "I will ensure that General Moragues knows of your efforts to support us all. It would be an honour if you will allow me to join your family in prayers, and then I will return to the Generalitat."

The siege settled into a kind of routine. Men were detailed to maintain the vigil on the city walls, whilst others went about their business. Apart from the occasional volleys of canon-fire, at first there was little evidence that they were at war. Trade, of course, ceased, and gradually the effect of this started to spread through the city. Shortages of meat came first, and then a lack of grain. Perez was concerned to guard his warehouse, leaving others to defend the walls; the warehouse had been full, awaiting the arrival of the Swan, and thus one of several warehouses able to provide food and refreshment for the city. As the population started to run low on stocks of food, the threat of looting became a worry, but General Moragues held a strict control over the men of the city and successfully averted widespread theft.

Perez and Rafael were summoned to the Generalitat for a public acknowledgement of their courage in trying to smuggle arms and ammunition into the city, but the ceremony seemed very ironic in the light of the disastrous explosion. They were extremely concerned to get a message to London to prevent the Woodbird from sailing with another cargo of explosives, and one of Carla's brothers agreed to make the journey overland, through France, to London. Although he was smuggled successfully out of the city, they never knew what happened to him, as he was never heard of again.

Now and again, a stray canon-ball breached the city wall, but no major damage was done, and the holes were quickly patched up by the general's team of carpenters and stonemasons. Occasionally a sniper successfully picked off one of the watchers from the walls, rarely killing them, but sometimes wounding. The women of the city worked hard to feed their men folk, and stop their diet from becoming too boring or inadequate, and as winter approached, started making little hoards of special treats for the Christmas Eve and Three Kings celebrations.

It was rare that anyone got in or out of the city, but a few spies managed it. They reported widespread discontent amongst the French and Castilian troops, with many tired of the makeshift lodgings on the mountain top, and anxious to go home for Christmas.

As the New Year approached, the people of Barcelona began to feel more and more optimistic; by maintaining their vigil on the walls, and hardly firing a shot, they felt they simply had to wait for the enemy troops to desert and melt away, and the victory would be theirs.

The family arranged for all to be home to see in the new year. Anna was particularly pensive. "I remember a year ago," she began, "we welcomed 1713. We looked forward to a year of peace. Little did we know we would spend so much of the year besieged in our city. Let us pray for peace in 1714. May God and the Virgin guard over us and bring victory to our dear Catalunya." The family sang many of their traditional songs that night, and even found a bottle of their increasingly rare Cava to share at midnight.

It was a clear moonlit night as Perot picked up his musket to walk to the walls where he was to stand watch. Perez stood to join him, grasping his Blanxart sword, and Rafael stood by him, his own sword at the ready. "My three lions," exclaimed Anna, "If the enemy could see you now, they'd run for their lives!"

"We will celebrate the arrival of 1714 together," stated Perez, "With my father and my son, we proudly defend our city."

Anna and Carla stood at the open door and watched as the three men set off for the walls. The moonlight glinted off their weapons, as they reached the corner, turned and waved, and disappeared from sight.

Anna turned to the rest of the family crowded around them. "Now, off to bed all of you. Nothing else will happen tonight."

As always in the moonlight, there were men walking in the streets as the three strode to their post. Some men were returning from watch duty, others taking their places, and a general atmosphere of goodwill existed in the streets. With the shortage of alcohol, and the seriousness of the situation, everyone remained literally and emotionally sober, but a general feeling of optimism remained. "Come the spring, they'll be gone," said one passer-by.

Perot, Perez and Rafael took up their positions on their section of wall, which was now very familiar to them. A neighbour, who had held the spot for the first part of the night, greeted them, wished them a peaceful new year, and told them that all was quiet. The three men stared out into the night. With a cloudless winter sky, the moonlight illuminated the barren land, shelled into craters, with its dead trees and shattered farmhouses.

Suddenly a voice, closer than usual, shouted, "Happy New Year!" in Catalan. Perot, fooled into thinking the voice was friendly, was about to shout a greeting in return, when there was a single rifle shot. The words froze in his mouth. The bullet hit him directly, and he fell back, instantly dead.

"Grandfather!" shouted Rafael. There was immediate consternation amongst the others nearby on the wall, as Perez darted forward, too late to comfort his father.

Perez enlisted the help of neighbours to carry his father back to the shop; Rafael ran ahead with the dreadful news, and Anna and Carla were waiting at the door, standing arm in arm, just as they had been a short while earlier watching the three lions marching away. The rest of the family, aroused from their beds crowded around as Perot's body was laid on the trestle in the shop. In just the same way that Elena had prepared Miquel's body for his funeral, so Anna prepared her husband. She spoke quietly as she washed him and wrapped him in a linen sheet.

"Well old man," she said, "you did well. Sixty-three ... a good age ... outlived all the rest of your generation ... Catalan through and through. The fight will go on in your name. And now we lay you to rest with your forefathers...." She paused and looked up. "But we can't, can we? The family tomb is on Monjuic and the enemy is there." She looked wildly around the room. "What do we do?"

"They are burying the martyrs of the cause in the cloister at Santa Anna. That's where we'll go in the morning," said Perez gently. "Now Rafael and I will stay with him tonight. The lions will hold a vigil for him. Now go to bed, and try to sleep. Carla, take her up."

Relunctantly Anna allowed herself to be led out of the room. Slowly and silently the family drifted away. Perez took the Blanxart sword and laid it beside his father. "Let him hold it one last time," he said, "before we use it to avenge his death."

The long night passed. Rafael slept for some of it, and Perez did not wake him. The house creaked and groaned around them, the usual nocturnal sounds. Faint sobs came to Perez as he sat beside his father: Anna, Carla, others of the family, all in private grief at the death of the head of the family.

At dawn, a sad little procession set out for Santa Anna, past the great grey bulk of Santa Maria, up the hill past the cathedral, and finally towards the Angel Gate and the convent. The citizens keeping vigil at the Angel Gate, turned to watch the funeral procession. The word went round, "That's Perot Blanxart, you know, the wine merchant in La Ribera. Hit by a sniper's bullet last night. Died as the stroke of midnight faded."

An elderly sister met them at the convent door. "We bring the body of my father," said Perez. "He's Perot Blanxart."

"Perot," said the nun. There was a long pause as she stared into the face of Perez. "I remember him well. He was my brother. The Lion of La Ribera." The sister paused again, and then smiled. "I imagine you are now the Lion. I believe that you must be my brother's son."

Managing a strained smile, Perez replied, "Indeed sister, I am Perez, the old lion now, and this is my son Rafael, the young lion."

"You both have the lion's manes," smiled the sister, touching Rafael's luxuriant hair with her thin fingers. "I remember my brother's. I never expected to receive a member of the family here, especially in such sad circumstances," she continued, "but you are welcome, and it is very suitable for us to provide a resting place for one of the lions. You must be my sister-in-law," continued the nun, turning to Anna. "May the peace of Santa Anna be with you at this time."

"Thank you sister," said Anna quietly. "I am twice blessed, as I am named after your patron saint; I also am called Anna."

The simple chapel of Santa Anna provided a quiet haven for the funeral party. The warmth and smell of the candles helped them to find some inner calm. As they knelt in prayer, they heard quiet footsteps behind them, and they turned to see Rafael Casanova joining them. Nodding, he knelt silently beside them.

After the mass had been said, the group went out into the cloister and watched as the gravediggers began to dig the grave. "A sad day for the Blanxart family," said Casanova.

"My father would expect and demand that we fight on," said Perez.

"The steadfast loyalty of your family has been well noticed," said the chief minister, "and will be rewarded after the war. Victory is within our sights, as we are sure the Castilians will soon withdraw. The Frenchies have no taste for the fight either. It is now just a matter of time."

But the citizens' army of Barcelona had underestimated the discipline of the opposing troops. Whilst the citizens were volunteers and not drilled as regular soldiers might be, the opposition was a well-disciplined fighting force, ordered to provoke and sustain a long siege. As 1714 dragged on from winter to spring, and then from spring into summer, the citizens could see no end to their plight. Food supplies were dangerously low, and General Moragues became increasingly worried that his stock of ammunition would not last through the summer.

Matters came to a sudden head on 11th September 1714, when the dawn patrols were horrified to see a huge army marching towards the city. In the night, canons had been brought forward, and were blasting a huge hole through the wall, killing men and throwing the nearby streets of the city into confusion. All those on watch rushed towards the breach, and climbing on anything high enough, started firing desperately at the approaching army. The bourbon soldiers fired back, kneeling in formation to produce terrifying volleys of small arms fire, and the citizens' army was rapidly decimated.

Perez and Rafael, alerted by the noise and action, rushed with all their neighbours to the centre of the fighting. Climbing to a high point on the remnants of the wall, and firing at random into the heart of the bourbon troops, Perez and his son were sure they had despatched several of the hated Castilians. When one of them climbed up to their vantage point, Perez launched himself forward with a roar, screaming, "This is for my father!" and ran the Blanxart sword clean through the soldier.

The Castilian and French armies continued to pour down from the mountain top; clearly for them a few hundred dead was of no consequence, and they were determined to bring an end to the action that day.

Both General Moragues and chief minister Casanova joined the troops at the front line and fought valiantly. By lunchtime, hundreds of loyal Catalonians lay dead. The deadly fighting continued, and Rafael Casanova, his horse shot from under him, was badly wounded. Moragues, observing the bloodshed and deaths in his volunteer army, and seeing the wounds of Casanova, assessed that the battle could not be sustained, and surrendered.

Seeing the general's white flag, Perez shouted, "No! Never surrender!" but Rafael pulled him back.

"Father, it's over. We are beaten. We must stop now before more die."

Standing back, and dropping their weapons, the dishevelled remnants of General Moragues's army stood defeated as the Castilian and French troops continued to pour into the city. By nightfall four thousand of Barcelona's citizens were dead, and twenty thousand soldiers had occupied the city.

Rafael stuffed his soiled and stained senyera under his shirt, and watched as an unknown officer of the victorious army, took the surrender from General Moragues, taking his pistol from him. He then arrested him. Wherever they could, the soldiers grabbed the offending senyera flags, and trampled them into the mud. Turning away from the sight of Moragues being dragged away, Rafael asked his father. "Is the sword safe?"

"Yes, it is, and stained with Castilian blood," replied Perez.

"Then let us take it home. The women will be worried sick. They need to know that we have survived."

Slipping away from the crowd, the two lions slunk away, metaphorical tails between their legs. The streets had become unnaturally quiet as everyone waited to see what would happen next. Patrols of soldiers marched around the main streets, and Perez and Rafael had to dodge into doorways to avoid them. At last they got home to La Ribera slum, and recounted the terrible news of the day.

A curfew was imposed, and the word went out that anyone seen in the streets at night would immediately be shot. For the first time since the canons' roar the year before, Barcelona was quiet. Once again, even the dogs sensed the impending doom, and hushed their usual night howling.

Unable to sleep, father and son sat up whispering together.

"Where did it go wrong? Why did we not see that final push? Were there no spies, no intelligence to tell us what was coming?" worried Rafael. "After so long. We thought we had defeated them, but they won the day."

"Rafael," said Perez, "I am still fit and young enough to wield the sword. This very day I sliced one of the enemy in two. But if anything should happen to me, the sword and all it stands for, and all the responsibility of it, falls to you."

"And I will gladly take it up," replied Rafael, "But speak not of such a disaster. I do not expect to lose you now. We may have been on the losing side, but we survived; we are still here, and our family is safe."

"But we are famous for our opposition to the Castilians. I am sure there are files about us at the Generalitat. I do not think we are safe. Remember, they will have released from the cellars those Castilian supporters who dominated the Generalitat before the war. They will be angry after a year in prison, and will be seeking revenge. They are not soldiers who were camping on the mountain, they are men who know our city well. They know exactly those of us who continued to remain loyal to the senyera."

An atmosphere of fear and loathing stalked the streets of Barcelona. The city officials who had been supporters of the Madrid regime had spent over a year locked in the filthy cellars of the Generalitat, and upon their release by the Madrid soldiers, they were indeed intent upon revenge. They were quick to unearth the records in the offices, and soon found plenty of turncoat spies to aid and abet them, reporting to them the details of who had done what during the siege.

From Madrid came extraordinary messages from the king, crowing about his success in crushing Barcelona, and celebrating the glory of a unified Spain. These royal statements inflamed the ardour of the Castilians now commanding Barcelona, and made them bold in their dealings with the defeated population. With a huge number of Castilian soldiers to support them, they were ruthless and speedy in their removal of the leaders of the city. The defenders of Barcelona, those who had held their Catalan heritage most dear, were branded as traitors to Spain, and were in fear for their lives.

The first and most prominent of the Catalonians to die was General Moragues. Following his arrest at the barricades, he was summarily tried by a military court, and condemned to death. He was hung in the Placa Sant Jaime, in front of the Generalitat building he had defended so nobly, and his body cut down whilst still breathing, and quartered. His head was hacked from his body and hung in a iron cage at the Portal de Mar where it would remain for twelve years. Following the brutal execution of Moragues, a reign of terror was inflicted upon Barcelona, with harsh and cruel repression imposed upon the people.

It was not surprising, therefore, that a few days after the defeat of the city, there came a thunderous banging at the door of the Blanxart wine merchant's shop. "Open up! Mossos!" came the shout. The newly formed brigades of Mossos were all former Madrid soldiers, and they prepared to break the door down and force themselves into the house.

Rafael stood beside his father as Carla pulled back the bolts of the big doors. The group of Mossos stumbled forward, surprised that the doors had been opened, and halted, momentarily silent, before Perez.

The leader found his tongue, and announced, "Perez Blanxart, I arrest you in the name of King Philip the Fifth of Spain, long may he live. You are charged with fermenting unrest and riot in the city; with displaying the Catalonya Flag, against the law of the land; with being one of the leaders of the illegal defence of the city against the loyal soldiers of the King; and with the murder of an unknown number of the King's men. Further you are charged with attempting to import arms and ammunition to Barcelona, with the sole purpose of supplying weaponry to the Catalan rebels."

Silently Perez pulled his sword from his belt. The Mossos took up a defensive stance, thinking he was going to attempt to attack them, but he did not. Instead, and without a word, he handed the sword to Rafael. Turning back to the former soldiers, he spoke loudly and clearly.

"I will defend Catalonya until the last breath leaves my body. I will never acknowledge your king in Madrid. I will accompany you with dignity, unarmed, and carrying my senyera. I beg you wait whilst I say farewell to my family."

The Mossos were unaccustomed to such a measured and dignified response to their boorish behaviour, and were taken aback. Carla walked unsteadily from the parlour doorway, where she had been watching proceedings, and handed the large bloodstained Catalonian flag, the one that Rafael had rescued from the final battle, to her husband. He kissed her, and embraced and kissed Rafael. Whispering in his son's ear, he muttered "The sword is yours now, my son." He hesitated, as if he wanted to say more. "Use it … well." Turning back to the Mossos, he said simply, "I am ready."

Whilst the Mossos had been in the Blanxart shop arresting Perez, word of what was happening had flashed around La Ribera, and the soldiers were shocked to find the streets lined with angry neighbours. Perez himself may have walked silently and with dignity, but the crowd voiced their opinion very loudly indeed. The Mossos shouted back, to no avail, and finally fired a volley of shots over the heads of the crowd to silence it. This was effective and the neighbours cringed back into their doorways. Poking Perez unnecessarily with their rifles, the Mossos pushed on towards the city.

As he left the Ribera slum, close by the walls of Santa Maria del Mar, Perez turned, raised his bloody senyera aloft, and called loud and clear, in Catalonian, "Long live Catalonya!"

The newly appointed officers in the city were known as "Botiflers" and had a background of the torturing methods used by the Inquisition, and indeed the tools and facilities used by that hated institution. Perez had no idea what horrors would be inflicted upon him, and although he walked steadily onwards, inwardly he trembled at the thought of what might happen. Pulling his senyera tightly around himself like a cloak, he prayed that he would die quickly, and not betray the part played by his son Rafael. He had heard terrible rumours of the tortures used, but had never known how much was true, and how much had been invented by the catholic inquisitors to instil fear into the people.

As they approached the doors of the Generalitat, the Mossos shouted "God Save the King!", and with an echoing shout from inside, the great doors were opened. Turning away from the great staircase which led to the council chamber above, the soldiers pushed him into a small cell, and slammed the door. He was surprised to find himself alone, in a tiny dimly lit room with light filtering from a small slit high on one wall. The cell was entirely empty. Perez, sat on the floor, pulled his senyera around himself, and waited.

In the stunned silence of the wine shop, it was Carla who had the presence of mind to bring together the older Blanxart children, and start to make a plan.

"None of us are safe," she began, "but you, Rafael, are the most vulnerable of all. The Mossos will be back for you, I am sure."

"I will be ready for them mother," replied Rafael. "Father gave me the Blanxart sword as he was being arrested, and I will cut down any Mossos who try to arrest me."

"No, you won't," said his mother, "as you won't be here. No, listen to me," she continued as Rafael began to protest, "You are surely their prime target. The rest of us are of little consequence, but they know you have been beside your father during the siege, and I am certain you are on their 'wanted' list. What's more, I am sure they will plan to torture your father, and as soon as he gives your name, they'll be here for you."

"Father will never betray me mother," said Rafael reproachfully. "He will never betray any of us."

"I know," replied Carla, "but who knows what agony he will be put through? He has never been tested in this way, none of us have, and we cannot be sure how he will be."

Some of the younger children, who were already crying softly, started to weep louder and cling to their mother. Anna sat with them.

"Your mother is right," said Anna. "You must go into hiding, and take the sword with you. They will surely search the house for you, and you must be gone. We cannot send you to San Cougat, as the house there is occupied by the Frenchies, but we must get you out of La Riberia. The city is not safe, but you can hide among the gypsies and vagrants in the sand dunes of Barceloneta. The girls will bring you food, and you can keep out of sight until it's safe to be seen again."

"Grandmother, I feel as if I'm running away and betraying father. I should stand and fight, not hide."

"You have no chance against these forces," said Anna glumly. "You are more use alive than dead."

"At nightfall, under cover of darkness, I'll come with you down to the sea. It's your best chance of survival," said Carla. "When the time is right, you'll come back into this house as the man of the house; meanwhile you must stay safe, my son."

There was a numbness in the house as preparations were made for Rafael to go into hiding. The Blanxart sword was wrapped in a Catalan flag, and then wrapped again in rags. Rafael fastened a belt around his waist, and hung the sword from it, under his clothes. Torn strips of cotton around his leg secured the sword. He could walk only rather stiffly, but the sword was securely out of sight. A black scarf tied bandit-style around his head, hid his golden curls. Pulling on an extra layer, and picking up the bundle of bread and dried meat Anna had prepared for him, Rafael was ready to go into the exile of Barceloneta. Carla pulled a black shawl over her head, and the two of them slipped out as soon as it was dark enough. The curfew was in place, and they knew the slightest move would be challenged by the bands of trigger-happy Mossos patrolling the streets. Dodging silently from doorway to doorway, they made their way across and out of the slum, and finally left the city by the sea gate, shuddering at the sight of General Moragues's head freshly displayed.

Perez, having fallen into a fitful sleep on the floor of the little holding cell, stirred at the sound of the bolts being drawn back, and was kicked awake by a soldier's boot. "Stand up, traitor," snarled the soldier, kicking Perez again.

Perez got to his feet, and found himself pushed and shoved to the grand staircase. To his surprise, it was clear that he was to go up, and so he did with a small party of Mossos close behind. At the top, the doors to the grand chamber of the Generalitat were open and he was pushed forward to a table, where he was confronted by a trio of Botiflers. One of them spoke in clear Castilian.

"Perez Blanxart, you are charged with a terrible list of crimes against his majesty, and against the royal kingdom of Spain. Let us start with the story of your ship, The Swan I believe. Tell us about the cargo it was bringing to Barcelona last year, the cargo which so spectacularly blew up. We do not think a few bales of English wool would explode with such an exciting effect. Perhaps you would like to tell us about your ship's cargo."

"I do not recognise this court, and I will answer no questions." stated Perez in Catalan.

"Then let us talk about something else," continued the councillor. "We have heard talk of singing coming from your shop, the wine merchant's in the Ribera slum. Singing in Catalan, we understand, songs in Catalan, the banned language. Would you like to tell us about the way you have been brainwashing your children against their king?"

"I will answer no questions," said Perez again, still responding in Catalan to the Castilian questioning.

"You are a strong healthy man, Senor Blanxart, but you will not stay that way for long when we have extracted the information we need. At the moment you are standing before us, but do not be mistaken, soon you will be unable to stand. Soon you will be begging to answer our questions, crawling on the floor to us, and desperate for death. But until that mercy comes to you, we will be diligent in asking many more questions.

Perhaps you are already changing your mind? Will you talk to us now?

"I will answer no questions," said Perez for a third time, and he stood up straight and adjusted his senyera cloak.

Turning to the band of Mossos, the Botifler councillor instructed them to take Perez down. Grabbing at his bloodied and torn flag, one of the Mossos propelled Perez to the top of the stairs, and quickly down. He was not returned to the tiny holding cell near the doors of the Generalitat, but down more stairs into the cellars which until recently had held the same men who had interrogated him. Grabbing a heavy iron cuff attached to a short stout chain which was in turn secured to a pillar, the Mossos secured the cuff around one of Perez's ankles, gave him a kick for good measure, and abandoned him. The door slammed, and he heard heavy bolts sliding into place.

At first, in the darkness, he thought he was alone, but he gradually became aware of low groaning. Shuffling around the pillar to which he was chained, he whispered into the gloom, "Hello. Is anyone there?"

"God and the Virgin help me," came a low, thin voice, little more than a whisper. "Water, water. I have been left to die."

"Who is there?" whispered Perez.

"Casanova, by the grace of God, barely living," came the agonised voice again.

"Chief Minister Rafael!" exclaimed Perez. "Do you remember me? I'm Perez Blanxart."

"Perez?" muttered Casanova.

"Yes, Perez Blanxart. It was my ship, The Swan, that exploded. Do you remember?"

"The Swan?"

"Yes, last year, at the start of the war. You came down to the beach."

"Yes, I remember," whispered Casanova. "Guns from London wasn't it? It seems a very long time ago."

"Have they tortured you?" asked Perez.

"No," came the reply. "I was injured in the final battle, and dragged in here to die. My arm was almost hacked off by a cursed soldier from Madrid, and I was hit in the leg by a stray bullet. I've been chained here ever since, hardly anything to eat, and only filthy water to drink. They thought I would bleed to death within a day, but I'm still here."

"Chief Minister, what can I do?"

"Tell me something, Senor Blanxart. Tell me about that sword. Is it true? True that your father took it to Madrid? Is it the sword from Corpus ...." but before he could finish, the old man groaned, "Bring me a swift death, Senor Blanxart."

"Alas, I cannot even see you, Chief Minister, and I fear I cannot help."

A sudden rattling of the bolts, the creak of the door, and a glimmer of light interrupted the whispered conversation. A harsh voice, accompanied by a swift kick, made Perez cringe.

"Only here a few minutes, and chattering like an old fish wife? Perhaps we're wasting time chaining you here. Come, let's take you into the light, and hear what you have to say."

The heavy cuff was removed from Perez's ankle and the gaoler led him out of the cellar. In an adjacent room, lit only by candles, the instruments of torture were laid out ready. Perez's clothes were hastily ripped from him, revealing his strong musculature. The gaoler sneered. "So strong, Catalan, you think you're so strong. But wait until we break this handsome body; you'll not stand there so bold; in fact you'll not be able to stand there at all." Perez's hands were tied together behind his back and the rope passed over a pulley hoisted over a beam.

He swung round as he heard the door open, and saw the three Botiflers enter. "Well, now," came the voice of one of them, "Perhaps you are ready to talk to us, just as you gossiped to that wretch Casanova. Guns, was it, that you tried to bring from England?"

Perez said nothing, but trembled in anticipation of what was to come.

"Now," came the voice again, in a smooth melifluous tone, "Tell us about The Swan, your lovely boat. What was its cargo when it exploded? Sticks of cinnamon? Soft silks, and woollen fleeces? I don't think so."

Perez continued to say nothing, and the gaoler hit him hard across his face, causing him to lose his balance and fall, with his full weight held by his arms and shoulders. Shrieking with the agony in his shoulders as his arms were wrenched from his shoulder blades, he tried to stagger back to his feet, only to fall again as the gaoler kicked his feet from under him. The agony in his shoulders was unexpected. He was horrified how quickly and easily such pain could be inflicted upon him.

"And how about that day you led your neighbours to the barricades? It was you at the front of the group, wasn't it? You, the lion of La Ribera. And who else was with you that day, marching against the king?"

Again Perez remained silent, and again the gaoler hit him hard, crushing his nose into his face, and sending him spinning, his arms and shoulders being destroyed by his own body weight.

Perez did not know how long he could stand this treatment, as the cycle of questions and pain continued. It was clear that the Botiflers knew a great deal about him and his family, and had information from a network of spies who had collected much evidence, before as well as during, the war. They knew a great deal about his life in la Ribera, knew much about his family, and clearly had more than enough to execute him as a traitor to the king of Spain. Before sentencing him, however, they were intent on securing a confession of guilt, and seeing how many others he would implicate in his activities.

Drawing on unexpected reserves of strength, Perez continued to refuse to co-operate, and the gaoler gradually reduced his face to a bloody mess. Repeatedly he was hit about the head, and his legs kicked from under him, and he collapsed, his own body weight torturing his arms and shoulders. At last, tiring of his obstinacy, the questioning stopped and he could stand on two feet again. When his arms were released they hung uselessly at his sides, both shoulders dislocated beyond repair. His bloody senyera lay on the floor under his feet, his own blood mingling with the stains of Castilian blood already soiling the flag. Naked but still defiant, he was unable to pick it up with his hands, so he grovelled at the foot of his torturer, and defiantly snatched up the ruined flag with his teeth.

He was led back to the cellar, the flag gripped between his teeth. Once he had been secured to the pillar and the door was bolted, and all was quiet, he spat the flag to the floor, and tried to speak again to Chief Minister Casanova, but this time there was no reply. 'Let us hope he is with his Maker,' said Perez to himself. In the darkness he could not see his flag, but he felt where it was, and lay down with his face on it. A fearful shivering racked his body as his blood continued to join the other stains on the senyera. 'Oh, Chief Minister Casanova, where are you now? I pray I join you there soon.' And he fell in and out of fitful sleep, unable to remain awake, and yet unable to sleep with the appalling agony of his destroyed shoulders.

Rafael and his mother had found their way to the scattered huts and hovels, the shanty town of Barceloneta which was home to various itinerant vagrants and dispossessed people. Here and there small fires burned and in the darkness the dunes appeared to be strangely peaceful. It would not look the same in daylight, but Rafael did not think about this. Leading her son to a quiet corner, darker than the rest, where even moonlight would not penetrate, Carla sat down. Rafael had limped beside his mother, walking as if he had a war wound, severely restricted by the sword strapped to his leg. With some difficulty, he managed to sit by his mother. "Stay here," said his mother. "I'll send the little ones to find you in the morning."

"They'll never find me," said Rafael.

"I have chosen carefully and know exactly where we are. I will make sure they know how to find you. Now try to sleep."

"Sleep? That's a joke mother. I'll be awake all night."

Kissing him, Carla vanished into the darkness. He lay back and stared at the stars, his head on the bundle with the bread and meat. Gripping the hidden sword, and despite his anxiety, he did sleep.

Despite his agony, Perez also fell asleep. He was awakened by a bucket of icy water being thrown over him.

Spluttering, he struggled up, his arms hanging useless at his sides. "Water for you," laughed the guard, offering him a cup. Unable to take it, Perez stood eyeing the man. "Oh well," continued the guard, "I don't suppose you wanted it anyway," and with a further laugh, threw the water to the floor. "Never mind, there's plenty of water for you today. Don't forget your rag, you'll need that." And he picked up the ruined senyera, and pushed the end of it roughly into Perez's mouth.

Rafael was wakened by a small child trying to steal his bread from the bundle under his head. "Get away," he hissed, and the child, startled by Rafael's voice, ran off. Half sitting and half lying, restricted in his movement by the sword tied to him, he looked around in the half light of dawn. He was in a narrow space between a tall structure and a sand dune. Shifting slightly he realised that the structure was a crucifix, and a shrine for those wandering in the confusing dunes. Thus, although well hidden behind the shrine, it would not be difficult for his mother or any others of the family, to find him.

Perez, naked and still clutching his precious senyera between his teeth, was kicked and pushed to the adjoining room, and manhandled onto a long narrow table. Coarse rope was wound around him, biting into his flesh, securing him firmly to the table. The ragged flag was taken from his mouth. The guard ripped a corner from the flag, wound it around the narrow end of a crude funnel, and rammed it back into Perez's mouth, creating a gag. A couple of the Mossos had come into the room to watch the torture and were soon joined by the trio of Botfliers. The guard started to pour water from a large jug into the funnel. Swallowing hard, and unable to breathe, Perez had the sensation that he would drown, and he choked and coughed against the onslaught of the water. Abruptly, the water stopped and the gag was pulled from his mouth.

"Ready to talk to us now?" asked one of the Mossos, in Castilian.

"What has happened to Chief Minister Casanova?" demanded Perez, in Catalan.

"What did he say?" the soldier asked his companion.

"No idea," replied the other. "He doesn't speak Spanish. Perhaps a little more water would help him."

The gag was pushed back in, and more water poured into the funnel. Perez's eyes opened wide as the water filled his lungs, and with a great coughing and shuddering, he died.

"Fool," spat one of the Botfliers. "You've killed him before he said a word," and he struck the gaoler hard enough to make him fall forward over Perez's body. "They will not be pleased with you upstairs." Turning to the Mossos, he instructed them to kill the gaoler for his carelessness and the bullet which despatched the unfortunate man, passed clean through Perez's body as well. The gaoler's body was slumped over Perez. The Botflier picked up the remains of the mangled and bloody senyera, and threw it over the bodies. "Pity," he said. "He was a brave man." Thus, in filth and squalor, did end the life of Perez Blanxart.

His son, Rafael, lost in the midst of the shanty town in the dunes, knew nothing of what was happening in the cellars of the Generalitat, and lay behind the shrine, waiting for something to happen. There was no sign of life in the immediate area and after a while he became bored with the inaction and cautiously stood up. Beyond the shrine he could see life stirring in the dunes. Here and there small fires produced wisps of smoke, and small figures in the distance scurried to and fro starting their day of scrounging and begging. He lay back against the slope of the dune, the coarse cloth securing the sword digging into him. He held the sword, the steel warm from his body, hard beneath his clothes. Somehow, grasping it this way gave him security and courage.

The sound of approaching horses sent him diving for cover, and he watched as a small troop of Mossos came by, nodding and crossing themselves as they passed the shrine, and failing completely to notice the hidden fugitive. He spent the day watching the life of the shanty town, and cowering behind the shrine whenever anyone came near. He munched the dried meat and bread he found in the bundle his grandmother had given him, and waited.

He was becoming increasingly anxious as night started to fall, the lack of information gnawing at him. So long without news of the family, and especially of his father, left him imagining all kinds of horrors. With the twilight it was harder to see who was coming, and he was startled when two small people in black cloaks suddenly appeared at the side of the shrine. Throwing off their hoods, two of his younger sisters laughed quietly at his alarm. "Mother said you would be here," they giggled, "hiding behind Sant Miquel."

"What news?" demanded Rafael.

"None yet," replied the older of the two, suddenly serious. "No word from the Generalitat about father, and the rest of us are barricaded into the house. Mother and grandmother will go to the city in the morning to try to find where father is. They say that you must stay here."

"How did you find me so easily?" asked Rafael.

"We used to play in these dunes when you were working with father in the shop. If ever we got lost, we would come back to Sant Miquel, and then we would know where we are."

"How will you get home? Is the curfew in place? You'll be shot, even if you are children."

"Rafael," said his sister severely, "we will be safe. We know the ways round here far better than the soldiers from Madrid, probably much better than you, and we know all the alleys and lanes of our slum. They will not catch us. Mother knows we can be relied on to find you. We will keep you safe whilst you hide here. Now, you must change your clothes. That's what mother said.

Here is a bundle of rags to put on. She says don't wash, and turn yourself into a beggar. That way you'll be able to wander the dunes and learn your way about. Just come back to the shrine at nightfall and we'll come to find you."

"You've got it all worked out, haven't you?" replied Rafael.

"Mother has," said his sister, "and grandmother. Now get out of those nice clothes, and put on these stinking rags."

Rafael smiled grimly. "I'll stink like the rags if I wear these."

"That's part of the disguise. And mother says, keep the sword tied tightly."

"It makes me walk like a cripple."

"I suppose that's another part of the disguise," said his sister as she helped him out of his own clothes and into the rags. Soon he was transformed, and stood half leaning on the hidden sword.

Producing another bag, the younger sister said, "Here's your supper. Now we must get back, or they will worry. You can wander about a bit tomorrow, and start to learn how to find your way round the dunes, but be here at nightfall."

His hair matted, his face filfthy and unshaven, and in soiled and ragged clothing, Rafael no longer resembled the young lion of La Ribera. His mother had done well with creating a disguise. He stood stiffly and watched his sisters disappear into the darkness, and then lay down to the food they had brought him. The coarse cotton securing the sword cut into him as he lay, and all the misery and loss of the last few days washed over him. Tears filled his eyes. "Oh father, father, will I ever see you again?" He nibbled the cheese, and pulled the stopper from the wine his sisters had brought. Gradually the tears dried as he sipped at the wine. "Father always taught us to pray to Santa Maria del Mar," he whispered to himself, "but now I think I need to thank Sant Miquel as well." Looking up at the crucifix above him, he crossed himself and prayed for his father, his family, and all of Catalonya. Finally, burrowing half into the sand at the foot of the cross, he fell asleep.

The following morning, Carla and Anna walked into the city. Stopping at Santa Maria del Mar, they went in and lit candles for Rafael and Perez, and then continued up the lane towards the cathedral. Finally arriving at the Placa Sant Jaime, they hesitated. Troops of Mossos, and squads of Madrid soldiers were coming and going, bringing wretched prisoners into the cobbled square, and delivering them to the Generalitat, before leaving, presumably to arrest others.

"What has become of Barcelona?" whispered Carla to her mother-in-law. "Everywhere there are Spanish boots marching, stamping on the heart of the city."

"I'm frightened," admitted Anna. "God knows what we shall find here."

They watched as other women went timidly to the great doors of the Generalitat, and were turned away. At last they plucked up the courage themselves, and hesitantly went up to the guard.

"We have come to enquire about Perez Blanxart," said Carla, suddenly bold as she spoke through the tiny grill in the door. "He is my husband."

"Wait," replied the guard. He turned and spoke to someone unseen. Turning back to the women he said roughly, "You can enter."

To their surprise, one of the great doors opened, and they were able to slip inside. As the great door closed behind them, they found themselves in the darkness of the gatehouse, with the great staircase before them. "You've come to see your husband?" sneered another guard. "No problem, he's through there. Carry on. Take your time." And he indicated the arch beside the great stair, leading to the inner courtyard.

Leaving the darkness of the gate house into the bright light of the courtyard, it took a moment for the women to understand the dreadful sight which confronted them. There, laid on the cobbles, were several bodies, mostly naked, and partly covered in dirty sheets. One body, however, could not be missed, as it was the only one covered by a soiled and ripped senyera. Carla clutched at Anna, and they cautiously negotiated between the other bodies towards Perez. Pulling back the flag, they saw his battered and bloodied face, and the mass of bruises covering his body. In his nakedness, he looked small and vulnerable, frozen into a child-like position.

For a moment, Carla thought she would swoon, and she knelt at her husband's head. Washing his face with her tears, she tried to wipe away some of the encrusted blood with the sleeve of her blouse. Anna put her hand on Carla's shoulder, unable to speak.

At last Carla looked up. "We must take him home," she said.

"Stay with him," replied Anna. "I'll get help."

She walked back towards the gatehouse, and turning, saw Carla lean forward to kiss her husband. "I'm going to get some help so that we can take him home," she said to the guard. It wasn't a question, it didn't even occur to her to ask if she could have the body of her son, she simply assumed she could have him.

Once outside the doors of the Generalitat, she realised she had no idea what she was going to do, and she stumbled numbly towards the cathedral. Groups of Mossos barged past her, bringing yet more unfortunates to the rough justice of the Botfliers. She walked across the cathedral square and headed blindly towards Santa Catherina market. At the notorious market cross where once witches had been hanged, she stopped. A barrow boy, who she vaguely recognised from deliveries of wine, was sitting cross-legged beside his cart.

"Will you help me," she began, "with a dreadful task."

The barrow boy stood up. "You make it worth my while, senora, and I'll do anything you want."

"Of course I'll pay you," replied Anna abruptly. "Just follow me. Bring your barrow."

With renewed strength she marched back up through the lanes to Placa Sant Jaime, and continued straight across the square to the doors of the Generalitat. "Hey, senora, I'm not going in there!" shouted the boy who had struggled to keep up with Anna.

"Then wait here," she snapped. "I'm paying you for this." Suddenly the tears welled up, her mood changed as the enormity of the situation gripped her, and she sobbed to the boy. "I'll pay you well. Just wait here."

Tipping his handcart on its end, the boy sat on the cobbles. "I'll wait, senora, I'll wait."

Anna went to the great door, and the guard let her in without a word. As before, she hesitated in the darkness at the foot of the stair. A hand placed on her shoulder made her jump, and she turned to find a more sympathetic guard looking down at her. "You've come for Perez Blanxart, haven't you? I'll give you a hand."

With a half smile and a nod, Anna went unsteadily and fearfully out into the sunlit courtyard. Carla had not moved, and was still kneeling beside Perez, sobbing quietly, and caressing his matted hair, as if smoothing it would bring life back into it.

As they stepped carefully between the bodies, the guard spoke quietly to Anna. "I remember your son," he said. "A good man. But on the wrong side. You Catalonians never learn. You should have known that Madrid would win in the end. Senor Blanxart has been a marked man for a very long time. He has paid a terrible price."

Carla did not look up when Anna and the guard reached her, but continued to stroke her husband's hair. "Let's take him home," said Anna, and she helped Carla to her feet. The guard lifted Perez and put the bloodied and naked body over his shoulder. Carla and Anna followed with the ruined senyera, and Carla supported the weight of Perez's head. At the gate, the guard stopped. "I can't go any further," he declared. "You'll have to manage from here on."

Carla tried to carry her husband over her shoulder, just as the guard had done, and she staggered out of the door, stumbled and fell. This collapse unleashed a fresh wave of howling as the two bodies, one alive, one dead, rolled on the cobbles. "Quick boy," called Anna, "help us here!"

The barrow boy brought his cart beside Carla, and they clumsily dragged Perez onto it. "By Christ and all the saints, it's Senor Blanxart," exclaimed the boy, as Anna hastily draped the flag over the naked body.

The boy pushed the cart, with its precious cargo, down the hill, past the cathedral, and down the lane towards Santa Maria del Mar, retracing the route taken by the Mossos with Perez when he had been arrested. Anna and Carla walked one each side of the cart, each with a hand on Perez, horrified by the coldness of his bruised skin, but reluctant to let go of him. At Santa Maria, the sad procession paused, and the women knelt at the door in a brief prayer for the soul of Perez, before moving on to the wine shop in the Ribera slum.

When they reached the shop, Anna indicated that Carla should remain with the body on the handcart whilst she went ahead to prepare the rest of the family. Neighbours, sensing the solemnity of the moment, gathered in silence around the cart, and waited with Carla for Anna to open the door. As Anna appeared, four of the men from the group of silent neighbours, stepped forward without a word, and carried Perez into the shop. The men lowered the body onto the table, bowed their heads briefly, and left. Anna produced a clean sheet, and covered Perez's body, and then laid what was left of the senyera over it. Once more, the old table in the shop became the resting place for the master of the house, another Catalonian martyr.

The younger children were led into the room and candles were placed around their father's body; Carla, however, would not let any of them lift the sheet to see him; she spared them the agony of witnessing how he had died.

The family settled into a restless vigil. With the shutters up, and the candles burning, it was hard to imagine the warmth and sunshine of the day outside the shop. It was as if the family was somehow cut off from the real world, trapped in a cave of sorrow. "So much death," mused Anna, looking around at her grandchildren. "Oh, my Lady of the Sea, do you really have to call them all to you? Can you not give us respite from all this dying, and let us live out our lives in peace?"

Carla remained close to her husband's head, and the children surrounded the body, some clinging to the winding sheet, others clinging to one another. Anna looked from one to another, and then noticed, in a shadowy corner of the room, the barrow boy was still with them. Moving quietly to him, she whispered, "You did my family a great service today. Wait while I find your reward."

"No, senora," replied the boy quietly, "I have had my reward. It was an honour to carry the body of Senor Blanxart. He was the lion, wasn't he? There are many who will be mourning his death this day, and I would like to stay for a while if I may." Anna leaned forward and kissed to boy on his forehead. "You may stay," she whispered.

The day passed quietly. Even the usual street noise was hushed, as if the whole Ribera slum was mourning the death of the lion. As the sun started to set, the older girls went to their mother. "What about Rafael? He has no idea father is dead. We must go and tell him. Shall we bring him back here with us?"

"No," said Carla. "This is too hard for you to do. It's my responsibility to find Rafael, and tell him he is now the head of our household. If he wishes to come and see his father, I will bring him here, but he will have to leave again before dawn. He carries the future of the family upon his shoulders, and until the city is safe, he must remain in hiding in the dunes."

Anna packed the little bag of food for Rafael, and Carla pulled the black cloak around her shoulders. "Stay quiet, and pray for your father," she told the children. "Lock and bolt the door behind me, and do not open it for anyone except your brother and I."

"I'll stay and guard the door," said the barrow boy. "I'll keep them safe, senora."

"Your reward will be in heaven," smiled Carla, as she prepared to leave.

"God speed you to Rafael," said Anna.

"God speed," murmured the children.

Turning to the family, Carla looked around the shop. Perez's body was covered in a clean cloth, with the tattered and bloody senyera draped over it; and the family sat mournfully and silent. "Lock yourselves in, bolt and bar the door, and don't answer it to anyone," said Carla.

She left the house, and paused to hear the bolts being drawn behind her. Creeping from shadow to shadow, she made her way through the silence of the curfew, out of the water gate, and into the dunes of Barceloneta. Occasionally dark figures slipped past her, intent on similar clandestine missions, but no-one spoke, nor did she venture any kind of greeting. She was aware that tears were still gently coursing down her cheek as she negotiated the maze of undulating sand. Skirting carefully around the few guttering fires, she found her way to the shrine of Sant Miquel.

"Rafael, my son," she whispered.

"Mother, is that you?" came the reply softly, as a dark figure rose unsteadily from behind the cross.

"Oh my son, how can I find words to you?" said Carla.

"Mother, you are crying. Is it father? What's happened to him? Tell me!"

"They've killed him," she replied, breaking into further sobs, and leaning heavily against her son. "Killed him in the cellars of the Generalitat. Your grandmother and I brought his body home this morning. We've brought him back to the shop. He lies just as your grandfather was lying, on the table in the shop."

"Mother, I must see him," replied Rafael.

"Yes I know. Come with me now, and I'll tell you what little we know as we walk. But you must return before dawn. The city, not even our own Ribera, is safe for you. I am sure the house is watched. Your grandmother and the children have locked themselves in the house, standing a vigil over your father. I have told them to open to no-one except us."

With the sword strapped to his leg, Rafael could move only with a heavy limping shuffle, and with the ragged clothing and matted hair, even his mother had had difficulty recognising him. Carla, beginning to feel the exhaustion of the day, was equally slow and clung to Rafael for support. Anyone watching their progress through the dunes would not have believed they were members of one of La Ribera's most prominent families.

Staggering to the top of the last dune, they could see the urban mass of La Ribera lying before them.

"Fire!" cried Rafael. "There's a fire!"

"It's in the slum," gasped Carla, "near to the winery."

"God help us, I think it could be the winery," cried Rafael, his heart beginning to beat faster.

"By the Virgin and all the Saints, let it not be the winery." said Carla, "For the love of Santa Maria, not the shop, not the house, not the family."

Stumbling and half-falling, mother and son staggered through the water gate, and into La Ribera. Neighbours, awakened by the commotion were hurrying towards the blaze, and a couple of soldiers, trying to enforce the curfew fired shots over their heads. Turning the last corner, their worst fears were confirmed. The winery was a raging inferno, the heat too great for anyone to get near. Pushing through the gathering crowd, Carla was crying out and moaning an almost animal-like howl, but the heat drove her back into the arms of Rafael.

"It's my fault," moaned Carla. "I told them to lock themselves in. They were trapped inside, the door was barred, oh God......."

A small group of Mossos, standing rigidly to attention, watched the conflagration impassively, rifles on shoulders, the flames reflecting in bayonets and buttons.

Rafael, held tightly to his mother who was in a state of complete collapse, and he felt another hand join his, helping to hold Carla. He looked into the face of Senora Macia, Carla's mother, his own grandmother. Behind her stood Grandfather Macia. "Rafael," said Senora Macia, "It is not safe for you here. Come away."

"I can't leave them," muttered Rafael, as if by watching the fire, somehow Grandmother Anna and his sisters would emerge.

"They are all with our Lady now," said Senora Macia. "Come away and save yourself and your mother before anyone recognises you."

Rafael and Carla allowed themselves to be steered away from the heat of the blaze and though the dark alleys to the Macia butcher's shop. Once inside, with the door and shutters firmly closed, Senor Macia lit a lamp. Their priority was Carla, who remained unable to stand or speak, but fell into a chair, muttering. At last, as she dozed into a fitful sleep, Senor Macia turned to Rafael.

"By Christ, you stink young Rafael. Where have you been? I hardly knew you, and recognised you only because I saw your mother. And you are walking so badly. I had no idea you had been injured. Tell me what's going on."

"Father was arrested, and tortured by the Botfliers. He died in the cellars of the Generalitat, and mother and Grandmother Anna brought his body back to the house this morning. Following his arrest, I have been hiding in the dunes of Barceloneta, disguised as a beggar. As for the way I'm limping," and he hesitated, uncertain if he should reveal the truth of the Blanxart sword, "it's an injury from the barricades. It's nothing."

"You must stay here; we will take care of Carla, and you. Too much has happened to you in the last days. You will be safe here for as long as you want."

"No we won't," replied Rafael, "and if they catch me here, or even mother, you will be drawn into their net. There is a price on my head. It's not safe for us, and it's not safe for you. I will return to the dunes, and take mother with me. I am the lion of La Ribera; perhaps I will be the last of the lions of Ribera, but I will always be dedicated to the cause of Catalonya. It may be that the Mossos think mother and I perished in the fire, but if I show my face in La Ribera, I will be recognised, and they will know I'm still at large. For now, it's best that I vanish. Who knows? Perhaps an army will rise up from the sands of Barceloneta to push the Spanish out of Barcelona once more."

"I fear we are witnessing the end of Catalunya," sighed Senor Macia.

"Never, as long as I have breath in my body," said Rafael. "I will continue the fight in the name of my father and my grandfather. I will not rest until Catalunya is a free country once again."

"We may wait a very long time for that," replied Grandfather Macia.

"However long it takes, it will take. But it will happen one day."

"You have a wise head on a young body," said grandfather, "and I pray you are right. Now if you are determined to go, let us find some provisions for you."

Carla stirred from her stupor. "In my sorrow, I have been listening. You are a good boy, my son, and I will come with you. You carry the future of Catalonya, and my duty is to support you. I've nothing else to live for, my life is over, except to be with you. Tonight we skulk away into exile, but one day you will return in triumph."

Grandmother Macia prepared a bag of food, trying to choose provisions that would last at least some days, trying to guess what they would need to survive in the dunes, and in the darkest moments of the night, Senor Macia watched them slip through the water gate, Rafael with his strange stiff limp, Carla bent, clinging to her son for support, aged before her time by the day's events. They disappeared into the dunes, and he wondered if he would ever see them again.

Edging up the soft, sandy hillock which signalled the start of the Barceloneta dunes, they turned and looked back at La Ribera. "Farewell old friend," said Rafael, straightening up, and gripping his mother with one hand, the other hand holding the hidden sword. "The young lion salutes you as he goes into exile." Carla looked wondrously at her son. Despite the desperate circumstance, she was proud of her son, still in his teens, carrying the future of Catalunya on his shoulders with dignity. They turned and stumbled into the unknown.

CHAPTER SIX

Carla and Rafael wandered on towards the beach, pausing briefly at the shrine of Sant Miquel to pray and pick up the meagre possessions and scraps of food Rafael had hidden there. The scattered rogues and vaga-bonds who lived in the shanty town amongst the dunes were used to the dispossessed and homeless seeking shelter, and took little notice of two people who appeared to be beggars. Rafael's filfthy state, and his strange gait, meant that no-one looked him in the face, and his mass of unruly blond curls had now become matted and greasy under a rough cap. The lion of La Ribera had truly vanished.

The two spent the first day and night wandering beside the sea, unsure what to do, or how to survive in such circumstances. The mild September weather, the warmth of the sun and the blue of the Mediterranean gave a false sense of peace and tranquillity, and it was hard to believe that such horror and mayhem lay only a mile away. As a child, Carla had often played beside the sea, and vaguely knew her way about the dunes. Rafael, busy in the shop, learning the vintner's trade from an early age, had rarely been there. They slept on the beach, still dazed from their experiences.

The second day they found an abandoned shack just at the edge of the beach. Consisting of little more than two walls and a roof which had fallen in, they decided they could make a shelter of it; and there was no sign of any recent inhabitant or anyone likely to be returning soon. They laboured to clear out the debris, vaguely hoping to find something useful amongst the rubbish, but apart from saving all fragments of wood for a fire, they found nothing of value. By the end of the day, they had a small clear space in which to sleep, but little else.

Unpacking the bag which Grandmother Macia had packed, they found a cooking pot, a dagger-like kitchen knife, and a water jug. These immediately became their most cherished and valuable possessions, and were hidden under the rags in the corner of the shack. Smiling grimly, Carla said, "Believe it or not, I know this knife. It's one from my father's butcher's shop. Here, in three possessions, is our entire life: a knife to butcher a rabbit, a pot to cook it in, and a jug to fetch the water for the cooking."

"Grandmother Macia did well for us," remarked Rafael. "Can we cook a rabbit in sea water?"

"I think it would be alright to cook with, but we need fresh water as well. There is a river north of here, polluted but not salty. Tomorrow I'll take the jug and see if the water there is safe to drink. Today, we'll manage on some more of the cheese." Rafael continued to have the Blanxart sword strapped tightly to his leg, enabling him to stand or lie down, but not to sit easily. Lying on the sand, with his mother sitting beside him, they watched the gathering dusk and ate a little of the precious cheese. "Yes," continued Carla, "We don't know how long we will have to live here, so we must behave as if it's for a long time, and become organised. Water will be the priority tomorrow."

With the sun setting behind them over the city, casting long shadows before them on the beach, the sea slowly turned from the bright blue of day into the deep dark blue, then black, of night. "We need time to recover, mother," said Rafael. "We have lost so much, but God has spared us." He paused and looked around. "It's so beautiful here, and peaceful. Our Lady of the Sea has guided us here; we must thank her, and Sant Miquel who watched over me for the last few days. As darkness fell, the pair slept.

Rafael was becoming used to sleeping in the stiff position forced by the sword, and at first he slept soundly. At some time in the dark of the night, he awoke to hear his mother sobbing gently beside him. Putting out his hand, he found hers, and whispered, "Take comfort, mother. The angels have my sisters in paradise; my father is there with them. Their pains and trials are over."

"You're a good son," replied Carla. "Without you I don't know what I'd do."

"Without me, you might be at home with Grandmother Macia," said Rafael, "So it's I who should be grateful. We are here to care for one another. Now try to sleep."

In the morning, Carla wrapped her black cloak around her, and set off with the water jug. Rafael watched her go with mixed feelings. He hated seeing his mother having to live like this, but her knowledge of the area, scant as it was, was a great deal more than he had. It was also safer for her than him to go wandering near other people and it was logical, if worrying, that it was Carla who went in search of water.

Rafael was determined to spend some time trying to improve the shelter, and hoped that some of the fallen roof could be put back. Limping stiffly, he moved around, hunting for longer timbers to heave up on top of the shack's two crude walls. He did not hear the horseman approaching until the last moment.

"And who have we here?" demanded the rider in Castilian.

Turning awkwardly, Rafael found a lone soldier looking down at him.

"By the Virgin, you stink!" announced the soldier. "I asked you, who are you?"

Rafael hestitated, pulling his cap down. "Joan Macia, sir," he replied quietly, in Castilian.

"What's that? Didn't hear you."

"Joan Macia," Rafael spoke a little louder, the unfamiliar Castilian sticking in his throat. "Sir."

Flicking his riding crop at Rafael, the soldier barked at him, "Speak up man. Who are you?"

Shouting loudly at the soldier, Rafael denied his name for a third time. "Joan Macia, Sir! God save the King!"

"Very well, Joan Macia," replied the soldier. "God save the King!" And he cantered away.

Rafael turned and hit his head against the side of the shelter. God save the King! How could he have denied himself three times? He was the lion of La Ribera; he was a Blanxart; and now he had fallen so far that he was afraid to admit even to his own identity. All those weeks on the barricades; all those promises to his father and grandfather; he felt he had betrayed them all. And yet what choice had he had? He must think of his mother and her survival; he must do all he can to stay alive, ready for the day when Catalunya began to fight back. He grasped the hidden sword, and vowed that one day he would hold his head up high again.

He spent the day shuffling around the immediate area of the hut, picking up driftwood and bringing it back ready for making a fire. The scrubby vegetation of the dunes seemed to him to have little possibility for anything to eat, and he hoped his mother would do better than him identifying edible plants. During the afternoon

Carla returned with the jug now filled with brackish water, and a bundle of green-leafed plants.

"There are soldiers everywhere," she declared as she arrived, and set down the jug. "In ones and twos, poking their noses into everyone's business."

"I had one here, mother," replied Rafael. "On his own, just the one, on horseback. Came right up close before I noticed him. Wanted to know who I am."

"What did you say?" alarm crept into Carla's voice.

"I told him I'm Joan Macia," said Rafael, with some embarrassment. "I betrayed father and grandfather."

"Nonsense," replied Carla firmly, "you did the right thing. If you had told him you're a Blanxart, he'd have arrested you immediately, and you'd be long gone from here when I got back. I was a Macia once; perhaps the time has come for me to be Carla Macia again."

"You're not angry at me for denying father and grandfather's name?"

"Certainly not," replied Carla. "In fact I am mightily relieved that you were quick thinking enough to do so. Our first duty to your father's memory is survival, and you did the only thing you could do to survive. The sword you bear is symbolic; and it is your responsibility to guard it now. At the moment, if anything should happened to you, there's no-one to hand it to. One day, perhaps generations from now, that sword will be carried in glory through the streets of Barcelona, heralding the rebirth of our great Catalonian nation. For now, you must do everything in your power to guard it and keep it safe." She paused, and smiled, "Oh, come here." And she hugged him just as she had done when he was a small child.

Pulling away, he asked her about finding water.

"It's a long way," she said, "and the water is very muddy. We must leave it to settle overnight and then see if we can pour off enough to drink." Rafael looked at the muddy water doubtfully, but said nothing. "And we must start to find food in the dunes and in the sea. There are rabbits, but they'll be hard to snare; there must be fish, but we have no line to catch them with; and there might be oysters. Let's go and see."

Slipping out of her worn leather shoes, Carla led the way to the water's edge where the sand gave way to a rocky shoreline. Rafael followed, but he kept his boots firmly on. Not only did he have to cope with the hidden sword, but he was not at all keen to walk into the water. "Yes," called Carla, "These are oysters. They're rather small, but they'll taste good. And there are other shell-fish among the rocks."

Carla collected enough shellfish to make a meal, and dropped them into the pot with seawater and some of the herbs she had collected during the day. "Rafael," she instructed, "Wander over the dunes and find someone with a fire. Ask them to let you light one of these twigs you've collected and we'll start a fire of our own."

Rafael returned with the twig glowing, and soon they were watching as their small fire grew and started to heat the pot in its midst. Once they were settled watching the cooking pot, Rafael said, "I got some news from the people I spoke to over there. There have been more fires in La Ribera. The Mossos have orders to burn any building showing the Catalan flag. No-one is safe."

"Grandfather Macia has a senyera in his butcher's shop," remarked Carla. "He'll be a target."

"Most of la Ribera is loyal to Catalunya, mother," observed Rafael. "Everyone is a target."

Each day Carla would walk to the stream for water. She would return with plants they could eat, and bits and pieces of rubbish she thought useful. One day, down at the edge of the stream, she found a cracked drinking cup and another day she returned triumphantly with thread and a bent pin, with which, she declared, they could catch fish – although, try as much as he could, Rafael never did.

Rafael ventured further afield and started to meet some of the other destitute inhabitants of the dunes. They accepted him as simply 'Macia', and mindful of their own doubtful backgrounds did not enquire why he and his mother were living beside the sea, nor how he had acquired his awkward limp. He began to learn which plants could be eaten, and the autumn yield of berries from some of the scrubby plants were a welcome addition to their shellfish diet.

On one memorable occasion, Rafael killed a rabbit by the simple and accidental expedient of falling on it, the hilt of the sword strapped to his side crushing its skull. Little of that unfortunate creature was wasted, but try as he may, Rafael could not repeat this bizarre way of catching a meal.

Mother and son settled into a simple routine for some days, until the morning they were woken by the shouting of some of the nearest residents of the shanty town. Stumbling out of the shack, they could see the western sky full of fire and smoke. Rushing up the dune to a vantage point, Carla could see clearly what was happening. The whole of La Ribera was alight, and an acrid smell of burning drifted across the dunes. Rafael came limping up behind her, and they stood with several of the others who lived in the dunes.

After the initial shock, Rafael spoke first. "What can we do?"

"Nothing," replied one of the other watchers. "Nothing at all."

"He's right," said Carla. "Let's hope they had some warning. Let's hope they've escaped. The whole place is on fire, the whole of the slum. My father's shop, all the shops, all the homes, everything caught up in one horrible great blaze." Turning to Rafael, she clung to him. "Haven't we suffered enough?"

Rafael put his arm round his mother. "I know what you're thinking," he said. "We must remain hopeful."

It was then they saw the beginnings of the huge crowd struggling towards them. Out from the water gate, and from other ways out of the city, the people of La Ribera were dragging handcarts and possessions away from the inferno. In attempting to salvage as much as possible, most had laden themselves with intolerable burdens, and the chaotic procession moved very slowly across the dunes of Barceloneta.

"There are hundreds of them," gasped Rafael. "They must have been given a warning."

"Let us hope Grandmother Macia and Grandfather are amongst them," said Carla.

The sorry mass of refugees continued to scramble over the dunes and through the rough paths, engulfing the scattered shacks and hovels of the existing population. As some got nearer to Rafael, he saw the wretchedness on their faces, and he remembered those first few lonely nights when he had fled the Blanxart shop inferno. Now, however, there were hundreds, of them. The ragged army continued to advance, wave after wave clambering up and down the dunes towards him. The landscape became a black mass of moving bodies, like a plague of locusts crawling across the land. Would they continue straight past him and into the sea?

Gradually, however, the mass of humanity disintegrated as one by one, and in small groups, they stopped, whether from exhaustion, or simply because they had found somewhere to make an encampment. As the sun rose, the creeping, hideous mass of people stopped, and turned, and looked back at the blaze which had been their home.

"Macia," said Carla, mindful of others within earshot, "go back to the hut and stand guard. We have but little, but we cannot risk losing anything, nor indeed, possession of our hut. I will go and hunt for my parents. Wait for me at the hut. If I find them I'll bring them to you."

Rafael, guarding their tiny shack, watched as others arrived on the foreshore, some with bundles of clothing and possessions, and some even managing to drag a handcart through the sand. Group by group, they set up small encampments, and sat, exhausted, among or on their bundles. Mostly they appeared to have brought some food with them, and once they had recovered a little from the stress of the evacuation, they took out various scraps of cheese and dried meat. Rafael was again struck by the incongruity of the situation. The autumn sun had risen into a clear blue sky, and the Mediterranean sparkled blue beneath it. Facing east into the dazzle of the sun, the scene was peaceful and idyllic; but turning west the clouds of black smoke, the crackle and roar of the flames, and most of all, the smell of the conflagration told of nothing but unspeakable horrors.

A young man, perhaps much his own age, came over to him. Rafael was eager for news, although frightened of what he might hear. The young man told him of how the Mossos had come in the evening and told them to be away by dawn. The whole of La Ribera was to be raised to the ground. King Philip, in Madrid, hearing the story of the siege and eventual defeat of Barcelona, was determined that no such insurrection against Spain could happen again. The king had decided that all the opposition to Madrid, and all the organisation of the Catalonians, originated in La Ribera, and so he had ordered the entire slum to be raised to the ground. The population had been given just one night in which to prepare to leave their homes, and most had spent the night desperately trying to work out what they could carry, and what would be abandoned to the flames. The youth knew the Macia butcher's shop, but he had no idea where Senor and Senora Macia might be.

In the middle of the day, Carla returned empty handed and with no news. "Everywhere was the same," she told Rafael. "Dazed people, sitting on bundles of possessions, no-where to go. There are hundreds of disposed people; the whole of the Ribera slum has come to the sea."

Carla set out again in the afternoon, and occasionally found people who knew of her parents, but none knew whether they had escaped the inferno, nor had seen them on the beach. With the sun setting, she arrived back at the sea's edge, south of their own hut, and was about to give up for the day, when she heard her name.

"Carla!" It was the voice of her father. She turned to see her father struggling towards her. Her parents had skirted along the southern edge of the dunes, dragging with them a fully laden handcart. "Your mother is exhausted," said her father. "We can't drag this thing any further." He stopped, too drained and empty even to show his relief at finding his daughter.

Carla flung her arms around her father, and then turned to the bundle of rags leaning on the back of the handcart. "Mother," she said, "I didn't think I'd find you. I have been imagining the worst all day. Thanks to the Virgin who looks over us, you're safe now."

"I think we are a bit too old for all this," said her mother weakly.

Carla held tightly to her mother. "You've done very well, mother. And now we've found one another, you will be alright. By a miracle, you have found me very near the shack, where Rafael is waiting. It's not much of a shelter, but it's a lot better than nothing. I'll bring you to Rafael – he'll be so pleased to know you are safe."

"We were always frightened of Hell when we heard about it in church," began her father, "but I never expected that we would see it. La Ribera is a vision of hell, fires burning on every street, frightened people running every which way, and a smell beyond description. If this is the Lord's plan for us, it's terrible."

"We watched the fire this morning. We felt so hopeless, just watching and unable to do anything," said Carla.

"Thanks to the Virgin, we got a warning. Most people escaped, just carrying what they could. Like everyone else, we have nothing left except what we could carry, or bring on the cart," said her mother.

"Dragging this cart has been a nightmare," said Carla's father, "but looking at what's happening around us, I'm glad we did."

"Whatever have you brought, father?" asked Carla.

Carla's father leaned close and whispered, "It's all the meat from the shop. I brought the lot. And if anyone tries to steal any of it, I've brought my best knives as well!"

"You'll be telling me your senyera is under there too," said Carla.

"Of course it is!"

Rafael was quite worried that it had taken Carla so long to get back to him, but he was delighted that she was bring his grandparents. He limped forward to help the other three drag the handcart to the shack. The old couple collapsed onto the beach by the hut, Rafael sat near to them, and Carla provided what little succour she could from their meagre supply of water. Oblivious to the magnificent sunset casting a warm glow over the beach, they huddled together, and slept fitfully.

In the morning, as another beautiful day dawned, they began to recover a little from the previous day's effort. Noting yet again the irony of such wonderful weather and the calm blue sea, Rafael looked at his grandfather. "So," he began, "what's the plan?"

"I've no idea," replied Grandfather Macia. "I just couldn't leave all my stock to the Spanish soldiers, so we loaded it all onto the cart. My knives are my most precious possessions as a butcher, so we brought them."

"I told him he was mad," said grandmother. "We nearly killed ourselves dragging that cart. Mind you, I would have been pleased to see the faces of the soldiers when they got to the shop, and expecting to find a room full of meat, found it empty instead."

"It's mostly dried and smoked meat," said grandfather, "and there is quite a lot of it, as you could tell from the weight of the cart."

"I was thinking after we pulled that load to the hut last night," said Rafael. "There's hundreds of people here, all refugees, and they've brought all kinds of stuff. They're sitting beside and on the bundles they've brought, mostly just waiting to see what will happen. They don't know where they will live, or even how they will live. We were like that at first. You're just so desperate and tired and distressed, you don't know what to do. Soon their food will run out, they'll all be hungry and they'll realise they have no way of cooking. Hopefully they've brought their money with them. With all this meat from grandfather's shop, we can set up a kitchen in the hut, right here on the beach, and feed at least a few of them."

"It would be really difficult, Rafael," said Carla. "We have no way of cooking anything properly. We have been barely able to feed ourselves. We can't begin to feed others. It's too hard. How could we do such a thing?"

"Tell us what you're thinking, boy," said his Grandfather.

"You've brought all this meat, Grandfather. You said you brought your good knives, so you can cut it for us, and we will cook it over the fire. That's the fresh meat, which will not last long anyway. The dried and smoked meats don't need cooking and grandfather is an expert at cutting them. We could ask those with money to pay with cash, or partly with bundles of firewood they collect on the beach. For those without money, we'd be able to barter for something they've brought, or found. If one or two of them could find some stone or bricks perhaps we could even build a kind of oven...."

"Slow down," smiled Carla, shaking her head. "Just cooking over the fire will have to be good enough at first."

"When we've unloaded the cart, it will make a table to work on, and with grandmother here to guard the hut and our things, I can go further afield to hunt for other stuff! What do you think grandfather?"

"Thank the Virgin for young people," smiled grandfather. "We are beset with terror and troubles, and you come up with a plan. We must try to make the best of a dreadful situation, young man. You give us hope, where there was none."

"Perhaps one or two of the refugees will be able to catch rabbits for us – that would be a good start for getting more fresh meat," continued Rafael.

"A kind of kitchen on the beach," mused Carla. "It might just work."

"Yes," repeated Rafael, thinking aloud. "A chiringuito, a little kitchen on the beach."

The afternoon was a lot more difficult than Rafael expected, as it was not simply a matter of unloading the cart. Grandfather insisted that all the legs of pig which had been hanging in his shop needed to be hung in the hut. This seemed to be the bulk of what he had brought out of La Ribera, and tying each hunk of meat to the makeshift beams of the tiny hut was very hard. Grandmother was convinced that the weight of meat would bring the whole structure collapsing down on them, but Rafael and grandfather worked hard and with enthusiasm.

As night fell, and the task was almost complete, grandfather produced the senyera he had hidden on the cart, and in the twilight, the four stood around it, each with their own silent thoughts about the horrors of recent days.

"We cannot hang it up for fear of our lives," said Rafael, "but we must keep it safe, with the ...." and he stopped, and looked at his mother for reassurance.

"Go on," she said. "It is the right time to tell the secret."

His grandparents looked at Rafael in astonishment as he started to tell the story.

"I was very lucky in the fighting," he began, " and was not injured. I walk with this strange limp for a very different reason. I am carrying the Blanxart sword; it is strapped to my leg to keep it hidden, and I have kept it safe and out of the hands of the Spanish by keeping it with me."

"I don't understand," said grandfather. "The Blanxart sword? What's that?"

"Many years ago, nearly a hundred, my great, great grandfather, Joan Blanxart was murdered in his baker's shop in La Ribera. His son Miquel, my great grandfather, kept the Castilian sword which killed his father, and vowed to use it to seek vengeance for the murder. The sword has been passed from father to son ever since from Miquel to Perot, my grandfather, and from Perot to Perez my father. My father Perez used it at the barricades of Barcelona. I was with him when he sliced a Castilian soldier in two with it. When he was arrested, he handed me the sword. I am the youngest Blanxart ever to carry the responsibility. One day, as we have said before, perhaps many years from now, the sword will be carried through the streets of Barcelona, when we celebrate the rise once more of our beloved Catalunya."

"An astonishing story, Rafael," said grandfather. "And you keep it on your person?"

"At all times. It literally never leaves my side. And until there is somewhere safe to hide it, it will remain tied to me. We must keep your senyera equally safe. One day our flag of blood will fly again in Catalunya. Father's senyera stayed with him through the torture and was burned with his body in the winery fire. Your flag has survived the destruction of La Ribera, and thus takes its place in the history of our nation."

"We never know when the Mossos will be coming to check up on us, and they'll certainly notice us when we start to try and sell the meat," said Carla. "The senyera must stay hidden if it is to be kept safe for the future."

"Grandfather," said Rafael, "with your permission, I would like to wrap the sword in your senyera. That way both will be safe."

"I can think of nothing better; but if you are found with the senyera under your clothes, you will be condemned. Anyone showing the senyera, or using our own Catalan language, or anything else demonstrating our loyalty to Catalunya, will be put to death."

With the bravado of youth, Rafael was confident. "I won't be caught, grandfather. I am the lion of La Ribera, and whilst I am in disguise now, I will rise again, and my children and children's children will preserve the traditions of Catalunya."

In the darkness of the hut, under the hanging meat, and surrounded by the only family he had left, Rafael solemnly peeled away the rags of his beggar's disguise, and revealed the sword. Hesitantly Grandfather and Grandmother Macia held out their hands and touched the sword as if it were a holy relic.

"May I hold it? asked grandfather, taking it reverently. "My, it's heavy," he exclaimed. "What a weight you are carrying."

"It's warm," muttered grandmother.

Carla smiled. "It's the warmth of Rafael's body," she said.

With a twist of butcher's string, grandfather helped Rafael wrap and secure the senyera flag around the sword, and Rafael strapped it back to his body. "It has started to feel like a part of me," he said. "I missed it when I took it off, and it's like an old friend coming back to me now."

Helping him back into his rags, grandfather joked, "You might be the lion of La Ribera, but you still stink!"

"I fear we will all stink, living here on the beach," said Carla.

"But we have the sea, the great blue Mediterranean sea, on our doorstep," remarked grandmother. "I, for one, intend to take regular baths!"

The next day, with grandmother guarding the hut, Carla took Rafael with her to collect water. Everywhere the beach was crowded with refugees, many of them still dazed by the abrupt loss of their home. On the whole they appeared to have little ability to cope with the distressing circumstances, and many were openly weeping. Few had realised that they needed to make the best of the dreadful circumstances, and despite his own terrible loss, Rafael hoped that getting the chiringuito started would help a little towards some kind of positive feeling amongst this sea of despair.

Returning with the water, Carla gathered more edible herbs and plants, and Rafael accumulated a large bundle of firewood. Arriving back at the hut, they discovered that grandfather had been busy on the shore-line picking up drift wood, and had even dragged a few large timbers back to start extending the shack. Together, they found and dragged several very large boulders to make a hearth, and by the end of the day, they were ready to start cooking. Various other people, drifting aimlessly, watched them at work, and asked what they were doing. "Come back tomorrow," they said, "and you will find out."

The chiringuito was a success, as so many of the hordes of people were desperate and hungry. Most of the refugees had some money with them and many were ready to collect firewood and pay for a slice of pork in exchange for a small coin and a bundle of sticks. Before the first day was over it was obvious that they would need to find a way to bake, and thus serve the meat wrapped in bread. As the small coins began to accumulate, grandmother counted them up and declared that she would venture out and buy flour.

Happily, several of the refugees proved to be skilled at catching rabbits, so quickly the stock of fresh meat was replenished.

From this tiny beginning, a small business developed over the next few weeks. Some of the refugees found employment, mainly in the massive work needed to rebuild the shattered city, and a strange calm came upon the shanty town on the beach. Once in control, the Spanish seemed to have no appetite to continue the purge against the Catalans, preferring, it appeared, to let well alone on the beach.

Each day saw a small development or improvement in the chiringuito. A wood fired bread oven was built, and the crude hearth for roasting meat was rebuilt and improved, and the hut extended. Carla was the driving force behind much of the daily routine of the chiringuito, with grandmother taking on the unexpected role of baker. Grandfather and Rafael spent much of their day assisting with chores at the cafe, but also had time to wander through the crowded camp. Grandfather found a number of their old friends and neighbours from La Ribera, and all had the same story to tell, of the dreadful flight in the night, carrying or dragging as much as they could, and everyone recalled that terrible moment when they turned and watched La Ribera in flames. For the time being, Rafael maintained his disguise, and told everyone he was Joan Macia.

As winter approached, most of the refugees contrived to make their huts and shacks into something weather-proof. The mild autumn weather assisted greatly as the displaced community came to terms with its loss, and re-grouped in a new, and not altogether unpleasant environment. Within a few days of the fire, some refugees had ventured back into La Ribera and returned with blacked pots and pans, but little else remained of what had been a flourishing and vibrant community.

Some of those visiting the charred remains of the slum reported mysterious activities with soldiers measuring and staking out what appeared to be a gigantic building. Rafael and his grandfather were watching from a sand dune near the sea gate, when a neighbour came rushing towards them.

"It's a fort!" the neighbour exclaimed. "They're building a giant fort!"

There followed a period of extraordinary irony, as many of the men amongst the refugees found work on the enormous building site. How odd it was to be digging foundations into the charred remains of their own homes. How strange to help with the obliteration of their own alleys and streets. How bizarre to be using stones from their own dwellings, or torn from their city walls, to form the foundations of the massive new structure.

During that first winter of 1714, the community settled into a routine of sorts, living on the beach and in the dunes of Barceloneta. With the income earned from labouring on the site of the new fort, some of the inhabitants were able to make themselves reasonably comfortable in their shanty town. The Botiflers, settled in a variety of local and government posts, were clear that their duty to King Philip included re-establishing Barcelona as a significant, and peaceful, trading port, and thus they continued to administer the city with a light touch. After the initial violence in the aftermath of the siege, they had no taste for further torture or execution, and most of the former inhabitants of the Ribera slum, began to feel safe, if not settled.

Rafael found himself in a dilemma. He had carefully carried the burden of the Blanxart sword, now wrapped in the Macia senyera, throughout the winter. His pride in the hidden symbols of Catalunya was undiminished, and his whole persona was dominated by the weight and restrictions caused by the length of steel strapped to his leg. As the winter passed, Rafael got to meet and know more of the neighbours, and began a network of business contacts to support the growing chiringuito trade. All of these contacts and friends knew him both as a disabled man, supposedly injured in the siege of Barcelona, and by his name of 'Macia'. Somehow the single word name had stuck since that day he had lied to the soldier to save himself; no-one questioned him for a Christian name, he was simply 'Macia'.

Nightly he slept with the sword strapped to his side; and daily he went about the business of the chiringuito with the limp which characterised him. It was as if the fit, young, active Rafael Blanxart had vanished, to be replaced by the crippled Macia. His disguise had probably saved his life, but now he was stuck in a situation he could not avoid. He had wandered up to the vast building site where so many of the refugees on the beach were now employed, but a guard had mocked him and shouted at him, "We need fit, healthy workers here, not cripples. Crawl back to your hole."

He considered leaving the sword under his makeshift bed in the hut, but it seemed to him to be a very insecure place to leave such a treasure; and the responsibility of ownership of the sword and its recently-acquired senyera, left him unable to take any risk other than continue to carry then both hidden beneath his clothes. He had gradually improved his appearance, and finally threw away the beggar's rags he had worn to escape the city. He kept his head covered, however, so that he would not draw attention to the unruly mop of blond curls which were the singular trademark of the Blanxart firstborn.

Grandfather and Rafael often walked to the edge of the dunes, to the same point from which they had watched the burning of La Ribera, where they could watch the building of the fort. It was indeed enormous, covering most of the area of the old Ribera slum. Huge earth works were being built up, reinforced with enormous stone walls, and the two men watched fascinated by the army of labourers toiling with wheelbarrows and carts, dragging the huge quantities of earth and stone into position. The hardest task of all was to dismantle much of the old city walls, and drag the huge blocks of stone to the new fort, for its outer walls. They became aware that the fortress would contain accommodation for a large army, and that Madrid was creating this vast warlike edifice, not to wage war, but to ensure that the Catalans had no chance of any kind of uprising against their Spanish conquerors. With the city walls dismantled, Barcelona could not defend itself, and the new fort ensured that Madrid would continue to dominate and rule.

"Poor Catalonya," said Grandfather Macia, "We stand little chance of fighting back against such a great machine as this."

"It is vast," said Rafael, "and I do not like to see so many loyal Catalonians forced to work, building this horror."

"They have little option but to work here," said grandfather. "With all the small businesses destroyed in La Ribera, they need the work; and some of the money they earn is being spent in our own chiringuito, so we cannot complain. We are as much complicit in reaping the benefits of this building site as any of those we are watching."

"All the more reason to keep safe the sword and the flag," replied Rafael, tapping the heavy steel concealed under his clothes. "Even the greatest fort will one day fall, and the sword will be ready for that moment."

Work on the great fortress continued for six years, until a great star-shaped monster dominated the city. Long before it was finished, troops of soldiers were moved in, and the flag of Madrid flew from the highest turret. The beach dwellers named the huge fort "Ciutadella", and discovered that King Philip himself visited a number of times to view progress in its construction. Whenever the king was near, however, the workers were roughly penned in the far distance, unable to see him; and with fully armed soldiers to keep order, the workers dared not shout abuse at the man who had obliterated their culture and desecrated their land.

Towards the end of the construction period, the beach people watched with astonishment as just to the north of their shanty town, a long causeway was built out from the fortress, all the way to the edge of the sea, giving the fort its own water gate, creating a barrier between the slum on the beach and its main source of drinking water.

During the construction years, life on the beach consolidated. Some of the inhabitants moved away to other parts of the city, or to family in other parts of Catalunya; but many survived in the huts and shacks on the beach. The Macia chiringuito continued to flourish, with the family busily involved in its day to day running.

Grandmother, who had been given a new lease of life by becoming the cafe's baker, was hardly strong enough to continue to cope with the demand for bread, and soon needed help. Carla had become friendly with another beach-dwelling family nearby, who had a son working on the fortress construction site and a pretty teenage daughter. The elderly parents were unable to work, and their daughter, Susana, spent much of her time collecting water and doing the chores around their tiny shack. Carla, sitting with the parents, watched as Susana brought some washing from a small line they had erected, and folded it carefully.

"You have a treasure there," observed Carla.

"We do indeed. Without her we surely would have perished. But she cannot get work like our son has, and cannot bring any money into the family."

"We need help in the chiringuito," said Carla, "and she is a good worker. Perhaps you could spare her for a few hours each morning when grandmother is baking bread. As grandmother gets older, she finds it hard, and Susana could quickly learn to mix and knead the dough. It would be a good skill for her to learn, and she can return at midday to run your errands."

When Carla reported this conversation to the family, the grandparents were very pleased, but Rafael was worried. "Mother," he began, "there was always a tradition in the family to employ no-one but people loyal to Catalunya. We may have lost our lands, but we are still Catalonians, and I believe we must maintain the family tradition. What do we know of Susana and her family, except that they fled La Ribera like we all did? We must find first if they are loyal to the flag."

"I will speak privately to her parents," replied Carla, "and if they are not loyal, we will not employ the daughter."

In fact Rafael's worries were unfounded, as Susana's family were as true to the senyera as the Macias and the Blanxarts, and thus Susana came to work in the kitchen. She learned quickly the art of bread-making, and soon was able to take the burden of the work from grandmother.

At first Susana was rather frightened of the mysterious young man she had seen only from afar. Busying herself in clouds of flour, mixing and kneading, strong hands and arms in the great bowl, she would glance at Rafael across the kitchen as he arrived with bags of flour, huge hams or bundles of logs. In the tiny space, they would brush against one another, and she would blush. He was the first man, other than her brother, that she had had close contact with, and she felt he was something of an enigma. He would greet her with a warm smile, and she would hesitantly smile back, but said little.

Carla and her parents had to be careful not to call Rafael by his real name when Susana was around, and she had no idea he was not Macia, but the legendary Lion of Ribera of whom she had, of course, heard stories.

With Susana working for them, and they themselves working long hours, the business flourished. Within a couple of years, they had almost completely rebuilt and extended the shack, and created a small but efficient working kitchen. Outside the hut, a group of rough tables and benches had been constructed by grandfather and Rafael. The fires under the roasting rack and in the bread oven were never allowed to go out, and the first chore of the day, long before dawn, was to stoke them with logs. Whilst it was still dark, Susana would arrive and begin the dough for the day's baking, and grandfather would be butchering some animal purchased the day before. Carla would start her day frying a huge pan of ham and oysters. Further along the beach, a small brewery had been set up, and Rafael's day started by dragging a small cart over the shingle along the shoreline to collect the day's barrel of beer.

Carla's mother tongue was, of course, Catalan; but she knew a fair amount of Castilian, and was able to serve the customers without using Catalan: with the current regime in place, it was feared that Catalan would die, and the language be lost, and certainly it was never heard in public. Carla, however, was determined to maintain it as the family's private language at home. She was pleased to discover that Susana and her family similarly maintained the language in private.

At daybreak, many of the construction workers would call in for a breakfast washed down with ale; the day would be spent in a variety of back-breaking chores – collecting water, purchasing bags of flour, stacking logs and stoking the fire, and generally coping with the hundred and one things needed to keep the chiringuito going. In 1714 the business had started small and tentative, but within a few years it had become well-established and well-known, and was even serving meals to soldiers who occasionally came riding through the shanty town. Rafael himself remained in the background whenever the soldiers were around.

The work was harder in the summer, with the long warm evenings encouraging patrons to linger at the tables, calling for more beer, and it was often well after midnight before the family fell into their beds, only to get up again before dawn. Susana was needed to work full-time, but her wages, with those of her brother, ensured her parents had a far more comfortable life than previously.

One late summer's evening, with the sky a panorama of rosy pink and orange, Rafael stood on the dune at the back of the chiringuito, admiring this busy kitchen they had built. Susana came out into the glowing light of the setting sun, and glanced towards Rafael. He waved and beckoned, and instead of turning shyly away, she sauntered up to him.

"Look at the sunset," said Rafael quietly, in Catalan.

"It's beautiful," replied Susana.

"It's a beautiful place," said Rafael. "I hated it when we were forced to come here, but now I love it."

"So do I."

The couple stood and watched the slowly changing patterns of the sky, Susana standing close to Rafael. Gently he touched her hand, and then held it more firmly. Susana did not flinch or pull away.

As the days passed the young couple found many opportunities to be together whether working in the kitchen or on errands for supplies, and gradually they become familiar, both of them losing that early shyness which had gripped them. Rafael found himself more and more attracted to Susana; and he particularly enjoyed courting her in his beloved Catalan language. Gradually he realised that his false identity would stand in the way of their relationship continuing. One evening, he decided to pour the whole dilemma out to his mother.

"I've watched you for some time," she said. "And I've also been pondering the problem. Susana thinks your name is Macia and that you were wounded in the siege; she has no idea of your real identity, or that you carry the sword, the senyera and the future of Catalunya hidden beneath your clothing. It seems to me that there is a clear choice: either you tell her the whole truth, or you turn your back on her."

"I cannot give her up," replied Rafael, "but I need your support and blessing to take the risk of telling the truth. Before she came to work for us, you talked to her parents about their loyalty to Catalunya. But are they loyal enough? Can Susana bear the burden of the truth, that I am a wanted man?"

Susana's family were confused and surprised by the invitation to supper at the chiringuito. Such an invitation was unknown in the shanty town, and when they discovered that the chiringuito unexpectedly closed early that evening, they were even more mystified.

Seated in the kitchen the visitors watched as Carla and Grandmother produced supper. There was small talk about the weather, recent visitors to the beach, and the progress on the massive Cuitadella fortress. Rafael, sitting awkwardly as he always did because of the sword under his clothes, held Susana's hand under the table, and surreptitiously smiled at her. A couple of times she started to ask him what was happening, but each time he stopped the question.

Finally most of the platters were cleared away, and everyone looked expectantly around. Carla broke the silence by turning to Rafael, and asking him to speak. There was a further silence as he stood, closed his eyes as if in prayer, and took a deep breath. As they watched, he pulled off the rough hat that he always wore, and his golden curls tumbled out. As he shook his head, the visitors gasped, and Susana muttered "Macia?"

Speaking very quietly, Grandfather Macia quickly interjected, "Use very quiet voices everyone. We don't want any of the neighbours to know what's happening!" Nodding, and even more amazed, Susana's family looked from grandfather back to Rafael. When he spoke, it was in Catalan:

"My name is Rafael Blanxart, the son of Perez Blanxart, and grandson of Perot; heroes both of them from the siege of Barcelona. I am the youngest of the generations of Blanxart to be called the Lion of Ribera. When he was arrested, my father handed me the sword of Catalunya. I hid in the dunes here in Barceloneta, and was hiding here when the rest of you were forced to leave La Ribera. I have kept the sword hidden ever since. When Grandfather Macia escaped from the destruction of the Ribera slum, he brought his

Catalonian flag, his senyera, with him, hidden in the meat from his shop. It replaced my father's senyera which was burned in the terrible fire at my father's shop. The Macia flag remains hidden with the sword." He stopped, took a deep breath again, and turning to Susana's father, continued.

"Sir, now that you know the truth, I wish to ask for the hand of Susana in marriage. I trust to God and the Virgin that you will consent to this marriage. I have told you the truth about myself, and hopefully await your judgement." Susana leapt to her feet, and putting out her hand to Rafael, she turned and faced her father. Rafael's face was grim and serious, but Susana was radiant, able to anticipate the old man's reaction.

Susana's father hesitated, and for a moment Rafael thought he had made a huge mistake despite Susana's tight grip of his hand. With a thoughtful face, the old man looked around the room, and then slowly stood up. There was a tense silence. Leaning towards Rafael, he held out his hand, and as he shook Rafael's hand his visage changed, and he smiled.

"Congratulations, young man; it is an honour that I give my daughter into your safekeeping. I had always hoped that she would make a good marriage, but I never expected such good fortune. In recent years I have agonised over the future of our nation, little knowing that you, young man, held the key. I am delighted to consent to my daughter's marriage to you, and give you my blessing. But wait, I wish to bring my own token of commitment to this meeting." And with that he rushed out of the kitchen. It was the turn of Rafael and the others to be mystified and they looked at one another. Within a few moments the old man returned from his shack, clutching a small black bag. His wife smiled, suddenly understand his intentions.

He opened the bag and pulled out a Catalan flag. "This is my senyera, and I bring it to the table as a token of my loyalty to Catalunya. My wife and I recognise the trust you placed in us in telling us your terrible, wonderful secret." Moving around the room, he placed the flag around the shoulders of Rafael and Susana, and placed his arms around the couple. "With my blessings, young man, I will see you wed." He paused, and grinned, "But first, I would love to see the sword! It would be an honour."

Rafael, grinning broadly, looked over his shoulder to the old man behind him. "You have the sword in your hand, father-in-law, just as Susana has embraced it many times before!"

Susana and her father stood back as Rafael started to take off his clothing. Stipped to his undergarments, the sword, wrapped in the Macia senyera, was revealed. Rafael, held the sword aloft, and with Susana's senyera round his naked shoulders, the Macia senyera in his hand, and his golden curls shaken out to their full glory, he stood, the embodiment of Catalunya; the Lion of Ribera.

"Long live Catalunya!" he pronounced.

"Long live Catalunya," they all responded.

"And long live the Lion of la Ribera," said Carla quietly.

"No," said grandfather. "La Ribera is gone. Long live the Lion of Catalunya!"

"Long live the Lion of Catalonya!" they chorused with enthusiasm.

Susana's mother, who had remained smiling quietly to herself throughout the momentous proceedings started to sing. Her gentle voiced filled the kitchen, as she sung one of the ancient Catalonian folk songs about the mountains and the sea; they turned to her and sung quietly with her.

Later that night, as Susana and her parents returned home, they were still full of wonder at the events of the evening; Rafael was equally enraptured, and the Macia family slept soundly.

Antoni Blanxart was born in 1729. There had been many babies born in the shanty town on the beach, but none who would inherit such a legacy. The boy was known as Antoni Macia, and it would be many more years before the secret carried by his father would be revealed to him, or that one day he would become the Lion of Catalunya.

CHAPTER SEVEN

In its own way, La Ribera had been a rather handsome well-established slum. Life on the seashore, however, was far more ramshackle. The various shacks which the Ribera people had erected after the expulsion from their home, remained chaotic. Here and there, additions and reinforcements had been made to create more permanent-looking establishments, such as the Macia chiringuito; but most remained little more than rough shelters.

The shanty town was a blot on the landscape. Much of Barcelona's old town around the cathedral had been repaired since the siege, and some newer properties near Santa Maria del Mar were rising to as many as five floors, with much-sought after accommodations for increasingly rich merchants. Since winning control of the city in 1714, the Castilian administration had gloried in its rich prize, and supported rapid growth of trade. After many years the city fathers, in surprisingly philanthropic mode, could no longer tolerate the chaos of the shack dwellers on the Barceloneta beach, and resolved to do something about it. Eventually building work began.

Work on the massive Cuitadella fort, and the long causeway out to sea, had taken many years. As the fortress neared completion, however, the military engineers had less work to do, and they were commissioned by the city to investigate building civilian housing outside of the city walls, south of the fort, replacing the seaside shacks.

There could not be a greater contrast between the chaotic way in which the shacks and hovels had grown up on the seashore, and the military precision of the new development. Straight roads were laid out, with uniform dwellings on either side. The foundations for a new church were laid, and a large open space for a market square identified. North of the housing, alongside the Cuitadella causeway, a large military parade ground was created.

The years had taken their toll of the older people of the shanty town. Susana's parents had died, and her brother had moved away from their shack which was now occupied, like many of the hovels on the beach, by fishermen and their families. Carla's parents had lived to surprising old age, but had died in the 1740's, leaving Carla, Rafael and Susana to continue with the chiringuito, assisted by Antoni and his brothers and sisters. The business had grown and flourished: at first busy with the workmen from the Cuitadella fortress, then the growing numbers of fishermen. By 1753 when the Barceloneta housing development began, fishing was the main trade for the residents on the beach, and the links with the old Ribera slum were few.

Rafael maintained his disguise as "Macia"; his son knew that his father's name was Rafael but he always called him Papa. Rafael kept his own curly blond hair hidden under a rough hat; and Susana cut Antoni's hair very short at all times, so although he was blond, there was no clue that he would have luxuriant curls given the chance. Rafael continued to carry the Catalunya sword, wrapped in Grandfather Macia's senyera, strapped to his body, and the community knew him as the cripple, injured somehow in the siege many years before. He would take the sword off only at night, when he and Susana climbed into the tiny box bed in the corner of the kitchen, and Antoni had never seen his father unclothed, or without the limp caused by the hidden sword.

Whilst the chiringuito continued serving meat and bread, more and more fish and seafood came onto the menu, and gradually the links with the fishing community strengthened. Living in terrible conditions in the shacks on the beach, many of the fishermen and their families would bring fish to the chiringuito to be cooked, and sometimes eaten there; often they would exchange fish for bread or dried meat. Susana found a source of rice, and experimented with paella. This rapidly became a favourite amongst those who could afford to eat at the chiringuito.

Antoni grew up on the beach and was well-known among the regular patrons of the cafe. He was one of many children in the area who were bi-lingual: speaking Catalan at home, and Castilian to customers. Like all in his position, he knew exactly when to use which language. As a small child, running freely along the shore, he made many friends with the fishermen and their families, and sometimes would return home triumphant, with a fearsome lobster or flailing octopus, exchanged for running an errand, or minding a baby. As he grew older, his parents saw that he had a fascination with drawing, mostly sketching with charcoal on any surface he could find; growing into adolescence, he used an old knife from his great-grandfather's butchers shop to whittle small sculptural shapes from driftwood. He seemed to have some skill with this, and the fisherfolk would often save unusual pieces of driftwood for him. The chiringuito was decorated with many of the fanciful sculptural shapes he created, which were a source of amusement, and occasional ribaldry from the customers.

Contacts with the customers had made him curious about reading, and he had gradually, but very successfully, learned to read and write both Catalan and Castilian, the first of the family to achieve fluency in both.

As he developed into a handsome young man, his skills developed, and his sculptures became larger and more accomplished; he made various tools from bits and scraps he found on the beach and he took much time smoothing the surfaces and creating an impressive finish. With growing confidence he begged his mother to let his hair grow, and with his blond curls, and blond beard, an outsider would have seen him as an artist at work, but he never thought of himself this way.

One warm summer's evening, a couple of rather grand gentlemen appeared at the door of the cafe, and asked for supper. One was a civilian in good quality clothing, and the other in a military uniform which Susana could not identify. Seating them on a beach table, Susana offered paella, and the men accepted. At that time Antoni was working hard as part of the chiringuito team. He carried a bottle of rioja and two glasses out to the men, and was intrigued by the language the military gentleman was speaking. Living in a fishing community, he was used to other accents, but he could not identify the language being spoken by the soldier. One of them was obviously Spanish and spoke educated Castilian, but the soldier was struggling with Castilian, and reverting to an odd gutteral tongue Antoni had not heard before.

Returning to the chiringuito, he asked his mother who the strangers were, but she could not identify them either; they agreed, however, that the uniform was not of the Castilian army. She served the paella.

Clearly the men were engaged in serious business as betrayed by the earnest conversation. From the snatches of Castilian, Antoni realised that they were talking about some kind of building or construction. Standing just inside the doorway, Antoni tried to hear the conversation and make some sense of it. Suddenly he was surprised by the military man coming into the chiringuito. The man had come simply to ask for more wine; but before he could do so he saw the mass of sculptures which filled the walls of the hut. In his strange tongue he exclaimed and pointed to them. Susana, guessing his question, pointed at her son, who smiled uncomprehendingly.

The soldier turned abruptly and called for his Spanish colleague. The Castilian joined them in the hut, and finally explained what was going on. The two men were, it transpired, architects, charged with the development of Barceloneta. The Spaniard was to design and build the church, and the soldier was to plan and oversee the housing. The Spaniard became very excited by Antoni's sculptural work, and said that he would be returning to talk to him.

The men returned to the table on the beach, with Susana following with another bottle of wine, and as the sun started to set, the men continued deep in conversation, occasionally turning towards the hut and clearly talking about Antoni. Rafael, who always remained well in the background when anyone military appeared, had also tried to listen to the conversation, and was equally unable to identify the language or nationality of the soldier.

The next morning, the Spaniard returned alone, and sat at the same table as before, setting down a large flat bag beside him. Susana went out to greet him, and he ordered a jug of ale, and asked to speak to Antoni. The young man stood beside him, but the Spaniard invited him to sit. Glancing back anxiously to where his father stood in the shadows, Antoni sat at the table, uneasy at the idea that he who usually waited at the table should be sitting with a customer.

"Tell me your name, young man," said the stranger.

"Antoni Macia, sir."

"And have you always lived here by the sea, Antoni, working in this cafe?"

"It's a chiringuito, sir, a kitchen on the beach. And yes, I've always lived here. I was born in that hut, in the kitchen. I've never known anywhere else."

"Tell me about the sculptures," said the man.

"It's just a hobby," replied Antoni. "I've been doing it for years. I only have an ancient butcher's knife and home-made tools. I use the driftwood from the shore."

"Can you show me one or two of your most recent pieces?" asked the man.

Antoni went into the chiringuito, and picked two large sculptures from a ledge on one side, one of a snail, and the other of the Virgin.

Susana whispered, "What's going on?"

"I don't know," whispered Antoni, and he carried the sculptures out to the man.

The stranger acknowledged the statue of the Virgin as well done, and caressed it slowly. To Antoni's surprise, however, he was equally enamoured by the snail, running his hands over the smooth surface, and following the spiral of the shell.

"These, young Antoni Macia, are beautiful," he declared.

"Thank you, sir," replied Antoni.

"Who taught you to work like this?" asked the man.

"No-one sir," replied Antoni. "I just picked it up as I went along."

"You have created some very special sculptures here," continued the man. "You have great understanding of the wood, both in your rendition of the Virgin, and this exquisite snail."

"I just work at it until it feels right in my hands," said Antoni. "And then I stop, and it gathers dust in the chiringuito. Mother threatens to throw them all into the bread oven sometimes."

"No, she must not do that."

The stranger looked at Antoni reflectively, considering his next question.

"Have you considered an apprenticeship as a sculptor?" he asked.

Antoni was astonished. "No sir, I've never given it a thought. I work here at the chiringuito; I work with mother and papa, and grandmother; and one day the chiringuito will be mine. I have brothers and sisters, but I am the oldest and will one day be the man of this house. This is my life, here on the beach. I have never thought of any other."

The stranger smiled. "I understand how the chiringuito is your family business," he said, "and I am sure you will make a great success of it. But you have a talent, a real talent. I believe you would make a good, perhaps great, sculptor. I am offering you an apprenticeship Antoni Macia."

Antoni put his hand out and smoothed the curves of the snail. He looked silently at the stranger, unable to know what to say.

"Go and fetch your father," said the man. "I will explain all to him."

Rafael reluctantly limped out to the stranger, who rose and shook him by the hand.

"Please sit," invited the man, "and I will tell you what we've been talking about, this young man and I."

Rafael sat, and looked suspiciously and intently at the stranger.

"Now," said the man, "My name is Joan Soler I Faneca. You should address me as Master Faneca. I am a master architect and one-time stone mason. I have been charged by the city fathers of Barcelona to plan and build a church for this new barrio of Barceloneta. You may even have seen the space allotted for the new church. I will have one master sculptor working for me, and I am recruiting one apprentice. I would like to offer that apprenticeship to your son Antoni."

Rafael opened his mouth to reply, but Master Faneca continued quickly. "Your son has a rare talent; and deserves to develop his ability. As an apprentice to the master mason, and if he works hard and diligently, he may one day become a master mason himself. Meanwhile, he will leave an indelible mark upon the new church of San Miquel del Port, here in Barceloneta."

"This is all very exciting, replied Rafael, "but who is the military man you were with yesterday? I am unsure how a soldier can be involved in such a project."

Master Faneca smiled. "He is a famous military engineer, and comes from the Low countries. His name is Prosper Verboom, and he is planning and overseeing the new barrio which is being built around my new church of San Miquel. My stone mason and his apprentice will work closely with him creating this new town by the sea."

Susana was lurking at the kitchen door, and Rafael beckoned her over and introduced her to Master Faneca. Seated unfamiliarly at one of their own cafe tables, the family watched as Master Faneca pulled a large parchment from his bag and spread it on the table. They were astonished to see a drawing of a very strange building, but Antoni was instantly enthusiastic.

"This is wonderful sir, a most magnificent plan."

"Thank you, young man," replied Faneca. "Not everyone responds with such enthusiasm for my ideas. This is the new architecture; it is called 'Academic Baroque'."

"The lines are so clear, and the decoration so clean. And there's my snail, twice on the facade!"

"Quiet, Antoni," interjected his mother, "listen to Master Faneca."

"No," replied Faneca, "let him speak. And this spiral is a classic part of the new baroque design. He betrays an artistic clarity which will stand him in good stead should he accept the apprenticeship."

"Oh yes, sir....." began Antoni with further youthful enthusiasm, before looking at his parents and hesitating.

"This is not your decision," stated Rafael sternly. "Go for a walk whilst Master Faneca and I decide."

Taking him firmly by the arm, Susana led him down towards the shore. "Be optimistic Antoni," she said. "Your brothers and sisters can work here with us at the chiringuito. I do not think your father will deny you this opportunity."

They stood on the shingle, and turned to watch the two men in earnest discussion, silhouetted against the bright morning sun. Rafael's black coat and hat, and his stiff seated posture was distinctive; and Master Faneca, could be seen to be seated and explaining the plan of the church to him. Once or twice they both turned to glance at Antoni. After a while, Rafael came limping down the beach.

"Go and shake hands with your new master," said Rafael. "There are papers to sign which I cannot read, so you must read them to me before you sign them."

With his father signing with a cross, and the young man signing as Antoni Macia, the bond was fixed. Work was due to start on the new church in the autumn, so Antoni would continue to work at the chiringuito for the summer. When September arrived, Antoni would be prepared to move into the master mason's house in Barcelona old town in accordance with the terms of his apprenticeship.

On the evening before his departure to his apprenticeship, Rafael took him to one side, and talked privately to him. In a speech which echoed the night he had asked Susana's father for her hand in marriage, he revealed the secret of the Lion of Catalunya to his son.

Pulling off his hat he shook out his blond curls, matching his adolescent son's unruly straw mop; taking off his long jacket he unstrapped the sword, and held it before him. Antoni, always ready with a quick answer, was for once speechless, as his father explained the significance of the precious Blanxart sword, wrapped in the Macia senyera.

"This is an evening you will never forget," continued his father, "for I have to tell you that your real name is not Antoni Macia. You are Antoni Blanxart, first born son and direct heir of the Blanxart family, once from La Ribera, now of Barceloneta. You have inherited the distinctive blond curls of the first-born Blanxart men; and you will inherit the sword and the flag. Remember, my son, whatever happens to you in the future, as you go out into the world, this sword, this flag and this responsibility will be your inheritance. You will one day be the Lion of Catalunya. Soon your hands will fashion the stones of our new town. Let each stone be placed in the name of Catalunya. In your apprenticeship, you will speak Castilian at all times, I know, but in your mind you must never forget your Catalan inheritance. One day our nation will rise again; I doubt it will be through me, and it may not be through you; but you and your first born son, and generations to come, will carry the future of the Catalan nation, ready for the time when our land is reborn and our language and culture are restored."

"I know not what to say....." began Antoni as tears filled his eyes. Rafael waited for him to regain his composure, and at last Antoni continued, "Little did I ever have any suspicion that you carried this burden; but I know that we carry a wonderful Catalan inheritance. I have learned Catalan songs from all of the family, and I am proud that I can read and write in Catalan as well as Castilian."

"There is a final burden for you to know about." responded Rafael. "It is a family tradition that all the first born men of the family should take as their wife a true Catalan patriot from a true Catalan family. I would never have married your mother without knowing her family to be steadfast. As time passes it will be increasingly difficult to be sure who is; but it is your task to ensure the inheritance continues. Oh, and another thing: you had better be sure that your first-born son has blond curly hair!"

Whittling pieces of driftwood was one thing; but chipping with a chisel at a block of limestone was quite another, and as autumn turned to winter, Antoni's hands became bloody and then calloused as he struggled to learn the skills of the master mason, and the nature of stone. Master Faneca would visit the stone yard regularly to inspect the efforts of his protege, and Master Verboom would usually accompany him. Antoni got to know both men well, and they in turn encouraged him in his endeavours. The stone mason, his master, had scant praise and much criticism for him, but grudgingly agreed that Antoni had talent.

All that winter, and for the next year, Antoni laboured in the stone mason's yard. When he was feeling frustrated by his efforts, the visits from Faneca and Verboom encouraged him, and he was flattered that they shared with him the plans and drawings. He was surprised to discover as an apprentice he had a couple of labourers available to shift the heavy blocks of limestone, but not surprisingly, his muscles soon bulged as much as their's. On his brief weekly visit to the chiringuito, he was invariably exhausted, and enjoyed a short respite from work whilst his brothers and sisters admired his physique.

In the spring of 1753, work started on the site. The Flemish engineer Master Verboom had designed a small new town along military lines, with fifteen long narrow streets, crossed at right angles by five avenues. The narrow streets, starting from just outside the old city walls, ran south towards the sea on the long peninsular of Barceloneta, and the widely spaced avenues gave eastern glimpses of the Mediterranean, and westward views of the bustling port of Barcelona.

The wide central placa, or market place, would be a focal point of the small town, with Master Faneca's new church at one side of it. The enormous parade ground was to the east, filling a vast space between the new town and the causeway which linked the Cuitadella Fortress to the sea.

From the port, the handsome western facade of the church of San Miquel del Port would one day be visible across a wide square of its own. Standing on the newly installed steps of the church, Antoni paused to look around at the bustling scene. The first long narrow street, named for San Miquel, had been laid out from the very steps he had himself carved back at his master's yard some weeks earlier. To his right the massive but crumbling walls of the city hid most of the buildings of the old town, except the towering mass of Santa Maria del Mar; to his left the new street stretched into the distance, stopping only at the edge of the sand dunes near his family's chiringuito. He thought he could see Master Verboom, with strings and measuring chains, checking the alignment of the streets. The military engineer brought a military precision to his work, and the setting out of the streets was taking a long time.

Turning towards the notorious sea gate of the city, he could see a pair of cart horses dragging a cart with a massive piece of octagonal stone on board. Seated like a king on the huge block was one of the mason's yard labourers, whilst another led the horses. Antoni smiled to himself as the first stone of the pillars which would support the roof of the church came into view. This was a truly significant day: it was not merely the base stone of the pillar, it was the base of one of the main supports for the whole building. Eventually an ornate keystone would crown the arch; but for now the focus was on this foundation stone. It had to be positioned with supreme accuracy. A shout from behind startled him. It was the master mason.

"Hey, dreamer, get yourself over here and check the scaffold with me. The stone will arrive before we're ready, and by San Miquel and all the saints we must move and settle it correctly."

Aware of the moment, Master Faneca appeared, and Master Verboom came striding up the newly laid Carrer San Miquel to join him. The labourers guided the cart round to the side of the church and into the nave itself. The heavy timber scaffold containing the block and tackle was waiting for its momentous load.

Work came to a halt in the surrounding area as every-one turned to watch the complex operation. The men pulled the ropes under the massive stone and up and over the pulleys in the scaffold. The horses were unhitched from the cart and hitched to the pulley ropes. Gently the labourers urged the horses to take the strain, the ropes creaked and groaned ominously, and very slowly the block of limestone lifted from the bed of the cart. Other labourers were used to manhandle the cart out of the way, and the job of swinging the stone into its position started.

The painstaking procedure took the entire day: but as dusk fell, both the master mason and Master Faneca declared themselves happy that the stone was truly posi-tioned. At the final moment of double checking, the mason indicated to Antoni that he should stand on the block and move around to ensure its complete stability. Antoni climbed up and jumped up and down. The stone beneath his feet was rock solid.

Glancing around, he saw his mother standing among the small crowd that had gathered. Antoni waved to her to come forward and Susana revealed a bottle of the best rioja. Master Faneca, remembering who she was, went forward to her, and she shyly handed him the bottle of wine. Pulling the cork, Faneca announced, "May San Miquel bless the foundation of this house which we build for him!" and took a long draught from the bottle. Faneca handed it to Verboom, and the Flemish man added, "Amen," and passed it to the master mason, who, adding his own "Amen", took a drink himself.

There was a pause as the master mason looked up at Antoni, still standing high on the new block of limestone, then smiled and handed him the bottle. "Drink, young Macia, you've earned it."

Antoni took the bottle. Looking at the three men through his long blond eyelashes, he was suddenly overcome. "Drink," repeated the master mason. Antoni drained the bottle and grinned, a dribble of the red wine running down his chin. "Now dance," shouted Faneca, and with everyone around clapping a rhythm, Antoni danced on the stone, his clogs beating out an insistent rhythm. His mother retreated and he saw her join his father who had been watching from the distance.

As he danced, Antoni pulled his apprentice's hat from his head, and shook out the blond curls which had been growing all through the winter and into the spring. As the sun started to set, it cast a golden glow over the young man.

"The Lion of Catalunya," whispered Rafael to Susana.

"He looks like a god," replied his wife.

"We have a worthy heir, my love," continued Rafael, "Soon will come the time to hand him the sword."

In the nave of the church, the master mason put out a hand as Antoni jumped down. "This is nothing, boy," he spoke quietly. "A year from now, you will be dancing on the keystone. Then we will have cause for real celebration."

Antoni had not noticed a young woman in the small crowd, admiring him from afar, but she had seen him. Watching him closely, her pulse quickened. If this beautiful man favoured the spirit of Catalunya, she would pursue him. Smiling to herself, she resolved to find out more about this blond god-like creature.

The building site for the new town continued to develop throughout the year. Verboom's revolutionary grid pattern of streets and avenues was completed, and the erection of the hundreds of uniform houses spread like children's building blocks across the new barrio. Strangers came from miles around to look at the odd new architecture they called 'academic baroque'. Reactions varied from appalled to enthusiastic. At the same time as the rows of stone houses were being laid out, the huge dressed stones were arriving one by one from the mason's yard, and the pillars of the new church were growing.

The building technique of the church was unlike that of the houses. The houses were built in a simple manner, from the walls up; but the church was constructed by creating the structure of support columns first, with curtain walls to be filled in later. Thus it was that the enormous timber scaffold contained a huge rib-like skeleton, with the outlines of the twin domes supported, it appeared, in thin air. At last the time arrived for the crucial insertion of key stones, after which the timber scaffold would no longer be supporting the stone.

The familiar cart pulled by the mason's two horses was inadequate for the job of bringing the enormous keystone to the building site. A larger cart, pulled by four horses had been employed. Antoni, stationed at the church as he had been to receive each of the stones of the pillars, watched as the horses strained to bring the first of the keystones from the old city, through the sea gate and out to the new town. Riding on the key stone was not one of the labourers as usual, but the master mason himself proud to be showing that his masonry was indeed high art.

Bringing the ornate stone to the site was all that could be accomplished on the first day; and it was the following morning before the mason and his apprentice supervised the beginning of hauling the mass of the key-stone to its position high over the chancel. Each day the horses strained at the ropes, and slowly the stone was raised. Finally, after four nerve-racking days, as the huge weight hung from the ropes, it had been hauled to the top of the scaffold. On the fifth day, the mason and Antoni climbed the now familiar ladders to the very top, and lowered the key stone into place.

The whole operation had been watched by Faneca and Verboom, joined by a growing throng, holding its collective breath as the stone was raised and then lowered into position. The procedure that they had planned and discussed endlessly, was a success. At last the master mason turned to Antoni. "Young man, I think we should call on your mother and take some of her excellent paella. And I'm sure your father will find a good bottle of rioja. Although it would be premature to celebrate too much, since we have two more such keystones to position in the coming weeks, I believe we deserve an evening of respite."

As they climbed down the ladders, Antoni felt a glow of pride; in the years of hard apprenticeship his master had never spoken so warmly, almost as an equal. Gathering Faneca and Verboom, the band of four, heady with the success of raising the keystone, marched down Carrer de Sant Miquel, now paved and completed, and insisted that Antoni sit with them and join them for supper, much to the amusement of his brothers and sisters who waited upon them.

The ritual was repeated twice more, the team of four horses dragging the next two keystones to the church, the long and painstaking hauling of the stones to the top of the scaffold, and the final nerve-racking positioning of the keys into the pinnacles of the stone arches.

"Now we take away the scaffolding," announced Master Faneca. "And heaven help us if my calculations are wrong."

Antoni had carved and fitted many small keystones over doors and windows for the new houses of Barceloneta, but he had no experience of the enormity of the stresses and strains which the pillars and keystones of the church had to support. Whilst everything seemed secure with the mass of timber scaffold surrounding it, the idea of taking it all down and leaving the stone skeleton standing high was terrifying. His fears were unfounded. As the scaffold was removed, the stone stood firm and tall, until finally its extraordinary silhouette was revealed.

Just one ladder remained, the tallest they possessed, reaching all the way to the chancel keystone. "Up you go, boy," said the master mason. "Dance."

Fearlessly Antoni scaled the ladder and climbed onto the top of the keystone. He breathed in the sea air, and looked about him. North was the ancient mass of Santa Maria del Mar still tucked inside the remains of the city wall; south the beach with its chaos of shacks and hovels and the chiriguito; below him to the east was the placa of the Barceloneta market, and beyond it the barren parade ground.

Slowly at first, Antoni started to dance, stepping lightly on the stone; then he grew bolder and stamped out the rhythm. Below him, the crowd listened, first to the rhythm of his clogs, and then to his voice as he sung out loudly and clearly from the very topmost point of the church.

Rafael turned joyously to Susana: "The lion sings in Catalan!"

Carla, his grandmother, was now a very old lady, and rarely left the chiringuito; she had, however shuffled along the unfamiliar street of Sant Miquel, leaning on Susana's arm, to witness this extraordinary moment. Quietly smiling to herself, she repeated under her breath, "Yes, the lion sings in Catalan. Yes, there was a crucifix on this spot once, where this church stands. Yes, a tall cross, and hiding behind it a young man, and his mother. It is good that this family is helping to build a church for Sant Miquel on this spot. Yes, it is good."

Verboom turned to Faneca, "What is he singing?" and Faneca feigned ignorance.

The crowd, however, knew, and clapped and cheered, and many joined in quietly with the old Catalan folk songs they had not heard or dared to sing for many years. Susana, tears trickling down her cheeks, smiled at her husband. "Our land is not dead. There are more here than I realised who have kept faith with our Catalan traditions. One day we will raise our Senyera again!"

Standing in the crowd was the same young woman who had admired Antoni from afar when he first danced upon the foundation stone. She had hesitated, unable to ascertain his allegiances, and nervous that as he was working for the Castilian local government, he would be a Castilian supporter, and know little or nothing of the Catalonian spirit. His wonderful singing dispersed all doubts. This beautiful man was a true Catalan, and she would pursue him with all her energies.

Finding him alone on the beach one evening, she nervously engaged him in conversation. Flattered by the attentions of such a beautiful young woman, Antoni found himself flirting with the girl. Nervously he invited her back to the chiringuito, and asked Susana for a bottle of rioja, which they shared in the setting sun. Rafael and Suzana watched the young couple from a distance, and hurriedly stopped Antoni's younger brothers and sisters from giggling and pointing.

When the time came for Antoni to walk back to the master mason's, Alissia, for that was her name, walked some of the way with him. Antoni explained that he escaped only once a week to visit his parents at the chiringuito, and Alissia replied that she hoped he would like to see her again on his next visit. Impulsively he put his arms around her and kissed her, and then pulled away, apologising for his behaviour. Alissia smiled, and pulled him back. "Next week, beautiful man," she whispered, and turned and darted away among the sand dunes.

It would be two more long years before the church was finished. Master Faneca's revolutionary design challenged both the master mason and his apprentice. Not only was the baroque facade unlike any other building in Catalonya, but the internal decoration of the church was equally new. The break from the Gothic tradition scandalised many older residents of Barcelona, but the excitement of the new baroque architecture of not only the church, but also Master Verboom's new town, created an atmosphere which was much celebrated by younger Catalonians.

Just as the new town of Barceloneta grew, so did Antoni's love for Alissia. They continued their weekly tryst, but Antoni knew he could not consider marriage as long as he was an apprentice. By careful questioning, however, he discovered that Alissia was true to the Catalan tradition, and would one day make a suitable wife. Rafael and Susana were not surprised when he told them he was in love with Alissia, and Rafael had secretly made his own enquiries to reassure himself that she was a true Catalan. Antoni had a further reason to be attracted to Alissia: she could read and write in both

Castilian and Catalan, matching him for skill, and they could exchange the few books they possessed, and talk about them together. Privately Antoni was overjoyed that their children, when they had them, would be taught from an early age to read the old stories of the Catalan heritage.

The facade of dressed stone of the church rose steadily, with Antoni responsible for many of the accurate smooth stones. The master mason consulted Faneca's drawings constantly, and considerable effort went into replicating the baroque ornamentation. One day Antoni looked across the mason's workshop to see his master working on a large stone spiral, much like a snail. It was at that moment that Master Faneca arrived, and laughed.

"That I should come at this moment!" he chuckled. "The snail. Macia come here and look." Antoni and the master mason stared at Faneca unable to understand the joke. "Do you remember all that time ago, years ago, when I discovered you working in the chiringuito? And do you remember the sculpture you showed me then, the sculpture that got you your apprenticeship?"

"The snail!" gasped Antoni, the remembrance dawning upon him.

"Master mason," continued Faneca. "You will remember that the facade requires two of these huge spiral sculptures. I propose a competition. You shall carve one, and Macia your apprentice shall carve the other. You shall each carve a face into the centre of the spiral. Master mason, you shall carve a likeness of yourself; Macia, you shall carve my likeness. We shall see if the apprentice can match the master's skill."

Turning to Antoni, he continued, "This shall be your masterpiece. Do well, my boy, and it will pave your way into the Guild."

It was the master mason's turn to laugh. "Very well, he is a quick learner and is doing well. But this is no challenge for me. You risk wasting a good piece of stone if he cannot manage the spiral – will you take the challenge?"

Antoni, who was rather horrified by the conversation, grinned nervously as he replied: "I'll take the challenge; by the Virgin, I'll carve my way into the Guild."

For the next two weeks, Antoni and the master mason slaved over their respective blocks of stone. Although Antoni was flattered by Faneca's confidence in him, he was very alarmed by the challenge. He was unsure what the master would think if he matched or bettered him in the creation of the spiral; equally he wanted to prove himself and justify Master Faneca's confidence in him.

At last the snail-like spirals were complete, and the delicate features of a face peered out from the centre of each. One of the labourers ran with a message to Master Faneca to come and see the results.

Faneca looked from one to the other. Both sculptures were superb. Faneca shook hands with the master.

"Excellent work, sir, I salute you. And I congratulate you on the way you have taught your apprentice. His work is equal to yours." Turning to Antoni, he continued, "I always believed you had it in you to be a master sculptor. You have proved your worth. You are a credit to your master and yourself. Well done Antoni Macia. I believe you will now be invited into the Guild."

Antoni shook hands with Faneca, and turned towards the master mason, unsure of his reaction. To his relief the older man was smiling. "This was your test," he said. "Match me in the spiral relief, and you will complete your apprenticeship. Today you have done that, and I welcome you as my assistant and master mason in your own right. I will sponsor your entrance into the Guild. Meanwhile, I believe Master Faneca has something for you."

"As an artisan and member of the Guild of Master Sculptors, you can no longer sleep in the workshop as you have been doing as an apprentice," said Faneca. "Congratulations Master Macia." And he handed Antoni a small ragged bundle.

Untying the rag, Antoni discovered a key. He looked uncomprehendingly from one to the other. Faneca grinned. "It's a house key," stammered Antoni.

"Master Macia, this is the key to a dwelling on Carrer Sant Miquel. You set the keystone over the door some weeks ago, and now the house is finished."

"You shall be its first tenant," said the master mason, "and with your new salary as a master mason, you will be able to afford the rent."

"No," stated Faneca, producing a small purse. "Here is your reward. You have proved your worth as a mason, and surpassed all expectations in your apprenticeship; but more than that, you have upheld the traditions of Catalunya. When I watched you dance upon the keystone, and heard your voice raised in the old Catalonian folk songs, I resolved to find, somehow, a way to recognise and reward you as best I can. With the contents of this purse, you can buy your house. Master Macia, you are now a man of substance."

With shaking hands, Antoni opened the leather purse and took out the coins, more money than he had ever held in his hands before. With a catch in his throat, he managed to say thank you to Master Faneca, as his eyes pricked with tears. Wiping his face with the back of his hand, he grinned and stammered, "I don't know why I'm crying. I don't know what to say. Was ever an apprentice so lucky?"

Slapping him good-naturedly on the back, the master mason grinned again, and said, "Take the rest of the day off, young Macia. Go tell your father of your good fortune; and go and look at that house."

Impulsively Antoni hugged the mason and kissed Faneca on the cheeks, before turning and running out towards the chiringuito. The older men laughed, and the mason turned to his grinning labourers. "Is this a holiday or what? Back to work you fools." Their faces fell, and carried by the euphoria of the moment, the mason relented. "OK, so it is a holiday. Just for one day. Go get drunk, but don't forget that you, and Master Macia, will be back to work tomorrow!"

Carrer de Sant Miquel was one of the longest of the narrow streets laid out by Master Verboom, starting near the old city walls in the northern end of Barceloneta, and stretching all the way to the beach in the south. The street was broken by the open placa of the church, and some distance south of the church was number one hundred. Antoni led his mystified parents up from the beach to his new house without telling them of the surprise he had in store. At the appointed dwelling, he pulled out the bundle and unwrapped the key. Grinning broadly, he fitted it into the lock, and opened the door.

Stepping cautiously into the cool shade of the interior, Susana looked around. The large room was rectangular with a window on either side of the door. The windows were heavily shuttered, and Antoni pushed the shutters open one by one and the midday sun filtered in. Turning to his parents, he told them the story of the completion of his apprenticeship, and his new status as a master mason. He paused as they congratulated him, but then they hesitated. "But why are we here in this house?" asked his mother.

"Because it is mine, mother," smiled Antoni. "Master Faneca gave me a reward. It seems he secretly is a supporter of Catalunya. In his position, he cannot be open about his beliefs, but he heard me singing, and became determined to reward me for it, and all that it symbolises."

Antoni was himself familiar with the layout of the house, identical as it was to many hundreds more in the Barceloneta new town development, but his parents were curious; they had never been inside one before. The classical symmetry of the frontages gave the new development a distinctive air. Above each window at street level was a classic keystone, mirrored by a similar but larger design over the wide door. On the upper floor the windows were repeated with identical keystones, and over the door, a tall, wide window of classic proportions, again with a grand keystone, gave a promise of a light, airy upper room. Above the upper floor was the crowning glory of the house: a huge cornice with a large triangular pediment, far grander than would be expected on a house of this size, and in complete contrast to the vernacular buildings of old Barcelona.

Everything about the architecture was clean, modern and revolutionary. Somehow the socialist ideals of Catalunya had been created in stone in the new town; the good citizens of Castilian Barcelona were taken by surprise; Masters Faneca and Verboom had created a new barrio in which all were equal. There was no grand big house for a rich merchant; the only grand edifice was the church of Sant Miquel. Every other dwelling was of equal size and status.

Susana climbed the steep staircase to the upper floor, and looked around the spacious airy room. "All this is your's?" she asked. Antoni nodded. "Then the time has come for you to make a respectable woman of Alissia. What a lucky young woman she is, to be coming to this wonderful new house."

Returning to the chiringuito for supper, Antoni's head was full of plans and celebrations. Chattering constantly, he told his parents that he would ask Alissia to marry him as soon as possible and that they would fill the new house with children. He spoke eagerly of how he would teach them all to sing the Catalan folk songs of old and how they would all read and write in both Castillian and Catalan. He spoke of furniture and linens, and how he would provide a comfortable home for his family.

Suddenly, in the midst of all this speculation, he stopped. "Father," he said, "you have told me that one day I will be the Lion of Catalonya."

"Yes," replied Rafael, aware of a sudden solemnity in his son's voice.

"Then when I marry Alissia, it should be as Antoni Blanxart, and our children should continue the Blanxart name and inheritance."

Rafael smiled and sipped the good rioja wine. "Well spoken, my son," he replied. "And when you become a Blanxart, you will become the Lion of Catalonya, and this burden I have born for so long will be yours." He tapped the sword strapped in its familiar place beneath his clothes. "By all the saints, after so many years, it will be strange to give up this bloody thing."

Antoni slept that night in his new house. Without a stick of furniture, he had nothing to sleep on except the floor, but he was determined to have his first night in his own home. Turning the key, and lying on the floor listening to the silence of sleeping alone for the first time in his life, he drifted off into a deep and dreamless sleep.

He was woken before sunrise, by a tremendous hammering on the door. The two labourers from the stone-yard, having spent their unexpected holiday getting drunk, just as the master expected, had been sent to wake the young master mason.

"Get up, get up," they chanted, "Master Macia, there's stone to be cut, with snails inside them. Master Macia, have you a woman in there? Have you been chipping away at her all night? Hey, Master Macia, the sun is rising. Time for all men of substance to be at their counting houses!"

Smiling at their jollity, Antoni whispered to himself, "Master Macia eh? What will you say when I am Master Blanxart, the Lion of Catalonya?"

Antoni spoke first to Alissia, and then with her parents, and all agreed to the match. A few days later, Rafael called his family together at the chiringuita for a meeting with Alissia and her parents. "This is more than just a marriage between a girl and a boy," began Rafael, standing in the old kitchen. "It is an important moment in the history of Catalunya." Susana smiled at the puzzled faces of Alissa and her parents, remembering a similar meeting years ago when she had been brought into the Blanxart family. "Today I share a great secret; a secret I have carried for many years; a secret shared only with a very few loyal Catalonians." Taking off his coat, he continued, "Just as my father, before he was murdered in the name of Catalunya, handed me the Sword of Catalunya, so the time has come for me to hand the sword to my son. And just as I was born a Blanxart, so my son now takes that as his name. I have hidden behind the name Macia to protect the sword, and hidden my son behind the name to keep him safe. The time has now come to reveal his, and my, true identity." As he spoke, he unfastened the sword from its senyera wrappings, and held it aloft. " I have hidden the Sword of Catalonya all these years, and kept it safe, so I now hand it on to my son Antoni Blanxart. With it I hand him the Macia flag, brought into the family by my wife Susana. And with them, I bestow upon him the title, Lion of Catalonya."

With a flourish, he removed his rough hat and allowed the long curls to fall free, the gold tarnished with silver in his old age. Alissia's father was the first to recover his composure after the fantastic revelations, and spoke with pride. "It is an honour to celebrate the joining of our two families Senor Blanxart. I salute your courage and fortitude. Long have I dreamed of a day like today, since the dark days of the siege. I believe my father and your's were acquainted, and he told me of the fierce battle on the barricades. He spoke of your father's sword, and how many Castilians were despatched with it. I never expected that I would see it for myself. It is with delight and pride that I give my daughter to your son. Alissia is a very lucky young woman, not only to be marrying the handsome man she loves, and to marry a man of the world, with a house of his own, but also to be carrying forward the hopes of our nation. May she have many children."

"And may her first born be as handsome as his father," smiled Susana.

"And with the Blanxart blond curls," said Rafael.

Antoni and Alissia put their arms around one another in a mixture of embarrassment and joy. Antoni went to kiss his future bride, but Alissia's mother intervened. "Enough of that!" she laughed, "Come my girl, we have a wedding to organise; and you, young man, have a sword, a flag, and a great new responsibility to deal with."

Later in the night, after the usual bottle of rioja had been shared, Rafael strapped on the sword for the last time, and limped with his son across the dunes and up Carrer de Sant Miquel. Entering the new house, he cautioned Antoni not to light a candle. "Here, my son, is your burden. It is not yet safe to reveal that we have this sword. Our duty is to keep it hidden, ready for the time when Catalunya shall rise again."

"For once, father, it is my turn to reveal a great secret." replied Antoni. Turning to a collection of his carving tools, he selected two stout steel bars, and inserted them into either end of a huge flagstone in the centre of the floor. Heaving mightily with all his stone mason's muscles, he lifted the flagstone. The floor surface was smooth, but unexpectedly the underside of the stone was also carved smooth. Levering the stone to one side, Antoni revealed a small dry chamber beneath the floor, lined in stone, rectangular in shape. Rafael gasped.

"Here is the chamber I prepared for the sword and the flag. No-one in the world knows it is here, and you will remain the only person to see it. Tonight we will lay the sword in its hiding place, and seal the chamber. I will tell no-one, not even Alissia, the secret. The next time this chamber is opened, it will be to reveal its contents to my first born son, and hand on to him the secret of the sword. Meanwhile, father, you must tell me all you know of its history, not only in the siege, but before that, so that I can in turn pass the story to my child."

CHAPTER EIGHT

Carla, now well over seventy years old, was determined to attend the marriage of Antoni and Alissia, and was brought on a handcart. The wedding was the first to take place in the church of Sant Miquel, which was as yet unfinished. Nine months later, a baby boy was born, and Carla lived just a few weeks more, celebrating the achievement of living long enough to have a great-grandchild. Her funeral was attended by almost everyone living on the beach, the large crowd filling Sant Miquel with solemn prayers for the old lady.

Francesc was one of the few Blanxarts to know all of his grandparents. Rafael, fifty-seven at the time of the baby's birth, was delighted to see the boy's blond curls, sealing his fate and destiny as the future Lion of Catalunya. Throughout his son's childhood, Antoni continued to work on the decoration of St Miquel; but he started to attract interest throughout Spain as a master sculptor. His skills and knowledge of the new classical architecture meant that he was much in demand as his reputation grew.

Rafael and Susana's chiringuito flourished, and without their illustrious brother, the younger children worked hard to assist their parents, and gradually take over the running of the beach kitchen. Susana would often steal away from the heat of her stove to the cool of Alissia's house to catch some time with her grandson, and soon his siblings.

It was early one evening in 1760, when Antoni brought Master Faneca to their home. Susana was playing with Francesa, and Alissia feeding the next baby, and supervising a rabbit stew; but Antoni and Faneca insisted Alissia return with them to the church. Leaving Susana with the children, they hurried her up the street. In the elegant placa outside the church, a small crowd had gathered, gazing up at the facade. Alissia followed their eyes and saw the attraction: the statue of Sant Miquel himself was finished, and placed in its proud position in the centre of the facade.

The angel stood tall and proud, his feet resting on a creature like a large rock. Twice the size of any man, the marble saint was wearing voluminous clothing, which opened to reveal a marvellous physique, muscled chest and stomach, with strong legs. A large halo hovered above, and the massive wings of the saint, with every feather in clear detail in the white marble, seemed almost to be beating in the summer air. In his right hand, a sword, and on his head a mass of curly hair.

Alissia caught her breath, and her thoughts crowded in upon her. This was the musculature of a mason; the sword of Catalonia; and the curly hair of her husband.

He had created himself in stone. She was not looking at a saint, but at Antoni Blanxart, master mason, the man she loved. Unable to express her thoughts, and fearful of betraying the secret of the sword, she could only gasp in astonishment. Gradually she became aware of Master Faneca's voice.

"... and with the installation of this magnificent statute of Sant Miquel, the church is finished. It is my masterpiece, thanks to the skills of Master Macia here..."

"Now to be known as Master Blanxart!" exclaimed Antoni; and his announcement sent a thrilling ripple of exclamation through many of the Barceloneta neighbours, who understood its significance.

Alissia swayed a little on her feet, and leaned against her husband. Putting her hand upon his arm, it was as if she was putting her hand upon the statue. Gazing up at the image, glowing in white marble against the grey limestone of the facade, she could think of nothing but to kiss Antoni and whisper, "It's wonderful, it's wonderful," over and over again.

At that moment, Susana arrived, carrying the baby, and with little Francesc clinging to her skirts. Her reaction was exactly the same as Alissia's: there was her son, a saint in white marble. Francesc looked up at the statue and pointed, and in his babyish voice he cried out loudly, "Papa!". The crowd turned to see the small child pointing at the statue, and Susana gulped. Alarmed by the little boy's honesty, she quickly picked him up, and with the boy and the baby both squashed together in her arms, retreated down the street.

Quietly, Antoni whispered to his wife, "A symbolic sword now stands in Barceloneta for all to see. Let people gaze upon it, and know that Catalunya will rise again from the oppression of Castile."

Feeling the arms of Master Faneca embracing them both from behind, there was a moment of stillness, and then Faneca's bass voice, quiet and confidential, "Amen to that." And in an even lower voice, the architect continued, "And is that a chained devil that our great Sant Miquel is killing, or is it Castile?"

Alissia gasped, and Antoni grinned. "Hard to tell from this distance," he said.

To the delight of Antoni and Alissia, Francesc was a quick learner and rapidly mastered reading Catalan and Castilian. Despite his youth, he started to devour the few books the household possessed, and when Antoni returned from working elsewhere in Spain on yet another classical masterpiece, he would bring books for the boy. The other children were pleased to receive toys from their father, and a homecoming was always a time of noise and excitement. Francesc would stand back from his siblings and watch them leap and screech at their father; and then when they had calmed down and recovered from the excitement of his return, he would come quietly forward, and his father would let him unwrap the latest book he had found. Anything printed in Catalan was a rarity, but Antoni was able to afford many Castilian novels, which Francesc vowed he would one day translate into Catalan.

As the family library grew in the upper room of the house, and Francesc entered his teenage years, he grew more demanding of his father's generosity: asking for books in French, which he mastered easily, finding many similarities with his native Catalan, and in English, which he found impossible at first. He was twelve years old when his father sat him down in the upper room, with the chest of books beside them, to talk to him.

"At your age, young man, I was working full time in your grandmother's chiringuito," began Antoni. "You have had a strangely easy life, but now the time has come to consider your future. You have shown no aptitude for the life of a mason." Francesc took a sharp intake of breath, but his father reassured him. "No, don't worry, my son, I am not about to apprentice you into my profession, but I must know how you see your life ahead of you. You have always been a studious and thoughtful lad, and I cannot think you have not pondered upon these things yourself."

"I have father, and I fear I will never enter your Guild of Master Sculptors. I may be a disappointment to you, but my dreams are elsewhere. Fearfully, I hesitate to tell you of my dream."

Antoni smiled into the serious face of his eldest son. "You should speak, boy. I will listen."

Francesc allowed a slight smile to hover around his face as he spoke. "I love to read, father, and you have given me a library beyond compare. I love the stories in Castilian, and I can manage to read and understand much of what's in the books in French and English; but most of all I love the few Catalan books I've got, and the stories of our own land. You and mother have given me knowledge of our heritage, and my brothers and sisters sing the Catalan folk songs you have taught us. We love especially to sing with our grandparents, knowing we are continuing the old and vital traditions."

Francesc paused, and Antoni was puzzled. He could not tell where this conversation was leading. "Go on boy," he encouraged.

His son took a breath, and then blurted out, "I want to be a teacher. I want to teach all the children round here the Catalan songs and stories; and most of all I want to teach them all to read and write our precious language." He paused and there was a silence. "Well father, what do you think? I have told you my dream."

Antoni continued to sit in silence, regarding closely his son, and struggling to find the best way to reply. At last he spoke quietly.

"You could not have had a better dream, my son," he said, "but I am fearful. What you ask is dangerous, illegal, against the law. I do not want to see my son imprisoned or punished as you surely will be if you pursue this goal. Your love of Catalunya pleases me more than I can say, and your desire to teach others is wonderful. I have carried a heavy burden all my life, knowing that at any day a knock may come at the door and I would be arrested for teaching the songs of our land, spreading the language which is banned. Heaven knows how hard it has been to find the few Catalan books I have managed to buy for your library, each one bought in dangerous circumstances. And you tell me you want to teach it. How can I answer with anything but pride and fear?

"Father, just now you called me thoughtful. I know I have youthful enthusiasm and optimism, but I have thought a lot, and I think I have a way. I should like to be a teacher of Castilian, and a writer, which should please the authorities and quietly, in the evenings, and to a very few people judged to be safe, I would teach and write in Catalan. There must be some who will pay me to learn to read. If our land should ever rise again, it will be though the effort of maintaining our culture secretly."

Antoni sighed. "You little know what you say, boy, but your words are wiser than your years. Let us start carefully: not as a teacher – yet – but as a reader and scribe. When I was apprenticed to the master mason, my father, your grandfather, could not read the words of the deed of apprenticeship, and I had to read it to him. You know that there are many in this situation. You could read letters to people, and write letters for them; and if it's all in Castilian, so let that be a smoke-screen. Your skills in French and English mean you could even translate for merchants receiving messages from foreign lands. And all the while, you'll be nurturing the Catalan, and ready to share it with those for whom it is safe to share."

"Will mother mind?" asked Francesc. "She's never told me what she thinks, but perhaps she wishes I was following in your footsteps."

"She will be more pleased than I can say, Francesc," said his father, "And your grandparents will also be proud and pleased. Talking of whom, I believe we must invite them all to dinner some time soon, and tell them your news. You may well be a little surprised by their reaction."

"Will it be a good surprise?" asked Francesc.

Antoni laughed, "Oh, I think it will be very good!"

A few days later, the four grandparents were excited to come to dinner at the house in Carrer Sant Miquel, and after the meal, Alissia was left downstairs with the other children, whilst the grandparents climbed the steep staircase to the upper room. Antoni and Francesc carefully carried lighted candles upstairs and Antoni looked around at the four old people. Rafael was now sixty-nine, he knew that, and although he was unsure, he assumed the other three all to be of similar age. The four old faces, in the flickering candlelight, lined and wise, beamed at their favourite grandson.

Antoni chuckled. "What have we here? Nearly three hundred years of Catalonia life!"

Susana smiled, "We may not be quite as old as that, but certainly between us there are many years experience."

"We could tell some stories," said Rafael.

"And that is why you're here," said Antoni. "Before you get too old to remember, or you die, you must tell the story to this boy who has all his life before him."

"Where do we start?" said Susana, "There is so much to tell."

"Let Rafael tell the tale," said Alissia's father. "After all he knows it so well. He was there at the siege."

"The story is older than that," began Rafael. "Let me think. My tale begins with my grandfather's grandfather. That makes him my great, great grandfather. His name was Joan Blanxart and I think he was born around the year 1600. He was murdered."

Rafael paused for effect, and Francesc's eyes became as round as saucers. "Murdered?" whispered the boy.

"Yes, murdered," went on his grandfather. "Let me tell you all about it."

Long into the night the tale was spun. With the children asleep downstairs, Alissia crept into the room with a bottle of wine, and Rafael told the family history. It was gone midnight when he reached the story of his own father, and how the sword was given to him on the night Perez was arrested.

Hardly daring to breathe, Francesc his voice hushed, interrupted, "So grandfather, you're the Lion of Catalunya?"

"No young man, no longer. I was once the Lion of Catalunya, but look now at my grey hairs. The Lion of Catalunya sits beside you there: the Lion of Catalunya is your father. See his golden curls!"

"But....." the question remained on Francesc's lips.

There was a silence, and they all looked towards Antoni. "Yes, boy," he said, "you will be next. You will inherit the mantle and the awful responsibility."

"So....." again Francesc could not finish the sentence.

"Where is the sword?" said Susana, finishing the question for him.

"Yes, where?" chorused Alissia's parents.

Antoni laughed. "Here in this house. But until the day comes to hand it to you, Francesc, only your grand-father Rafael and I will know exactly where it is."

Long after everyone else had fallen asleep in various chairs and corners of the room, young Francesc lay awake, his mind a turmoil of all he had heard. One day he would become the Lion of Catalunya, inheriting a sword hidden somewhere in the house! And his grand-father had spoken of the Catalan flag, the senyera. He had never seen one, and was full of curiosity that there was one, in the house, hidden with the sword. He vowed that he would write the story... somehow... secretly... he would write it in Catalan, he knew the language well enough. He knew such a document would land him and his family in trouble if it were ever found, but he was resolved that the story must be preserved for the future.

One day the people of Catalunya would escape the yoke of Castile; he dreamed that he would be the one leading his people to freedom, the sword in his hand, the flag round his shoulders, and he would show his people the book, the book he had written himself, giving them back their history... he tossed and turned, his imagination running riot as he marched, in his dreams at the head of a Catalan army.

Antoni, also awake and watching his son, pondered on the events of the night. How would this thoughtful, bookish boy take on the mantle of history? Antoni knew that he himself had been an active carefree youth, and had grown into a strong and muscular man, able to handle himself in any situation. Hadn't they called him a 'man of the world' when he achieved his apprentice-ship? He had travelled far and wide in Spain, fulfilling the commissions of the rich and fashionable Castilians who had the money to pay for grand new churches in the revolutionary baroque style. He had what others called 'charisma' and he revelled in his secret status as

Lion of Catalunya. But this boy? This delicate son, this Francesc? True he had the blond curls of the first born Blanxarts, but he was a quiet, studious lad, more interested in books than anything else, and he wanted to be a teacher. Perhaps the fire of Catalunya smouldered in him.

Life in the barrio settled. The new houses gradually filled up, and then filled to overflowing. With their usual casual cruelty, the Castilian-controlled city authorities cleared all the old beach shacks and had a huge bonfire on the beach. Rafael, now an old man, watched the blaze. His own home, the chiringuito, was saved from the conflagration, since many of the Mossos liked eating there. The acrid smell of burning homes brought back to him that day, nearly sixty years ago, when he had watched La Ribera consumed. Francesc, sixty years younger, stood with him and watched the fire, aware that tears were trickling down his grandfather's face.

"You're right, boy," said Rafael. "Someone must write down the story. Oh, our poor Catalunya, such a fragile country. We cannot lose our heritage in smoke and flames. The countryside is ravaged, the city oppressed..." the old man's thoughts trailed off.

"I've started," replied Francesc, "And I would like to read it to you, grandfather. I must get the story right, I must have it clear. If no-one else is writing it, what would become of us if I fail?"

Later that day, with the old man carefully seated with a glass of wine in his hand, Francesc started to read.

He had got no further than the opening few pages, than he slipped in a question, as casually as he could, "By the way, it would help me to write about the sword, I mean, to describe it, if I saw it, wouldn't it?"

His grandfather roared with laughter. "You'll not catch me as easily as that, young man, although you may be right. I will talk to your father. But read on, you are bringing Joan Blanxart to life!"

It came about, after that first reading, that grandfather and grandson spent much time together as Franscesc pieced together the story, and Rafael rummaged through his memory. In trying to remember the words of songs, they had to bring Susana in, who had a better memory, and Francesc was able to include many of the folk legends and the words of the songs even if he had no way of writing the music.

An agreement was reached with Antoni, that Francesc's book, when it was finished, would be hidden with the sword, and at that moment, the sword and senerya would be revealed to the boy. With this additional motivation to get the words onto paper, Francesc wrote industriously whenever he had the time. His chores for his mother still had to be done, and his few Catalan books were much read and reread as he developed his own writing style and ability to express himself in Catalan.

As a reader and scribe he was much in demand, and started to establish a profitable business. He resented the time he was taken away from writing his family history, but was delighted to be adding successfully to the family income. From reading and translating, he started teaching a very few to read themselves, and he constantly watched for the moment when he encountered someone keen to learn Catalan. He worked at his own skill in the language, referring often to the few books his father had found for him, and started to make some notes, as best he could, of the complex grammar of the language. He found links with French as well as Castilian, but he found many aspects of the grammar very challenging.

He loved the way in which people started to recognise him as a teacher, and his quiet studious personality, whilst not as charismatic as his famous father, was strong and distinctive. His mother would sometimes look at him and wonder if she had produced a son who could be called wise.

It was not just the languages that fascinated Francesc. The more he read, and the more he learned of the world, the more he came to hate what the Castilians stood for. Castilians were slothful and greedy, and enjoyed oppressing others. In one highly valued book written in Catalan, he discovered that the aristocrats of Madrid were called the "occupying leeches." He liked that phrase. He believed that he was trapped in a lowly position in a massive spider's web of social conventions; a whole social system based on subjugation to a foreign king in Madrid. He thought of himself as a Catalan citizen; citizen of a state which did not exist, speaking a banned language, reading books that the authorities, given the chance, would burn; a citizen unable even to fly the flag of his country, in his country. Although at the time he did not know the word 'socialism', in his mind he was forming the kind of socialist ideals which would one day influence the future Catalunya. Occasionally a book would fall into his hands which helped him understand these things, and clarify his own thinking; and he was mightily frustrated by his poor English when such a book arrived from London.

Meanwhile, the population of Barceloneta was mushrooming. The clean lines of Prosper Verboom's elegant classical houses were rapidly become destroyed by the resident's efforts to enlarge their homes. Master Verboom had provided flat roofs, suitable for drying washing, and sleeping on hot summer nights; these were the first casualties of the itinerant building: even Antoni's own home had its residents on the roof, two of his sisters and their families had arrived when their shack on the beach had been destroyed.

In despair, Prosper and Antoni experimented with removing the heavy baroque cornice, and building some of the houses one more storey high; they then replaced the cornice above the second floor. This looked elegant at first, but then, inevitably, another family would appear on the roof of that dwelling, and another shack would be built on an even higher level.

Slowly Master Verboom's sunlit streets turned into shady canyons, and the washing, no longer discretely out of sight on the roof, was hung across the streets in a riot of underwear and bedlinen. As time went by, some of the buildings had grown to four floors high, and

Antoni and Prosper wondered how they could remain upright, with their shallow foundations on sand. The place did remain standing, but the architect and sculptor decided that if one fell, they would all fall like dominoes, each one dependent upon its neighbour for support.

With his family history book finished, and Rafael becoming a very frail old man, the time came for Francesc to be shown the stone chamber under the floor containing the sword and the flag. Antoni's legendary great strength was also beginning to wane, and he strained to lift the great limestone slab. Although most of the family had been banished to the chiringuito for the occasion, Francesc asked for his mother to remain and learn the secret of the hiding place, and so Alessia also watched with baited breath as the slab was raised.

Kneeling at the edge of the small chamber, Alessia smiled. "To think I've been walking over this spot for all these years," she reflected. "Just beneath my best rug. Antoni, how clever."

"Well done," said Rafael. "You created a dry safe place for the sword to lie in hiding. See how the colours of the flag remain bright. I am sure the sword will still be sharp and shining."

"Let us see the sword!" exclaimed Francesc impatiently.

Antoni carefully lifted the bundle and handed it to his father. "I may be the Lion," he said, "but I would like you, father, to unwrap the sword."

Slowly and shakily, Rafael unwound the senyera, the fabric still strong and the yellow and red stripes glowing in the dim light of the room. He turned to Francesc, and draped the flag around his grandson's shoulders. "Future Lion of Catalona," he declared. Antoni took the sword from his father and held it silently for a moment.

"I have been strong and steadfast in my love of my country," said Antoni, "but I do not think I will live long enough to see Catalunya rise again. When you are a man, my son, this sword will be yours. It may not be that you are chosen to be there when the yoke of Castile is finally destroyed. Perhaps it will be you, maybe it will be your son, or even your son's son. Who knows? But with this sword, and this flag, and now your book, we continue to dedicate ourselves to the cause of our homeland."

Spontaneously the other three put their hands upon the sword, and swore, "Our Catalunya." Francesc stepped forward with his book. Completed and bound in leather, it was a precious document. He had read the entire manuscript to his grandfather, who had approved of every detail. Rafael, his hand shaking, touched the book lightly as Francesc handed it to his father, and then Antoni wrapped the sword and the book carefully in the senyera, and lowered the precious bundle into to the tiny stone chamber. In silence, Antoni levered the flagstone back into position and Alissia replaced the rug.

After the ceremony of the secret chamber, Francesc was silent and thoughtful. Antoni and Alissia looked from him to Rafael who was sunk into a chair. Suddenly the old man seemed small and even more frail. Francesc moved quietly to his grandfather's side, and sat on the floor at his feet.

"What is it, my son?" asked Antoni quietly. Francesc looked long and hard at his grandfather, and then at his father. Then he spoke.

"It's serious, isn't it? It's not just a story. We really hold the key to Catalunya here in our hands, in our house, here beneath the floor of this room. Castile would destroy us. Who am I to inherit such responsibility? You, grandfather, who fought at the siege of Barcelona, and carried the sword for so long; and you, father, singing the folk songs of Catalunya in defiance of all, a great sculptor and a famous man, now the Lion of Catalunya; and now me. I don't have grandfather's courage or father's strength. I could not even lift the slab to reveal the sword. How can I be the Lion? How can this responsibility be mine?"

There was another silence as the three older members of the family looked at one another; and then Rafael spoke, slowly and quietly, with the wisdom of an old man at the end of his life.

"We all have our strengths. Oh I was strong and foolhardy in battle, and obstinate in my guarding of the sword, and your father is physically strong and commands great respect wherever he goes, both at home and throughout Spain; but you, dear boy, have an inner strength that surpasses us both."

Rafael paused to gather his thoughts. "We were merely the bearers of the sword and senyera, but you have contributed your book, the story so far, the very lifeblood of Catalunya. This is a great achievement. Your mother and father and I have often watched you and spoken amongst ourselves. We are proud of you, enormously proud, and we know the future is in safe hands. The future may be symbolised by a sword, but it will be persuasion and knowledge which will win in the end. You are a thinker, and one day may be called a philosopher. I see already the beginnings of a political understand beyond the thinking of your father or I."

"I was a humble working man," he continued. "Working long hours to sustain the family on the beach, coping with the daily grind of the chiringuito. Your father broke away with his talent for drawing and sculpture, the first of our family to become a master craftsman, the first to be welcomed into a guild. But you have gone beyond, the first to be really educated. Your father got called a man of substance, and he was; but you are destined to be a man of the world."

"Oh grandfather," replied Francesc, "you must help me. Thinking of the future scares me."

"No, you will not need help," said his grandfather. "You will have the support of us all, but your own knowledge and learning is all the help you will require. Besides, I am a very old man, and not long for this world. I die smiling, knowing that all I strived for was worth it. I'm leaving Catalunya in safe hands."

With that, the old man closed his eyes and seemed to sleep. Francesc, leaning against his thin legs, slept also, and Antoni moved quietly to the other side of the room where he lay on a rug and slumbered. Only Alissia remained awake, watching the three lions: the former, the present, and the future Lion of Catalunya. In the silence of the night, she listened to the three breathing: Francesc's youthful easy breath, Antoni's heavier deep breathing, and Rafael's troubled and rattling chest. And as she watched, she saw Rafael's breathing ease, and with one long sigh finally stop. Gently she shook her husband awake. "He's gone," she whispered, "the old lion has left us."

CHAPTER NINE

If anyone had asked Rafael, when he was a young man, if he thought he would die peacefully at home, surrounded by family, as an old man, he would have laughed. Through the turmoil of his early days, the trauma of the loss of his father, and the flight to safety on the beach, so much had happened in his youth that he hardly expected to survive twenty years. He had lived with a false name under the nose of the Castilian authorities, and had survived long enough that the Mossos had forgotten they were hunting him.

Francesc and his father sat and watched the old man until dawn, and then Antoni went down to the beach to collect the rest of the family and tell them the sad news.

Rafael was the first of the family to be taken to rest in the old graveyard at Monjuic since the siege. Traces of the old family burials had vanished, but Francesc was adamant from the stories he had listened to, that it was right and appropriate to take the old man's remains there. He also insisted that after the prayers at Sant

Miquel, they should also go to Santa Maria del Mar, reviving another old family tradition.

Francesc named his first-born son Xaudaro, an old and traditional Catalan name. Soon after his grand-son was born, Antoni passed the title of Lion of Catalunya to Francesc. This was the first time the title was held by a man of education rather than physical strength, and it would set a pattern which would recur more times over the years. Francesc's writing did not stop with the family history; he attempted a simple grammar of Catalan, struggling to make sense of the confusing patterns of language in the few books he cherished so much. He started to write his political thoughts, and talked with his father Antoni, and elderly Master Verboom the designer of the barrio of Barceloneta, who, coming from the Low Countries, had much sympathy with Catalunya, and was eager to explain his radical socialist ideals. Francesc ensured his son Xaudaro understood not only his inheritance as a Blanxart, but also the significance of the way Verboom had designed Barceloneta, giving everyone the dignity of a well-proportioned house, with no dwelling larger or smaller than any other. Xaudaro, whilst still young, looked at his father and declared, "We live in a model town, don't we father? It would be much better if all of Barcelona was like this! We should tear down those palaces in Montcada and build more homes for ordinary people!"

Francesc smiled. "The enthusiasm of the young," he said to himself. He looked fondly at his bright son: the boy's golden curls mirroring his father's. Xaudaro grew up as multi-lingual as his father – he had, after all, the best teacher in Catalunya to teach him – and he followed happily in his father's footsteps as a teacher.

The family business, reading and translating in the front, with a little Catalan teaching out of sight at the back, in Carrer de Sant Miquel, was thriving in safe hands with him. It seemed to be a happy pattern that the first born, who would one day become the lion, should develop the Catalan side of their business enterprises, whilst the rest of the family would work in the growing chiringuita enterprises. As Antoni grew older, and lost his great strength, he loved to watch his grandson's progress as an intellectual and linguist, just as Rafael had loved to watch Francesc. The day came for Xaudaro to be shown the hiding place, and its precious contents. Unlike the time years before, when Antoni could lift the flagstone on his own, this time it was a struggle for the three of them, Francesc and Xaudaro assisting Antoni, to lift the great slab of limestone.

The years passed. Antoni and Alissia joined Rafael and Susana in the Montjuic graveyard, and Francesc in his turn became an old man. As each generation passed, the values of Catalonya and socialism began to merge, and each first-born Blanxart boy fulfilled his obligation of finding a true Catalonian girl to marry, and then of teaching his family the songs and ballads, the poems and stories and the great longing for the revival of their homeland. Xaudaro grew up not only a fierce advocate for Catalunya, but also a passionate socialist, a combination of the innovative wisdoms which defined all true Catalans.

At the turn of the century, Xaudaro and his wife had their first child and he was named Alejandro, another traditional Catalan name: and as 'Alejandro Blanxart' his inheritance, and culture were stamped upon him from the day of his birth. And, of course, he had the extraordinary blond hair, which made every Blanxart first-born stand out from the crowd. At the time his son was born, Xaudaro was made the Lion of Catalunya by his aging father.

Little did the neighbours in Barceloneta know that every few years, an extraordinary ritual was taking place in the house in Sant Miquel. The stone would be raised, the sword, book and senyera taken out and displayed to the next Lion of Catalunya. The 1700's merged into the 1800's and little changed outwardly in the barrio.

Political storms raged throughout Europe: alliances were forged and broken; waves of immigration took Catalan families to the Americas, fleeing oppression from unknown foreign conquerors. Napoleon came and left, bringing another reign of terror to Barcelona, but the city remained intact. It became the cradle of the Spanish industrial revolution, and thus continued its role as the economic jewel in the Castilian crown. Despite all efforts to attract wealth to Madrid, the real wealth and business of nineteenth century Spain was in Barcelona. Whilst other regions fell into poverty, the people of Barcelona were always busy and enjoyed periods of full employment.

With money in their pockets, even the working classes could afford to visit the Blanxart chiriguita on the beach, and with increasing trade, the family opened new and larger beach kitchens, until the shore line was dotted with busy steaming chiringuitas, their stoves heating vast pans of paella, ovens producing fragrant flat loaves, and brew houses pungent with hops as great flagons of beer were brewed.

The everyday business of maintaining the busy chir-inguitas meant that all the Blanxarts were working hard. It was a long day, starting at dawn, stoking the fires for the ovens and stoves, until late into the evening, cleaning the pots and pans by candlelight. The income from the chiriguitas ensured that the family were comfortable, and immune to the political tides of boom and recession which made life so unpredictable for working people elsewhere in the city, or indeed throughout Spain.

Hardly had the new century dawned, when the country was struck with more conflict and upheaval. The Carlist Wars, so confusing to the ordinary working man, sent waves of soldiers of varying nationalities across the land, often finding rest and refreshment on the beach and in the humble chiriguitas of Barceloneta. Riots in the growing industrial suburbs similarly caused groups of homeless workers to appear temporarily on the beach, and the socialist ideals of the Blanxarts ensured that all were cared for and fed before returning to their suburban slums, and new opportunities for employment.

The traditional of education, created so strongly by Francesc, was fiercely maintained within the family.

Over the years, with each generation, the future head of the family would learn the stories of Catalunya and the legends of the Lion; for each of them the time would come to reveal the sword and the senyera, and to read Fransesc's book; and sometime after that they would inherit the title and obligations of becoming Lion of Catalunya. As the century progressed, and the implications of the industrial revolution became clearer and clearer, the Blanxart men added more socialist idealism to the inherited understanding of Catalan culture, and the two became intertwined.

Barcelonans lived in a constant state of chaos: working class riots led to a bombardment of the city from Montjuic; and later class struggles saw the indiscriminate burning of monasteries. Alejandro founded a socialist magazine, written largely by himself and his father Xandaro, printed on a little hand press in the upstairs room at Sant Miquel, and distributed very discretely in the factories and mills which now dominated the city landscape. Alejandro's secret knowledge of the forbidden Catalan language and culture underpinned his work on the magazine, but he was careful not to reveal too much about the sword, the senyera or the book.

As Alejandro grew older, he was raised into an atmosphere heavily charged politically: he was saturated by both socialist ideals and Catalan culture from the time he was born, and dreamed of becoming the Lion of Catalonia who would do more than keep the sword hidden: he dreamed of revealing it to his people. He dreamed of flying the senyera; and he dreamed of printing his grandfather's book. He chose his wife with the traditional care of the Blanxart family, and in 1835, Emilia Perez came into the family. She brought as much anti-royalist passion, and hatred of Castile as Alejandro had, and they became a formidable couple.

After so many stable years, fate then dealt an unexpected blow. After several miscarriages, Emilia produced the first-born son Alejandro was so desperate to have. The boy was named Jordi, born in 1840, and had the wonderful head of golden curls, strong limbs and open smiling face of all the other Blanxarts. And he was blind.

Emilia was distraught; Alejandro despondent. How could this fine inheritance, all this important culture, this knowledge and experience fall upon the shoulders of a blind boy? Emilia had another son a year later, but Juan was born with the straight black hair of his mother's family, and could hardly take the place of his blond brother.

In the evenings, with Jordi and Juan asleep, Emilia and Alejandro would weep together. "All my longings and ambition dashed on the rocks," Alejandro would say. "We will love and cherish our little boy, but how can he be the Lion of Catalunya? The time will come when father hands the sword to me; all I have ever wanted is the honour of being the Lion of Catalunya, but now I dread the day. Will I be the last Lion? Will the title, and all it stands for die with me?"

As had happened in many previous generations of the family, it was a grandfather who came to the rescue.

Xaudaro, now an old man just past his seventieth birthday, sat with the blind Jordi, and started to sing to him all the old Catalan folk songs. Jordi would smile, and sing along. Xaudaro then bought the boy a small guitar, and from the first moment it was put into the little boy's hands, it was clear he had talents and gifts beyond the fears and hopes of his parents. Struggling to reach around the body of the toy instrument, Jordi would work at the guitar in the way other children learned to read, or run with a ball, or all the many other skills a blind boy would never have, with long dedicated hours, daily conquering the complexities of the instrument.

"Listen to your son," Xaudaro would say. "In his darkness he absorbs the Catalan culture. No Lion's son has had such a wonderful voice, and learned the folk songs of Catalunya so easily. Have faith, my Alejandro, that your passion will flood the boy just as our music floods him now. The Lions of Catalunya have all been different. We know of the legendary strength of my grandfather, the sculptor Antoni, whose image stands at the church of Sant Miquel; he was followed by the wisdom of his son, the bookish Francesc, my father, who gave us our written history in the secret book we keep with the sword; you and I have been hard workers, building up our business empire, strengthening our position in financial terms; perhaps the time has come for another kind of Lion, one who will return to the culture and lead it into the light he cannot see. This little bond boy will learn through his fingers and his ears what others learn with their eyes, and he will celebrate our heritage in a unique way. Be strong for my grandson, Alejandro. Juan will be his eyes, and he will make his way in the world."

Emilia embraced her father-in-law, and whispered quietly to him, "May God grant that you are right." Alejandro nodded silently. It was hard to be so optimistic.

Jordi soon outgrew the child-sized guitar, and recognising his talent, his father took advice, and bought him a high quality full-sized instrument. Again Jordi struggled to reach around the fat body if the instrument which was as big as he was, but from the moment he strummed the new guitar, something magical happened in his fingers. A sound like none heard before in the barrio, emerged from the guitar, sweeter, stronger and more lyrical than any of the rough street music which was all the neighbours had heard in the past. Soon his life fell into an unplanned routine. His mornings would be filled with learning all the languages which surrounded him, the Castilian and Catalan, and the beginnings of French and English; and often he would sigh with the exhaustion of so much memorisation, and turn to his guitar. In the afternoons, one or other of his grandparents would sit with him and tell the stories of Catalunya, and he never tired of hearing them again and again, and when the grandparent fell asleep over the words, he would strum softly again, picking out familiar tunes, and inventing new ones.

In the late afternoon, with the sun setting, Juan would appear, as if by a given signal, although there never was one, and carry his brother's stool out to the corner of the street. He would return and lead Jordi to the stool, and the young guitarist would sit and sing and play. Neighbours would open their windows to hear the sweet sounds, and strangers would stop in astonishment, listening to the beautiful music coming from the little boy. As he grew older, his clear soprano would soar above the chords, bringing new life and excitement to the songs of sailors, and of the mountains, and of the troubadours. People would offer money, but Juan was under strict instructions from his father not to accept it. "Take my brother's music into your heart," he would say, "And when the time comes, sing with him." Many people were puzzled by this cryptic comment, but a few, recognising the Catalonian melodies and words, understood and smiled knowingly.

The brothers made a striking pair: Jordi with his mass of blond curls, and Juan with his jet-black locks tied back from his face. Jordi would be smiling as he sang like an angel, and Juan would smile quietly, sitting proudly at his feet. Somehow the boys created a feeling of peace and tranquillity, even though the folk songs Jordi sang were often telling the trials and tribulations of the Catalan people. As the sun set, and a cool breeze blew down the lane, the time would come for the brothers to go home, into the warmth and safety of the cosy house.

Jordi had been born into a tumultuous time for Barcelona. The railway had arrived from France, carving a tortuous route through the Pyrenees, and terminating in the great station of Franca. The old boundary of the city had defined Barceloneta, which was entirely outside and south of the wall. The railway replaced the old wall with iron tracks, and became the northern limit of the barrio. The great Franca Station, with its curving arched roof, was visible even from the beach, glimpsed in the distance at the far end of Carrer Sant Miquel.

Whilst all this railway work seemed enormous to the people of Barceloneta, it was as nothing compared to the gigantic endeavours taking place elsewhere around the city. Vast tracks of farmland were laid out in a fantastical grid pattern, creating L'Eixample, thousands of superior dwellings for the rapidly expanding middle classes. Hundreds of slum hovels were swept away to create a wide road from L'Eixample to Franca Station: passing close between the old cathedral and Santa Catarina's market, the Via Laietana was named for the ancient tribes who first settled on the little hill at the centre of the city, older even than the Roman occupation.

The muddy stream west of the old town had been paved some years earlier and had turned into an extraordinary boulevard, which quickly gained the collective title of Las Ramblas, although in fact each section of the street had its own descriptive name. The rich businessmen of the city had built themselves an opulent opera house, and those who had made the greatest donations gave themselves large boxes which they decorated lavishly. They ensured that working people of the city could also attend the opera, building a huge gallery, which they nicknamed the henroost, high above the boxes and stalls.

All this expansion of Barcelona took place though a period of continuing political unrest: indeed such unrest was the norm for the city, and the mushrooming developments were on the whole unaffected by the complexities of the politics. It was as if the businessmen of Barcelona would thrive whatever happened: and they did. The humble house in Barceloneta was visited by many people, especially the leaders of the Catalan workers, including one Josep Barcelo, who was eager to learn as much as he could about his Catalan heritage. The family liked Josep, and shared many stories with him; in turn he talked about his political ideals, and for the first time they heard the word communism. The Catalonians felt braver than before, and for the first time in many years, the language and culture began to emerge from the shadows. A great deal of the responsibility for this emerging Catalan life lay on the shoulders of a little blind boy singing his heart out in Barceloneta.

The barrio of Barceloneta remained a stable and static point in the rapidly changing universe of the city, and whilst everywhere seemed to be expanding, the restrictions of the railways line to the north, and the sea on the other sides of the triangular district, meant that there was nowhere to expand, except upwards, and, as was traditional in the area, this was what happened. The canyon of Carrer Sant Miquel saw the sun only for brief moments in the middle of the day, and whilst the grandees of the city took their promenade on the fashionable Ramblas, the people of Barceloneta strolled the sandy shoreline in the evening, inspecting the fishermen's boats and lines between the chiringuitas, and admiring the larger vessels crowding the harbour to the west.

As they grew into their teenage years, the inseparable brothers Jordi and Juan explored their changing city. Juan, as eyes for both of them, would describe the richly dressed patrons entering the ornate foyer of the Liceu Opera House, before the two would clamber up the steep stairs to the hen roost. The boys were able to experience much Italian opera, and occasionally even German pieces were performed. They also attended concerts, and Jordi's astonishing ear for the details of melody and harmony ensured a constantly expanding and extraordinary repertoire for his impromptu street performances back in Barceloneta.

The barrio remained obstinate in its refusal to modernise, and the tiny houses, teeming with inhabitants were in stark contrast to the rest of the city. It remained, however, a hotbed of political intrigue, and the small bars and domino clubs were the centre of much heated debate. The businessmen of Barcelona, secure in their grand apartments in L'Exiample, were aware of the power of the Catalan culture over their workers, and the prudent amongst them sought to cultivate friendly links with the leaders of the Barceloneta population. Inevitably, these links led to Alejandro and his sons Jordi and Juan.

One summer evening, following a performance of an opera by Donizetti, Jordi and Juan were leaving the opera house from the side entrance, and turning into the crowds of Las Ramblas, when they were accosted by a well-dressed businessman leaving from the grand foyer.

Politely the man interrupted their enthusiastic chatter about the opera. "Excuse me, but are you the sons of Alejandro Blanxart?"

"Yes, sir," replied Juan, "I am Juan and this is my brother Jordi."

"Then you are the famous guitarist, who sings and plays like an angel!"

"I don't think of myself as an angel," replied Jordi, "but it is I who plays and sings. My brother here is my eyes. Who are we talking to, sir?"

"My name is Miguel Roca, and I am a businessman here in Barcelona. Many of my workers have told me about your music, young man, and that you know and sing the old folk songs of Catalunya."

"It is our family's tradition, sir, that we learn and sing the songs and stories of our heritage. Without the fathers and sons of the Blanxart family, many of the old songs and stories would have been lost," replied Jordi, with pride. "They have been passed down the generations, and currently I am working to learn them, ready to pass to my children when the time comes."

"I believe the time has come to pass them far and wide beyond your family, Master Blanxart," stated Senor Roca. "I believe the time has come for Catalunya to stand up as a culture in the world. The politics are in place!"

Puzzled by this final cryptic remark, Jordi felt that this was a conversation for his father, not himself, and so he invited Senor Roca to visit them in Barceloneta the following day. Giving him the address in Sant Miquel, the boys said farewell to the businessman, and hurried home, unaware of the significance of what seemed to them to be a chance encounter.

Not long before, Senor Roca had been talking with his business colleagues, and had agreed to seek a meeting with Alejandro Blanxart. He was keen to see if all the rumours were true that he held the key to the richness of the Catalan culture. So much of what Senor Roca and his colleagues knew was in the realm of myth and legend, and they were anxious to know the truth.

In preparation for the visitor, Emilia had tidied the upstairs room, and prepared wine and pastries. Xaudrao, ancient and frail, slumbered on a low chair with his blind grandson sitting on the rug nearby.

Alejandro could not guess the importance of the meeting, but felt it appropriate to show considerable dignity with such a visitor. It was a shock, therefore, when Senor Roca arrived with three other well-dressed businessmen beside him. Emilia fussed to get them all seated, and sent Juan running to the nearest chiringuita for extra wine and refreshments. Jordi sat quietly listening to the unexpected commotion, recognising the voice of Senor Roca, and puzzling over the other strangers.

Once introductions had been made, Senor Roca took the initiative. "Senor Blanxart, you will know that many political changes are swirling around our city. You will know of the waves of unrest in the factories, where despite many offers of employment, our workers are often disgruntled with their situation; you will know that Barcelona is booming, leading all Spain in industrial development and output; and most of all you will know that under all of this, the desire for a strong and independent Catalunya fuels the feelings of revolution."

Alejandro nodded, unwilling to show his hand at this stage. "Go on," was all he said.

"Not all the leaders of industry favour the Castilians; some of us have Catalonian backgrounds and we sympathise with the workers. We are concerned to develop our factories into fair places where all men earn good wages. We are not communists, but we reject the cruel Castilian form of capitalism. We believe the workers will be galvanised into a new kind of unity if they are united as Catalonians, working in their own country, an independent and free Catalunya!"

Jordi gasped. Such words were treasonable only a few short years before, and even now, in the 1850's were dangerous. That such sentiments were coming not from the grumblings of the workers in the local barrio bars, but from respectable city businessmen was indeed extraordinary.

"What have you heard," continued Senor Roca, "of the mood of the workers? We have had so many piecemeal strikes, discontentment is rife, and yet the city is alive and expanding. The arrest of Senor Barcelo has made matters a great deal worse. We come to seek your advice."

Choosing his words carefully, Alejandro replied. "Yes, I hear of much unhappiness. We know Senor Barcelo well - he is a good man. Chatter in the bars and in my own chiringuitas turns constantly to the conditions of the workers, and their hatred of Castile. It may seem an echo from the past, but memories are long, and the scars from previous battles remain. Josep Barcelo is a man of the people, and you would do well to befriend him."

"I fear it is too late for that. The authorities in the Generalitat have condemned Barcelo to death," continued Roca. "We are fearful of what will happen."

"They are the puppets of the Castilian government," came Jordi's voice from the corner of the room. All turned towards him, and even sightless he could tell he was the centre of attention. "When Senor Barcelo is executed, and he will be, any day now, it will be the signal for a general strike. I listen a lot, and I hear much. Your factories will be devastated, and your machines smashed. Who knows what conspiracies are at work? Is Madrid simply out to destroy Barcelona business, or are they naïve enough to think executing the workers' leader will subdue the desire for independence? Gentlemen, the opposite will be true. The death of Josep Barcelo will give us another Catalan martyr, and be the rallying cry for Catalans everywhere to unite."

"It is as we feared," said Roca slowly and with a heavy heart. "We have tried to intervene and save the life of Barcelo, but he is to die within the week. Then I fear, our beautiful city will be subject to the laws of anarchy. What is to be done?"

"Without a focus or rallying point, you may be right," said Alejandro. "The same old battles will be fought all over again. Castile will continue to attack Catalunya, and we will continue to fight back. Little has changed since the days of my ancestor Joan Blanxart, and he died at the hands of Castilian soldiers more than two hundred years ago. He was the first Catalan martyr, and there have been many more. Hundreds died during the great siege, all martyrs for Catalunya. Barcelo is yet one more in this sorry catalogue of death."

"But the politics are different now, father," said Jordi. "Perhaps the time has come to rally the people behind the senyera."

There was a silence in the room. Alejandro needed time to think: had they arrived at the time when the flag of Catalonya would fly again? Roca and his colleagues waited without understanding: they had never heard of the senyera. Juan looked around wondering who would speak first. And Jordi sat quietly, smiling at the effect of this words.

Slowly, and with dignity, the old grandfather Xaudaro sat up and opened his cloudy eyes. "Blood was spilled when our senyera was created, and blood will be spilled again. There have been many martyrs to the cause of our beloved Catalunya, and there will be many more. Now is the time to be brave, and unfurl the flag. Now our time has come."

There was a further silence, and then Alejandro spoke. "Gentlemen, I beg your patience at this time of crisis. I must speak to my father and my sons privately. We must be sure that this is the moment. If you return this evening, we will give you our answer."

Mystified, Roca and his friends agreed to return, and climbed carefully down the steep stairs. Alejandro saw them to the street, and then returned to his father and his sons. "Is this the moment?" was all he said.

Xaudaro replied first. "Let us proceed with caution. We will reveal the senyera and the book. We shall keep the sword hidden. The flag will give a rallying cry to the workers, as we have discussed, and the book can be printed for all to read the true stories of our land, not just the myths and legends of childhood. But the sword is ours, sacred to the memory of past Blanxart martyrs, and not to be revealed until the situation is clear. With Barcelona full of so many different factions, including many anarchists who will enjoy an opportunity for trouble-making, the time is not ripe yet for the sword."

"Grandfather is right," exclaimed Jordi. "We shall listen to his wisdom. Let us give them the senyera; let us give them their history, but let us keep the sword until that glorious moment when the world celebrates the re-birth of our nation."

Grandfather continued, "The sword is no longer a weapon of death and destruction; it to be carried solemnly by the Lion of Catalunya, at a time of celebration, not general strike or strife. Alejandro, my son, I passed the title to you a few short years ago. It may be that you will carry the sword to the people, before your time is out, or it may be that Jordi here will carry it. But that time has not yet come." The old man paused and laughed. "And now you youngsters have a task! Between the three of you, you have to reveal the hiding place."

"The sword!" exclaimed Jordi. "Am I to hold the sword at last?"

"For a moment only," replied his father. "We will lift the stone, remove the book and senyera, and return the sword. I hope to God we are doing the right thing."

Alejandro and his sons descended the steep stairs, leaving grandfather listening from above. All the rest of the family except Emilia were sent to one of the chiringuitas, and told to stay away until Juan came with a message. Alejandro looked around. Juan's face was illuminated with excitement; Jordi was solemn and Emilia, who knew nothing of the conversation in the upstairs room, was puzzled.

"The timing of this ceremony has been thrust upon us by events in the city beyond our control. I pray we are not making a mistake. Emilia, please roll up the rug."

Still puzzled, his wife did so.

"Now Jordi, kneel with me on the floor. You feel the outlines of the flagstones beneath your fingers? Can you feel this stone? Can you feel all around it?"

"Yes, father, and I feel small holes, like slots alongside it."

"This is the hiding place. Your great, great grandfather, the sculptor Antoni Blanxart, fashioned this sleeping place for the sword, and here it has rested these many years. The secret will be revealed today to you, my son, and you, Emilia my wife, and for the first time to someone who will never be the Lion of Catalunya, but who will be the eyes of the Lion, to you Juan. These small slots you feel, Jordi, are the secret to lifting the stone."

Alejandro rose and fetched iron bars from the fireplace. Handing one to each son, he told them to find the slots and insert the bars. Jordi feeling with his fingers, and Juan searching with his eyes, each found a slot, and pushed the bars in. Alejandro handed another lever to his wife, and told her to find another slot. "It's hardly women's work, I know," he apologised, "but we'll need your help."

Inserting a fourth bar himself, he instructed them all to heave. Slowly the slab rose, and they carefully slid it to one side. Juan gasped and went to touch the wrapped sword, but Alejandro signalled for him to stand back.

"Jordi, my son, one day you will be the Lion of Catalunya. It is right, then, that you have the honour of taking the sword from its chamber."

Jordi's fingers moved forward slowly, feeling the edge of the hole that had now been revealed in the floor. First he found Francesc's book, and lifted it up. "That is the book with the stories of our land," explained his father. "The stories your grandfather has told you. With luck, Senor Roca and his associates will have that printed and distributed soon. But give the book to your brother who can read it to you, and now grasp your inheritance, the sword of Catalunya."

Jordi's fingers moved again in the cavity, and soon found the fabric of the senyera, wrapped around the cold steel of the sword. He lifted the weight, and groping carefully, found the hilt. Although he could not see the flag, he unfurled it easily, and Emilia caught it as it dropped. Slowly, Jordi stood up and held the sword revealed in all its simple glory.

From upstairs, came grandfather's voice. "Have you got it, boy? Grasp it well and feel its shape. Bring it to me, that I may see it for one last time. The chamber will not be opened again in my life time." And Jordi carefully carried the sword up the steep stairs and handed it to his grandfather. The old man caressed it, and then called for Juan. "Juan, eyes of the Lion, you should hold the sword also, as the time may come when you wield it for your brother."

Finally, when the sword had been passed to all, even Emilia taking it for a moment, it was wrapped in a new cloth, and returned to the stone chamber. The lid was levered back into position. Emilia unrolled the rug, and the crowbars were returned to the fireplace.

When Senor Roca and his friends returned in the evening, the Blanxart family were ready for them. A small stool had been placed in the centre of the room, and the senyera hung from the roof beams. Emilia now joined her husband as Juan waited below to bring their guests up.

Roca arrived in a state of agitation and excitement, rushing up the stairs ahead of the others, and speaking before he sat down. "Calamity," he exclaimed, "Barcelo has been executed, even as we were speaking this morning, he was being led to his death. He was garrotted at noon. I believe we are on the brink of civil war."

"Then there is no time to lose," said Alejandro. "Has a strike been called?"

"Yes, a general strike, immediately. The city will be at a standstill."

"Will the people rally to the flag?"

"I believe they will, and we must do all we can to encourage them. We need pamphlets printed and distributed, and we need copies of the senyera. The moment has come when leadership matters most. From the disaster of this morning, and the ashes of the pending strike, we have the opportunity to rise like the phoenix. Senor Blanxart, are you with us?"

Pulling a large cloth to one side, Alejandro revealed the small printing press they used to print pamphlets. "I will produce the pamphlets here. You must use your contacts to print flags - we need hundreds. The strikers will rally on Las Ramblas tomorrow. They must be carrying the senyera, and understand the message of solidarity we can print in our pamphlet!"

One of Roca's friends, called Fernando, who had spoken little, stepped forward. "I have a mill in Vilassar de Dalt where we can weave such a flag on one of our great looms. I can produce a hundred in an hour. Let me take this one as a sample, and we will work through the night. I have a small group who are fervent Catalonians and will not see this as strike-breaking, but as support for their fellow workers."

"No," said Alejandro, "This is an ancient senyera, and it must stay here. If ever it leaves the house, it will be with me or my sons. You can see the simple design. Four stripes of blood across the yellow background. Remember it well, and make your copies sir."

Roca interjected, "I understand Senor Blanxart, Fernando. It is a powerful design because it is so simple. Just remember as you have four fingers to dip in the blood, so there are four stripes on the flag. Now go and make flags!"

Fernando, charged with his task, left quickly. The others settled urgently to agreeing the wording of the pamphlet. Once that was done, they turned their attention to Francesc Blanxart's book. Jordi held it and caressed it. "Gentlemen, I cannot read a word of what is in this book, but my grandfather and my father have told me the stories so that I know them by heart. If one of you has a printing press that can print this book, let it be done with all speed. My brother Juan will come with you, to guard the book, and to assist with setting it in type. He will guard it with his life. In giving you my brother for this task, I am giving you my eyes, so I urge you to send him, and the book, back again quickly, as without him I am truly blind."

Josep Barcelo was executed in 1855. The general strike which followed rallied public opinion away from Castile, and created a vision of the future Catalunya as an independent state. In less than twenty years, Catalunya was declared a federal republic, independent from Spain, with its distinctive flag, the senyera with its four blood stripes. Juan had returned his great-grandfather's book, and together with the original Blanxart senyera, it was returned to lie with the sword in the special chamber under the floor.

Jordi thus grew up in a period of rapid change. Suddenly everyone wanted to read Francesc's book, and then when they discovered it was available only in Catalan, wanted to learn to read the language. From being the whispered underground chatter of subversives, Catalan became the language of choice for those who could manage it, and workers throughout the region met in the evenings to learn the language which they felt should have been their mother tongue. In Barceloneta, where many people spoke Catalan fluently, the demand was to learn to read and write, and the Blanxart house abandoned all the other activities of translation and coping with Castilian in favour of constant Catalan reading and writing lessons at many levels. A senyera hung from the first floor window: the first time since the destruction of La Ribera back in the early 1700's that the flag was displayed openly. All over the city, senyeras appeared, and with them a cult of Catalan culture.

Xandaro died peacefully in 1866; unaware that he had reached the greatest age of any member of the Blanxart family so far, and unsure of his surroundings. His funeral procession to Montjuic was, however, distinguished by the brilliant new senyera draped over his coffin, with his grandsons walking either side, each holding a corner of the flag.

Many of the activities which sprang up had little or nothing to do with the history of Catalonya. A new dance, the sardana, developed, and was taught as if it had a long history. Standing in sedate circles, holding hands in unity, the dancers would dance intricate steps to 'traditional' Catalan music, which had only recently been composed. Francesc's book gave them a solid historical basis for their culture, but without records of music and other aspects of the culture, the Catalan nation had to invent much of its own history.

Jordi himself was much in demand as a concert performer; although self-taught, he had achieved a standard far beyond the street buskers. He still sang on the corner of Sant Miquel, but he encouraged Juan to accompany him far and wide across the city, to sing not only in churches and bars, but often in squares and on street corners. The Liceu opera house presented many mixed programmes of song and dance as well as opera, and Jordi was a popular attraction at these events, sharing the stage with a wide variety of other artists, including circus acts like sword swallowers and jugglers. Jordi's performances were always focussed on the folk songs of Catalunya and talk began of the Catalan people building their own concert hall. To Jordi this seemed very fanciful and unlikely.

The festival of San Jordi was revived, and annually, on 23rd April, men would go out and buy flowers to present to all the women in their lives. Women, to reciprocate, would hunt for books written in Catalan to give to their men. Francesc Blanxart's history of Catalunya was a popular choice, and ensured that amongst the growing celebrations of Catalan culture, many of the real traditions and history of the nation were preserved. The romantic revival of Catalan culture grew from strength to strength during the rest of the century, and became known as the "Renaixenca".

Jordi was keen to teach the reality of all this. Not for him the artifice of the sardana or other new "traditions": he was concerned to teach Catalan with good and accurate grammar. He would sit and talk through the ideas and conventions, whilst his brother would show how the rules appeared in writing. He was also in great demand as a singer, famous for his wonderful tenor voice. He was one of many performers at the celebrations in 1868, following the Glorious Revolution, which sealed the destiny of the region.

Finally in 1873, a tentative declaration of independence was made: Catalonya was now a Federal Republic, with lands stretching from Perpignon in the north to Valencia in the south. Senor Rosa, who had become friends with the family, and especially with Jordi, came to visit in advance of the declaration of independence.

"Young man," he said addressing Jordi. "You have become the leading singer of Catalan Folk song in our land. A group of friends, many of whom you know, want to celebrate our independence in a very special way. We have come to seek your advice. We want you to sing, of that there is no doubt. But we want more. How can we solemnly begin this new country of ours, this re-birth?"

Jordi thought for a moment, and then replied, smiling, "You have read the book. You know the significance of the great church of Santa Maria del Mar in the history of Catalonya. I believe the Virgin will smile upon a celebration held in her great cathedral of the sea. We have a magnificent organ and we have a great choir: let them sing a solemn mass of thanksgiving that our country is at last independent. And then I will sing."

All were thankful that the day of republican celebration was free of bloodshed despite warnings from anarchists and Castilians. The day dawned with the Blanxart family, and others from Barceloneta gathering at their local church of Sant Miquel. Following the prayers, the family stood in the sunshine of Placa Sant Miquel, and Juan whispered softly to Jordi, "Sant Miquel is smiling."

"If only I could see the statue," said Jordi, in a rare moment of self-pity. "If only...."

The family then walked to the wide square outside the Generalitat building, where the announcement of the republic was made. Again many were fearful of violent interruptions, but for once the trouble makers stayed away.

It was then time to go to Santa Maria del Mar. Almost everyone gathered in the square planned to attend the church service, and so it was a joyous procession that marched down the hill, passing the Mediaeval cathedral, across the new scar of Via Liaetana, and to Santa Maria. As they walked, more and more of the population joined the throng, and at the doors of the church, a silence fell as they filed inside.

Whilst others knelt at their favoured side chapel, Juan led Jordi directly through the gathering throng to the choir, where his guitar was safely waiting for him. The brothers sat quietly waiting for the mass to begin.

"There is a delay," whispered Juan.

"I can tell," replied Jordi. "Can't you feel the place filling up? There have rarely been this many people here."

"Thousands," suggested Juan. "It seems we have to wait whilst others find somewhere to stand."

"What an extraordinary atmosphere," whispered Jordi. "I can feel the people. There is a rustling and movement in the air, like none I have known before."

At last the mass began, the organ and choir leading the celebration, and the huge crowd responding with enthusiasm. Finally the moment arrived that all were waiting for. The priest placed a stool in front of the famous statue of Our Lady of the Sea, and Juan led his brother, with his well-worn guitar, to sit on it. At that moment, the sun came out, shining as it always did upon the statue; but this time including Jordi, and his aura of golden curls, in its dazzling glow. The audience gasped, such was the drama of the moment.

In the silence that followed, Jordi started to strum, quietly and gently at first, but then with a passion and fervour unknown in this solemn place of worship. The chords rang out, tumbling over one another as they echoed into the high vault. And then he started to sing. He sang of the mountains and the sea, he sang of fishermen and troubadours, he sang of the senyera, and he sang of the heroes of Catalunya's history. His voice rang out, and the stones and pillars of the church reflected the glory of his music and the achievement of the people.

When the music finished, there was a long silence as the sound died away into the stone. Then came a stamping, roaring noise as the people showed their love and affection for the blind young man. Alejandro and Emilia, standing to one side with Juan, tears flowing at the adulation for their son, were speechless. Jordi himself simply sat and smiled and waited for the noise to fade.

CHAPTER TEN

The peace was short-lived. If anyone thought they would walk away from the celebration at Santa Maria del Mar into a new dawn of independence, sweetness and light, they were very much mistaken. Political groups of all kinds sprang up, some opposed to Catalan independence and wanting Castile to intervene, some unhappy at the liberal socialism of the industrial areas, jealous of the prospering middle classes, and passionate in their communist ideals, and others simply without any philosophy or foundation, who schemed for nothing more than anarchy.

Alejandro had often worried if he had missed his opportunity, and should have carried the Pujol sword to Santa Maria that day of music and celebration, but as the political wrangling and bloodshed resumed, he was glad he had not. Another worry had entered his mind, and he took Emilia to one side to talk to her.

"Our son is now thirty-three years old," he began.

"And unmarried," Emilia completed the sentiment.

"You have been thinking as I have been," said her husband.

"Indeed, and I reach no conclusion."

"I am past my sixtieth birthday," continued Alejandro, "and it is time to pass the title of Lion of Catalunya to Jordi. But without a wife or child, what will happen? Does this fragile independence mean the end of the line? Shall I, or shall Jordi, be the last Lion?"

"And what of Juan? He also should have the chance to marry and have a family. He has spent his whole life being his brother's eyes. Should we find a match for Jordi, will Juan continue to be his brother's eyes? And if we should find a match for Juan, what will happen to Jordi? It is a puzzle, husband, and I was turning it in my mind long before that day at Santa Maria."

"Indeed, I watched our son that afternoon, his golden curls bathed in our Lady's sunshine. He is truly beautiful, and there were many young women in the church who would make good wives, and could love him," continued Alejandro. "Many of them have taken to hanging around the street corner, hoping he'll sing to them. But he does not see them, and I can hardly tell him to start singing love songs to see what happens!"

"I do not think we can wait for chance or fate. We must take matters into our own hands. Husband, you must talk to the boy."

Alejandro was nervous, and hesitated before talking to Jordi. He arranged for Emilia to take the rest of the family to the beach, for supper in one of the family chiringuitas, and told Jordi that he needed to have an important conversation. Jordi immediately was suspicious that his father was about to hand over the title of Lion, and became nervous, but when Alejandro started to talk about finding a wife, he burst out laughing.

"You forget, my dear father, that Juan is my eyes in every way. Do not think I am unaware of my many admirers when I sing; Juan has described them all. There's Nuria with the long black hair, who always wears a red flower for passion; there's Elena with squinting eyes, and pouting lips for kissing; there's Amelia shyly fanning herself; there's Alissia, who Juan is keen on for himself, but she only has eyes for me; there's Clara, the most persistent, who comes every night and brings fragrant flowers so that I can smell their perfume...."

"Stop, stop, Jordi." said his father, starting to laugh with him. "I had no idea. So what's to be done?" He paused, and then nervously asked, "Have you been with any of these young women, Jordi?"

"I'm not sure if a father can ask such a question!" chuckled Jordi, "and I surely will not give you an answer, except that neither my brother nor I are inexperienced."

Alejandro laughed some more, and then checked himself, saying, "This was supposed to be a serious conversation. I suppose now you'll tell me which of the ladies you prefer!"

At that moment, the street door crashed open, and Juan came running up the stairs, laughing. "Mother has told me what you two are up to," he laughed, "and you should know that as the eyes of my brother, I should be here also. I've left mother and the others on the beach. Now how far have you got?"

"Nuria, Elena, Amelia…." began Alejandro.

"Alissia, Clara…." laughed Jordi.

"Anna?" asked Juan, "Or her sister Violeta?"

"I was coming to them," replied Jordi. "I was bringing father round gently to telling him our plan." He stopped, and Alejandro waited.

"Alright," Juan broke the silence, "of all the girls who have eyes for my handsome brother, Anna is the one he knows and trusts. It happens she has a sister, Violeta, who has shown great interest in me."

"They love us, father, and want to marry us!" blurted out Jordi. "Have you heard of it before, brothers marrying sisters?"

"I am sure it will not be the first time," said Alejandro slowly, "But first we must talk, and then I must talk to the girls' father. What do you know of this family?"

"They are the daughters of Senor Valdes, father, a wine merchant in the old city." Began Juan. "You have met him many times, as he is one of the suppliers of wine to our chiringuitas. He was with his daughters at the independence service at Santa Maria's. You spoke to him briefly at the end of Jordi's music, and whilst you were distracted we were talking to the girls. Behind your back, Anna took Jordi's hand and kissed it and then let him touch her face. She has always understood how to communicate with him by touch instead of sight. It was about that time that Violeta admitted her interest in me, and we started meeting the girls together." Juan stopped and looked at his brother, who was nodding vigorously and grinning.

"That's all very well," said Alejandro severely, "Bur there are obligations which must be fulfilled. You know that Jordi will one day be the Lion of Catalunya. As such he must marry a girl from a known Catalan family, a girl committed to the cause of our nation as much as we are. How can we be sure about a family from the old city?"

"There is no problem, dear father," said Jordi.

Juan continued, "No problem. You know that we check all our suppliers for the chiringuitas, always have done, and only take supplies from families loyal to the Catalan cause. The Valdes family have supplied us for some time, and have celebrated our country's independence with much enthusiasm."

"Very well," agreed Alejandro. "I will seek a meeting with Senor Valdes, and your mother can meet Senora Valdes. This is a far more complicated liaison than one ordinary marriage, and there must be clear marriage contracts, arrangements for dowries and clear understanding of all the obligations."

Alejandro asked around the barrio, and in all the chiringuitas, for information about the Valdes family, and was greatly relieved that all he heard about them was positive. They had come from Girona some two generations ago, when that town was becoming more impoverished, and Barcelona was beginning its boom. The Valdes in Girona had maintained the Catalan language quietly at home, bringing Catalan-speaking servants with them when they came to Barcelona. They had bought one of the big houses in Montcada, and set up a flourishing wine cellar, echoing the Blanxart business of many years before. Once satisfied that their credentials were impeccable, Alejandro arranged a meeting with Senor Valdes, at which generous dowries were agreed. The sisters had only one brother, Oscar, who would inherit the wine business, and thus Senor Valdes was able to indulge his daughters lavishly. Emilia was equally delighted to meet Senora Valdes, and they quickly became friends. Although the Blanxarts were financially very secure with their chain of chiringuitas, they were not as sophisticated as the Valdes, and Emilia enjoyed her visits to the big house in Montcada, with its grand chamber on the piano nobile. She was excited to see that there was a large senyera hanging at one end of the huge room..

Alejandro then surprised the Valdes family by arranging a meeting of all four parents, and all four children. They were to meet in the upstairs room in Carrer Sant Miquel, and Emilia found herself preparing refreshments for another exciting gathering. In the morning, Alejandro summoned his wife and sons, and they opened the secret chamber, taking out the sword, wrapped in the original senyera, and the history book. The stone was returned and the rug rolled back, so that the visitors would not know where the hiding place was when they walked over it.

Jordi waited anxiously at the door, listening for the voices of Anna and Violeta, and soon grinned eagerly when he heard them approaching. He led Anna upstairs, and Juan, with a similar grin, led Violeta. Senor Blanxart greeted Senor and Senora Vales and escorted them up the steep stair to the upper room, where Emilia was waiting to greet them. A small table, covered by the ancient senyera, stood in the centre of the room. Once all were seated, parents on tapestry-covered chairs, and the youngsters on stools, and wine glasses filled, Alejandro cleared his throat, ready for his speech.

"Senor and Senora Valdes, welcome to my home. Welcome also to your beautiful daughters. The Blanxart family have lived in this house in Barceloneta for many generations since it was built by my great-grandfather, the famous sulptor Antoni Blanxart. Our fortune has been built on the chain of chringuitas along the beach, a humble trade, but an honest one! And since my grandfather, Francesc, author of the famous history of Catalonya, we have also given much importance to education of our young people, especially reading and writing our difficult Catalan language."

The Valdes family began to wonder where this preamble was leading.

"Great-great-grandfather, Rafael, survived the siege of Barcelona, bringing with him, from the flames that devoured La Ribera, the old sword that had been in the family for generations before him. Partly due to his blond curls, and even more due to his bravery, Rafael was known as the Lion of Catalunya..."

Jordi gasped, anticipating where this was leading.

"The Lion of Catalonia. The sword and the title have been handed down the generations ever since, to the first-born Blanxart; and by an extraordinary stroke of destiny, each first-born has had the same blond curls."

Anna, sitting close the Jordi, ran her fingers through his long curly hair. Alejandro, seeing the gesture, smiled, and went on.

"At this time of celebration, we anticipate a double wedding, and since Senor Valdes lives so close to Santa Maria, in that great church. Anna, I turn first to you. You are an extraordinary girl, falling in love with a man who will never be able to see you, and who will be unaware of your blushes; I know you will care for him and cherish him, but the obligation will be greater than you expect. For, my dear, you will be marrying the Lion of Catalonya!"

At this everyone gasped and exclaimed. Jordi jumped to his feet and Alejandro dramatically pulled the senyera off of the table to reveal the sword.

"Jordi, my son, through your music and your knowl-edge of Catalunya, you are a worthy successor to the line of ancestors who have been Lion before you. I hand you the sword, I place the ancient senyera around your shoulders, and declare you to be the Lion of Catalonya!"

Jordi stood, savouring the moment, and desperately trying to think of the best way to reply; to make the speech he had prepared so many times in his head, but which now he hesitated to put into words. Anna jumped up and put her arms around him, as he took a breath.

"Friends, father, it is hard for me to put into words the emotions I feel. May I always be worthy of this honour, and with your support, carry forward the love of our nation." There was another pause, and the others could see he was thinking carefully about what he would say next. "Without sight, I cannot hold the sword alone: I feel its strength and power, and even through my finger tips, I feel its history; but I know I must share its burden with my loyal brother. Come Juan, stand by me, and hold the sword with me." Juan stood with one hand on his brother's arm, just as he had guided him for the last thirty years, and the other hand on the sword.

"Violeta," continued Jordi, "You will have to share your future husband with me, for he is my eyes; but your sister, when she is my wife, will take some of that burden from him. Are you standing with us, with a hand for Juan?"

"I am here, dear brother," said Violeta.

"Now let me thank you all and pledge my life to both the sword and my future wife, in the best way I know."

Juan, instinctive as usual, led Jordi back to his stool, and handed him his guitar. Just as he had played in Santa Maria, he started with slow quiet chords, but unlike the vast echoing spaces of the great cathedral of the sea, he was now in the intimate confines of the upper room, and he did not need to crescendo into strident strumming. The gentle music filled the room, and then his voice, singing a passionate love song, an ancient Catalan song from the mountains, telling of love of the high snowy peaks, the rippling streams and green meadows of Catalonya, carrying a hidden message of love for Anna and her family. Perhaps it was as well that he could not see the tears forming in the eyes of every person in the room.

On the day of the double wedding, Alejandro led his family, as always, first to their own church of Sant Miquel for prayers, and then onto Santa Maria del Mar for the marriage mass. Anna's father accompanied her down the aisle, and Violeta was brought to the altar by her brother Oscar. Jordi did not sing at the wedding, as he felt it was a day to be shared equally with his brother, and a performance from him would focus too much attention on him, detracting from Juan's day. From the church the newly wed couples walked with their parents to the big house in Montcada, where the Valdes servants had prepared a sumptuous wedding breakfast.; and then in the evening, for the first time, Jordi and Juan went their separate ways, Anna bringing Jordi back to Barceloneta which was to be their home, and Violeta taking Juan upstairs to his future home in Montcada.

The brothers and the sisters were, however, inseparable, and most of the ways in which they spent their time, they were together; whether wandering to a chiringuita for supper, or taking a promenade along Las Ramblas, whether attending mass at Santa Maria or shopping in the market of Santa Christina, the four would be together, chattering and laughing.

Enric was born a few days before Eduard. To Anna's great relief, she brought blond, curly-haired Enric into the world, whilst her sister gave Juan a swarthy, dark-haired Eduard. Jordi held his son, delighting in the tiny, frail baby in his arms, singing gentle Catalan lullabies to him, and a few days after the birth, Anna was able to tell him that his son had beautiful blue eyes. She could tell from the way Enric's eyes followed her around the room, that he could see.

Anna and Violeta set to work, remembering their obligation to the Catalan inheritance, to sing in Catalan to the babies, and as they grew, to teach them all the songs and stories of their nation state. Thus the next generation started to absorb the folk tunes and the culture which the Blanxarts had preserved down the generations, and with Jordi in the background, the greatest of all Catalan folk singers, they couldn't fail to understand the importance of their unique culture.

Senor Valdes had been a successful wine merchant, inheriting a booming business from his father, and he had celebrated that success by investing in the rebuilding of the grand opera house on Las Ramblas, which had burnt to the ground in 1862. His box at the opera was always well stocked with his best wines, and his daughters and their new husbands regularly attended the exciting seasons of opera presented at The Liceu. Jordi was very pleased one evening to recognise the voice of Senor Roca, and discovered that he was the owner of the adjacent box. When Jordi was not himself performing, the brothers and their wives enjoyed a busy social life centred on the Valdes box at the opera.

As Senor Valdes' success grew, he bought many vineyards throughout Catalunya. Oscar Valdes took a major part managing the family business, and was rapidly becoming a well-known businessman in his own right. It seemed the two families, Valdes and Blanxart, were enjoying a golden age. Jordi would lead his rather timid mother to the Valdes box, where she began to enjoy the music of Verdi: she declared La Traviata to be her favourite, and every time she saw it, she cried softly through the last act. Juan, on the other hand, took his father to Don Giovanni, and Alejandro, unused to such musical excesses, decided that he rather liked the music of Mozart. In the evenings, back in their humble house in Sant Miquel, Emilia and Alejandro would lie in bed whispering.

"Did you ever imagine we would become so grand? Going to the opera, and supper afterwards in Montcada? Two old people in the twilight of our lives, living such lives? Our sons have done well!" But they never let go of their working class background, and whilst enjoying the entertainments given them by their sons, they never aspired to such middle class behaviour as demonstrated by the Valdes family.

It was Oscar Valdes who brought news of the shadow which was to fall across their middle class lives. Returning from a visit to one of his father's vineyards, he spoke grimly. "The harvest is failing everywhere, the grapes are not ripening, but dying on the vines. I fear we have a disaster on our hands, father."

Senor Valdes immediately sent for his horse, and the two galloped out to the vineyards along the muddy Llobregat River. Sure enough, the vineyards were a sorry sight, and jumping down from his horse, Senor Valdes grabbed the first handful of shrivelled grapes on the first line of vines. "This is terrible," he groaned. Re-mounting father and son rode swiftly into the small town of Vilafranca del Penedes, centre of the Llobregat wine-growing country, and spoke to many of the despondent inhabitants. All had the same story: far and wide, the harvest was failing; far and wide there was nothing but shrivelled and blackened grapes, fit for nothing.

Speaking to the manager of one of his biggest vineyards, Senor Valdes learned the truth. "An insect of some sort has attacked the vines. They are all dying. We have no choice, but to uproot them all, and burn them. There will be no harvest this year, nor for some years to come. The Catalan wine industry may never recover."

Father and son rode home a little more slowly. After a long silence, as they reached the slopes of Montjuic, Senor Valdes reigned in his horse, and they sat overlooking the vast metropolis. "We have had our golden years, my son," stated Valdes, "and now they are over.

You are aware of the debts we have from simple things like paying glassblowers for bottles and printers for labels, to the huge burden of wages and the costs of our presses. Without grapes this year, we would be struggling, but without grapes for many years, we are finished."

The house on Montcada was closed up, and the proud senyera on the high wall of the great chamber taken down and folded. Debtors queued to remove furniture before the house was sold, and tearfully Senora Valdes left her beautiful home. Juan and Violeta, with little Eduard, moved into the Blanxart house on Sant Miquel, and Senor Valdes with his wife and son found a vacant shack on the roof of a nearby tenement in humble Barceloneta. Senor Valdes was most upset about losing his box at the opera: his pride and prestige were hurt by such public humiliation as putting an opera box on the market. Jordi and Juan pleaded with their father to buy it, but it was too extravagant, and too middle class, an investment for the old man to contemplate.

Oscar was, however, given work at one of the chiringutas, one which needed his managerial skills, as it was the only one not turning a good profit. He found the work hard after his exalted managerial position in the family firm, but quickly showed an understanding of the business and rapidly turned the chiringuita into one of the most profitable.

Emilia loved having her house full, and particularly enjoyed the company of her two lively grandchildren, the cousins Enric and Eduard. Except for a rare invitation from Senor Roca, visits to the opera became a thing of the past for the old couple. Jordi, Juan and their wives still attended regularly, and for the young men, it was simply a matter of returning to the hen-roost where they used to sit. Their wives were unsure at first, sitting with the ordinary people, without a comforting glass of wine, but once the lights had been lowered and all had focussed on the music and spectacle, they forgot their apprehension.

Regardless of political strife and tensions, the glorious opera house stood as a glowing tribute to the commercial success of the city. The brothers had particularly enjoyed introducing their wives to the splendours of the house – Juan describing the golden chandeliers and the bright reds of the velvet seats. Jordi remained mystified by the concept of colour, but was especially appreciative of the brilliance of the singing, whether it came from works by Mozart or Verdi.

The four of them had an extraordinary experience up in the hen-roost in 1883, when the company presented a long and difficult opera by the controversial German composer Wagner. Not only was the story in Catalan in their programmes, but the singers were singing in their beloved language. This was one of the first translations of the opera, and extraordinarily it was into their beloved Catalan. Jordi drank in the modern music with all its unexpected harmonies and soaring melodies. At one point Juan thought he would explode with excitement, when he whispered urgently to Jordi, "The hero, Lohengrin, he has a sword like ours!" By the second interval of the interminable opera, the girls were uncomfortable and wanting to leave, but the brothers were entranced, and determined to hear every note.

Afterwards, outside on Las Ramblas, Anna and Violeta needed fresh air and refreshment to recover, but their husbands were plotting how they could get to see the opera again. Turning to walk towards the sea, they met Senor Roca.

"My God," exclaimed Roca, "That was hard work. I don't think I need to sit through that again. Give me Verdi any day!"

"Do you mean your box will be empty tomorrow, Senor Roca?" enquired Jordi.

"It certainly will, young man, there is only so much that a man can endure, and this Wagner has gone well beyond my endurance. Certain parts of my anatomy are quite numb!"

"Then can we have your box? It would be a shame for it to go to waste."

"Very well, although I confess I find it hard to imagine that you would want to hear all that again."

"Again and again and again!" exclaimed Jordi. "It was wonderful!"

"I'll never understand you young people, always so excited by the strange and new. The box is yours' whenever Herr Wagner's music comes to town!"

Time would show that Senor Roca's assessment of Richard Wagner was wrong. Wagner's operas came to be great favourites amongst the Catalan audiences, and soon many of the German works had been translated into Catalan, and the operas were performed regularly in the local language at the Liceu Opera House. Jordi, however, was frustrated that he couldn't transpose any of the Wagner operas on to his guitar. "How does he write such complicated stuff?" he asked his brother.

The old lion Alejandro took to his bed in 1876, and died peacefully, aged seventy; he was quickly followed by his wife, and within the year by Senor and Senora Valdes. Jordi, Juan and their wives thus made four sad journeys to Montjuic, reflecting that their parents had lived through extraordinary times. Barcelona had flourished and become the powerhouse of Spain, only to rebel and become the capital of an independent state. From hiding their senyeras in case of punishment, they now flew them with pride, and a senyera was draped over each coffin as it made its slow way to the burial ground.

The chiringuitas remained busy at all times, and the brothers were pleased to promote Oscar to have a managerial eye over all of their many busy workers; this gave Jordi and Juan the chance to put their own effort into the teaching of Catalan. The busy house on Sant Miquel, swollen already with the many brothers and sisters Anna and Violeta gave to Enric and Eduard, was teeming with anxious young people eager to read and write their mother tongue. One day Juan had a bold suggestion to make to his older brother. "We have a chain of chiringuitas, all busy and making money for us. Let us enlarge them, and at the same time close one down."

"You are speaking in riddles, brother," replied Jordi.

"No, listen. If we enlarge them all but one, we can take in more customers; and the one we don't enlarge, we will turn into a school. A school dedicated to teaching Catalan. That way we increase our income from the beach kitchens, create a proper school for our students, and give Anna and Violeta more space here at home to care for our children. We will have a school on the beach. We cannot fail."

Oscar was charged with the task of expanding all but one of the beach kitchens, and Juan became fully engaged renovating one of the oldest, at the end of Almirall Aixada, to become the make-shift school. Jordi was frustrated that Juan would not let him visit the chaotic building site whilst the renovation was in progress. "You'll fall over something and hurt your hands," Juan told him, "And we can't have that!" Later, however, when the work was finished, Anna took Jordi and his guitar down to the beach, and into the schoolroom.

"This is quite a big space, isn't it?" asked Jordi.

Sitting him on a stool, Anna said to him, "Sing and play, my love. You will tell how big it feels from your music."

Jordi started to play, and then sung a few lines. Stopping, he laughed, "We have a little concert hall don't we? A little Catalan concert hall by the sea!" As he returned to the song, he could tell that others were creeping into the schoolroom, and sitting quietly at his feet. He reached the end of the song, and there was a scattering of applause. Laughing again, he said, "OK, sometimes it will be music; but more often it will be speaking and listening, reading and writing. Let us open our school as soon as we can. And Juan, are you nearby? For us, there will be much to learn as well, as I am determined to conquer German, so that we can understand Senor Wagner's operas!"

Life in the 1880's settled into a routine, if a life punctuated by constant terrorist attacks could ever be called routine. The vast majority of the population were delighted to be living in their own republic and the senyera flew in the breeze over many homes and businesses. But this was Barcelona, and the constant undercurrent of restlessness never went away. Whether right wing royalists or communist cells, there were always groups set upon assassinating someone, or calling a strike, or simply enjoying tearing up part of Las Ramblas to practise building barricades. The middle classes in their grand apartments in L'Eixample were certain that all the plotting was happening in Barceloneta, and to be fair, Prosper Verboom's elegant new town had taken on the appearance of a Dickensian slum.

In fact, this reputation as a hotbed of dissent was unwarranted; the residents were loyal Catalonians, but peaceable, and given to argument with words not weapons, more likely to clash over a dominoes board than with guns and bombs. The real terrorists and agitators came from the margins of the sprawling city, and from the grim outlying industrial areas like Sants. Cells would spring up overnight, target their particular grievance, cause whatever gratuitous violence they favoured, and melt away again as quickly as they had appeared.

As young teenagers, Enric and his cousin Eduard, had taken to exploring the city, returning with amazing tales of change and development. Anna and Violeta had trouble separating the truth from the exaggeration. Enric claimed they had been into exotic gardens in L'Eixample; Eduard spoke of huge fountains gushing coloured water; and the two were fascinated to watch the building of Placa de Catalunya, the enormous square at the western end of Las Ramblas.

None of the adults believed the boys, but then one day in 1887, they came home with extraordinary tales of the demolition of La Cuitadella. The hated fortress, symbol of Castilian oppression, remained a huge carbuncle close to the city centre. New developments had grown up all around it, but the ancient lump of earthworks remained, an anomaly in the changing landscape. "If you don't believe me, you must come and see for yourself!" challenged Enric, and grabbing Anna by the hand, he dragged her urgently to the beach. "There!" he said. "Didn't I tell you?

Shading her eyes from the sun, Anna could just make out, beyond the railway, that a large gang of men with wheel barrows, were indeed taking the fortress apart. A huge steam shovel roared and whistled as it moved the earth. "Oh," she gasped, "Won't your father be pleased?"

Back at the house, Juan had arrived with more exciting news. "Have you heard?" he said, "They've started work on La Cuitadella. The whole thing is to be flattened."

"We've seen it," boasted the boys.

"A nice big space for a factory, I suppose," grumbled Violeta.

"Or even rebuild La Ribera slum," suggested Jordi.

"No, much better than that!" replied Juan. "They're going to make a park, you know, with trees, and a boating lake, fountains and statues."

"Can we go and watch?" asked Enric.

"Don't get under the workmen's feet," replied their mother, "And don't come home covered in mud!"

At the edge of the old fortress site, they watched as the great steam shovel dragged lumps of the earthworks away and into the filthy water of the old moat. Men with wheelbarrows carted large pieces of stone to one end of the site where they were stacked, ready to be used again elsewhere. Bricks were being stacked neatly into piles, also ready for re-use. The boys noticed an old man with a broad brimmed sun hat, watching the scene just as they were.

"Hey senor, is it true there's going to be a park, with fountains and statues?"

"Yes boys, one day there will be; and watch - you see where that old flagpole is, just being taken down? That's where the lake will be."

"To swim in?"

"No," replied the man, "I shouldn't think so. But I think there will be boats. And you see those bricks and stones all neatly stacked?"

"Yes."

"They're going to be used to build our great Universal Exposition."

"Our great what?"

"Universal Exposition! This will really put Catalunya on the map. It's what will be here first, before they make the park."

The boys looked at one another uncomprehendingly, wondering if they could remember the strange phrase 'universal exposition' when they got home, and how it was going to be there before the park. It seemed very mysterious. Jordi would know what it meant, he knew everything even though he couldn't see, and they would ask him about it. The man was still talking to them.

"Yes, all this will certainly put us on the map! And where we're standing now, this side, near the railway, will one day be a zoo. In fact I think you two are in the monkey house!"

"No! Now you are joking with us, aren't you sir?"

"Go home and ask you father. Tell him you met Senor Roca, and he'll tell you I don't joke. As sure as there are four blood-red stripes on our flag, I tell you there will be a zoo. Watch out, there's one of the bears behind you now!"

The boys jumped around, and laughed some more. "Very well Senor Roca, we will tell our fathers."

"No," continued Roca, "better than that, bring your father here, and describe it all to him. Tell him about the steam shovel, tell him how the earth is being flattened. He'll like that. He'll love to stand here and hear all these sounds: sounds that represent the demolition of this hated fortress."

Enric looked curiously as Senor Roca. "You know who we are, don't you Senor? You know my father."

Senor Roca laughed, "I've known your father since before you were born young man. Now I'm serious, go and get him. He'll not want to miss this."

By the time the family got back to the little vantage point where the boys had met Senor Roca, a crowd was gathering, and cheering each time a particularly large piece of masonry fell.

"Jordi!" called Senor Roca, "Over here! You mustn't miss this!"

With his wife to guide him, Jordi was soon by Roca and shaking his father's old friend by the hand. "A great moment, Senor Roca, a great moment!" And the old man and the young lion continued to clasp their hands together as the sounds of demolition filled their ears.

Later that evening, Enric asked his father about the "Universe thing, that Senor Roca spoke about." Smiling, Jordi explained to his son, "Catalunya is a new country, just a little older than you, my son; but we are lucky enough to be a rich and successful industrial nation. Or, to be accurate, we live in a rich and industrial city in the middle of a rural and rather backward land! The city fathers want to show off their wealth, and put Catalunya on the world map, and to do so, are holding a great exhibition, inviting other nations to bring exhibits of their achievements, but more importantly to show what we have achieved in our country. There will be many exhibits about the factories and the goods they produce. There was an exhibition like this is London some years ago, and we will have one just as good."

"It sounds a bit dull, father," replied Enric.

"I expect it will be dull to you, looking at looms and machine tools; and it will be very dull for me also, listening to the machinery with no idea what it's doing. But we must remember we are flying the flag, the senyera, for all the world to see, and that's what's important. Perhaps there will be a machine which plays the guitar!"

Despite the boys' insistence that they would be bored, and Jordi's scepticism, the two families, with Oscar Valdes with them, made an expedition to the Universal Exposition. The boys were very excited by the unexpected route they took, along the beach and over a long bridge which spanned the new railway and landed them in the middle of the exposition. Coming from the slums of Barceloneta, they were very impressed by the sheer scale and size of everything. Centrepiece of the exposition was a giant horseshoe of warehouses, following the curving line of the railway track. Large formal gardens lead them to a range of exotic pavilions set amongst palm trees. They rode the new trams, and watched huge looms producing enormously long lengths of cloth. One machine was turning out the longest senyera in the world! Even Jordi was impressed, and the boys remained engrossed all day. There wasn't a machine that played the guitar, but there were several that played organs and pianos, which greatly excited the boys.

After the excitement of the demolition of La Cuitadella and the visit to the Universal Exposition, life returned to its daily routine. Oscar was an excellent manager of the chiringuita business, and very happy to let Jordi pursue his career as a singer and guitarist, and Juan run the language school on the beach. Enric grew into a handsome young man, proud of his blond Blanxart curls, and Eduard his cousin remained his best friend.

After the excitement of Wagner, the brothers were eager for the next sensation to come to the Liceu, and were eager to be at the opening night of Rossini's William Tell. Although Wagner's star was still in the ascent, there was still a great deal of loyalty to the Italians, and a Rossini opening was an event which brought out all the wealthy of Barcelona in their finery and jewels.

The opera season opened late in 1893, and it was the first week of November before the new opera was to be played. The glittering audience took their places, and Jordi and Juan, with their wives were up in the hen-roost nervous with anticipation.

Anna and Violeta had asked their husbands to explain the story of the opera to them. "It's very complicated," said Juan, "but the most important thing for you to know is that William Tell is a revolutionary, fighting to rid Switzerland of Austrian occupation."

"It seems like an echo of our old Catalonian struggles against Castile," said Jordi. "We know from our own history what that's like. I expect the Swiss hated the Austrians, just like we hated the Spanish."

"I think we're in for a memorable evening," said Anna, not having any idea that her words would be prophetic in a way no-one could possibly imagine.

Jordi could tell the atmosphere was one of great excitement, and Juan told him that he could see everyone from Barcelona high society, many ladies in new dresses, glittering in their jewels. There was a hush as the orchestra attacked the unfamiliar music, and as the overture grew to its breathless climax, Jordi whispered, "That's a tune I can transcribe for the guitar!" and all around them went "Shush!"

After the first interval, during which everyone seemed to agree that they were at the first night of a very exciting opera, the audience settled down for the next act. A sudden commotion close to the brothers and their wives up in the hen-roost, turned everyone's attention away from the stage. A wild-looking man in the front row had stood up, screamed incoherently, and flung some kind of package over the balcony rail. Immediately there was a terrific roaring explosion, and the opera house filled with smoke. Anna and Violeta clung to their husbands, and hid their eyes. Juan looked around desperately, to see how he could lead his brother and the two women to safety. The safety curtain came crashing down and suddenly the glamorous audience was reduced to panic and confusion. No-one had any idea what had happened, and amid the chaos, the crowd was faced with the horror of finding a way out through choking smoke and blinding dust.

Juan shouted to Jordi that the place was on fire and no-one could see where to go. Jordi was used to negotiating the place without sight, and despite the confusion, realised he would find it easier than the others to find the way to the stairs and the fresh air. He yelled to his brother, and their wives, and others near-by to cling to one another, and he would lead them to the stairs. The throng of shocked and confused people leaving the top gallery made progress very slow, but finally they made the staircase and groped slowly down. Coughing and spluttering, they found their way out into the side lane, and then onto Las Ramblas.

Las Ramblas had become a vision of hell. Rich patrons were stumbling out of the foyer, faces blackened with smoke and dust, debris in their hair, clothing torn, and bleeding from multiple cuts. Shocked husbands were desperately trying to find wives separated in the melee, and many, both men and women, were crying in their distress. Some of the injured simply collapsed onto the pavement. Anna and Violeta, being younger than most of the patrons, recovered quicker and once in the fresh air, began to see what was needed. Despite their own feelings of shock, they attempted to help some of the injured. After his calmness leading the family to safety through the smoke and dust, Jordi collapsed to the ground with a fit of shaking, and his brother could do nothing but cling to him and reassure him he was safe.

"A bomb, it must have been a bomb," was the word which spread through the crowd, as more and more of the distressed audience emerged from the building. Passers-by on Las Ramblas helped to comfort the victims, most of whom were trembling and incoherent with shock.

After a while, a number of improvised stretchers were brought from the auditorium, some of them with people alive but badly injured, some of them with a sheet or item of clothing covering the face of the dead. Even for a city used to terrorism and violence, the atrocity was shocking.

With a single bomb, a mad anarchist, later identified as Santiago Salvador, had murdered twenty members of Barcelona's richest families. When the opera house reopened two months later, the seats those twenty victims had occupied were left unsold.

Having done all they could, and ascertained they were themselves unharmed except for the shock, Juan helped Jordi to his feet, and urged them to hurry home. "Enric and Eduard will have heard the news, it will have travelled faster than we can, and they will have no idea we are safe," said Juan. "Clearly we will not able to get a carriage, so we must walk." Looking at his wife, he went on, "Are you sure you are unharmed? There is blood upon your skirt!"

"I'm alright," said Violeta. "It's not my blood, but someone else's. My sister's dress is also ruined, and we have both ripped our petticoats to shreds making bandages to staunch wounds. Oh, the poor people!"

Strangers turned and stared at the group as they made their back through the warehouses and sheds of the quayside. Hearing what had happened, many wanted to stop them and ask for details, but they headed on, worried about the children. As they turned into the Placa of Sant Miquel, Enric and Eduard and all the children came running, and great was the tearful reunion. Oscar, bringing up the rear, embraced his sisters and their husbands. "My God, we feared the worst," exclaimed Oscar. "From what we heard, it seemed the whole audience had been killed."

Later than night, when all had stopped shaking, and the children reassured that all was well, Jordi took Juan to one side.

"We must talk," he said, "seriously."

Juan led his brother to a quiet part of the beach, and found them a bench to sit on.

"We could have died this afternoon," said Jordi. "Both of us together. And if we had, the secret of the sword would have died with us. Our wives know the sword exists, but have no idea where it is. I believe the time has come to reveal the secret chamber to our wives and to Enric. Perhaps even to bestow the title of Lion of Catalunya upon him."

"And Eduard?" asked Juan.

"Yes, and Eduard. He should know the secret also. He and Enric are as close as brothers, almost as close as we are dear brother, and he deserves the knowledge of the sword, and to be brought into our confidence. I feel that the dangers of the secret are not so acute as they were when Antoni Blanxart created the chamber beneath the floor, and in this age of sudden death, we cannot afford to lose everything our forefathers believed in. I would hardly be an honourable Lion if I allowed the tradition to vanish without trace."

"What about Oscar?" enquired Juan. "It seems odd to miss him out. Since the collapse of the Valdes business, and the deaths of his parents, he has become like a brother to us, and indeed the business is flourishing because he manages it so well."

"If we had had this conversation yesterday," said Jordi, "I would not have considered breaking the tradition; father to first-born son, and no-one else to know the secret."

"Or in our case," said Juan smiling, "father to first-born son and his brother!"

"Precisely! But after the events of today," continued Jordi, "I am shocked to know how close we came to us both dying together, and with us the secret of the sword, and the knowledge of the Lion succession. So yes, we'll bring Oscar into the secret as well. It will be quite a gathering, and a considerable surprise. The sword has never been revealed to so many at once."

"And you mean to pass the title to Enric? He is still young."

"But he knows the songs, even if he cannot sing them as well as I can, and has read great-grandfather's book so many times he knows the stories by heart. Others who have read the book do not know who the Lion of Catalunya is, but Enric is shrewd, and will have his suspicions. He may even have wondered if he is being groomed for the honour."

"How soon will you tell him, and reveal the sword?" asked Juan.

"Why wait? We could have died today, we may die tomorrow. Imagine a bomb like that thrown into the school on the beach. We are as much a target as the opera house for a fanatic. We will sleep one night only, and then reveal the secret. Can you gather all together in the lower room during the afternoon?"

"Will you not open the chamber in the morning, and have the sword on the table upstairs, as father did?"

"No," replied Jordi. "I will explain that we are about to reveal the sword, then everyone can gather around the chamber and watch it being opened. All present shall learn the secret together. Once the sword is in my hand, I will hand it to Enric and pass the title to him." Jordi paused, thinking about the coming ceremony, and changed his mind. "Juan," he said, "I'm wrong. You must act out the ceremony with me. Once the sword is in our hands, we will pass it to Enric. You have been the eyes of the Lion, and thus you must be a part of the ceremony of handing the sword and title to the next generation."

"I wondered if we should have taken the sword to the great Universal Exhibition. After all, that was supposed to be putting Catalunya on the world map." said Juan.

"And I wondered if we should have taken it to the demolition of La Cuitdella," rejoined Jordi, "but it was right that we did not. Today's bomb at the opera shows how fragile our freedom is, and how easily we could lose it. The sword remains hidden until we are sure and strong. It will be part of Enric's responsibility to decide if the sword should be revealed, but I will caution him to be very hesitant, and think long and hard, as we have had to do."

The following afternoon saw the family assembled in the Sant Miquel house. Once more the little ceremony of revealing the secret chamber was enacted; once more reactions varied from complete astonishment to unbounded joy, and Eduard was the first to regain his composure and make a sensible comment. "Oh Uncle Jordi and Uncle Juan, what excitement, what an amazing thing!" Turning to Enric, he continued, "Congratulations, my brother, for as you know, I think of you, cousin, as my brother. We have both read our ancestor's history book, and know it by heart. I had long wondered who is the Lion, and now, as Uncle Jordi hands the sword to you, I discover that the Lion was right here in our family. I was suspicious, seeing that Uncle Jordi has such unusual curly hair, and so have you, Enric! How wonderful!"

"I believe that I feel today, as all my ancestors have felt," stated Enric, " overjoyed, and humbled, delighted and frightened. From our ancestor's book, we know of many years of oppression and struggle, and today we have our fragile republic. Our senyeras fly boldly in our streets, and we hear Catalan spoken at every turn. This sword represents the courage of countless Blanxarts gone by: of the brave Perez, tortured and executed by Castile; of the fortitude of Rafael, concealing the sword from the Mossos; of the legendary strength of sculptor Antoni, who we see daily masquerading as Sant Miquel in his great sculpture; the wisdom of Francesc, writing our history, so that we know of these great ancestors; and now the brilliance of my father, who has sung the songs of our nation and told the stories, so all far and wide know the name Blanxart, and the legends of our land. And then dear Uncle Juan, we all know you as the eyes of my father, and we salute you too, for now we know you as the eyes of the Lion."

"Others before me fought to gain our nation state; my task is to hold onto it, and strengthen it against all the forces of evil which would see it destroyed. As we return this noble sword to this extraordinary secret chamber, I swear to up-hold and defend our nation; to stand and be counted in the line of Lions who have gone before me, and tell the world, 'We are Catalunya!'"

There was a silence, then Jordi said simply, "Well spoke, my son. Amen to all."

Oscar, who had stood with growing astonishment and amazement throughout the simple ceremony, then said, "To think we have been walking over this secret chamber all these years. I must thank you, Jordi, for the honour of including me in this special moment. I have a bottle of my father's best vintage, hidden in my room, almost the last of the Valdes wines. I have wondered why I was keeping it, as there seemed to be no reason. Now I know what it is for! Pray organise glasses whilst I run and fetch it."

CHAPTER ELEVEN

The atrocity of the opera house bomb made the city vigilant, but determined that life should continue. The chiringuitas remained as busy as ever, continuing the simple fare of well-cooked Catalan dishes, mainly seafood based, with paella as the basis of much of the menu; and with long draughts of locally-brewed beer to wash it down. It was a characteristic of the beach kitchens that all the customers mixed together, humble workmen would sit at the long benches rubbing shoulders with doctors and lawyers; even the Mossos, formerly so distrusted and hated, could come for supper and take part in the joking and ribaldry. No-one was turned away despite some fierce and angry political arguments, there were few fights, and the characteristic of the steamy atmosphere was more one of laughter than dissent.

An undercurrent of commitment to the cause of Catalunya remained strong, however, and even the Mossos realised the strength of feeling against Madrid. These political police, recruited and trained by Castile, watched warily, and secretly dreaded the day when they would have to quell any further uprising. They were aware more than most, certainly far more than Enric Blanxart, the new Lion of Catalunya, that Madrid would remain angry, and would not rest until this upstart state had been returned to Spain. When this happened, as the Mossos knew it would one day, they knew they would be in the front line, and would be arresting or even executing these genial friends with whom they daily laughed and ate their meals.

The school by the sea flourished, and remained the focus of learning the history of Catalunya and its culture. In addition to the teaching of the language, a great deal of effort went into translating books from other languages into Catalan, and everything, from opera libretti and popular songs, to the great classic novel of the time by authors such as Charles Dickens and Victor Hugo, were painstakingly translated. Jordi himself, struggling with German, assisted in translating Richard Wagner's operas, but even such a gifted linguist found the task daunting and difficult.

A regular visitor, at first as a student, and then to assist with teaching, was a young man called Pompeu Fabra. He would sit with Jordi and Juan, listening intently, and making copious notes. He gained a reputation for checking the spellings of the growing Catalan vocabulary, and pointing out when there appeared to be more than one way to spell a certain word. No-one took a lot of notice of the bookish and slightly pedantic young man, as he scribbled away in his notebooks, but on meeting him, you could not fail to be aware of his passion for the language and his growing expertise. Jordi developed considerable regard for the young man, and spent much time encouraging his enthusiasm.

From the concentration of the day, the evenings were spent making music, and the schoolroom became a little concert hall on the beach. Enric suggested to his father that they should buy a piano, as not everything they were singing could be accompanied by the guitar, and Jordi agreed. The arrival of the piano caused a great ripple of excitement for everyone, and Jordi was puzzled that his wife had left the house early to go to the market on such a day. Anxious to hear the new instrument, Enric accompanied his father on the familiar walk along Almirall Aixada to the schoolroom. As they approached the beach, they could hear someone playing the new piano. They stood beside an open window to listen.

"That's Mozart. Who's playing it so early in the morning?" asked Jordi.

"I cannot imagine," replied Enric.

"I wish your mother hadn't gone out so early. She would have loved to be with us."

They turned the corner and crept silently into the schoolroom. Juan was sitting listening, and indicated to Enric to be quiet.

"Juan is here," whispered Enric to his father.

"Is he playing?" asked Jordi.

"No," giggled Enric, looking around. "Just sit and listen."

The notes rippled and flowed for a few moments more, and then suddenly slowed and ceased. "I can't remember any more," said Anna aloud, imagining that she was alone.

"My wife, my dear Anna, is that you?" jumped up Jordi.

Anna jumped at the sound of her husband's voice. Enric laughed at his parents, "What a surprise!"

"Yes," said Anna, "I wanted to surprise you all, but I can't remember any more. We had a piano in the house at Montcada, and I played regularly. It went with all of mama's things when we lost the vineyards, and I had no idea if I could still play."

"How did you organise this?" said Jordi.

"Juan was here to see the piano delivered early this morning, and I came down here to see it with him. I didn't go to the market. I told him to keep it a secret whilst I experimented to see what I could remember."

"What a treat," said Jordi. "Play some more."

"I can't remember much without the sheet music," said Anna, "But I'll try. I played this hundreds of times, so I might get through."

So saying, she played the first few bars of Fur Elise.

"Beethoven," whispered Jordi.

"I know," said Enric.

But as before, Anna started to falter and soon stopped altogether. "I'm sorry, but I need the music," she said.

"Come here, my clever wife," said Jordi. "You have hidden this talent from me. We shall buy all the music you need, and you will be able to play new music to me. But first, let me try this instrument."

"Have you never played before?" asked Anna.

"Oh there were many opportunities. There is a huge grand piano at the opera house, and I have walked around it, feeling its bulk. But I was never alone, and could not just sit and see if my fingers could find the keys. I could not experiment with an audience. What if I cannot do it, how would people think of the great Jordi Blanxart if they heard him stumbling about on the piano?"

"Well there's no-one here now," replied his wife as she led him to the piano stool. Jordi sat, and felt for the keys. He played a few single notes and stopped.

"You three must go," he announced, "I can't do this even with you here."

After a pause, Enric and his mother turned to go, motioning to Juan to go with them, although he didn't move. Anna quietly closed the door.

"Am I alone?" called out Jordi. There was a silence. "If anyone has remained, I will hear your breathing!"

"Brother, let me stay. I promise there is no-one else," came Juan's quiet voice.

"No-one else? Very well, but remain quiet. I'm strangely nervous as I do not know what will happen now."

Jordi turned to the piano. With his right hand he started to hunt for the notes, beginning with scales and arpeggios, his long tough fingernails clattering on the keys. After a while, he started to explore with the left hand, and gradually began to find harmonies which were familiar from his more complex guitar pieces. Slowly a sound started to emerge, not of Mozart or Beethoven, but of a syncopated, grinding rhythm, the beat and thump of flamenco. As he continued to improvise, he started to laugh. And then he suddenly stopped.

Turning to his brother, he joked, "I can make music of a sort on this machine, but it does not take easily to the folk rhythms I know. I think others will do more with it than I!"

Juan laughed with him. "It was not so bad, dear brother, and I think you have a career waiting for you in the bars and brothels of the old city. Sitting in a smokey corner, thumping out such improvised tunes and melodies, will give you a new and altogether different reputation."

"One, I fear, I do not want!" laughed Jordi. "You must take Anna to the music shops of the city, this very afternoon, and buy the music she needs. And what of your wife? Does Violeta also play the piano? You must take her also, if she does."

"I am ashamed to say I do not know," replied Juan, "but I will go directly to find her and find out."

Students were arriving for the day's language work, and puzzled to find the door closed, they knocked, and waited to come in. "That's our signal to stop," said Jordi. "Let them in, I'll get the day started here, but you take some time away, and take our wives to the music shops."

Each day, the students would stop for lunch, and accompany Juan and Jordi to one of the chiringuitas. Thus the room was empty when Anna and Violeta arrived back from the music shop. Excitedly they opened the packages they had brought from Senor Alio's dusty shop in the lane behind Santa Maria del Mar, and hunted quickly for the book which was giving them such a thrill of anticipation. Pulling an extra stool to the piano, the sisters sat together and opened the book, "Duets for four hands and one piano."

Cautiously, struggling to remember their technique, and embarrassed that they were not doing very well, they started to play. Slowly the skill returned, and they boldly attacked a second and a third piece. They laughed when they muddled sharps and flats, and giggled over mistakes of tempo, and emboldened by their growing success, started to play louder and louder. Such was the volume of their playing that they did not hear the door opening and the students, with their husbands, creeping in. At the end of a particularly noisy piece by Liszt, simple enough for them to sight-read with gay abandon, they came to a crescendo, and stopped, laughing together. Abruptly the group of students broke into loud cheering and clapping, and the sisters spun round, horrified and blushing, that they had been caught.

Musical soirees became regular events at the school on the beach, and many new talents were developed there. Jordi founded two choirs, one for men only and one for mixed voices, and Juan revealed an unexpected talent as a conductor. Their wives worked hard at their piano technique, and so were able to accompany the choirs in some of the great oratorios of the day. When the accompaniment proved too complex for one of them, they would share it, breaking the score into the right hand for Anna and the left hand for Violeta.

At home the women and their older girls were busy sewing elaborate banners for the choirs, as no self-respecting Catalan choir performed without displaying its banner, proclaiming its name and date of formation.

The wives, determined to add more musical contributions, as well as their sewing skills, ensured that all their children learned to read music and play. Enric and

Eduard said they were too old to start playing the piano, but their mothers dragged them reluctantly to it. Enric, painfully aware that he did not have his father's talent with the guitar, became a proficient pianist, and eventually Eduard, all fingers and thumbs with both guitar and piano, obtained an old trumpet and drove everyone mad on the beach as he struggled to master it.

Enric and Eduard, with the enthusiasm of young men, organised the language students and the musicians into all kinds of sporting groups. And when they weren't declining verbs or struggling with strange melodies, the students would be found playing games of football on the beach, practicing gymnastics on the sand, or cycling in groups around the city. Excursions were regularly organised, and the most popular and regular of these was an overnight camping trip to Montserrat.

Juan and the sisters became regular customers at Alio's Music Shop, searching for some of the great classical pieces, as well as new music, especially new Catalan music. Francesc Alio, owner of the shop, was a diffident man, and reluctant to sell his own compositions to the women. As they became more familiar with him, the sisters persuaded him to visit the school on the beach, and soon he was a rather shy but interesting player in many of impromptu evening concerts.

Jordi especially enjoyed Alio's playing, as the latter would take an old folk tune, sometimes well-known to Jordi, sometimes new to him, and improvise a piece which was both original, but had an echo of the past.

March 1892 saw the next step in Catalan independence with the Catalanist Union, and the publication of the aims of the state. Catalunya declared that it would become a sovereign country, divided into districts, with Catalan as its official language, and a volunteer army of its own.

One evening in the same year, Alio arrived with a new tune he had been working on, and before the evening's entertainment started, he played it to Jordi. It had a difficult rhythm, partly like a slow waltz, but then jerking away with unexpected four beat bars.

"You have a powerful melody there, Senor Alio," declared Jordi. "But I don't know the tunes, nor where they come from. What's it called?"

"The Reapers," said Alio. "And the tunes are very old, fragments from the sixteen hundreds, from the time of the Reapers' War. Your ancestor wrote about it in his book, the Corpus de Sang - 1640 wasn't it?"

"Are there words?" asked Jordi.

"Some fragments," replied Alio, "but not much. There's a kind of chorus which speaks of a good blow with a sickle. It represents Catalunya's triumph over all. The reapers are cutting the chains of oppression with their sickles."

"My brother and I were talking earlier about this declaration of Manresa. If we are to go on striving for our sovereignty, we will need an anthem, as so many

European countries are doing at the moment. Play it again: perhaps you have stumbled upon just the right piece of music."

Francesc Alio played the piece again for Jordi, and then again at the evening concert. His original compositions always received a very favourable response, but none more so than the tune of the song of the reapers. At the end, he told the audience that there was a need for words to fit the tune, and many people were very interested in this, and offered to contribute.

It was through Francesc Alio that Jordi met members of the biggest and most influential choir in Barcelona, the Orfeo Catala. The choir was too big to fit into the little schoolroom by the sea, and rehearsed in warehouses and churches around the city. It gave many successful performances in the Liceu Opera House, as well as the old cathedral and Santa Maria del Mar. In a similar way to Jordi's music school being funded by the chiringuitas, the many choral societies of Barcelona had their industrial sponsorship; and the greatest choir had the greatest resources backing it.

Tired of such an important organisation being peripatetic, the directors of Orfeo Catala met with their wealthy backers with an outrageous and expensive plan: to build their own concert hall. Musicians such as Jordi and Francesc Alio, who were known to be sympathetic to the promotion of Catalan music, were invited to assist with artistic contributions and fund-raising. Soon it became clear that there was enough goodwill to be very ambitious with the scale and design of the new auditorium, and the controversial young architect Lluis Montaner was recruited.

Montaner started by visiting many of the choral societies and immersing himself in the musical traditions of his city. Jordi was keen to play him some of the music of Isaac Albeniz, who had produced many piano works which Jordi himself had transcribed for guitar. Montaner also listened to pieces by Francesc Alio. As he travelled around the city, however, he found a music scene with far more in it than Catalan folk tunes. He found advocates for Palestrina, Beethoven and Bach, and was slightly alarmed by the passionate esteem with which Wagner was held in the city.

In 1906, a ceremony was held on a slum-clearance site close to the Via Laietana to lay the foundation stone of the new concert hall. Jordi was invited to the ceremony, but declined. At over seventy years, he was beginning to find public events a strain, and sent Enric in his place. Enric was by now married to a good Catalan wife and they had produced the required first-born son, Rafael, named for one of his famous ancestors, at the turn of the century. Jordi had delighted in his grandson, and Juan had watched his brother with the tiny baby in the arms of the blind old man. The baby was perfect with blue eyes and blond curls.

Enric with his wife and son stood with Senor Alio to watch the positioning of the foundation stone. Alio was, like Jordi, feeling the strain of old age. "I fear I may not live long enough to see this great venture finished," sighed Alio, "but at least I was here at the start."

Much was made of the new-fangled invention of photography, and the ceremony of laying the foundation stone for the new concert hall was well documented. At the appearance of the photographer, all the small boys rushed to be in the official photograph, and they can all be seen, including the six-year-old Rafael in his sailor's suit. With so many small boys clustered together, the foundation stone is almost obscured in the photograph.

Enric was surprised to hear his name called as his little party were about to leave the building site. "Enric, it's Enric Blanxart isn't it?" said the man, and coming forward he introduced himself. "I'm Pompeu Fabra, do you remember me?"

After a pause, Enric recognised the man as the serious student who had made such copious notes with Juan some years before, and had assisted with some of the teaching at the school. "Why Pompeu, I'm sorry I did not recognise you. This is my son, Rafael." And turning to Rafael, he explained, "This is Senor Fabra, who used to come to the school by the sea, and worked very hard at learning his Catalan spelling and grammar."

"Just as I have to!" replied Rafael, shaking hands solemnly with Fabra.

"It is providence that we have met, my friend," continued Fabra, "as I have been meaning to come and visit your school on the beach. How is it? Does it continue to thrive? And do you still have those wonderful musical evenings?"

"Indeed it thrives, and yes there is still much music making. Do you remember Senor Alio whose music we still enjoy to play?"

The small-talk and introductions continued for a while, until Enric said, "I think it is time we tried to catch a tram down the Via Laietana. Rafael will be getting tired, and I have promised to see Senor Alio safely home."

"Come and see at my office," said Fabra. "I'm at the Institute of Catalan Studies, everyone knows me there. Try and bring your father, and Juan, if they can come. I'd love to see them and show them what we're doing."

Just as the Mediaeval and classical church builders built the skeleton first and then clothed the skeleton with walls and roof, so the temple to music was similarly constructed; but whilst masons spent months and years piling stone on stone, not only for masterpieces like Santa Maria del Mar, but also for more recent structures like Sant Miquel in Barceloneta, the skeleton for the new concert hall leapt skywards in just a few days, the stone of old being replaced by the latest technology in steel.

Lluis Montaner may have looked back to Mediaeval times for the decoration of his building, but he used the most modern construction methods available, fascinating to both Enric and Rafael who visited regularly to watch the progress. Rafael knew the story of his illustrious ancestor, Antoni the sculptor, and how he had danced high on the keystone of Sant Miquel, but he didn't offer to go up to the top of the new hall and dance on the thin steel beams!

Enric would return home to report to Jordi the exciting developments. He described the huge windows which seemed to be hanging from the steel skeleton: "Curtain walls they're called," he told his father. And young Rafael watched with bated breath, as the huge sculptures which were to be part of the structure were carefully unloaded from trucks.

"There are many great horses," he told his grandfather breathlessly, "with riders. They are called the Ride of the Valkyries. And there are great pillars supporting whole trees."

Enric explained that these huge sculptures would form a massive proscenium arch: traditional music being represented by Beethoven with trees and pillars, and modern music represented by Wagner with the Ride of the Valkyries. Rafael's grandmothers no longer played the piano in public, but they tried to give the boy some idea of the music in question. They could manage several of Beethoven's themes, and the boy particularly liked the great ending of the ninth symphony, the Ode to Joy, but they gave up with Wagner. "One day," laughed Anna, "you will hear the Ride of the Valkyries at the Liceu Opera House, and you will know why my sister and I cannot play it!"

As the great sculptures were hoisted into place inside the hall, similar massive sculptures were erected on the façade. One day Rafael was very excited to meet Senor

Miguel Blay as he was supervising his great carving being placed at the corner of the building.

"Look young man," said Senor Blay, "my sculpture represents all Catalunya in music. We are a nation of singers and players."

"I know we are," said the boy confidently. "My grandfather is Jordi Blanxart, the guitarist. He plays in the schoolroom on the beach, where I go to school!"

As the building nearer completion, Rafael was allowed to travel on his own, by the tram, up the Via Laietana, to watch progress. The day he came face to face with a line of huge busts, he was very excited. As he reported back to the family, "I have met Senor Palestrina, Senor Beethoven, Senor Bach and Senor Wagner! They are all there, waiting to be placed in their places. Senor Blay has made them all, and will be there to watch them being hoisted up."

Many other Catalan characteristics were built into the fabric of the building: huge ceramic flowers decorated the pillars, and even the electric lamps were constructed to look at if they were growing organically out of the walls.

Rafael insisted that his father came with him to watch the crowning glory of Montaner's design being inched into place. The extraordinary inverted dome, with its sun design and circle of singers, had to be lifted high above the curtain walls and lowered gently into place. Although its steel frame made it strong, as it rose in the air it appeared fragile, and work on the entire site came to a halt to watch it being positioned. Enric remembered the history of Antoni, and imagined that the lowering of the great keystones at Sant Miquel must have been just as nerve wracking as watching this great glass construction lifting high into the sky.

Once the roof was in position, an army of workmen moved into the hall to start the internal decoration. Rafael was frustrated that he was not allowed in - "not safe for little boys!" - and had to be content with watching the arrival of all that was needed. Organ pipes, more sculptures, and hundreds and hundreds of seats all passed by the boy, and the day drew near when the hall would be finished.

On the day of the grand opening, a carriage was arranged for Jordi and Juan and their wives to be taken to the new concert hall. Rafael went with his mother and Eduard by tram, and no-one would tell him where his father was. Rafael became upset that his father would miss the great event, but he was reassured his father would not be missing it, and had a special task to perform.

Rafael was particularly pleased that he had been chosen to lead his grandfather in the grand procession to the stage. The ushers directed Jordi and Rafael upstairs to the elegant hall overlooking the street, where they sat waiting for the moment to arrive. Jordi was particularly excited to meet Senor Albeniz, and promised him a good performance of the piece he had chosen. Rafael was puzzled by an introduction to a man called

Senor Erard, and afterwards Jordi told him that he was the famous builder of pianos in Barcelona and had made the piano they played on at the school on the beach.

Other musicians joined them, and soon all the great and good of the musical world of Barcelona were together in the room. The great choir, Orfeo Catala took its place on the stage amidst much cheering from the capacity audience, and the new organ was heard for the very first time. The ushers invited the honoured guests in the platform party to line up. Jordi, with Rafael as his eyes, was almost last in the line.

As the organ swelled into a solemn march, the procession began. Rafael whispered a commentary to his grandfather as they shuffled slowly towards the stage. As each celebrity reached the stage, they climbed the few steps and turned to acknowledge the audience, whereupon the audience produced a great cheer.

"Senor Montaner and Senor Blay, the architect and the sculptor, are leading the procession, grandfather," whispered Rafael. "In front of us are many other musicians, but I cannot name them. We are following behind a Cobla Band."

"We come through the great glass doors and across the top of the grand stairs. Now we are entering the auditorium. Gosh grandfather, there are so many people here, and they are all standing up. Now we go down the slope of the audience. I have your hand grandfather, you will not fall, although it is quite a steep hill. Everyone is looking at us grandfather. Now I can see the stage. The choir are all standing round in their places and the front of the procession has already got there and they are going to their seats. Oh grandfather, nod to your right for there I see Senor Fabra, you know the one who is writing a spelling book of Catalan. Oh and now nod to the left for I have seen Senor Alio. He must be very excited that we will sing his song soon. Senor Albeniz has just reached the stage. That extra loud cheer was for him."

The cobla band, immediately in front of Jordi in the procession, received a great ovation when they mounted the stage. They took their places in a semicircle around the remaining empty chair, the one with a guitar resting on it. Rafael, as he had been instructed, waited for the band to be seated, then guided Jordi up the steps and onto the stage. The cheer for the blind musician was the greatest yet, and he stood for a while acknowledging the acclamation. Rafael picked up the guitar, guided Jordi to the seat, and he sat down. With a sigh almost of relief, the audience sat and silence fell.

Jordi started as he so often did, with gentle strummed chords, but then as his volume increased, a melody started to emerge. It was Francesc's Reaper's Song, played quietly once, and then as he reached the chorus, much louder. It was then that the great organ took up the theme, playing the verse on trumpet stops, and although Jordi continued to play, his guitar was drowned. When the chorus was reached the choir leapt to its feet with the great words, "Let us swing the sickle, let us swing the sickle, defenders of our land, let us swing the sickle!"

At that the audience stood once more, and the words rang out.

"Triumphant Catalunya, will once again be rich and full!
We must not be the prey of those proud and arrogant invaders!
Let us swing the sickle!

Only Rafael knew how hard Jordi was strumming his guitar as if bringing all the passion he could from the instrument. Upon the second chorus, the cobla band entered with their shrill rhythmic sound.

"Now it is the moment, oh reapers! Now is the moment to be alert!
Awaiting the arrival of another June, let us sharpen our tools!
Let us swing the sickle!

With the third chorus, a line of young men entered from the rear of the auditorium carrying huge flags, the red and yellow senyeras of Catalunya, on tall poles. As they came out from under the balcony they raised the flags and swung them over the audience. At the same time another troop of men appeared in the upper balcony and took places behind the audience up there, again swinging large senyeras.

"May our enemy tremble on seeing our noble flag:

Just as we reap the golden corn, may we also cut free of the chains!

Let us swing the sickle!"

Jordi was the only one not standing for the performance, sitting strumming. At the end he handed his guitar to Rafael, who had been standing proudly beside him in the centre of the stage, singing his heart out, and unsteadily stood up.

Another roar of applause, another rustling and sighing as everyone sat down. Jordi remained on his feet. He coughed quietly and then spoke:

"My friends, my Catalonians…" Another cheer interrupted him. "This is a great day in the history of our nation. This extraordinary achievement, this great palace of music, stands as a symbol of the glory of Catalunya and her people. We are a great nation, with an illustrious history. We have a culture which comes from the mountains and the sea, a culture and heritage older than Castile…" Another great cheer, "Many of you will know our history from the book written in secret and in dangerous times by my great grandfather Francesc Blanxart. You may know of the old tradition of the Lion of Catalunya."

There was a murmuring of agreement.

"We have always had a dream. My friends, God is willing and the dream is coming true: you all know the story that there was a symbolic sword carried by the Lion of Catalunya. Perhaps you felt this story, and other such stories, was a myth, a mystery to amuse our children."

Jordi paused, and the audience whispered. There was nothing of this in the official programme.

"I can reveal to you that Francesc Blanxart, author of that great history, was himself one of the Lions of Catalunya. He received the title from his father, the great architect Antoni, and he handed the honour to his son Xandaro, and so it passed to his son, Alejandro, my father. Each of them was the Lion of Catalunya, and my father in turn handed it to me."

The audience started to applaud, but Jordi held up his hand.

"No, I am no longer the Lion of Catalunya, I am too old and lack the strength. I have passed the title to my son. Please welcome him, my son, Enric Blanxart, the Lion of Catalunya, revealing, at last in the daylight, the Sword of Catalunya!"

The audience turned as Enric entered and marched down the central aisle. Round his shoulders, the ancient Macia senyera, in one hand Francesc's original hand-written history book, and in the other, the sword. As he reached the stage, he stood between his father and his son. The sun, shining through the great glass dome, illuminated the halo of white curls of the former lion, the golden mane of the present lion, and the youthful locks of the future lion. In the roar of applause, no-one heard what Enric said to the other two.

"Today the fight is over, and we stand, the previous Lion, the present Lion and the future Lion, shoulder to shoulder. The fight may be over, but there will still be many battles to come."

As he finished speaking, there was a great clap of thunder, rain started to pour as clouds covered the sun, and the great Palau de la Musica darkened. There would indeed be many battles to come.

Lightning Source UK Ltd.
Milton Keynes UK
UKHW041520240119
336125UK00001B/20/P